CAPTAIN OF THE CARYATID

Also by Richard Woodman

ACCIDENT
ACT OF TERROR
THE ANTIGONE

CAPTAIN OF THE CARYATID

Richard Woodman

PAN BOOKS

Captain of the Caryatid first published in Great Britain 1997 by
Severn House Publishers Ltd
The Cruise of the Commissioner first published in Great Britain 1998 by
Severn House Publishers Ltd

This omnibus edition published 1999 by Pan Books
an imprint of Macmillan Publishers Ltd
25 Eccleston Place, London SW1W 9NF
Basingstoke and Oxford
Associated companies throughout the world
www.macmillan.co.uk

ISBN 0 330 39298 0

1 3 5 7 9 8 6 4 2

A CIP catalogue record for this book is available
from the British Library.

Printed and bound in Great Britain by
Mackays of Chatham plc, Chatham, Kent

For the ship's company of the lighthouse tender *Alert*,

and the keepers of the lighthouses at Lundy,

1967–1970.

Contents

A Quiet Sunday Evening

Captain Septimus Macready dozed in front of the fire. His consciousness swam slowly from its refuge among the foggier recesses of his brain towards the warm reality of a Sunday evening. It was the incessant clicking of knitting needles that compelled him to abandon his reverie.

The knitting needles belonged to his wife. The recollection brought him back to full consciousness. He surreptitiously opened both eyes and without moving his head stared from under his brows across the hearth.

Opposite the Captain the small bird-like person of Mrs Gwendolen Macready sat with the immobility of a coiled spring. The Captain regarded his wife. Their marriage had existed for twenty-three years. For twenty-two of them, matrimony had resembled the lines of a railway track, running smoothly parallel, interdependent as an entity yet independent in part.

There had been romance; a brief, intense experience that had forged a mutual link between the two, then faded, leaving them individual and only slightly, guiltily, dependent upon each other. Thus their twin lives ran abreast, the distance between them impeccably exact, an absolute constant.

The Captain's eye roved over his wife: the sensible slippers, lisle stockings and plaid skirt; the cardigan and glasses retained by a bight of cord around her neck. He watched her nimble hands click-click the needles as she knitted yet another woollen garment for the interminable children that Porth Ardur produced.

Captain Macready closed his eyes again and sighed gently. Children. Maybe that was the trouble. They had never had any children. Neither was wholly to blame yet each bore a fragment of guilt and it was an unmentioned barrier between them. The Captain wondered what it was really like to be a parent. Most of his crew were. Mrs Morgan was.

At the thought of Justine Morgan and her daughter his heart kindled. The widow was everything his wife was not. She was brassy, drank gin and laughed explosively. Where his wife's brownish hair was greying, Justine Morgan's became blacker. Her ample bosom conveyed an infinite prospect of comfort and her thick, well-formed legs carried her stockily voluptuous frame with a pride that busy Mrs Macready dismissed as vulgar self-indulgence.

Mrs Morgan was the Captain's official dancing partner. Between them they had carried off several local trophies and were hopeful of completing their repertoire by collecting the regional prize for Latin American dancing that winter.

At the thought of dancing with Mrs Morgan Captain Macready smiled slyly to himself. He had never stepped, nor ever attempted to step, beyond the strictest bounds of propriety in five years. In a way this added a piquancy to his relationship with the widow who had, whilst yielding in the most sensuous embrace of the dance, never sought to encourage the Captain's attentions extramurally. In the town Mrs Morgan was considered 'fast', a largely unjust judgement by those jealous of her way of life. In truth it was as unkind as it was incorrect for despite her apparent sociability in The Feathers, dancing was her pleasure and the adornment of her own body her especial vice.

In a curious way the Captain and Mrs Morgan were ideally suited partners. They were both short, stocky and well-formed, inclined to a middle-aged thickening, but healthily and athletically confident in their own physical power. They therefore danced well and had recently been chosen by their team-mates as Porth Ardur's leading couple.

Mrs Macready viewed her husband's dancing with cool rationality. He had, after all, a certain social position to maintain in Porth Ardur and he was a fine figure of a man, setting off a brass bound uniform or evening dress extremely well. Gwendolen Macready was a pragmatist from her plaid skirt to her avuncular attitude towards her husband's dancing, with a sense of purpose that enabled her to ignore such innuendoes that the Captain's choice of partner had fostered. Besides in five years they had died down, having nothing – beyond malicious speculation – to feed upon. Mrs Macready considered her husband deserved some pleasure and seemed content that he was, himself, contented. After all, he was a sailor and the dancing provided sufficient innocent evidence to support the romantic image his profession had acquired. Besides, it allowed her to support a slightly martyred attitude as much as it gave her freedom to preside in the town as the Captain's Lady and attend the organisations she enjoyed.

These were the Ladies' Circle, the Mothers' Union, Women's Institute, the League of Hospital Friends, etc,

etc, for the list was apparently endless. None, she quietly asserted to herself, could function without her tireless energy. Gwendolen Macready was one of Porth Ardur's Principal Wives, one of those powers behind the various thrones in the little seaport's hierarchy that knew that they, and they alone, made the town function at the human level. Certainly their husbands might occupy the offices of Town Clerk, Mayor, Chief Inspector of Constabulary, Estate Agent, Rector, Collector of Customs and so forth but it was their wives who exercised influence and guided affairs into the 'proper' channels.

Within this structure Gwendolen Macready occupied a unique niche, for she was *the* Captain's wife of Porth Ardur. Oh, there were many sons of the town who earned their livings at sea, every street boasted at least one Board of Trade Certificate. Many still lived in the town, or at least their wives and families did, having married local girls with the homing instinct of the true sailor. Many too were masters of merchant ships, captains in their own right, but they were not the Captain known best in Porth Ardur.

That distinction was indisputably held by Septimus Macready, Master of the Lighthouse Tender *Caryatid* which, with all its 900 gross registered tons, dominated the tiny granite inner harbour of Porth Ardur at weekends. The *Caryatid* berthed regularly on Friday as the tide served for, as the Bosun never failed to remind the Carpenter as the steamer warped into her berth: "There'll be dancin' tonight, Chippy!"

Bernard Foster, First Mate of the *Caryatid*, threw the last wall-eyed, one-legged teddy bear into the wooden box and

4

thankfully slammed the lid shut. He collapsed into a chair and stoked up his pipe as the gurglings of his children, subsiding into sleep, floated down to him from upstairs.

His wife, haggard with the effort of trying to bath two robust boys, entered the room. She too slumped into a chair.

"I'll make a pot of tea," she muttered, closing her eyes.

"Don't worry, I'll do it," he answered. For a long while neither moved.

"Monday tomorrow," she said at last.

"M'm." He agreed with the obvious, knowing the implications in the trite remark. Monday meant him being away at sea until Friday. It was not long but Anthea Foster groaned mentally at the prospect: the two boys, four evenings on her own, it was enough to wilt the strongest spirit. She thought of something else.

"You'll be tired next weekend, I suppose?" She got up from her chair.

"Sorry?" He looked up at her, uncomprehending, seeing her fading good looks sadly heightened by her exhaustion.

"You'll be working extra next week with Barry gone." Her reference to the Second Mate, who had that week decided to rush off and ship out on a tanker, brought comprehension to him.

"Oh that, sorry love, no you don't have to worry: there's a new chap coming down on the overnight train, name of Farthing, Charles Farthing . . ." He puffed his pipe. "Going to make tea?" She nodded, brushing a wisp of hair back from her forehead. There was more than a touch of grey in it, he noted wistfully. Oh well, one could only bow to the inevitable, but it was a shame that such a beauty as Anthea should wither so soon . . .

She came back into the room with a tray.

"It's an odd coincidence. I mean, Porth Ardur so rarely has any new faces that to get two in the same week is a real bonus . . ." She tried to smile.

"Two?" said her husband.

"Yes, Mrs Humphries told me that the new Harbour Master was expected this Monday. She's been cleaning for old Captain Edwardes' widow; such a pity about him, he was such a gentleman . . ."

"Mmmmm," agreed her husband, emitting clouds of aromatic blue smoke.

Charles Farthing was not, as his name tended to imply, a round man. He was an extremely gaunt twenty-year-old with a penchant for cavalry twills and shapeless sweaters which gave him the appearance of an itinerant scarecrow. Some two hours after the conversation between Mr and Mrs Foster, Charlie was struggling out of a taxi in the capital's west-bound railway terminus cursing the rain. Behind his cab another drew up and from this stepped out a man little older than Charlie but in an immaculate suit. With an instinct peculiar to such persons, the porters who were dubiously approaching Charlie switched their attention to the newer arrival and, with the motivation of true snobs, unloaded the man's baggage. As the two taxis drove away Charlie was still standing in the rain cursing.

Unbeknown to the two men they were the very persons Anthea Foster had been discussing, for the immaculate gentleman was Porth Ardur's new Harbour Master. He was an ambitious fellow, one of that professional breed of mariners that go ashore early and, having the right background and the right connections, become authorities upon matters maritime, write books about the sea and ultimately become consulted for dreadful films about seafaring. They studiously insist on being called 'Captain', though frequently commanding nothing more manoeuvrable than a large mahogany desk. Such was the man destined to become Harbour Master of the little Celtic port of Porth Ardur. His name, if we ignore his self-styled title, was James St John Stanier.

While Stanier was being tenderly tucked into his extortionate first class sleeper, Charlie was struggling down the platform in search of a third class compartment empty enough for him to occupy a whole banquette in a horizontal position. When he eventually found one and had stowed his cases he was running in perspiration. He therefore decided to indulge himself in a little ritual he used to perform as a child. He strolled casually down the platform until he reached the locomotive. Then he inspected the gleaming beast, its green paint throwing back the platform lights, steam rising from the piston glands and a wisp of smoke from the funnel. He read the locomotive's number and the name in brass letters over the wheel arch: 'King Charles I'. Was that a good or a bad omen? Good for Charlie Farthing or a dismal reference to the doomed King? He turned away and stared ahead to where the lines, catching the yellow station lights, tangled in points beneath the gaudy reds and greens of the signal gantry, then straightened out into the four tracks that faded into dark distance. The magic iron road to the West. He muttered the word in the gloom, pleased with its sibilance.

He had a faerie image of towering cliffs with Tintagel-like fortresses defying the Atlantic swells, of mists and maidens and wind-buffeted trees clawing for existence against the southwesterlies that scoured the rugged coast. Was it the land of dragons, of Merlin and the legendary Arthur? He chuckled inwardly at himself. Cynicism rose up in him. Why did he always dream these stupid romantic dreams? He had been at sea for eight years and still, if he was going somewhere he had not previously visited, thought that this might be the place where legend and fact mingled in a dream-like reality to which he could surrender his soul and settle.

As he walked back to his compartment he remembered that first, shattering blow to his preconceived notions. For two months he had listened to his shipmates' stories about the beauty of Japanese women. He had been sixteen, on his first voyage, receptive to every emotive chord anyone wished to pluck. He had augmented these tales with fantasies. At last the ship berthed and at last young Charlie got ashore. He swaggered into a bar in Izesaki-Cho and an almond-eyed beauty of indescribable delicacy had sat beside him. She had gazed longingly into his eyes, bathed his hands and face in hot, scented towels and brushed her sandalwood scented hair in black waves across his cheek. As she spoke Charlie fell in love and as she stroked his thigh he felt the heat of passion combine with an unbearable crescendo of longing. 'Are you cherry-boy?' she had asked. Charlie could not believe such poetic imagery existed in speech, used as he was to a terse Saxon formality. But this was the land of cherry blossom, this was the Orient, the Mystic East. He nodded, transported with happiness.

"I love you for free . . ."

Charlie's breath was coming in ecstatic sobs. His cheek was being stroked, the girl's nails scratching it with the same delicacy one taps porcelain, her other had found that hitherto innocent part of him that was now betraying him shamefully. He surrendered, suddenly aware that the girl's breasts were pressing into him, perfumed orbs of the most celestial delights.

"I love you for free . . . free fousand yen?"

Charlie was laughing as the train pulled out of the station. As it came clear of the great arch of the terminus he saw the sky was clearing. The rain had stopped and over the jumbled roofs of the capital rose a yellow moon. Orbs, mused Charlie. Those bloody orbs . . . and he began to settle himself for the night.

Further down the train James St John Stanier also saw the moon. He leant nonchalantly out of the window, smoking a last cigar before retiring.

Spring tides, he thought, musing on the technical details of the port upon which he was determined to stamp his personality. Lunitidal intervals, maximum rise and fall, the neap range, the off-lying dangers to the port . . . he turned over the technical data in his mind. Navigational aids . . . he was not too sure what existed on that score . . . at any rate there was bound to be some room for improvement. After all, there was that pier called on the chart 'Lighthouse Pier'. Odd that, because there was no light upon it other than the statutory two fixed reds that appeared on all such projections. He tossed the cigar into the darkness and pulled his head in. He was looking forward to tomorrow immensely. It was all such a tremendous challenge.

*　　*　　*

9

The same moon that rose over the capital shone down upon Porth Ardur. As the night wore on it cleared the shadow of Mynydd Uchaf from the sleeping town, bathing it in light. It woke Justine Morgan from her favourite dream and she lay a while trying to recover the lost shreds of happiness. She had been dreaming of her late husband, Brian Morgan. A pillar of a man with the vitality of a bull, eager as a lover, strong without roughness and yet with such a well of softness within him that his sudden death in a mining accident had left his devoted wife with a lasting image of immortality. It was as though the removal of the physical presence of his body had only been a metamorphosis. Brian Morgan remained eternally enshrined within the remembered gentlenesses of his person and these he had passed to his wife to cherish forever.

Justine smiled in the darkness. It was impossible to explain to others. That was why she had come here, twenty miles from her mining village, as a widow. Why she had stayed a widow, earning herself a decent and reasonable living first as the assistant and later as the successor to a lady who ran a small business selling garments to the ladies of Porth Ardur. But Justine remained in love with her husband, devoted to a memory that would not fade with age. That was why she held herself not only with the confidence of youth but with the certainty of experience. That was why she did what, in the eyes of other women in the town was reprehensible: she 'preserved herself'. But there was only a kind of radiant joy in this vice. For Justine Morgan preserved not only the voluptuousness of her own body by her onanistic ministrations, but the infinitely delightful sensuous memory of a vigorous and tender lover.

The moon poured into the bedroom and Justine Morgan rolled languorously onto her back. Her black mane was caught up in a scarlet ribbon, pale in the moonlight. Her breasts, large, still firm, spread across her rib cage under the *décolletage* of a nightdress her lady customers never saw in her window, and her hands fluttered reminiscently over a belly flat with tension.

Very slowly she moved her hands downwards and felt again the urgent insistence of Brian Morgan.

Calico Jack was aware of the moon only for its illuminant properties. The broad swathe of the Lighthouse Pier bucked in his vision, the ordered symmetry of its granite masonry impossibly distorted by the alchohol in his system. Despite the chill of the night Calico Jack wore upon his elderly, gaunt frame the full dress uniform of his trade. The white cotton peaked hat, the cotton sweatshirt and the faded blue denims of a steam ship fireman adorned his thin, sinewy body. He staggered with unerring purpose to the narrow plank that served as access to the *Caryatid*. He groped instinctively for the rope handrails and in seconds was aboard, swallowed up in the shadowed recesses of the silent ship. Below, he found the oil-lit messroom, where able seaman John Evans sat pouring a second mug of orange tea with the confidence of long practice. Evans was one of six Evanses on board but the only other John, and so was also called Jack. A keen fisherman, he was known to the ship's company as Mackerel Jack to differentiate from Calico Jack, whose unvaried clothing, always the same, always spotless, had earned him his own qualifying soubriquet.

No word was spoken by either of the men. Calico Jack sat down and drank the tea. After a little he writhed somewhat, then rose, flung himself at the ready-opened port and spewed into the night.

When he withdrew his head from the port he was paler but steadier. He wiped his mouth and, with a hand that trembled only slightly, lit the rolled cigarette that Mackerel offered him. Then he lurched out of the messroom and disappeared. Seconds later Mackerel heard the clang of the boiler room door and the rasp of a shovel as Calico Jack revived the banked fires in *Caryatid*'s Scotch boilers. When the sun came up Calico Jack was stone cold sober, the alcohol sweated out of him. A dark haze rose from the tall vertical funnel of the *Caryatid* and a white wisp of steam showed that the ship's whistle gland was still leaking. But it had done so as long as anyone could remember and now it no longer seemed important.

Matters of Routine

It was not immediately apparent to anyone in the town that that particular Monday morning was in any way significant in the history of Porth Ardur. There were individual beginnings but these, at the time, seemed not to impinge upon the ordered life of the sea-port.

The first to experience such an initiation was Charles Farthing. In a chilly dawn he had bundled out of the overnight express, stumbled across the junction platform and into the four-wheeled carriage of a branch line train. At a more leisurely pace, attended by a porter, James St John Stanier had traversed the same platform and, with evident distaste, sat himself down in what passed on the branch line for first class accommodation. It was not long before a pannier tank engine had been coupled up and at 6.55 a.m. it jerked out of the station.

The branch line route lay across the seaward ends of several well-defined valleys. The pithead wheels of mines showed up above the lines of small houses that ran parallel to the valleys as though stuck to the two hundred feet contour. It was a fresh spring morning, cold enough for the smoke from a thousand range fires to rise above every town through which the train progressed. At each station the train stopped. Newspapers and mail bags were flung out onto the platforms before the tank engine hissed, hooted and jerked its creaking rolling stock into further motion. Charlie was fascinated by the little towns, each isolated from the next by the massive spine of mountain into which, by way of smoky tunnels and high cuttings, the train plunged. What fascinated Charlie most was the strangeness of it all. It was as though he was in a foreign land, a sensation heightened by the unpronounceable names borne by the stations through which he passed.

After about an hour the train turned in line with a valley and ran along its side. A mile or so later it again began to turn, bringing a stupendous view of blue water flecked with the white caps of breaking waves and shadowed darker patches where the sun threw the shadows of cumulus clouds.

For a quarter of an hour Charlie was captivated by the view. In the distance was the dim line of another shore and here and there islands, one of which bore the white column of a lighthouse which gleamed in the sunshine as though it had been of burnished metal. "Delightful . . ." he breathed to himself and then remembered his thoughts of the previous night. A tiny tight knot of excitement began forming in the pit of his stomach. After all that globe trotting was he really about to discover a land of enchantment? Or merely a land of cynical disappointment? If a man was not meant to romanticise, why the devil was he equipped to do so? He ran his hand through his tousled hair and frowned, an annoyed and surprisingly fierce expression crossing his face.

He was interrupted from his reverie by a sudden gloom in the compartment. The train had plunged into a cutting. Sheer on either side granite rose, dripping with water, fissured by frost and time with tufts of thrift and the fresh curling green of ferns: hart's tongue and maidenhair. He was suddenly convinced that he might indeed be on the threshold of magic, some lost magic still left in the world, when the train pulled out of the cutting. Behind them, on a craggy eminence, the gaunt, fantastic outline of a castle was silhouetted black against the morning sky.

A few minutes later the train pulled into the station of Porth Ardur.

'Captain' Stanier descended from the train unaware of the morning's promise. His senses informed him that there was three eighths cloud cover of Fairweather Cumulus, that the wind was sou'west force four and that the wisp of cloud over the mountain behind him was orographic in nature and probably presaged rain. He took a taxi to the best hotel.

Captain Septimus Macready, dressed in full uniform, strode down the hill towards the harbour accumulating the same information as Stanier. In addition he also noted the state of the tide. When he reached the harbour he leaned over to look at the inner boat steps. The swell gently rose and fell, covering, then exposing two complete steps. Things did not look too good. He strode on to the ship, tossing good mornings to left and right of him as he passed fishermen and his own seamen, whom he had met here every successive Monday morning for the last decade.

Septimus Macready stepped aboard *Caryatid* noticing only details: the cleanliness of the decks, the hand-rope tension, the presence of a safety net under her gangway. Charles Farthing, arriving a few minutes later, saw the ship as a whole. She had a bar stem straight enough to rake

aft when the ship trimmed by the stern. Her tiny high
fo'c's'le flared outwards and then dropped abruptly to a
low well-deck. This deck was dominated by the foremast
which boasted two derricks. A smaller one forward, over a
small hatch and a larger one aft, over an open deck. This
latter seemed to be of some sort of wood, a massive spar
about two feet in diameter, he guessed. At the end of the
well-deck the bridge rose, abaft which a clutter of boats and
tall, bell-mouthed ventilators were just visible. The bridge
was high and of varnished teak with a large athwartships
wheelhouse and small, open wings. At the forward end a
small brass bell gleamed. He looked back at the fo'c's'le
to where its partner, large, imposing and equally polished,
bore the just legible legend 'CARYATID, 1910'. So the old
lady was already twenty-five years old. He should have
guessed, though, by the incredibly tall funnel that rose as
vertically as the stem, a buff column emitting a dark heat
haze from its top where, too, a wisp of white steam escaped
from the whistle. Charlie was pleased with the look of the
ship. She was certainly old but on that particular morning
she was whimsical enough to suit his mood. He gathered up
his bags for the twentieth time since leaving the station and
went on board.

Stanier reached the harbour two hours later. Being a man
of importance he had checked in at his hotel, changed
and, having had a decent breakfast, made his way to the
harbour office. It was a good time for the new Harbour
Master to arrive, he reflected, as it was just coming up
to high water. He patted the Admiralty tide tables a little guiltily, slightly ashamed that he needed to consult

them at all. Oh, well, in a day or two it would not be necessary.

The first blow to his self-esteem came when he viewed the Harbour Office. The beautifully chiselled granite that formed Porth Ardur's sea wall and inner harbour swept seawards in two embracing arms. The outer one extended a little further in a mole to break the effects of a swell from the bay beyond. Where the two arms met, the caissons that formed the tidal gates were situated. Next to this, under the shelter of the adjacent sea wall, was an ugly, squat brick building. So eager was the new Harbour Master to sight his eyrie that he barely noticed the two coasters, half dozen fishing boats and the *Caryatid* as his taxi took him along the pier.

He was met by Thomas Jones, who was technically the Harbour Master's Coxswain but who in fact filled the offices of Dock Master, rope man and fresh water agent to ships using the port. Stanier noticed the peeling sign over the badly pointed brick work, which bore the legend 'HARBOUR MASTER, CAPT T EDWARDES, TEL: 29'.

"'Aven't painted it pendin' your arrival, Cap'n," Jones explained. Stanier was soothed by the unsolicited use of his title. He nodded curtly and went inside.

Here Jones explained that the building had been erected for the Naval Examination Service during the Great War. Had the Captain served? But no, how foolish of him, the Captain was too young.

Stanier listened as patiently as he could while Jones conducted him round the various files and boxes that constituted the Harbour Master's office. Eventually the coxswain's loquacity died away and Stanier spoke for the first time.

Pulling his watch from his waistcoat he said, "Thank you, Mr Jones. I see it wants but ten minutes to high water; would you be kind enough to tell me what movements we have?"

Jones waved his hand airily towards the harbour entrance. "Fred and Stan have the c'soons open now, the fishin' boats are already out an' there goes the *Carry* . . ."

For the first time since entering the building Stanier looked out. A spinney of gaily painted masts was visible round the end of the sea wall where the departing fishing boats puttered out of the harbour. One or two were already hoisting sail, each skipper's course slightly divergent from the next as they headed for their own favourite grounds.

Stanier was next aware of the dominating bulk of the *Caryatid*. The high tide caused her to tower over the granite quay and though only a small ship, in a tiny harbour like Porth Ardur her hull was imposing.

Her black top sides were badly rusted below her anchor boxes and half-way along her well deck, where four or five brightly painted buoys sat. Seamen were busy lashing them down. Stanier, for all his experience, had never seen a ship like her before.

"What ship did you say that was?"

"The *Carry*, Cap'n, *Caryatid* properly, see. She grosses nine hundred tons and lies weekends on the lighthouse pier."

Stanier thought fast. Nine hundred made a tidy packet in dues and she was obviously a buoy tender here in his harbour.

"What amount of dues does she pay, Mr Jones?"

"Why bless you, none, Cap'n, she's a lighthouse tender an' exempt." Jones chuckled to himself as if he found

18

the idea of Captain Macready paying dues vastly amusing. Stanier was annoyed with himself for betraying his ignorance.

"Ah, yes, I was forgetting, Section 357 of the Merchant Shipping Act. So she works out of Porth Ardur . . ."

"Port' Ardur, Cap'n . . ."

"Pardon?"

"It's 'Port', you don't sound the 'h' but pass quickly to the name, so you sort of run the two together."

"I see," said Stanier, colouring.

Jones ignored the Captain's discomfiture. "Aye, she runs out of 'ere most weeks, just occasionally she's away over a weekend, then you'll get all the wives and sweet'earts coming down for news. Drives a man bloody crazy. Sometimes she goes out at weekends for emergency calls but not often. Captain Macready tries to avoid it as most of the crew either fail to muster or are too drunk to be much use."

"I see. That's Captain Macready up on the bridge, is it?" Jones looked up.

"That's 'im, Cap'n. They call him 'Ebb-Tide Macready' as 'e's always going out." Jones chuckled again and quietly noted the humour was lost on Stanier. Odd, he thought, how a man could have education and no sense of humour. Stanier was looking up at the portly bulk of Macready, arrogantly self-confident, the gold braid at his cuffs flashing in the sunlight as he rang the engine room telegraphs.

"My God, he looks like the Master of the *Mauretania!*"

Jones laughed again. "Oh, they run them lighthouse tenders really tiddly like. You wait 'til the Commissioners come, Cap'n. Oh, she's a smart little ship an' no mistake."

"Does she tend our buoys?"

19

Jones nodded. "We've two in the bay she renews 'em ev'ry year. You have to pay rent for 'em, about three pounds I think it is."

"Rent? But surely we have jurisdiction over the *Caryatid*?" Stanier looked surprised.

Jones suppressed another laugh. "Oh no Cap'n, nobody has jurisdiction over old 'Ebb Tide', excep' the Commissioners – and as they only come once a year . . ." He shrugged and tailed off, further explanation seemed superfluous.

Stanier was beginning to dislike Captain Macready. In his miserable brick hut he was beginning to feel that the real kingdom of his harbour had been usurped by another. "What about my predecessor? How did he get on with, er, *Captain* Macready?"

"Oh, very well, sir. They were close friends. You don't want to worry, Captain Stanier. Just treat the old *Caryatid* as a matter of routine."

Bernard Foster took over the bridge from Captain Macready before *Caryatid* was clear of the bay. Macready went below and summoned his new Second Mate. Charlie was charmed both by the Captain, whose attitude was avuncular, and by his cabin which was richly panelled, with bright chintz curtains looped about polished brass ports. The twin barrels of a matching clock and barometer were secured to the bulkhead above the diminutive knee-hole desk. Beyond, Charlie sensed rather than saw the Captain's tiny night cabin.

"Well Mr, er, Farthing, so you've decided to join the Lighthouse Service?"

Charlie nodded. "Yessir."

Macready looked hard at the young man. He was thin, yet

his wrists seemed sinewy enough. The grey eyes met his own coolly, the tall body swaying as the steamer met the first of the Atlantic swells rolling in from the open sea. Macready questioned the new officer as to his past experience.

"Mate's Ticket, sir. Most of my time in cargo ships, a little in coasters including two passages in ketches."

"D'you get on all right in small boats?"

"Yes, sir."

"Good. Now if you go up to the bridge Mr Foster will outline your routine duties and explain the broader points of our job. You can't expect to learn it in a day, there's *no* teacher like experience . . . right, thank you Mr, er, Farthing . . ."

Up on the bridge Charlie found the ship had cleared the bay completely. The headland that guarded the approaches to Porth Ardur was falling astern, a huge jagged escarpment of fissured rock that seemed to jut out into the sea like a vast fist.

The fresh southwesterly breeze had set up a choppy sea that opposed the ebb tide now sweeping the *Caryatid* westwards. Ahead on the port bow, blue with distance, Charlie could just make out the hump-backed outline of an island. Foster took him into the chartroom. Picking out a general chart of the area the Mate described the area tended by the old steamer.

"This is our principal operational area," began Foster, tapping the chart with a pair of brass dividers. "The Channel is about eighty miles long. The main commercial port is at the narrow eastern end here." He tapped a spot that Charlie recognised as the junction through which he had passed that morning. "The south shore is mainly steep-to,

21

though with many off-lying dangers." Foster indicated buoys marking rocks and banks. "The north shore is more complex. There are coal exporting ports here and here." Charlie remembered the pithead gear. "There is a lower coast further to the west, plenty of agricultural land which slopes into the sea and produces a large area of sand banks and bars which we mark, but only local fishermen use. Then the country becomes more mountainous again with our base there at Porth Ardur and only small fishing ports to the west where the coast swings away north again. There's a regular archipelago off these headlands and we supply two lighthouses there. The main channel is pretty deep. The main offshore danger is the Hellweather Bank marked by buoys and a lightvessel. Then further down to the west the island of Ynyscraven, that's it fine to port, we're bound there now, that's got a lighthouse, and further west still is the isolated rock station known as Buccabu lighthouse."

"And it's our job to maintain all the buoys and supply the lightvessel and the lighthouses?"

"That's about it. There are the four principal lighthouses and the Hellweather lightvessel, a number of lesser lighthouses, most actually unwatched beacons, four granite daymarks we land and paint annually and eighty buoys, some lit, some not."

Charlie nodded. Foster went on to tell Charlie of his duties aboard and explained the procedure for landing. "I'll come with you to Ynyscraven today and show you the ropes. After that you'll be on your own, though the boat's crew'll help, alright?"

"I think so, Mr Foster."

Foster lit his pipe. "Call me Bernard, for heaven's sake, reserve the 'sirs' for the old man."

"What's he like?" enquired Charlie, adding hurriedly, "He seemed pleasant enough to me."

Foster puffed ruminatively on his pipe for a minute, then he said, "You'll not find a better seaman anywhere but don't emphasise your foreign exploits too much. What certificate've you got?"

"First Mate's," replied Charlie. Foster nodded. "Good, I've a Master's but I like a quiet life and I don't much talk about it, or how I got it. I'd advise you to do the same."

"I'm sorry Mr, er, Bernard, I don't think I quite understand."

Foster drew again on his pipe and moved away onto the open bridge out of earshot of the man at the wheel. He motioned Charlie to follow him.

"Captain Macready joined the Service as a boy. He's had no qualifying time for Board of Trade certificates but in the old days Lighthouse Service officers were self-examining. The Masters sat on a board with one of the Commissioners and set exams for the likes of you and me. They were specialist exams in our work and quite tough. But the bureaucrats don't recognise such practical things. Now we all have to have tickets like you and me. A few old-timers are left, like Macready, and many of them resent us as interlopers. So be a bit diplomatic. D'you savvy now?"

"Yes, yes of course . . ." Charlie sounded a little dubious.

"Mind you," asserted the Mate, stabbing his pipe stem in Charlie's direction, "you won't find a finer seaman than our Septimus. I've seen him do the most fantastic things with this ship and the men love him, you wait until tonight, you'll see. Just because he doesn't have a bit of paper doesn't mean he's no sailor, and it doesn't mean he isn't Captain and Master of this ship. One or two smart-arses have made that mistake." Foster chuckled reminiscently to himself and turned away into the wheelhouse, leaving Charlie musing on the bridge wing.

What an extraordinary day it was turning out to be. He had never thought he would stand on the bridge of a ship whose master had no qualifications. Or at least, no formal ones, he hurriedly corrected himself, mindful of the Mate's admonitions.

A patter of spray flew round the break of the fo'c's'le and streamed across the well-deck. Instantly the stays and guys were bedewed with tiny drops that gleamed in the sunshine.

Perhaps, thought Charlie, I have found fairy-land after all.

Stanier spent the remainder of the day being shown round by Mr Jones. In the main his enthusiasm waned. He was shown the *Caryatid*'s berth which was always to be kept clear. That alone seemed an infringement of his authority as the Harbour Master. Even more infuriating, when compared with his little brick caboose, was the Lighthouse Authority's compound. At the inner end of the Lighthouse Pier a stone wall enclosed a large area above which could be seen the tops of several score of buoys. They were red, green, black, chequered in various combinations and of differing shapes. There was also a store and an office building which housed the administrative staff of two old clerks and several girls and women. Outside was a flagpole from which the Authority's ensign snapped sharply in the breeze.

"Quite a set-up," Stanier muttered more to himself than to Jones, but the latter detected the envy and chuckled quietly to himself. They completed the circuit of the inner basin and walked out along the mole. At its outer end there was another flag-pole with a yard.

"'Ere we 'oist the shapes and lanterns to show the port's open or closed, Cap'n Stanier. Two lanterns 'orizontal means open for outward movements, four in a square means open for inwards. Fred and Stan look after them altering them according to the c'soons. I usually tells 'em when there's enough water on the sill, unless of course you'd like to do that in future?"

Stanier looked up at the yard, swaying slightly in the wind. If he did not do that he would have very little to do except fill in forms in the brick caboose. He was suddenly angry. "Yes! Yes, of course I'll take that responsibility. You'll do nothing about hoisting signals or moving the caisson without my instructions. Do you understand, Mr Jones?"

"Perfectly, Cap'n," said Thomas soothingly, already preparing the rhetoric he would use later to explain the new Harbour Master to the lads in The Feathers.

Stanier turned away then stopped, swinging abruptly round on Jones. "And furthermore, we'll carry out a survey of the harbour approaches starting tomorrow morning . . ."

By evening, however, two things had soothed Stanier's battered pride a little. The first was his launch. This was a splendid teak boat some thirty-six feet long. It was steam propelled and agleam with polished brass, miniature ventilators, and lined with scrubbed teak gratings. Every cleat and fairlead gleamed with polish and the varnish was similarly bright.

But the greater boost to his morale came as they traversed the inner harbour. This area was filled with a few rowing boats and yachts, and a larger number of open, inshore fishing boats. It was tidal and dried at low water springs. At the end was a small dry-dock which Stanier had missed earlier. A small coaster squatted on the blocks, old pit props acting as side shores to hold her ample tumblehome secure.

"This 'elps a bit of revenue into the port, Cap'n," explained Mr Jones. "And it does you a bit of good on the side, like." Jones leered at the Harbour Master.

"Does it?" queried Stanier.

"Of course, Cap'n, as Harbour Master you're also pilot, both for the basin and for the dock. Can't fail to make a bit out of that, now, not to mention the odd bottle . . ."

After they had returned to the abhorred brick caboose and pored over accounts and dusty documents, from which Stanier gathered that Edwardes had been as lax over his paperwork as over the correct procedures to be adopted when running a port, Jones suggested a drink. It was just after six when the two men entered The Feathers. Stanier had only intended to have a sociable drink with his underling and then return to his hotel, or to be correct, Porth Ardur's only hotel. However, about half an hour after his arrival another person came in. Tegwyn Morgan, eighteen-year-old daughter of Justine, slipped behind the bar and in sliding out of her coat destroyed Stanier's hitherto impeccable self-possession.

Having spent the succeeding hour contemplating her body as she bent to oblige successive customers, he realised he was succumbing to lust as much as to alcohol. In a wave of self-revelation he made his apologies, thanked Mr Jones for his time and wove, with as much dignity as his twenty-six years could muster, his way out.

Straightening up and smoothing her dress over her hips, Tegwyn smiled at Mr Jones. "Who's your new friend, Tom love?"

"That, my dear, is the new 'Arbour Master. Captain bloody Stanier."

"He's young, isn't he; quite good looking too."

Avalon

If, in the last hours of Sunday, Charlie Farthing had idly ruminated on the possibility of discovering a land of enchantment somewhere west of the railway terminus, by the early hours of Tuesday he was almost certain. His certainty was incomplete for by this time, although delighted with the situation he found himself in, his breast was racked by emotions more immediate and desperately assertive than the simple realisation that he, as an animal, had stumbled upon the perfect habitat.

The *Caryatid* let go her anchor in fifteen fathoms off the north-east corner of Ynyscraven at about four in the afternoon. The breeze was dropping but the sea was still lively. It was already past low water but the flood was yet young and the rocky, grey cliffs showed exposed and shiny lower slopes where slime and weed marked the full tidal range. Ynyscraven's northern tip bore the white lighthouse that *Caryatid* had come to service. It was situated below the highest point of the island, precariously balanced upon a shelf of rock from which the cliffs dropped away in broken, creviced rock, old as time and inhabited by little tufts of thrift and a million sea birds. Kittiwakes, fulmars, razorbills and guillemots were the most numerous, but here and there squat

28

little puffins, with their bright coloured beaks and their web feet trailing like hastily stowed under carriages, whirled their rapid wing beats across the sea. The air was alive with the screams of the birds but Charlie's thoughts were broken into by the Captain. Macready had been studying the foot of the cliffs through binoculars. Alongside him Foster was doing the same.

"About four foot lift," Foster muttered helpfully.

"Yes, I think as you're going in it'll be alright. Anyway, see how it goes."

The Mate turned to Charlie. "Come on, we'll show you what this is all about." Charlie followed Foster down the bridge ladder and along the boat deck. With a deceptively casual activity one of *Caryatid*'s boats was being prepared.

A few minutes later Charlie found himself bobbing over the sea, the motor boat lifting effortlessly over the ground swell and flinging aside spray from the wind sea. Tidal eddies further complicated the wave patterns so that the boat seemed like an ancient war canoe picking its way between Scylla and Charybdis. This illusion was heightened by the black rocks that rose on either side of them as they approached the landing. To one of these massive outcrops was secured the end of a wire.

"The hoist wire for landing stores," explained Foster. "Boat lies underneath and signals to the winch house . . ." Charlie looked up to where, perched on a rock outcrop, a little cement hut stood next to a gantry over which the other end of the wire ran. He nodded. Ahead of them the cliff shut out sunlight and they motored into a cool gloom. All around the suck and whirl of the swells lifted and dropped them as though they were gliding over the back of some vast, sub-aquaeous monster that respirated gently beneath them. The landing was in sight and in a sudden bemusing flurry of activity a stern anchor had been pitched over the boat's stern, its hemp rope smoking over an oak king-post. White water was all around them and Charlie's heart beat suddenly faster. He was aware too that the boat's crew now worked with a concentrated energy, though scarcely a word was passed between them. A heaving line snaked through the air and was quickly caught. Charlie could see two keepers above him on a granite platform from which steps vanished up the towering cliff above and behind them. Another line came aboard, there was the rattle of chain where the boat ropes ended in chain snotters to prevent chafe on the rocks and suddenly the boat was secured, surging forwards and backwards, rising and falling, held by the snapping ropes that confined her like a fractious horse. Foster, Charlie and the working party leapt ashore and began the long, breathtaking climb up the steps.

The next two hours proved utterly fascinating. The boat returned to *Caryatid* and ran successive loads of oil barrels in under the hoist wire from where they were winched aloft. Once the seamen had started work Foster took Charlie off to see the lighthouse. They strode through the immaculately kept quarters and ascended the lantern tower. Foster showed Charlie the enormous optic and demonstrated how easily it was turned by an overgrown clockwork motor. At the centre of the foci the paraffin vapour burner sat, an innocent-looking apparatus of great importance and reliability. With something akin to a shock Charlie realised how he, in common with most seamen, took the wink of a lighthouse so utterly for granted.

"It's most interesting, Bernard," said Charlie as they came

back out into the daylight. "How often do we bring oil and water?"

"We don't need to bring water very often, the lighthouse has a flat roof over the dwellings to act as a catchment. We deliver oil about once a quarter."

"One other thing, I noticed the lantern level was well below the highest point of the island . . . that seems a bit odd to me . . ."

The Mate nodded. "They built the first tower on the highest point but found that ten months out of twelve it was in cloud. This one's just below the level of normal orographic cloud and has a range of twenty-four miles in all but fog or very heavy precipitation."

They began the long descent to the boat. Around them the sea birds whirled and screamed. "They're nesting," explained Foster. Tufts of thrift, moss, fern and heather gave way to lichens as they descended and at the foot of the cliff they waited once more. The smell of ozone was invigorating in Charlie's nostrils and he inhaled it enthusiastically. He watched the boat come in, impressed with the confidence with which the coxswain relied upon the keepers, though equally careful of his stern anchor line as his only escape should a swell pick up the boat and surge it forward. There was only sheer rock ahead and Charlie was beginning to appreciate some of that 'experience' Macready and Foster had been emphasising.

They returned through the swirling waters; the tide was much higher now. On several isolated pinnacles of rock cormorants and the greener crested shags sat drying their wings. They looked like Teutonic eagles atop pointed helmets. Charlie smiled to himself. He liked the imagery. They were the helmets of giant warriors hurled from the cliff-top by some Arthurian vedette long ago.

Charlie had one last surprise. As the launch rounded *Caryatid*'s stern he looked up. The steamer's stern was in considerable contrast to her workmanlike bow. A counter that would have graced a sailing ship extended out over the rudder post. Knuckled twice it bore a handsomely carved set of trail boards painted in gilt, red, green and blue. A scroll work of seaweeds and fishes terminated in naked females who bore flaming cressets and between these two devices, one on either quarter, was the name *Caryatid* and her port of registry. Foster saw his fascination. "It's poetic licence really," he offered by way of explanation. "Caryatids are supposed to bear up the roofs of temples but . . ." he shrugged, "the idea of supporting, in their case, seamarks is quite apt . . ."

Charlie nodded. The next minute they were alongside and hooking on. Seconds later, with a clatter of the steam winch and a creaking of manila falls, the launch was being hoisted into the davits.

The *Caryatid* was brought to an anchor for the night some three miles south of the lighthouse off the southern end of Ynyscraven. As was his custom Captain Macready announced to his officers after dinner that the off duty watch could have a run ashore. Charlie, who had no idea whether or not he was on or off duty when at anchor, enquired of the Mate. Bernard Foster puffed his pipe, a twinkle in his eye. "Strictly speaking it's your turn, the port watch being off tonight, but I think you'll benefit more from a run ashore. I'm not bothered about going and the Chief and I'll have a game of cribbage. You go off and gather some local colour."

It was already dusk when the motor launch left *Caryatid*'s side. The last man into the boat had been Calico Jack who had slid down the man-ropes to the jeers of his fellows waiting thirstily in the well of the boat. Somewhat impatiently Charlie watched the boat go. He had been told by the Mate to wait for Captain Macready. When the boat returned Charlie slid into it and waited. A few minutes later the portly backside of his commander swung into view. Half suspended, the Captain exchanged a few words with Foster then descended into the launch.

The boat turned away from the ship and approached the island some three and a half cables distant. Macready stared appraisingly at *Caryatid* then abruptly turned and viewed the land.

Ynyscraven lay like some enormous dragon. The lighthouse was situated on its north point, where the dragon's head might be imagined to lie. The greater, higher part of the island, little better than heather-covered moor, formed the beast's back, gradually sloping away to a slightly lower plateau.

As if reading Charlie's thoughts the Captain said, "Beautiful spot, Mr Farthing."

"Yes it is sir, I was just thinking the same."

"There's a bit of farming done this end," he waved to the south where a few low houses could be seen by their lights. "Mostly sheep, although they domesticate the wild ponies for a living."

"Much of a population, sir?"

The Captain shook his head. "No. There's the owner's

reeve, two or three shepherd families and a couple of crackpots. In the summer you get the visiting ornithologists, probably a few there now since the birds are breeding."

The boat slowed and came alongside a low stone jetty. The Captain and Charlie jumped ashore. They were in the shadow of a steep hill and in almost total darkness.

"There's the path, you go on ahead, I just want a word with the coxswain."

Charlie started off. He had a sudden desire to be on his own and began to walk briskly upwards. Gorse and bracken spurted out of little hollows in the rock but everywhere granite outcrops predominated. The path led up the side of a small valley. Below him to his right Charlie could hear a little stream and he could see where denser and more luxuriant vegetation grew. The air was scented with damp, pleasant odours and he continued upwards for several minutes without any sound of the Captain behind him. He failed to notice a fork in the path where it crossed the head of the valley. A fairly large stone house stood in a little coombe. He continued climbing, the path winding round behind the house. Ahead of him he could see open sky, and realised he was reaching the summit of the island. Just before he emerged from the vegetation onto rough pasture the figure of a girl stepped out in front of him. The encounter was abrupt, with the quality of ambuscade about it.

"Hullo," she said. He could barely make out her features since she was silhouetted against what daylight remained in the western sky, but her voice was low and self-confident.

"Oh, hullo," he replied, taken aback.

"Did I startle you?" There was a note of mockery in her voice.

"A little," he replied.

"Only you're going the wrong way . . . to the pub that is."

"Am I? Oh, I'm sorry. I didn't really know that's where I was supposed to be going."

"You *are* off the *Caryatid*?" she asked suspiciously.

"Yes," he replied.

"Well," she said firmly, "the *Caryatid*'s people always go to the pub." There was such an emphasis on 'always' that Charlie began to assume he was trespassing.

"I beg your pardon, I was really just walking, following the path, I didn't know I was trespassing."

She laughed, a light refreshing laugh. "You're not," she said reassuringly, "it's just unusual to see one of *Caryatid*'s crew not on the pub path. I expected you to take the path to the right of the reeve's house, it runs alongside his garden, you go through the old monastery wall and the pub-cum-post office is right there."

"Oh, I see." He pondered a minute. "What did you mean when you said you 'expected'?"

She laughed again. "Oh, I was watching you and Mr Foster up at the lighthouse this afternoon . . . through my glasses from the crags above the hoist gantry."

Charlie vaguely remembered some huge rock outcrops behind and above the little lighthouse plateau.

"Then you have the advantage over me. Name's Charlie Farthing. I've just joined the *Caryatid* as Second Mate. This morning as a matter of fact."

He held out his hand feeling rather foolish since they could now hardly see each other. He was instantly hurt when she ignored it. A note of asperity came into her voice: "What do you think of Ynyscraven?" she asked. For a minute he was tempted to reply, "not much," since the manners of the inhabitants left much to be desired but there was that hint of interrogation in the question that made him think he was being tested.

"I think it the most beautiful place I have ever seen," he said without falsehood. "Now will you tell me who you are and shake my hand or are you really a sprite about to disappear?"

His intuition had been correct but the girl's response exceeded his expectations. She grasped his outstretched hand, suddenly leant forward and brushed her lips against his cheek. Then, still holding his hand, she pulled away laughing. "Come *on* then, I've been waiting ages for you."

In the next hour and a half Charlie lost his heart. He was comfortably euphoric after a poor night's sleep and the exertions of the day. The girl took him across the spine of the island to the cliff-tops of the western side. At this point Ynyscraven was only three hundred yards wide and the walk across a springy turf being cropped by the ghostly forms of sheep seemed to him to take but a few seconds. They sat down below the sky line.

To left and right of them the broken, precipitous cliffs of the island stretched away. Far below the restless Atlantic pounded at their feet, a white filigree of foam lacing the shore. The westerly wind was deflected upwards so that here they were in total peace, above them the pale shapes of ridge-soaring gulls screamed into the night. Before them the infinite vista of the dark ocean and the vast canopy of sky as the planet plunged into night seemed quite personal to them.

"Quite the most beautiful place I have ever seen . . ." muttered Charlie.

The girl hugged her knees then turned her head towards him.

"And have you seen many places, Mr Farthing?" she enquired mockingly.

He shrugged. "Bits of four continents, but always as, well, a visitor."

"But you are a visitor here."

Charlie shook his head. "I am to you. But as a sailor that," he indicated the ocean below them, inky blue in the night, "that is my home until I choose somewhere to swallow the anchor. Besides, I'm a bit of the *Caryatid* and she seems to be part of the seascape hereabouts."

He heard her chuckle softly in the darkness.

"Tell me why is this island *so* important to you?" he asked, sensing rather than seeing her shrug.

"I was born here. Perhaps I was taught as a little girl to dislike the outside world. I am told many people of my age wish to leave the places they are born in but I have no wish to leave this place. Ever!" Her voice, which began dreamily, ended emphatically, as though warning Charlie. It made him think of an earlier remark.

"And why did you say you had been waiting ages for me?"

"You ask too many questions, Mr Farthing." She was laughing at him again.

"But I want to. I don't even know your name. Is it Guinevere or Morgan le Fay?

She rounded on him sharply. "Why did you say that?" The sharp, interrogative, even imperious note was in her

voice again. He told her. He told her of his wry fancy
that had started the previous night at the railway station
and had persisted as the train had brought him nearer
and nearer to Porth Ardur. He told her how no single
incident that had occurred during the day had destroyed the
feeling that he was approaching a land of magic and the
conviction he had felt when seeing the jettisoned helmets of
the defeated warriors. He ended feeling the merest pinprick
of cynical self-ridicule. Her reply laid his wandering heart
at rest. Quietly she said:

"That, Charlie, is why I said I had been waiting for
you."

Very slowly she rolled over him. They kissed cautiously,
not wanting to break the magic of the night with the dross
of physical contact but as their lips met they both knew that
a passion existed within them that seemed bottomless. After
a little she drew away from him and rose to her knees.
The next minute she was pulling him protesting to his feet.
"Come on," she said, "we must go to the pub. They'll be
missing you by now and when they find you they'll accuse
you of doing unspeakable things with sheep."

Charlie roared with laughter. It was an accurate assessment. "Hold on a minute," he pulled her back. "I still don't
know your name."

"It's Sonia," she said daring him to laugh. "It's Slavic,
you know, now *come on*!"

The public house which went under the grandiloquent title
of the Craven Arms was a large, open, stone hall. It had a
wooden bar along one side and barrels of spigoted beer on
cradles. Three small kegs of spirits were similarly rigged

and the walls were decorated with the nautical paraphernalia which has since become so popular but which was, in the case of the Craven Arms, entirely plundered or washed ashore from wrecks. In the sense of being a public place the Craven Arms fulfilled its function admirably. When the *Caryatid* anchored the little island usually went *en fête*. Almost its entire population was present. The atmosphere was thick with smoke, loud chatter and the clink of glasses. The oil lamps caught the sheen of perspiration on rosy faces and the slopping amber of beer in glasses. The atmosphere was decidedly convivial.

When Charlie and the girl arrived they were greeted with cheers which Charlie found embarrassing, as much for Sonia as himself but looking at her, as she shoved her way to the bar and returned with two pints of beer, he realised she was quite used to it. He was able to see her clearly for the first time. Like himself she wore wellington boots. A pair of slacks were mostly covered by an Aran sweater. At her throat a knotted kerchief of emerald green was the only item of personal decoration she wore. Her features were regular and broad, her hair was reddish, neither auburn nor carroty, and a pair of level green eyes looked at him from beneath arched brows. On each slightly prominent cheekbone her creamy skin was slightly wind-burned and freckled.

"Disappointed?" she asked handing him a glass of beer.

"I don't answer *that*," he laughed, "and you?"

"You forget I've been watching you this afternoon."

Charlie rubbed a bristly chin, wondering what on earth she saw in his unremarkable features. He shrugged. "Good," he said and they smiled at each other.

This intimate conversation was carried out at a shout

whilst the two lovers were being gently jostled by the other inhabitants of the bar. These were well on the way to intoxication and Charlie looked round for Macready. The Captain, still in his brass-bound reefer sat in a corner. Before him were a large glass of brandy and his hat. With him sat a tall, florid man and they were in conversation. There was a tiny, yet distinct, gap around them as though the company acknowledged the social difference of the two gentlemen, conceded them a trifling privacy before proceeding with its own merriment.

"Your Captain's talking to the reeve. He's the agent of the owner. The island belongs to the estate of the Earl of Dungarth. I believe Mr Hamilton was his adjutant in the war. He and old 'Ebb Tide' always chinwag like that."

An accordion started up. Mackerel Jack began to play a reel and there was a move to dance. A little space was cleared at the end of the bar and two of the locals and their women spun into the ring. Next was Calico Jack, jerking energetically around an odd little woman to the cheers of his shipmates. The woman wore a fur coat that had seen better days. She appeared not to notice the sweltering heat in the place, though her grey hair hung in wispy disorder about her head.

"Who on earth is that little old woman?" Charlie asked Sonia.

"That's Mother. Come on, we'll dance now!" Charlie's surprise had not turned to protest before he found himself whirling alongside the old woman. Calico Jack's happily inebriated face came and went around the bulk of her fur coat like an alcoholic moon as *Caryatid*'s crew pounded out the rythmn, nodding and smiling to each other that their new Second Mate seemed a good lad and a sport and a lucky bastard to have got the daughter.

"Give 'em a fuckin' waltz, Mack," yelled one of the greasers and Mackerel Jack, to the accompaniment of knowing leers and winks, slowed down the music so that all the gyrating partners lost their timing then melted into linked couples. Calico Jack disappeared into the vast fur coat, the shepherds grabbed their women tightly, possessively, with so many seamen in the room. One off duty lighthouse keeper held his affianced shepherdess with a discreet tenderness and two seamen, who had been dancing an improvised hornpipe between them said, "Oh, fuck it!" and sat down, grinning into their beer.

Mackerel excelled himself, slowing the waltz down to a melancholic chanty tune that the men hummed. Some of them had sat in the horse latitudes on the decks of windjammers humming the tune of 'Leave her Johnnie' as their vessels idly rolled in the calm; all of them were affected by it and all watched the dancing couples without ridicule.

Charlie was lost in the perfume of Sonia's hair; feeling her thighs against his he gently pushed his pelvis forward and was met by an answering thrust. He felt her breasts against his chest and leaned his body closer to hers, trying to keep the revelation of his own arousal private between them. As the music slowed to its end he kissed her, briefly but publicly. There was a moment of silence, then a storm of shouts and cheering. Glasses were banged on the table and booted feet stamped on the granite flags of the floor.

Mackerel swung into another jig and the locals relinquished their women as the Caryatids swept into the next dance. Somebody pulled Calico Jack out of his furry burrow and demanded he bought the next round.

Sonia pulled Charlie back to the bar. "It's your turn too," she said. They were laughing at each other like children. While he stood at the slopped wood surface he looked about him. "It's like a Viking hall," he said. She nodded.

"Or Camelot?" he went on. She frowned and shook her head.

"No," she replied seriously, "no, Camelot was corrupted, this is Avalon."

They clicked glasses, laughing again.

Charlie looked several times at the old woman Sonia had described as her mother. She was sitting quietly with Calico Jack, taking no part in the conversation of the fireman and his mates but staring ahead of her. He turned to the girl.

"Your mother, is she alright?" Sonia looked quickly at her mother and nodded.

"She's alright. I'll explain one day."

Charlie was going to press her but someone was up and singing now. It was a popular and sugary ballad that evoked enthusiastic applause. Other songs followed in which the company joined or talked through, according to inclination. At last Mackerel Jack played an obviously familiar chanty. Charlie was beginning to join in when he felt the girl's hand on his arm. "You'll be going soon, they always play the chanties when the Captain tells them. Everyone knows it's time to go . . ." She trailed off. He bent and kissed her, feeling someone behind him slopping beer down his back. "Will I see you again?" he asked, wondering if he was being played with in a manner he was not unacquainted with.

"Of course," she breathed at him; then she looked away

and, in a clear, strong voice, joined in the chanty. Charlie could have sworn afterwards that there were tears in her eyes.

They sang 'The Hog's Eye Man' and the 'Arethusa' then broke into 'Spanish Ladies'. At the last verse, 'Now let every man fill up his full bumper . . .' glasses were drained for the last time. The chanty, old when Nelson was a midshipman, finished in cheers which gradually died away. Sonia nudged him and nodded in Captain Macready's direction. Macready had risen and made a great show of looking at his watch. "God bless my soul, it's midnight," he intoned and from the assembled grins Charlie guessed it was a ritual. The Captain looked up. "Mackerel!" he said sharply.

"Sir?" mocked the able seaman back.

"My song, please." If Charlie had expected some ghastly piece of self-aggrandisement he was pleasantly disappointed. In a remarkably fine baritone Septimus Macready launched into the most plaintive of all sea chanties:

'Oh Shenandoah I long to see you,

Away you rolling river,

Oh Shenandoah I long to hold you,

And away, we're bound away 'cross the wide Missouri . . .'

Charlie found himself clutching Sonia's waist as the whole company swayed gently to the haunting tune. There was no applause at the end of the song. The Captain paused a second to swallow, jammed his cap on and, waving to the barman flung open the door and strode into the night. His alcohol-bemused and happy crew followed him, trailing out into the moon-flooded night.

Sonia held Charlie's hand while they followed the file

of men. They passed through the old monastery wall and descended the path by which Charlie should have come up earlier. In the moonlight Charlie recognised the bifurcation and here Sonia said goodnight. They clung together for a long while. He longed to squeeze her breasts but had an intuitively repressive thought not to sharpen his desire further. At last they drew apart. "Good night, Charlie darling," she whispered and turning away into the undergrowth she disappeared. For a minute he stood there in the moonlight. Was it the same moon he had seen rising over the capital's jumbled roofs and chimneys? He shook off the thought and turned away, hurrying down after the retreating crew.

He caught them up as they tumbled into the boat. Aft with the cox he saw Captain Macready. "Mr Farthing!" the Captain called.

"Sir?"

"Officers aft, if you please." With much scrambling Charlie pushed aft. The men drew good-naturedly aside, not interupting their conversation as he passed.

"D'you hear what Calico says there, Harry boy-o?"

"Whash tha'?"

"The old 'un. Under that mountain of fur she was naked . . ."

"Cor fuck me . . ."

A Disagreement

Captain James St John Stanier, Harbour Master of Porth
Ardur, had by the middle of his first week in his new job,
got his feet well under the table. Having insisted 'his staff'
kept him fully informed and made no moves to berth, shift
or unmoor ships without his express permission, he was to
be seen strutting about the quay side at tide time full, as
Thomas Jones told the lads in The Feathers 'of piss and
importance.'

Thomas, Fred and Stan were convinced the new broom
would soon get tired of its clean sweeping and went along
with their new governor's ways. All of them sensed a change
in the weather and anticipated the passenger-ship trained
'Captain' would not favour dirty weather half so much.

Unaware that he was also the butt of jokes amongst the
fishermen, Stanier pressed on regardless of the sly glances
and smirks he engendered. On Tuesday afternoon one of
the *schuyts* sailed. The skipper sent for a pilot and Stanier
duly went aboard. The Dutch skipper took no notice of
Stanier and seemed content that the pilot was simply there.
With a massive paw on the wheel, another on the engine
room telegraph (which he appeared to be about to break
with every swing) and a string of roared commands at

his mate on the fo'c's'le, the Dutchman got his coaster warped across the basin. Once lined up with the entrance he slammed the telegraph full ahead and the *schuyt* steamed straight through the lockheads, swung round the end of the mole and slowed to disembark the pilot. Leaving the wheel the Dutchman proffered a paw to Stanier. "Dank you, pilot." They shook hands, Stanier took his signed chit and the Dutchman disappeared into his wheelhouse again. Stanier beat a hasty retreat. At least his launch was a credit to him, he thought, jumping into it.

"That was as neat a piece of ship handling as I've seen, Captain," said Jones innocently when Stanier sat beside him. "Yes, thank you," replied Stanier, his blush told Jones what the latter already suspected.

Despite this blow to his pride, Stanier soon forgot it as he made progress on another front. In coming to Porth Ardur it was not his intention to become romantically entangled. His one intention was to enhance his career. However, as a junior officer in a passenger-liner his life had encompassed a fair amount of sexual activity. It was therefore logical that he should seek a compliant and discreet bed-partner with whom he could establish a casual relationship. Although his experience in such matters was not inconsiderable his assumptions about the female sex were apt to be naively based upon the atmosphere on board passenger-liners sailing under sexually awakening tropical skies. The metamorphoses experienced by women in such circumstances were unlikely to occur on the home ground of Porth Ardur, even given the handsome features of James St John Stanier.

On the other hand the sailor was himself susceptible to certain females. He had stared with shameless candour at

Tegwyn Morgan because she had walked into his life and fulfilled his ultimate dreams of sexual fantasy. As he had striven to do his duty by the shipping company with matrons approaching the autumn of their lives he had improved his performance with a little harmless (and encouraging) day-dreaming. Tegwyn Morgan exactly fitted his image of a *femme fatale* and Captain Stanier took to drinking in The Feathers regularly.

It was not until Thursday night that Stanier also met Justine. She was pleasant chatty and, discovering that Stanier was a dancer, invited him to the dancing group's club night the following evening.

"Does your daughter dance as well?" Stanier asked, too casually to fool Justine. She shrugged, "Occasionally, when she's in the mood."

She laughed, a rich bubbling laugh so that Stanier looked from mother to daughter and licked his lips. He did not notice further along the bar several elderly men apparently abstractedly supping pints. Their concentration was riveted on Stanier.

Tide time on Friday was 1148. Punctually at 1130 *Caryatid* appeared in the bay. The weather had turned. After leaving Ynyscraven the ship had steamed west southwest to where the Buccabu Reef rose from the bed of the Atlantic. The eroded residue of a once mighty escarpment, it was barely covered at high water and on its largest rock summit human ingenuity had eventually succeeded in erecting a tower lighthouse.

The Buccabu lighthouse consisted of nearly 6,000 tons of fully interlocking granite blocks, from the summit of which a mighty optic shot out the beams of light that it collected from the paraffin vapour burner at its focus. It had no adjacent dwellings, rising like the bole of an oak tree to its immense height of 139 feet above high water. Charlie had been terrified and then impressed at the expedition with which his boat's crew had removed one of the keepers. Slinging over the stern anchor he had seen them use at Ynyscraven, the boat had run in with the swell under it. At a shout from the coxswain the line had been checked. The keepers on the set-off tossed their heavy lines and, as if by magic, the boat was suddenly secured by two head ropes. If the stern anchor dragged the swell would pick the boat up and . . . Charlie shivered, suddenly thinking of Sonia.

An hour after *Caryatid* had recovered her boat the first rain began to fall. It swept in a grey curtain from the west, shutting in the visibility and towing a rising wind in its skirts. Charlie remembered the old doggerel:

> 'Comes the rain before the wind,
> Then your sheets and halyards mind.'

Within a further two hours *Caryatid* was running before a southwesterly gale. Captain Macready decided to take his ship back to Ynyscraven until the weather moderated and *Caryatid* spent nearly twenty-four hours anchored under the lee of Charlie's private Avalon. But there was no shore leave while the gale blew. Charlie was miserable for the first time, staring disconsolately ashore in the forlorn hope he might see Sonia. Further along the boat deck he was astonished to see the figure of Calico Jack similarly lovelorn. Then, late in the afternoon, he caught sight of her. A tiny figure high up, leaning against a rock, the white sweater clear against the dark stone. He picked up the long glass and trained it, steadying the telescope against a stanchion. She had her arms about her neck. She seemed to be adjusting something at her neckline. He saw her pull her green silk scarf clear of her throat and shake her hair free. Then she walked further uphill until she stood on the skyline and stood, arm upstretched, her scarf and russet hair an oriflamme against the grey backdrop of the sky.

Charlie watched her for several moments before he granted her the courtesy of a reply. Grabbing the bridge semaphore controls he set the wooden arms whirring on the monkey island above him. He spelled out 'I love you'. Behind him a voice chuckled. Spinning round he found Captain Macready regarding him with some indulgence.

"Like to be ashore, eh, Mr Farthing?"

"Er, yes sir, very much."

"Sorry about that. You deep-sea mariners are apt to think we coastal men spend all our lives in someone's bed. Sometimes one night out here in a gale in circumstances like yours are worth thirty drinking gin in the Indian Ocean." He smiled sadly. "Young love, Mr Farthing is a *very* misleading emotion—" The Captain broke off as if he had already said more than he intended. Charlie looked back to the island but Sonia had gone and another rain squall was sweeping, like a final curtain, over the scene.

"Inform the Chief we'll weigh at oh-five-hundred for Porth Ardur, let Mr Foster know as well." Charlie left the bridge and Captain Macready paced up and down until he heard the steward ring the gong for high tea.

Captain Macready relieved his First Mate as *Caryatid*

steamed round the point and entered the bay. He shaped a course of north as he had done a thousand times before, the seaman at the wheel spinning the spokes effortlessly as *Caryatid*'s patent steam tiller responded to the hydraulic pressure of the telemotor.

"Steady on north, sir," he said.

"Very good."

The gale still blew and despite the shelter of the land a long swell rounded the point and the steamer rolled lazily as she ploughed towards the mole of Porth Ardur. Bernard Foster finished talking to the Bosun down the voice pipe and turned idly to look out of the wheelhouse windows, waiting the few minutes until he was needed on the fo'c's'le for berthing.

He noted with pleasure the orderly state of the foredeck. The ropes coiled in their appointed places, the blake stoppers curled round their securing lugs, and the spurling pipes stopped off to prevent the sea from pouring into the ship's chain hold. He looked up and something unusual caught his eye. He picked up the glasses.

"The new Harbour Master's got the signals up against us."

Macready uttered a grunt and lifted his own binoculars. "Well I'm damned!"

"Perhaps he's got a coaster coming out."

"No masts moving over the mole, Bernard . . ."

"You don't suppose he's boomed the gates against the swell?"

Macready shifted his binoculars. "There's hardly any lift along the outside of the mole. Besides, it's a sou'westerly not a bloody sou'easter. No, strikes me the new broom is trying to sweep clean. This is the first time we've had this without getting notification from the Coast Guard." Macready stepped out onto the bridge wing and rang the engine room telegraph. The bells tinkled faintly in the engine room then jangled the acknowledgement on the bridge.

"Is Mr Farthing there?" Charlie had just come on the bridge.

"Yes, sir."

"Mr Farthing, you're a dab hand with the semaphore, call up the mole and ask what time we can berth." Charlie did as he was bid. He was not to know that ashore his transmission was causing a certain amount of confusion. Thomas Jones and his mates, seeing that their new boss was full of reforming zeal and refused to delegate any responsibility, acted dumb when asked if any of them could use semaphore. It was Captain Stanier, therefore, who was thus compelled to stand conspicuously on the wind-swept mole and wave the yellow and red flags, hoist by his own petard into a position that threatened to unseat both his person and his dignity.

He read *Caryatid*'s whirling semaphore arms with some difficulty. By way of reply Stanier transmitted, 'You will enter as convenient'; he was rather proud of the last long word. By way of sealing his personal authority upon the scene he followed this up with: 'Watch for my signals'.

Stanier saw the *Caryatid* swing into the wind and the anchor ball rise at her forestay. He smiled with satisfaction.

"If we wait here too long we'll miss the bloody tide," Macready observed to the wheelhouse in general. A hissing rain squall suddenly descended upon the ship, the wind with it lashing the little ship and tearing up the water of the bay into a million white streaks. Macready swung round with sudden decision.

"Right, let's get the launch away and land that poor bloody keeper. Mr Farthing, you go in and find out what the delay is. The men'll be wanting pay and their wives will be pestering the clerks for housekeeping and God knows what if we miss the tide . . ."

Charlie clambered out of the boat and gave the grinning lighthouse keeper a hand with his gear. "Cheerio lads," said the keeper to the boat's crew.

"Piss off, Larry boy," said the coxswain without malice.

The keeper laughed again from the top of the steps. "Give her one for me then," added the bowman. The keeper turned and looked down into the boat: "I've two months' worth of my own to get rid of first; you'll still be waiting when I've finished." He went chuckling off down the quay.

Charlie found Captain Stanier in his brick caboose. "Good morning," Charlie began. "Can you tell me how long the *Caryatid* is likely to be kept out?"

Stanier made a great show of looking up. He regarded Charlie with some hostility. As an emissary of the magnificent Captain Septimus Macready he was somewhat unprepossessing.

"Are you an officer?" Stanier asked superciliously, staring at Charlie's plain pilot jacket, blue serge trousers and sea-boots. Charlie was annoyed.

"Captain Macready isn't in the habit of sending his cook on such errands."

Stanier went white with suppressed fury. "I think you had better call me 'sir'. And I'm sorry to mistake your identity.

52

I'm used to seeing officers in a collar and tie." Charlie flushed with irritation. He thought his white polo-necked sweater rather dashing. Who was this bastard anyway?

"I expect you learned your seamanship in the passengers' bunks," he said, "but it doesn't matter. I'm looking for the Harbour Master—"

"*I* am the Harbour Master, Mister bloody Mate, and I'll be lodging a complaint against you when your ship berths."

"Well, Captain," replied Charlie with heavy emphasis, "perhaps you'll be kind enough to tell me when that will be?"

"When I signal. Now please return to your ship."

"That was a bit strong, you know, Captain," said Thomas Jones who had silently witnessed the entire proceedings. Stanier leaned back in his chair, perfectly composed again.

"Mr Jones, *Caryatid* is not the only ship using this port. She must wait her turn. There is the *Sea Dragon* to sail yet."

"But she's a blooming motor yacht, she can slip out after the ebb's away." Jones's voice rose on a note of disbelief.

"She belongs to Sir Hector Blackadder, chairman of the Cambrian Steam Navigation Company. She dry-docks on this tide and I have been personally asked to move her round into the dock at high water. When I have cleared the gates you may signal the *Caryatid* to enter. Is that clear, Mr Jones?"

"Perfectly clear, Captain. But you're asking for trouble."

Stanier did not hear the last remark. Donning his bridge coat, resplendent with its four bars on each shoulder, and his hat, which sat at an angle popularised by Admiral Beatty, he strode purposefully into the windy day.

It was not that Captain Stanier, wearing his other hat as Porth Ardur's pilot, made a mess of moving the *Sea Dragon*. In fact he manoeuvred strictly in accordance with the recommendations of the Board of Trade for turning vessels in a confined space. He laced the inner harbour with warps until it resembled a spider's web and gently hove the *Sea Dragon* round until her bows were in line with the gates, then he steamed gently ahead and not one inch of the yacht's paintwork was scratched. This time there was no master to interfere, since that worthy had not then been appointed. Neither was Sir Hector in attendance, so Stanier felt his responsibility keenly.

It is true that some damage was done to the cross trees of the trawler *Cheerful Boys* but it was only the mizen mast and her owner was neither a shipping magnate nor a knight of the realm. When the little dock tug, really no more than a motor boat, came and got hold of the *Sea Dragon*'s bows and tugged her across the inner harbour to the dry-dock gates, Stanier felt his pride restored. This feeling was augmented when he saw at the door of The Feathers the voluptuous form of Tegwyn Morgan.

The main problem caused by Stanier that morning was that by the time Thomas Jones signalled the port clear for *Caryatid* to enter, the ebb was away. It was a spring tide and within an hour and a half of high water there would not be enough depth for the lighthouse tender to get over the sill.

Caryatid might have made it if she had not fouled an old trawl wire with the anchor that Stanier had made her let go by the delay. So it was thus that the *Caryatid* was compelled to remain at anchor until the next high water, around 0100 on Saturday.

It was not the first time it had happened. Occasionally the gates were boomed against a southeasterly gale, sometimes the opening mechanism failed to work, but under any circumstances it was a bitter blow to the crew of the *Caryatid*. Accustomed to arduous labour, they held their weekends sacrosanct, to be interrupted only in emergencies. For Captain Macready it was a dilemma. He would be entitled to go ashore until tide time, but scarcely felt the effort involved in a wet boat passage worthwhile. But it was Friday night and his night for dancing with Justine Morgan.

At seven o'clock *Caryatid*'s boat left the ship with half the crew. Foster watched them go. Anthea would not be pleased, but with the Captain ashore and a new second mate he felt he ought to stay. Perhaps he had an exaggerated sense of responsibility, or was it that he felt himself indispensible? He shrugged resignedly. It was just too bloody bad. He turned for his cabin and the log book.

Charlie was quite glad to stay on board. He walked quietly round *Caryatid* after the empty boat had been hoisted. The ship lifted easily to the swell that rolled into the bay. His hair was tousled by the near gale. It was definitely moderating, he thought to himself. Aft, leaning on the teak taffrail that ran round *Caryatid*'s elegant counter with the ensign cracking and snapping above him, he looked to windward. Somewhere just over the horizon, upon the island of Ynyscraven, was that strange wild creature that he was hopelessly in love with. Half-Celt, half-Slav, a combination so extraordinary that he had never heard of it before. But then he recollected that he had never been in love like this before, so perhaps it was not so very extraordinary. It was rather nice to discover a new, fresh sensation in a world which one had grown blasé about. He too shrugged and strode forward to the monastic isolation of his tiny cabin.

Justine Morgan stepped out of her bath at about the same time that Captain Macready made up his mind to go ashore. As she rubbed under her breasts she abstractedly felt their weight with a small pleasurable ripple. She smoothed the towel down over her belly, vigorously drying her thighs and legs. She slipped on a wrap and walked into her bedroom. Below she heard a key in the door-lock.

"Is that you, Tegwyn?" she called in her low mellifluous voice.

"Uh huh," her daughter called in the fashionable transatlantic syllables.

"Come up, will you?"

Friday was Tegwyn's night off from The Feathers. She came into her mother's bedroom and flopped down on the bed.

"What is it, Mother?" she asked.

"I was just wondering if you were coming dancing tonight?" replied Justine, sitting at her dressing-table and brushing her hair. At the same time she scrutinised her daughter for telltale signs. Tegwyn yawned and shrugged, then lay back and stretched like a cat. Her mother's eyes narrowed. There was fire in the belly of that one, thought Justine, as she saw the half-smile curl upon her daughter's lips.

"I might. And then again I mightn't."

"And that means you will and you've designs upon some unsuspecting fellow."

"Mother, how could you?" said Tegwyn, sitting up in mock indignation.

Justine stopped brushing her hair and stood up. Undoing her wrap she stepped into a pair of knickers. Tegwyn watched her mother's figure in admiration. An odd pang of unaccountable jealousy pricked her.

"And what if I am? You're not beyond a flirt yourself."

Her mother threw off the wrap and began putting on her brassiere, deftly arranging her cleavage. She laughed.

"I'm old enough and wise enough not to get into trouble, my girl. I've seen you and that new Harbour Master making eyes at one another. He's unscrupulous, you know. A girl like you is not in his class but he'll use you and then when he's finished he'll chuck you to one side." She picked up a slip and a pair of stockings.

"Rubbish, Mother. I can take care of myself."

"Just make sure you can, that's all. Now go and get ready. It's black tonight. I've a pair of black stockings you can borrow in the second drawer."

Tegwyn got up from the bed. "I've my own black stockings, thank you." She flounced out of the room.

By the time he had been home and chatted to his wife over a cup of tea Captain Macready was late at the Tudor Tea Rooms where the dancing club held its weekly meeting. He was also unprepared for the sight that met his eyes.

In coupled pairs the members were dancing a tango under the direction of Justine Morgan as leading *danseuse*. Except that they were not exactly doing that. Only one couple was

57

actually dancing while the others watched, and Justine, leaning on the gramophone with her lips slightly parted and a rapt expression on her face, took no part in directing the couple. For a minute the Captain gazed at Justine. He had never seen her so provocative off the floor. One hip jutted out, eloquently supported by one of those fine, sturdy legs. The other leg was in repose, her high-heeled shoe tap-tapping to the rythmn. Although still, her whole body seemed coiled round the music and it was only when the Captain realised she was motivated not so much by the beat of the tango as by the spectacle before her that he looked at the couple that was generating all the electricity.

Now at this precise point Septimus Macready had no idea who the young man was. He simply saw a broad-shouldered, fair-haired male, following the erotically formal movements of the tango to perfection. He was leading a splendidly arrogant girl whose out-thrust breasts seemed, in a nautical simile, like the bow wave to the curve of her throat. Her head was thrown back and a cascade of hair tumbled from a black ribbon done up on the crown of her head. For a second Macready was confused. The girl seemed a suddenly metamorphosed Justine, dancing with the mature confidence he so much admired. Then he realised it was Tegwyn and he too stood transfixed until the final chord and the abrupt halt to the dance.

A storm of quite spontaneous applause burst from the eight or nine couples standing about the tea room. Stanier and Tegwyn walked off the floor hand in hand like lovers from a formal dance floor. The others gathered round with cries of enthusiastic comment. Macready entered the room and went up to Justine.

"Sorry I'm late, m'dear. Damn ship's kept outside . . ." he smiled, puzzled at the tears in her eyes. He had never seen tears such as these before. Tears of laughter quite a few times, but never of pathos. He blundered on, embarrassed at the effect they were having on him.

"I see we'll have to watch our laurels . . . who is the young fellow?"

Justine had recovered herself and smiled. "Him? Why I thought you'd know him." She saw Macready frown slightly.

"He's the new Harbour Master, Captain Stanier, old Tom Edwardes' successor."

"Well, I'll be damned. So he's the young jackanapes who got me locked out, is he?" It was Justine's turn to be surprised at her partner's expression.

"Septimus, what is it? You've gone quite red!"

He let out his breath in a long, slow exhalation. He shook his head. "Nothing."

Justine's eyes sparkled again. She touched Macready's arm. "They danced well, though, didn't you think? Tegwyn was beautiful," she finished in a whisper and Macready caught her mood, unconsciously setting words to his thoughts.

"Yes," he said, his voice low and unusually sensual, "she reminded me of you."

Their eyes met and they exchanged a glance such as lovers of long standing exchange. And yet to them it was like the first time. For five years they had matter-of-factly danced with the team, a natural pair who danced together well. Between them there had never been the slightest hint of intimacy beyond the contacts prescribed by the formalities of various steps. Now something profound had occurred in that electric atmosphere of the Tudor Tea Rooms, in the shadow of aspidistras and piles of bentwood chairs.

Septimus Macready leant over and turned the handle of the gramophone. He lifted the needle and the record began to spin. He carefully lowered the needle and led Justine out to begin the tango. In the room the rest of the club turned from Stanier and Tegwyn, silence fell and the air crackled.

Aboard the *Caryatid* Bernard Foster finished his log book, completed his stores lists and sat back, relighting his pipe for the twentieth time. Along the alley-way Charlie still sat ruminating, lost in the fantasies of young, romantic love. It was uncanny the way he had preserved the feeling deep down inside himself that there was, in this tired old world, love such as the ancients enjoyed, such as poets wrote of and playwrights immortalised. Not for everyone, of course; the evidence of his experience suggested the vast majority of people rubbed along with a mixture of affection and lust. He mused on the problem, it probably explained the discontent apparently inherent in the human situation. He sighed with utter contentment. That he should be one of the lucky ones seemed incredible. And yet that tiny feeling of certainty he had experienced as he had looked west down the railway tracks had, despite himself and the cynical patina the years had laid upon him, been vindicated.

He spoke her name softly, whispering the syllables, laying emphasis upon differing parts of it, secretly teasing it with his tongue as he might her nipple.

The sun went down and about nine thirty a knock came on Charlie's cabin door. It was Mackerel Jack.

"'Scuse me sir, we're ready to take the boat in for the lads."

Charlie looked at his watch. "Shore leave doesn't finish until eleven," he said.

The seaman winked. "I know sir. But we gen'rally run in a bit early, see, and wash our mouths out." Charlie comprehended.

"Well, I'm not sure."

"That's alright, Charlie," it was Bernard's voice from the next cabin who was well aware of what was going on, "we call it usage of the service – it's a long established tradition."

Mackerel Jack smiled happily. Charlie smiled too. A few minutes later the launch left the ship's side. Charlie heard the hiss of spray as she plunged into a wave and thought that perhaps the wind had not moderated further.

In the Tudor Tea Rooms Macready had at last come face to face with Stanier. The Captain and Justine had danced the tango superlatively well. To the onlookers it had seemed a competitive performance; as if the older couple were confirming their right to remain the club's leaders, to re-establish their precedence in the pecking order.

As they finished, Stanier, who by now knew the identity of the stocky well-built man dancing with Tegwyn's mother, walked over.

"My congratulations, Captain Macready. May I introduce myself? I'm James Stanier, the new Harbour Master." He held out his hand, an urbane and charming smile upon his face.

Macready grunted. "So you're the young jackanapes that

locked my ship out tonight." It was more a statement than a question.

"Sorry, Captain. Had a tidal job docking the *Sea Dragon*; you left it just too late getting your anchor up and . . ." he shrugged, a peculiarly foreign gesture, or so Macready thought.

"Now you listen here, young man, don't you ever mess me or my crew about again. When I signal my ETA to the Coast Guard you make sure those damned gates are open. I'll worry about whether there's sufficient water on the sill, I'm a damned sight more familiar with this port than you are—" Justine watched, alarmed at the Captain's apoplectic colour. She turned and made violent 'come hither' motions to Miss Byford who looked after the tea arrangements. Miss Byford, who assisted Justine in her shop, was dressmaker to the club, a small, shrivelled, rather asexual little person with the energy of a ten-year-old boy. She bustled up and the intrusion of her tray with its cups and saucers and its ritual of 'Do you sugar, Captain Stanier? But of course Captain Macready doesn't,' at least soothed the irate Macready.

Stanier was unruffled by the outburst. That was the trouble with these Celts he thought, they never held their tempers long enough for their brains to work.

"I shall never give one ship preferential treatment, Captain, yours included. I should perhaps remind you, though this is scarcely the place for gentlemen to argue, that I *am* the Harbour Master of Porth Ardur." Stanier sipped his tea.

Macready opened his mouth to speak, thought better of it and shut it again. He had not liked the inflection of the word 'gentlemen'.

"Perhaps, Captain Stanier, I could remind you, because I

know Captain Macready is too much of a gentleman to do so himself, that as Master of the *Caryatid he* is a Harbour Commissioner for Porth Ardur." Justine smiled warmly at the younger man. Macready's heart went out in gratitude to the lovely widow.

Stanier coloured and Tegwyn shot her mother a look of pure venom. However this sally had restored Macready's ruffled feathers and he tried, filled as he was with love, to pour oil on troubled waters.

"Come, come, Captain, if you'll be good enough to have the gates open in," he looked at his watch, "two and a half hours, we'll berth *Caryatid* and say no more about it." He turned away and he and Justine lined up the club for one of their routines. It was only Tegwyn who heard Stanier mutter, "I'm damned if I will."

Those members of the *Caryatid*'s crew that had enjoyed a watch ashore usually assembled in the public bar of The Feathers about closing time for a quick half pint before they scrambled down to the boat. A few had spent the entire evening there and the boat's crew had been sinking pints for forty-five minutes.

Calico Jack had come ashore with the boat's crew and managed to consume eight swift glasses by the time the landlord called time. At ten twenty-nine Captain Macready had entered the lounge bar with Justine. They both had gin and tonics.

"You bringing her in tonight, Captain?" enquired the landlady serving them.

Macready nodded. "I don't envy you that rowdy lot in the public."

"They're alright. They do everything automatically." The landlady sniffed. "I'll go and cash up then." She left them alone, for the rest of the bar was empty. The Captain looked at Justine and she smiled back.

"Thank you for putting that youngster down." Her smile broadened. "I didn't like the way he talked to you and I'm not sure I like what he's doing to Tegwyn."

"I didn't know you really cared what anybody said." Oh dear, Macready thought, this sounds as hackneyed as a film. But he need not have worried.

Justine shrugged. "I don't think I did until this evening."

"Odd, isn't it? I mean, all these years we've known each other . . ." he drew a deep breath, feeling like an adolescent, ". . . and I've never wanted to kiss you like I do now." She looked up at him and he bent over her and very lightly, tentatively, half-expecting an outraged rebuff, he kissed her. Justine slowly opened her lips. Messages flashed from brain to brain, loins to loins, immediate urgent messages. But maturity triumphed and they drew apart before the landlady returned.

"Do you love your wife, Septimus?" asked Justine.

"Gwendolen?" he replied surprised. Justine laughed her open gay laugh that defused the question.

"Of course Gwendolen, you don't have any more, do you?" Justine laughed again. "But do you love her?"

"We've been together a long time. It becomes a sort of habit, I suppose. It's not a question that one often asks oneself . . ."

"Or mentions?"

Macready shrugged, then nodded, "I suppose not."

It was Justine's turn to take a deep breath. "Septimus, you

are probably not going to believe this given my reputation, but since my husband died I have never slept with another man. Oh I've flirted, led them on, had them take me to dinner and the pictures but never . . . you know . . ." She was blushing now.

"I never believed those stories anyway . . ." he began gallantly but she waved him to silence.

"Septimus, what I'm trying to say is will you . . . do you want to sleep with me?" She buried her delicious mouth in her gin and tonic.

Macready had answered before he had thought about it – much as Stanier might have expected of an impetuous Celt: "Yes!"

It was nearly time for the boat to leave and the glasses were almost all emptied in the public bar.

Calico Jack was happily drunk and for the tenth time in the hour since he came ashore was telling the story about his island love being naked under an old fur coat. It would appear to have been the high spot of his life except that his ship-mates had heard other equally extravagant yarns. The landlord was thundering time and eventually *Caryatid*'s crew drifted out into the darkness towards the waiting boat.

They were singing lustily when Captain Macready descended the steps.

"It's alright, my dear," said Stanier solicitously, "I'll ask the clerk to get me a drink then, while he does so, up you go. He does it every night so he'll not think anything's amiss."

Tegwyn looked up at the damp exterior of the Station

Hotel. Damn her mother, she thought impetuously. She looked at Stanier. He was smiling at her, patiently, solicitously. A real gentleman.

She nodded. "Alright."

Deadly Sins

It was as well that at least one man in Porth Ardur that night committed the sin of disobedience. Thomas Jones, fully aware of the locking out of the *Caryatid*, braked his bicycle outside the Harbour Master's office at a quarter past twelve. He reappeared with a handful of oil lamps and disappeared into the rain-drenched darkness along the mole.

At least several of *Caryatid*'s crew therefore benefited by his action. It is true that had he not turned up, in accordance with Captain Stanier's instructions (to wit that no signals should be made to ships in the bay without his express order and presence on the quayside), what later occurred between Captain Macready and Justine might not have. But it is more likely that it would only have been postponed. In any event Jones's actions had no bearing on the frantic activity in the Station Hotel except to ensure that neither mother nor daughter discovered the other had slept out that night. So from that point of view Thomas Jones rendered a public service by retaining peace in one household. That he also indirectly sheltered Captain Stanier was not likely to be recognised by that overzealous young man as a personal service. But we anticipate.

Caryatid berthed at 0108 on the Saturday morning. Within minutes of securing her ropes she became like a morgue. The main engines were shut off and the fires banked. Even the steam generators were closed down and the 'bulkhead dynamos', as the oil lights were called, were lit by those remaining on board. Seamen and firemen, some in shore clothes, others in working dungarees, hurried ashore. Last to go was Bernard Foster. By the time he left, Charlie was stripping off and rolling into his bunk. For perhaps ten minutes *Caryatid* lay like a dead thing. Below, the nightwatchman poured himself another cup of tea, moved the oil lamp nearer the penny dreadful and idly wondered how long it would be before he dozed off.

At the end of those ten minutes a late observer might have noticed a movement in her wheelhouse and another in the shadows of the quay. But there were no observers, for the night was still blustery and another rain squall drove over the port. Even our first transgressor, Thomas Jones, had reached home and was at that moment letting his dripping self into his cottage.

Thus it was that Justine Morgan tripped across the gangway, aboard the *Caryatid* and into the waiting arms of Septimus Macready, unobserved by anyone save her eager lover. When they reached the cabin he took her coat. She threw off her scarf and shook her hair, kicking her shoes off in one sensuous movement. Her eyes were bright and he looked at her in admiration.

"Where did you wait? I'm sorry to have been so long!"

She giggled. "You'll never guess."

He shrugged. "I've been waiting in the church," she said. He laughed softly, "Well I'm damned . . ." then, realising what he had said, they both laughed softly together like conspiratorial children.

Justine could not truly say what made her enter the church for she was no practising Christian. But St Iseult's church stood just behind the buoy compound, slightly above the harbour and she knew it would be unlocked, for the vicar had views about the House of God remaining open. And in a way Justine needed that refuge, not just from the rain but for her soul. Great had been her love for her husband, so great that she had kept it as a memory so personal and intimate that only she and her husband's shade knew about it. And God, of course. There had to be God otherwise her husband's soul could not exist and her nocturnal practices would have been no more than self-abuse. She did not believe they were.

But something had happened tonight. She was not sure what, or that she wanted to know, except that the sight of her little daughter aroused and in the arms of a man had ignited some latent kindling in herself. The only man who occupied any sort of permanency in her life was Septimus Macready and seeing him there, she had suddenly realised that very sense of dependability that Septimus radiated was attractive. Of course, he had been attractive for years and it was this that their bodies had recognised from the start, this that had made them such superlative dancers, and fed the perceptive gossips of Porth Ardur.

For Septimus too, after half a century of life, he felt lust as painful and as sharp as his brief physical relationship with Gwendolen. His pores opened at the prospect before him. He turned the oil lights down very low and drew Justine into his tiny night cabin.

A deck below them Charlie Farthing slept. He dreamed of

69

a holy land of heather that lay like velvet under his destrier's hooves. Stark granite outcrops pushed through the heather and there was a megalith older than measured time breaking the skyline. He felt his hauberk rasp his neck and his helmet, slung at his hip, rubbed his thigh, but the damp west wind was in his face and ahead of him lay the road to Avalon . . .

Two decks down the nightwatchman slumped over the messroom table and dozed, dreaming of nothing . . .

Justine lay back on the tiny bunk. Septimus leaned over her. He was trembling.

"My God, Justine, you are beautiful . . ." She smiled at him, feeling her own flesh quivering. She felt the weight of her hips and parted her thighs as he knelt between them. He had a good body, she thought, still taut, a fine down of wiry hair across his square chest . . . and lower down he was as eager as a boy.

Charlie Farthing dreamed on. His destrier was eager too, searching for the smell of a mare. The heather plateau went on and on. He searched himself, straining in the saddle for a sight of she whom he had come to seek. The destrier slid into a depression. As they rose on the farther side a standing stone came into view. They approached it and suddenly the destrier whinnied. A pale horse stepped forward and upon it sat a green-eyed maiden, russet hair streaming in the wind. Charlie dismounted, clumsy in his harness, and knelt at her feet. The ground was hard, hard . . . Charlie awoke on the deck, tangled in his bedclothes . . .

At the Station Hotel Tegwyn was eagerly exhausting James Stanier. But the honour of a gentleman is sacrosanct in the discharge of his duties to a lady and Stanier was on her and off her in a welter of sexual abandon . . .

At about the time that Charlie fell out of his bunk one other sinner was active. Calico Jack, being a practical man, had sinned deliberately and accepted the consequences of his action philosophically. Trained in the matter of sinning he was not so abandoned as to urinate in his bunk, but the consequences of his greed led him to rise from it. In any case his pillow had apparently been gently revolving around his head for upwards of an hour or so. He went to the head and emptied his bladder then crawled back along the alley-way only to see a half-empty bottle of whisky in the messroom. He staggered in and picked it up. He remembered some drollery about a pessimist seeing a bottle half-empty, while an optimist saw it half-full, and chuckled at his own optimism. Then he tipped it down his gullet.

The price of his greed was repaid with interest. The stream of his yellow vomit shot across the mess table and Calico Jack passed out on the deck.

Sins are usually reckoned to be actions that transgress arbitrary moral codes laid down by religious writ. Immoral acts, on the other hand, are less clearly defined since the viewpoint of the observer, or arbiter, has great bearing on the subject. It is generally accepted that an immoral act is one in which people are hurt, whether directly in the committing of the act, or indirectly as a consequence of the act.

Thomas Jones's action in disobeying Captain Stanier's order was a sin, since Stanier was his superior. But no church would condemn him for an act that he conceived a kindness to his friends on the *Caryatid*. Yet Stanier would be hurt by the act, his pride wounded, perhaps some bilious combination in his body's constitution would hasten his eventual demise by, perhaps, two minutes? Who knows?

But Stanier was young and would revenge himself if he was that upset, to pushing the treadwheel of human futility round another half-revolution.

The activity in the Station Hotel was another dance nearly as old as time, but it was a fornication, a sin the Celts indulged in themselves and condemned in others. But if no one was hurt where was the harm? If a child was the result of this union then condemnation might be justified, but Stanier was a young man with a high sense of his dignity. No one was going to trap him into a hasty marriage to legitimise a bastard and he, in his cold, Saxon loving, was too efficient to be totally overruled by lust.

But the sweet, ripe loving of Septimus and Justine carried with it the full knowledge that someone was most certainly going to be hurt if she found out. Gwendolen's shadow hung between them as a strange, dolorous barrier, giving to their love a piquant sadness, a foredoomed premonition that increased towards the morning.

At last Justine rose and cast about for her clothes. Macready watched her.

"Will we do this again, my dear?" he asked softly.

She shrugged, tears starting in her eyes, "Oh yes, my darling, yes, yes . . ." she sobbed in his arms. He stroked her hair as Justine pulled herself together. "I've an idea," she said, suddenly brightening in her old, cheerful way. "Do you go anywhere where you could spend several nights?"

"You mean in the ship?"

"Mmmm."

Macready thought. "Ynyscraven, a little island about sixty miles away. But Justine, you couldn't come on board . . ."

"No, no, silly. But I could take a holiday there and you could . . . you know . . ."

The idea caught his imagination and he grinned delightedly, "What a splendid—"

"But we'd have to be careful. I don't want a scandal in this place." She pulled up her stockings and fastened them. Septimus caught a final view of her thigh as she pulled down her skirt.

"Alright," he said. "We'll carry on just as normal here. I'll try and work some sort of long job at the lighthouse on Ynyscraven." She nodded, fastening her scarf. He held out her coat.

"I'll slip ashore alright," she said. He saw her to the gangway. For a second the big oil lamp caught her face then she was gone in the night. Septimus returned to his cabin. On the deck a white patch caught his eye. Justine had left her panties. He caught them up, a smile upon his face. It was replaced by sudden worry. My God! What if Gwendolen found them, he thought, finding himself stuffing them in his pocket. Supposing that bloody gossip of a steward found them . . .

He flung open his wardrobe. He was likely to wear any of his three uniforms . . . ah! that was the answer. He pulled out his mess jacket and slipped the silky thing away.

Justine noticed the omission before she reached the end of the quay. A sudden panic seized her too. It was on just such details that marriages foundered, how could she have forgotten, she who was so careful about her appearance? But she had been as eager as a young virgin tonight, so

perhaps there was some excuse. She shrugged, relying on
Septimus's dependability and hurried up the steep street.
She wondered if it were possible to conceive at their ages.
She found herself smiling at the thought. She slipped into
bed within twenty minutes of leaving the ship, and was fast
asleep when Tegwyn let herself into the little stone cottage.

The Wages of Sin

Thomas Jones woke the following morning with that uneasy feeling that something was wrong. It was not a very disturbing feeling, more an itch marring the even tenor of his life. He stirred, the bedclothes twisting round him uncomfortably. He sat up irritably. And remembered.

Stanier.

God blast the Saxon boor, but Stanier would want to know why, contrary to his orders, the *Caryatid* lay in the harbour.

Jones swore again and rose to put on a kettle and brew a cup of tea. While thus occupied he had an idea. It was not an original idea, most recently it had been propounded by the founder of the Boy Scouts movement but was older than Jones's Celtic warrior forbears. Certainly Stanier's Saxon antecedents had outwitted those same forbears and with that recollection Jones resolved to act. He would attack. On impeccable military authority it was the finest form of defence. Thus Thomas Jones turned aside the wrath of Captain Stanier and was able to avoid any retribution for his disobedience.

In truth Jones's own action did not really avert Stanier's wrath. Tegwyn Morgan had already done that. James St

John Stanier lay abed late, replete with loving and satiated with recollection. Jones' note (that there were no intended movements other than the berthing of the *Caryatid* to which he would be pleased to attend without bothering the Captain) hardly had any effect upon Stanier who had already resolved not to stir from his bed for several hours. He slipped into sleep smiling.

After years of moral behaviour Captain Macready found his conscience irksome throughout the weekend. His was not a nature that dissembled easily. He bumbled solicitously after his wife, like a gull in a ship's wake, but that worthy woman, practical to the end, simply assumed he was unwell. She therefore reciprocated by mollycoddling him which increased his guilt. It was with considerable relief that Macready found himself climbing the stairs to bed on Sunday evening in the knowledge that when he next woke he could escape to the clean sea air which forgave the sins of men as being things of little moment.

Neither was it part of his wife's make up to enquire closely into her spouse's motivation. If he accepted her ministrations then she assumed she must be alleviating the ailment. With that little touch of martyr's wormwood she knew that by Monday Septimus would, like Richard on the morning of Bosworth, be himself again.

It was left to Calico Jack to pay in full the wages of sin. His hangover on Saturday morning was prodigious. Not even a pint with a whisky chaser bought in the public bar of The Feathers at eleven o'clock sharp, cleared the pain from his head. Calico Jack was, however, inured to such pain. Years of dedicated drinking had made him accept the consequences with a degree of stoicism that would have done credit to Epictetus had that worthy not disapproved of the cause.

The *Caryatid* was the latest in an incredibly long list of ships that had provided Jack with home and employment for half a century. Alone among them *Caryatid* also promised him the golden hope of a pension, for Calico Jack was one of a breed of men who toiled in the boiler rooms of steamers for decades and, at the end of the day, when their sinews were weakened and their breath came in pants, could walk ashore with their entire possessions in the bottom of a half-filled kit-bag.

To such a man drinking had become as much a way of life as another's fortnightly visits to the public library or the golf course. Calico Jack had drunk in every corner of this tired old earth; could be relied upon for a verdict on the inebriative qualities of alchoholic beverages from arrack to ouzo, and could tell you where, in each sailortown from Archangel to Yokohama, you could purchase the *vin du pays*.

It was not the worst hangover that Jack had ever experienced but there were other, more disturbing symptoms that his 'liveners' in The Feathers soon masked. Calico Jack did not know that the malfunctioning of his liver was reaching a critical point. It could not be said that he drank to forget pain, only that when he drank somehow he just forgot anyway.

So he spent his weekend in customary fashion. Having no family in Porth Ardur he slept aboard the ship and spent

most of his waking hours, not to mention his entire weekly
wage, in The Feathers.

But it should not be thought that Calico Jack was a simple
man for his fund of experience ran back too far and was
too diverse for that. Even at his age he was not without a
certain vivacity. He surprised many a youthful engineer by
reciting lengthy sections of romantic poetry such as it had
once been fashionable to cram into the heads of infants at
Board Schools. Jack had received most of his education in
the great Varsity of the World which is the unequivocal
alma mater of every merchant seaman.

Neither was Jack an unhappy man. He was the most
undeceived of all men, knowing full well that naked he
had come into this world and naked he would go out of it.
Perhaps that was the root of his philosophy, for he worked
hard, in the primeval conditions of a stokehold, his lean
body corroded without by coal dust and sweat, and within
from a great universality of booze. And he played hard,
as much a part of the great rut as the Canadian moose,
and far more honestly than James Stanier. Certainly Calico
Jack had loved. He had been the victor of many an affray
with bar and brothel girl; he boasted of having done the
impossible with the unspeakable (or was it the other way
round?) and had collected several scars to prove it. But best
of all he nurtured the memory of his first voyage when, as
a boy of fourteen, he had shipped out on a whaler that had
called unexpectedly at the fishing port where he lived. Jack
had sailed in her on a four-year cruise into the wide blue
Pacific and there he had been privileged to love a dusky
maiden. He was one of the last of those old sailormen who
had stormed their way into that promiscuously innocent

ocean and despoiled its islands with a truly Viking ferocity, taking spirits and syphilis into the lives of the innocently, charmingly compliant natives. In the cruise the whaler had five times recruited in the Marquesas and Calico Jack, the least significant figure on that old auxiliary barque, had disported himself with the carnality that adolescence and too much bad adult example produced.

But Jack had not simply lusted in the Marquesas. He had loved, absolutely, romantically, even fantastically. For he had discovered his maiden bathing in a pool, had seduced her, or been seduced by her, and they had lived and loved under those tropic skies of dark velvet for three delirious weeks. And thus it had been on each visit, until the whaler turned for home, her holds crammed with the sperm oil that industry then wanted. Jack had felt sorrow at his last departure, half-promising to return, half-knowing he would not. He had seen during those five visits the waist of his woman thicken, had seen small dusky children multiply about the island, and seen her breasts lose their pointed sauciness so that his passion had cooled. In that early initiation into the natural law of decay lay his determination to wander; yet the memory of that first, pure love came to him now as an old and almost broken man. It shone in his memory as Rigel Kentaurus had burned in that Marquesan firmament all those years ago.

It was this stirring of this memory that caused him to think himself in love with the madwoman of Ynyscraven. *Caryatid*'s crew had known Sonia's mother for years as the 'madwoman'. The old lady had lived on the island for about fifteen years, arriving one day on a fishing boat with three cabin trunks and a small child. She was some kind of artist and considered a harmless lunatic. The islanders all liked her daughter and she was inoffensive, paid her debts and kept out of anyone's way. For a long time she had always exchanged greetings with Calico Jack, even danced with him once or twice. They seemed to be capable of sitting silently together, wrapped in each other's company, though exchanging not a word. It was clear to even the most mule-headed observer that they were both slightly cracked. Or perhaps they knew they had both drunk at a well of loneliness and suffering that those who have visited, never afterwards mention.

It was love that triumphed over Calico Jack's physical decay that weekend, and Sunday night found him again staggering from The Feathers in time to flash up the two scotch boilers and raise steam for Monday's tide.

It is a curious quality of divine retribution that it is often absent from those whom others think best deserve it. In the neat stone cottage that housed Mrs and Miss Morgan there was no hint of sin or its concomitant consequences. Indeed both women were able to maintain that ambiguous attitude to their individual behaviour that chiefly characterises their sex from that of the simpler, more brutal male.

Both women considered they were in love. This in the first place exonerated all subsequent peccadilloes. In Justine's case it was probably true, whereas in Tegwyn's, love was not quite the right word. Nevertheless from the individual standpoint their hearts sang in their ample breasts that no woman had ever loved like this before.

But there lurked the tiny worm of guilt, a particularly Celtic worm, for it fed on other people's good opinion, and therefore the Morgan household was one of extraordinary amity and concord as daughter sought to please mother and mother tried to make up for that gap in her maternal vigilance that had occurred as she lay in the hairily masculine arms of Septimus Macready. As a consequence of their individual preoccupations with these deceptions, neither noticed anything odd about the other's behaviour and the weekend passed very pleasantly. This alone they attributed to being in love, each thinking only she was experiencing it, which circumstance fed their own self-conceit delightfully.

Men who rarely mar the even tenor of their lives, rarely experience the pangs and expectations of adventurous souls. This was true of Bernard Foster, whose weekend consisted of a dutifully performed sexual coupling with his wife, a walk with two sons and a spaniel and a duty visit to the ship to pick up Charlie Farthing for 'a quiet Sunday evening with my family'.

It is not true to say that Bernard lacked a sense of humour. His spaniel, for instance, was called Windlass. One, because it was a bitch, and two, because of an unfortunate propensity it had for breaking wind in public. His wife did not quite see the joke, however, which was becoming increasingly true of poor Anthea's whole outlook on life. But Bernard was a dedicated father, a good seaman who enjoyed his work and a pipe smoker. None of these occupations, particularly the last which consumed vast quantities of matches, seemed to leave much time for excessive hilarity.

Charlie's visit was a success. He was good company and

presentable enough to cause Anthea to take some pains
with her appearance, so that Bernard felt a trifle jealous
of young Charlie . . . Oh well, he sighed and reached for
his matches.

Alliances Are Made

The next few weeks passed with only a few catspaws
disturbing the tranquillity of Porth Ardur. Since few of
these were in any way public, no one could have supposed
that there was anything amiss in the town.

There had been an unpleasant interview aboard *Caryatid*
between Captain Stanier and Captain Macready. For once
the former's cool headedness had deserted him as he had
chosen to bait Macready on the latter's home ground. Voices
were raised and it was difficult for both Foster and Charlie
not to hear what was being said. Charlie Farthing listened
with particular interest since his name, not to mention
his manners, seemed to be the chief topic of Stanier's
complaint. It is true that by the time Stanier had finished,
Charlie's appearance and demeanour had been unfavourably
linked with Macready's, and *Caryatid* had been reduced in
maritime importance to less than a Thames lighter, but in
so doing Stanier signed his own death warrant. Charlie
could not understand why Foster kept digging him in the
ribs as the two officers stood like schoolboys at the foot
of the companionway leading up to the bridge. Suddenly
he realised Stanier was pushing Macready onto ground
which the older man regarded as highly contestable. At

last Macready began to reply as Stanier ran out of steam. Charlie listened spellbound and next to him Bernard Foster was fairly hopping up and down with a glee that Charlie had not suspected of him.

". . . And in future, Macready, I'll trouble you to take note of the fact that I'm in charge here, that you and this old coal-bucket you call a ship berth here by courtesy of the fact that the port allows it and don't think you can frighten me by waving your commissioner's badge at me because you only sit on the board by courtesy of the Parliamentary Act as a *representative* of the Lighthouse Authority and that cuts no ice with me. I remain the Harbour Master and you'd better not forget it!"

There was a pause, then:

"Mr," (Macready emphasised that title derogating it as only a Celt can when mouthing the English tongue), "Mr Stanier, I have stood here and listened to your bloody nonsense long enough. In my opinion, which is based on the trifle of thirty-nine years on this coast, Mr Farthing is as promising a young officer as *I* could wish for. If he failed to come up to your passenger-liner expectations I suggest you return to poodle-faking on promenade decks and fornicating with the cargo rather than running down *my* officers on *my* ship after you have exercised your trifling authority by locking this vessel out quite unnecessarily. You quite plainly demonstrate your complete inability to command anything larger than a motor launch by your pettiness and if I hear another word from you, sir, I shall have you forcibly removed from this vessel. D'you understand me, damn it, for I'm going out on this tide and be damned to you!"

Neither Charlie nor Foster heard Stanier utter another

word but they both stood smirking in the alleyway as the apoplectic features of James St John Stanier passed them.

For some time after this the *Caryatid* entered and left Porth Ardur as she had done for years. Macready assumed that Stanier had grown up and even went so far, by way of conciliation, as to smile at the brick caboose. Stanier, however, saw this as a gesture of defiance and pondered on the possibility of revenge.

To this end he was unexpectedly assisted from an unusual source and fell to more pondering as to how to put new allies to the best use. In part this deepening of the feud between the two men was caused by Gwendolen Macready. It was an inadvertent move on her part but was nevertheless instrumental in driving an influential party into Stanier's camp.

For many years the housewives of Porth Ardur had complained about the excessive amount of sooty black smoke that spewed from *Caryatid*'s funnel as she fired up and steamed out of Porth Ardur on a Monday morning. This unfortunate emission often coincided with the hanging out of a vast acreage of sheets and pillow slips, not to mention unmentionables. Several times deputations had besieged the Lighthouse Authority office where the head clerk, untrained in the best methods of putting down riots by irate women, had locked himself in his office until the fuming crowd had dispersed. Protests to Captain Macready himself had been made, but the Captain had simply deplored the occurrence and mentioned it to the Chief Engineer. That worthy was a bachelor and did not give a monkey's damn about all the women in the world, since one had once infected him with the clap. He therefore did nothing about it except smile savagely and recollect that Calico Jack was usually on duty when *Caryatid* sailed since he lived aboard. This fact would happily ensure that the practice continued to torment the goodwives of Porth Ardur.

The wives, many of whom were married to men in *Caryatid*'s crew, had tried various ploys including one inspired by Lysistrata and her friends. This had, however, been a one-sided sacrifice that had led to several nasty bedroom mêlées, not to mention a revealing argument in the queue of Beynon's Butchery. Consequently it had been abandoned. The simple expedient of washing on a Tuesday never seemed to occur to any of the parties concerned, unless it was a matter of principle, in which case neither party could, in all honour, compromise.

Something of Macready's disagreement with Stanier reached the ears of Gwendolen through the agency of Anthea Foster. Gwendolen attributed her husband's preoccupation to this cause and not to any burgeoning romance with Justine. Mrs Macready in turn made enquiries about Captain Stanier in her own circles. It seemed common knowledge that the new broom was sweeping clean and she let slip an innocent remark that her husband seemed to be receiving something of the treatment. This was quickly seized upon by Mrs Beynon, the butcher's wife, who astutely saw in it an opening ripe for exploitation by the careworn wives of Porth Ardur.

In the days of Captain Edwardes they had no luck in attempts to get the Harbour Master on their side. Captain Stanier, on the other hand, seemed to be a different proposition and Mrs Beynon quickly whipped up some support. The ladies deputed to approach the Captain swallowed their dislike of him being an 'outsider' and reflected that he was a handsome embellishment to the social scene and might be worthy of their daughters. A deputation therefore met the Captain at the Station Hotel where he generously bought them all gin and tonics.

"Now ladies, what exactly is it that I can do for you?" he began, his masculinity asserting control at the outset. He smiled urbanely round at the circle of faces.

"It's like this, see, that old ship makes a great deal of smoke and we ladies, all of us, that is . . ." The problem was outlined to Captain Stanier who, though privately nursing a snigger, agreed the ladies had a point of view and promised most sincerely to consider what he could do to help them.

It proved a difficult problem for the young man. To be fair he had little time for such considerations since his affair with Tegwyn was still burning with an incandescent fire. Besides he had another problem, that of accommodation.

Under the terms of his employment he was allowed a month in an hotel after which he was expected to make his own arrangements. He eventually settled on a furnished house in the poshest part of Porth Ardur: Glendŵr Avenue. This tree-lined road with its neat rows of Victorian villas was ideal for Stanier's self-esteem, compensating him in part for his miserable brick caboose. The house's owners were on extended service in the colonies and the place was full of oriental bric-a-brac which exactly fostered Stanier's image of himself as a great white empire builder. It was also a delightful place for further fornication with the beautiful Tegwyn who adorned a tigerskin rug so delightfully. Stanier had never realised that a stool made from an elephant's foot could be such an object of sexual stimulus or that an oxhide shield and an assegai could be used for erotic purposes.

All in all, despite the unpleasantness with Macready, Stanier was beginnning to feel established in Porth Ardur.

This sensation was augmented by the presence of Sir Hector Blackadder who had arrived in the middle of June to inspect his refitted yacht. *Sea Dragon* was a modern diesel yacht 105 feet long. Sir Hector was very proud of her and usually manned her from the unemployed of Porth Ardur who, desperate for work, were capable of debasing themselves with sufficient submission to please the millionaire and make him justify the maintenance of *Sea Dragon* as a kind of employment institution for the deprived.

Not that Sir Hector should be considered a hard man. He lived in times when such simple ideas were quite permissible, indeed a large section of the town's population agreed with him and regarded him as a benefactor. This further pleased Sir Hector who regarded capitalists as the new aristocracy and was rather fond of saying this in public. He was equally fond of saying that anyone could get where he was if he worked hard, and that his knighthood had been conferred by an impressed monarch as encouragement to others of his class. He was never heard to explain how he had started to amass his fortune but there had been a story current in Porth Ardur when Sir Hector first started holidaying there, that he had always gone to school with a pair of scissors. With these he had snipped flowers from middle-class gardens and after school had stood innocently outside hospital gates reproaching empty-handed expectant fathers with masses of chrysanthemums and irises.

Whatever the origins of his wealth it was now legendary and Sir Hector regarded it as incumbent upon himself to own a yacht. Although the proprietor of the Cambrian Steam Navigation Company owned twenty-three rusting and profitable ships he was not overfamiliar with matters nautical. He therefore found it necessary to employ a yacht-master and it was with this in mind, as well as to inspect his recently refitted yacht, that he had come to Porth Ardur.

While he was walking round the yacht Stanier had strolled along the quay and, of course, introduced himself.

"Are you a master mariner, Captain?"

"But of course, Sir Hector."

"What company were you with?"

"Isthmus and Occidental, sir," replied Stanier, slightly outraged that the other should have to ask the question. After all there was the I&O and there was the rest of the Merchant Marine . . .

"Ever consider serving in the Cambrian Steam Navigation Company?"

Stanier sensed a trap and looked quickly at Blackadder. The millionaire was regarding him with a level, inquistive gaze.

"No, sir."

"I suppose you've heard it has a few old and rusty ships that feed badly and hire and fire indiscriminately . . . come now is that it?"

Stanier smiled deprecatingly and shrugged, "Something like that, Sir Hector . . ." Blackadder laughed, "Well at least you are honest. It may be true, Captain, but they are profitable ships. I *know* they make more profit per voyage than your I&O liners and, in the long term, that's what matters. If the I&O lost its government mail contracts it would fold in ten years. Yes, it would. Don't protest."

"Well, that's unlikely Sir Hector."

"Don't be a damned fool, it'll end in two years once the aeroplane takes over, that's the field to watch next. I'm considering expanding into it myself." Sir Hector raised his gaze above the rooftops of Porth Ardur and the mountains beyond as if searching for an aeroplane amid the cumulus. It was the look of a visionary.

He returned his gaze to Stanier. "Would you like a job here, Captain?"

"I'm sorry, Sir Hector, I don't understand?"

"Oh I know you're tied up here but you must be due some summer leave. I'm inviting you to take a working holiday as master of the *Sea Dragon*. You can plan a three week cruise around the coast here, there are some lovely spots. What d'you say?"

"Well, Sir Hector, I'd like it very much but . . ."

"But me no buts, Captain, I've a little influence hereabouts that can get you time off. You can dine at my table and bring your wife, d'you have a wife, Captain?"

"Er, no, Sir Hector."

"I don't doubt an I&O officer like you has fixed himself up in Porth Ardur, eh?"

Stanier grinned, "Well as a matter of fact I, er—"

"That's settled then, as long as she doesn't eat peas off a knife and knows the difference between champagne and claret she'll be alright. Is she pretty?" Stanier coloured, thinking of Tegwyn and the assegai. "Oh alright, Captain, I'm sure she is, just fix her up with a decent evening dress and bring her along, Now, let's have dinner at my hotel this evening and we can discuss details, bring a chart up with you . . ." And so Captain James St John Stanier was officially appointed to his first sea-going command.

By the time June turned to July several sets of plans had been made in Porth Ardur. Stanier, Blackadder and Tegwyn Morgan were preparing to sail during the first week in August. Stanier had not found it easy to persuade Tegwyn, for she would openly acknowledge her liaison with Stanier by sailing on the *Sea Dragon*. Tegwyn knew many of the crew of the yacht would raise eyebrows at her presence, so she hit upon the idea of going as Stanier's guest and made much noise about the formality of the invitation. She was still apprehensive about telling her mother but was amazed by the reaction when she eventually did so.

"Of course, *cariad*, you go and enjoy yourself. I shall shut up the shop, I think, and take a few days off myself." Justine smiled at her daughter. "You'll need some evening clothes in the latest mode . . . we'll see what we can do there."

"Oh Mother, you are absolutely wonderful!" Tegwyn threw her arms around Justine.

But Justine's heart leapt on her own account. When she next saw Septimus at the Friday dance she gave him the go-ahead for their own plot. As they left the Tudor Tea Rooms she hurriedly whispered the dates she hoped to be on Ynyscraven.

"How will you get there, my dear?" asked Macready.

"I'll take a train to Aberogg; that's where the mail boat goes from, isn't it?"

Macready nodded, smiled and squeezed her arm.

"It's not long to wait now, my dear."

"No, my darling, not long."

Charlie Farthing had seen Sonia several times since that
first meeting and was more in love with her than ever. The
Caryatid had spent odd afternoons working at the lighthouse
on Ynyscraven and Sonia had appeared over the crest of the
island every time he had landed. They had exchanged kisses
and meaningless endearments while the *Caryatid*'s seamen
exchanged leers, winks and suggestive gestures.

Charlie was delighted when Captain Macready mentioned they would be spending some time at the island
in August.

"We'll be renewing the hoist wire at Ynyscraven in
August. It'll mean at least a week there. That should
please you, Mr Farthing." Macready smiled, nursing the
greater part of the smile for himself.

"Yes, sir, it does indeed."

After the Captain had gone below, Charlie asked Foster
what exactly was involved. Foster lit his pipe and puffed.

"Well, we have to cut the old wire out and remove it, then
stretch a new one, cut and splice it, set it up taut. When that's
done we renew the traveller and hoisting wire itself. It's a
big job. If everything goes alright, five days. If we get any
snags it may take longer." He puffed again. "When that's
all set up, the engineers will overhaul the hoisting engine.
They can't do that while we are working since we need it
to heave things about. They'll start when we've finished.
That'll take two days, so we'll probably be the weekend
away. All the wives'll moan but the lads'll have a great
time. The Old Man won't work after six o'clock, so by

seven the boat'll be away to the pub," he puffed again, "and you'll be in seventh heaven." Foster smiled at Charlie who grinned back.

"Sounds like a bloody holiday," he said ingenuously.

"It's bloody hard work; you earn any free time you get."

In this way plans were laid by the various parties for their own pleasure and amusement. Anticipation ran high in the breasts of those involved. Several members of *Caryatid*'s crew were delighted with the news, Calico Jack chief among them. Justine Morgan congratulated herself on the way things had turned out while Tegwyn, writhing in the uncontrollable excesses of sexual abandon, furnished herself with a wardrobe not strictly for *evening* wear from the more outrageous recesses of her mother's shop.

Stanier approached the whole exercise as a cold professional. He acted as though it were the *Mauretania* that he was taking command of and subconsciously relegated Tegwyn to the status of a passenger. It has to be remembered that James St John Stanier had had a surfeit of passengers.

Macready happily prepared for several nights of idyllic love and salved his conscience by busying himself around the house during the intervening weekends, tidying up a number of jobs that Gwendolen had long ago abandoned any hope of getting him to do.

And Charlie Farthing dreamed dreams of love . . .

This euphoric state of affairs might have continued until the *Caryatid* and the *Sea Dragon* sailed from Porth Ardur and the Ynyscraven mail boat slipped out of Aberogg, had not an unforeseen event occurred which upset the judgement of one of the vessels' commanders and ruined the equanimity of another.

A Declaration of War

Clausewitz maintained that war was the continuation of diplomacy by other means. If by diplomacy he meant the posturing of factions whose ambitions are in opposition, then he may have been right. War is war whether at the international level or around the parish pump and it follows the usual pattern of human disagreement, a series of small incidents that culminate in an outbreak of hostilities. But historians like a *casus belli* and it should not be supposed that this factor was absent from the clash of personalities that ruptured the peace of Porth Ardur.

A few days prior to commencing his cruise with Sir Hector, Stanier had decided to take the field against Macready. His alliances were holding and a curious piece of information had come his way. Armed with this intelligence, which he considered to be an irresistible reinforcement, he intended to attack Macready over the distressing matter of *Caryatid*'s boiler smoke. Stanier smiled to himself as he walked down from Glendŵr Avenue that morning. He could see the harbour below him and *Caryatid*'s tall woodbine funnel belched black smoke which the wind caught and drove inland, up the shallow valley where the majority of the population lived.

His smile turned to a grimace as ahead of him he caught a glimpse of the stocky rolling figure of Captain Macready dressed in reefer jacket, with its bars of braid, and a small crowned hat, its peak adorned with the 'scrambled egg' that denoted a vessel's commander.

"Bloody charlatan," muttered Stanier, recollecting the conversation he had had with Sir Hector Blackadder.

He had dined quite frequently with Sir Hector when the millionaire had come down for a weekend to Porth Ardur. The talk had been of the forthcoming cruise and Sir Hector had been enlarging on the manning of his yacht.

"Oh, the crew are never a problem," said Sir Hector, puffing on a large Havana. "You see, I bring the cook and cabin staff, they're my own permanent domestics. The engineer I retain, as you know, almost full-time. The couple of greasers and six seamen I pick up every year from the unemployed fishing hands hereabouts. The problem comes when I want a skipper . . ." Stanier winced at the terminology but Sir Hector ploughed on through a haze of blue smoke, unaware at the savage knocking the younger man's pride had just received.

"Usually I get someone in the port who's on leave, between ships and run out of money, old Edwardes often knew of someone with a ticket of some description. Of course they don't all get invited to dine at my table," he smiled at Stanier who smiled back, his wounded pride salved a little.

"And none of the previous skippers have *ever* been invited to bring their mistress." Sir Hector drew on the Havana.

"I'm very flattered, Sir Hector . . ."

Sir Hector grunted. Then he looked up. "I like you,

Stanier, you've a ruthless streak and I'm on the lookout for a junior partner."

"I'm, er, quite overwhelmed Sir Hector, I, er . . ."

The knight bachelor waved aside the younger man's protestations of undying loyalty. "We'll see, we'll see . . . anyway as I was saying, it has often been a problem since I don't really know a great deal about navigation and I'm advised the tides hereabouts are rather tricky. One year I had a dreadful chap. Name of Evans, not that that means much round here. He was the best old Edwardes could trawl up for me. He was a damned trawler skipper. Swore he was the finest skipper on the coast but'd had a disagreement with his owner. Trouble was I'd not much time to check his credentials and I had a rather lovely Italian contessa in the party and my judgement was, huh," Sir Hector laughed condescendingly as if about to reveal a great secret, "well, impaired. Don't ever let a woman impair y'r professional judgement, young fella. It don't do and the bloody damage is done before you realise it." Sir Hector puffed again at the cigar.

"The stupid bastard got us tangled in among some rocks with a tide race running like a river in spate. Beautiful afternoon somewhere down off that lighthouse, the, er, whatsitsname? Bucka-something . . ."

"Buccabu, Sir Hector. Decanter?"

"Buccabu! That's it! Er yes lad, not a bad port, eh, even for this place. Buccabu. I shall never forget it. I thought we'd had it. I smelt a rat when the bloody fool was in the wheelhouse with a bottle of rum but, Christ alive, we were in the middle of hell then. White water all around us hissing and sucking at us. The *Sea Dragon* generates nine hundred and eighty-six horse-power and it was like farting against thunder . . ."

Sir Hector drew courage from his port glass, blenching at the recollection.

"What happened?" asked Stanier, fascinated. All this was so far from the ordered bridge routine of an I&O liner.

"One of the seamen burst into the wheelhouse, said he knew the place and would pilot us through and would one of us throw the bloody skipper off the bridge and take the wheel. Well, I couldn't steer but I had no compunction about getting that old soak off the bridge. When I turned round there was my beautiful contessa, her hair flying and her arms spinning that teak wheel as the sailor shouted directions from the bow. I can see her now," Sir Hector gazed at the whorls and arabesques hanging almost motionless above the table as the cigar smoke rose languidly.

"God, but she was stunning. Her eyes cracked fire and she had nostrils that dilated when she was excited," he sighed nostalgically. "Turned out she'd been an Olympic yachtswoman. Ever since then I've taken a trick at the wheel." He drew on the cigar butt then ground it out.

"I hope that you are not expecting any such excitement on this cruise, Sir Hector," said Stanier also stubbing out his cigar.

"Not of that nature," said Sir Hector winking lasciviously.

"But I should have thought one of the *Caryatid*'s mates might have been a suitable candidate," volunteered Stanier, pouring another glass of port.

Blackadder shook his head. "They get little leave although Foster brought *Sea Dragon* round here. That's when he found out about their lighthouse service. By the way, d'you know old Macready?"

Stanier made a face. "Yeees," he said warily.

Sir Hector smiled. "Funny man. Been in those ships man and boy, I believe. He always looks more of the typical skipper than any of the lot I employ, what do you think?"

Stanier was flushed with the wine. "He's all wind and a brass-bound uniform. Struts about that old coal bucket like an admiral. I don't suppose he's been anywhere other than round this coast."

"You're right there, my boy. Old Macready hasn't a Board of Trade ticket to his name. Are you surprised? It's true! He comes from a generation that didn't need 'em, but don't be fooled. He knows his onions where seamanship's concerned."

James St John Stanier missed the last remark. His inebriated heart was singing in his breast, for now he had a weapon with which to chastise the upstart, charlatan Captain Septimus Bloody Ebb-Tide Macready.

The recollection of that conversation put vigour into Captain Stanier's stride as he fairly flew over the cobbled approach to the harbour. His lip curled derisively as he passed alongside the white-washed granite wall of the Lighthouse Authority's compound.

Thomas Jones met him with the morning's sailings. "Usual stuff Cap'n; fishing boats and the *Carry* at high water. Macready's sent along to say that he'll leave the moment there's water on the sill, some emergency buoy job on the Hellweather . . ."

"Yes, yes, very good, Mr Jones. Now I'm going aboard the *Caryatid*. I've a thing or two to say to Captain Macready." He turned on his heel and strode off towards the gangway of the *Caryatid*. Behind him Jones chuckled.

Captain Macready was also in fine spirits. In the first place he was deliriously happy with anticipation. The approaching sojourn of *Caryatid* at Ynyscraven and the prospect of five whole nights with Justine almost caused him physical pain. Secondly it was a beautiful morning and the Captain had come to appreciate such things lately. Finally the challenge of an emergency job always stimulated him. It was with an impish delight therefore that the Captain riffled the papers on his desk and stared down onto the foredeck where the hands were securing a new buoy for the Hellweather Bank. He hummed light-heartedly, a man utterly contented with the world.

Captain Macready was vaguely aware of some cloud looming on the horizon of his dreams as the noise of a disturbance penetrated his conscious mind. Somewhere below an argument had begun. The Captain listened. He recognised Foster's voice, low and reasonable.

"But I am sorry, Captain, we are sailing as soon as possible and Captain Macready is rather busy. Captain, I really must insist . . ."

"Get out of my way, man, who the devil d'you think you are?"

There was a scuffling noise then a pounding of feet on the companionway and Captain Stanier pulled back the door curtain from Macready's cabin.

Macready was still standing at the port-hole. He turned slowly and confronted the invader. Stanier was hot from his argument with Foster and catching his breath from a too-quick ascent of the ladder.

"Ah, Captain Stanier, good morning. I am sorry they did not teach you to knock at cabin doors when you were an apprentice . . ." Macready watched with pleasure as Stanier's flush deepened. But the man quickly recovered both his breath and his composure.

"My apologies, Captain Macready, but I wished to speak to you before you sailed and your chief mate has been less than helpful."

Macready shrugged. "Well, what can I do for you?"

"Would you mind stepping out onto your boat deck for a moment, Captain?"

There was a persuasive plausibility about Stanier that disarmed Macready. The Captain was not to know that the Harbour Master had planned his approach as he had walked down to the harbour.

The two men emerged onto the boat deck. Stanier looked up. *Caryatid*'s tall buff funnel rose above them, flanked by two enormous cowl ventilators. From the brass whistle the permanently leaking steam escaped with a faint hiss. The steam was white, the condensing vapour the colour of samite, pure against the pall of dense black smoke that spewed out in thick convolutions of partially-consumed carbon. It rose, then spread out, drifting sulkily away over the rooftops of Porth Ardur.

"*That*, Captain Macready, is what I wished to see you about." Stanier's gesture was dramatic. It was the first piece of histrionic display he had allowed himself since he arrived.

"*That* is what I have received constant complaints about

101

since taking my post as Harbour Master. I have to insist that you instruct your engineers and firemen that making that much smoke is entirely unnecessary . . . it is quite obvious that the rudiments of stoking are unknown to your staff."

Macready was willing to tolerate the complaint about the smoke, even from Stanier. He accepted the criticism since it was not new and had clearly been resurrected by persons who considered the new Harbour Master was able to help them. He was even prepared to meet Stanier half way and say that he would investigate the matter. But he was not prepared to accept *any* criticism of *Caryatid* or her ship's company. There was only one person qualified to carry out such a task and that was the person of her master, Captain Septimus Macready himself.

"Why, you young jackanapes, what in God's name gives you the idea that you could stoke a boiler one whit better than that?" Macready delivered the last word with such vehemence that a blob of spittle hit Stanier.

Macready waited for the younger man's reply, his face colouring rapidly as he prepared further invective. But Stanier was a model of Saxon coolness.

"Captain," he replied, labouring the title with heavy sarcasm, "I hold a Master's certificate. You do not. I scarcely think *you* are in a position to lecture *me* on anything!" he stared at Macready triumphantly.

Macready let out his breath slowly. He was discomfited. Beaten. The wind he had saved to blast this whippersnapper from the holy ground of *Caryatid*'s deck exhaled itself so that he seemed to shrink. With a great effort he struggled to draw another breath. Between clenched teeth he hissed at Stanier, "Get off my ship . . ." and trusting himself no longer he blundered back into the accommodation.

Stanier strutted slowly from the *Caryatid*. It was indeed a perfect morning.

Macready slumped on his settee. Stanier's barb had struck his heart. Not even the thought of Justine's body could lift this sudden depression. This was how Foster found him when he came to report the ship ready for sailing.

"Are you quite alright, sir?" he enquired anxiously, bending over the inert, crushed figure.

"Eh? Oh, er, yes, yes of course I am."

"Shall I ring the engines to 'Stand-by'?"

"What? Oh, yes, by all means; go ahead."

With a great effort Macready pulled himself together. "Courage," he muttered to himself as he straightened his reefer jacket. "I've lost my equanimity," he thought wonderingly to himself. He took a deep breath, his cap from the hook and headed for the bridge. Oddly he found himself thinking of Gwendolen, and when he touched the engine room telegraphs his hands were quite steady again.

Stanier nursed a feeling of quiet contentment after his victory. For the first time since arriving in Porth Ardur he felt he was a man who had his finger on the pulse, that his life was well-ordered and successful and that his future prospects were good. He put into his preparations for the cruise all the enthusiasm that youth could muster. His seamen were recruited and on pay and the yacht was approaching a state of maintained perfection that even the most demanding Master in the I&O would approve of.

His affair with Tegwyn was outwardly discreet and privately abandoned, which suited his own particular demands. As far as Stanier was concerned there was no cooling in his ardour, yet an astute observer, had there been one, might have detected a regularity occurring in the couple's sexual activity which was the precursor of a lowering in temperature.

As far as Tegwyn was concerned, Stanier was becoming an obsession in her life. She had never met a man who outwardly showed a woman such attention, who acted with such gallantry and yet in private demanded and delighted her. Used as she was to the hot passion of Celtic manhood, where ardour was everything and privacy irrelevant, Tegwyn felt like a duchess. She was also ravished by the prospect of the cruise in the *Sea Dragon* and was happily aware of having stimulated a certain amount of disapproving jealousy among the other women of Porth Ardur.

Tegwyn Morgan would never have passed so far down the path of moral disintegration had her mother been unpreoccupied. Justine lived in a rosy glow of anticipation. She saw Macready only once a week as she had always done, yet felt no pang of jealousy when he was home with his wife. For years Justine had nurtured her secret, unnameable passion for her dead husband. It was not difficult for her to fantasise over the Captain and even, in moments of rare and delicious delight, over both of them.

Her whole voluptuous frame seemed to ripen during those summer weeks so that she resembled a fruit at the very fullness of its promise, an instant before it fell from the tree, to bruise and wither upon the ground.

*　　*　　*

Caryatid plunged into a grey swell, pushing her bow into it, thrusting and rising as she lifted to it. A patter of spray came aboard and the white water of her wake hissed away on either bow. "There must have been a blow somewhere to the westward," offered Charlie to no one in particular.

"M'mmm," agreed Bernard Foster, staring through his glasses and still wondering what Stanier had said to upset Captain Macready.

"Look, Charlie," he said suddenly. Charlie picked up the telescope and levelled it to the north.

Caryatid was steaming slowly west, along the line of the Hellweather Bank. The sandbank ran for eleven miles roughly east to west and was about two miles wide at its greatest breadth. At its western end the lightvessel of the same name bobbed up and down, its red hull defaced by the huge black and white letters that told mariners totally ignorant of their position where they were. A mile east of the lightvessel and on the very tip of the shoaling water the West Hellweather Buoy was situated. Or it should have been. On this occasion it appeared to have parted its chain mooring and driven ashore onto the bank. Bernard Foster had seen it, a red and white can lying on its side on the top of an exposed section of the shoal.

He blew down the voice-pipe and Captain Macready came up to the bridge. The ship was stopped and the three men stared to the north while the quartermaster idly spun the spokes of the wheel, privately betting whether or not the Old Man would go in and get the stranded buoy.

Charlie suffered a sinking feeling in his stomach as he looked across at the buoy. There was a light westerly wind and the sky had become overcast. The day was not greatly inspiring. But to the north of them the sea seemed to lift and heave as the swells hunched up and flung themselves thunderously at the impeding sand bank. Suddenly the name Hellweather seemed horribly apt. The exposed sand was only visible now and then, around it white water and spray foamed and dissipated its latent energy in a roar that was audible to the three observers over half a mile away. At last Macready spoke.

"It's an ebb tide. We'll lay the new buoy then steam in from the other side. It may be possible to get a boat in on the lee side of the bank. Alright, Mr Farthing?"

"Aye, aye, sir," said Charlie, suddenly realising why seamen never used the word 'Yes.'

An hour and a half later, the new buoy was laid at the West Hellweather station and *Caryatid* steamed away from it. The gleaming, unweathered newness of its paint made it a bright jewelled spot against the grey back-cloth of sea and sky.

The spot got smaller and smaller and Charlie was aware of a quivering feeling in his stomach. It increased when he noticed the seamen congregating around the motor boat. Bernard Foster was earnestly giving the coxswain some instructions and momentarily Charlie resented the implied lack of faith in his own judgement. Then the butterflies reasserted their presence in his stomach and he acknowledged the wisdom of the Mate.

Foster came forward.

"I've just had a word with Mackerel Jack, Charlie. He's the best boat handler in the ship, you can rely on him, okay?"

Charlie nodded. "What's the urgency to get this damaged buoy back?"

"They don't often break adrift. We ought to know why. Besides it won't stay there, it'll probably drift off and float about to the confusion of all, a danger to navigation." He smiled reassuringly and added in a lower voice in which there was just a hint of pride, "Besides, we don't like losing them, it's a bad advertisement."

Charlie looked back at the *Caryatid* as the motor boat chugged away. Her low freeboard disappeared behind a swell, leaving only her bridge, masts and funnel visible. She reappeared on the crest, her straight, workmanlike stem looked incongruous compared with her elegant counter and he found himself smiling, admiring the plucky little ship that went about its difficult business without fuss. He looked into the well of the boat where an enormous coil of three and a half inch manila hemp had been carefully coiled. The bowman, muffled in black oilskins and sou'wester, his stocky frame augmented by a life jacket, whistled softly to himself. The coxswain stood at the tiller, the only man compelled to stare ahead.

As the boat approached, Charlie saw the buoy. The tide had ebbed considerably and a fairly large area of sand was exposed. Beyond the buoy the swells thundered eight or nine feet in the air as they reared up, toppled and broke upon the sand in a thunder that drowned the boat's engine. On this side of the bank, however, the effect was broken. The swells rolled along, suddenly covering and then exposing the sand as trough succeeded crest. There were no breakers and Charlie heaved a sigh of relief. But it was short-lived, for the rise and fall remained significant. He was aware that the bowman had grabbed the boat hook and was stabbing downwards as the boat fell into a trough. He was periodically looking aft and shaking his head. The third member of the boat's crew was busy aft and as soon as the bowman nodded that he had a sounding, an anchor flashed overboard and a grass line snaked after it.

Charlie felt redundant and bit his lip.

Suddenly the boat bumped hard, the whole of her keel slamming down on the rock-hard, impacted sand. There was a shout from aft as Mackerel Jack gunned the engine into reverse while the third seaman quickly recovered the anchor warp to avoid fouling the propeller.

"I can get no further, Mr Farthing," Mackerel yelled at Charlie. That much was obvious. There was an instant's pregnant silence while the boat's crew waited for their officer to make his executive decision.

"Shit!" thought Charlie. Then stung into action by his impotence he grabbed the manila line, put a bowline in it and slipped the bight over one shoulder.

"I'll go," he yelled. "When I've gone, back her off a bit." Then in a quieter voice to the bowman, "Pay the line out." He jumped over the side.

Despite the season the water's chill shocked him. It came up to his chest and he floundered, dignity disappearing as he saw the grin on the bowman's face. That worthy had assumed he would be ordered into the water and had been contemplating how one disobeyed an order given by Mr Farthing.

Charlie suddenly felt the swell lift him. His lifejacket buoyed him up and he kicked out his legs, rolling onto his back. He was already twenty feet from the boat. He thrashed out, feeling the drag of the rope, kicking with single-mindedness. He looked up at the grey wrack in the sky and thought of Sonia. He kicked harder until suddenly he felt a swell depart and he grounded flat on his back, a large untidy seal.

He stood up on water-logged sand. His sweater and serge trousers dripped water and both socks had come off.

Waving at the boat he pulled in some slack rope then trudged across to the buoy, the sand sucking at his feet. The base of the buoy was towards him, weed-encrusted like a great hairy mollusc. Charlie saw at once what had happened. No chain was attached to the buoy for the lug to which it was secured, the arse-iron as it was called, had fractured. He dragged a bight of rope round to the other end of the buoy and secured the rope to the nose iron. The topmark and staff were missing. Pulling all the slack rope with him he turned back towards the boat.

Mackerel edged the boat in and the bowman pulled the rope as tight as he could so that Charlie half swam, half hauled himself back out to the boat. With a great effort the seamen dragged him dripping aboard.

"You must be fuckin' freezin', Sec," said the bowman matter-of-factly. Charlie grinned. He no longer felt such a beginner.

Mackerel backed off into deeper water and turned the boat. The anchor warp was transferred to the bow and the manila snaked out the transom as he edged back to his anchor. A few grunting jerks and it came home.

The motor launch chugged slowly back towards *Caryatid*.

The steamer had come close in now and anchored. Charlie could see she was in shallow water as her roll was exaggerated. He looked anxiously at the length of rope remaining in the boat and the distance still to go. But Bernard Foster was far too careful a man to be caught on that score, and there were still ten fathoms in the boat when the end was passed up onto the *Caryatid*'s foredeck.

"That's most extraordinary, Mr Farthing," said Captain Macready, looking Charlie up and down.

"Sorry, sir?" said the younger man, uncomprehending.

"Your clothes are soaking wet, yet your seaboots are comparatively dry," Captain Macready was smiling.

Charlie laughed. "Oh I never swim in my boots, sir."

"You'd better get dried off, Mr Farthing," said Captain Macready who had almost recovered his composure. Except, of course, when he actually thought of Stanier.

Stanier had a phonecall on the Friday morning to inform him that Sir Hector's party would arrive on Sunday night. He immediately set about the final preparation aboard *Sea Dragon*. His first priority was to turn her in her berth so that she could be steamed out of the inner harbour with the least possible fuss and the maximum panache.

During this operation the dock gates were opened for several fishing boats as it was within half an hour of high water. Across the dock Thomas Jones put down the telephone receiver and tossed off his mug of tea.

"*Carry*'ll be here in about an hour," he said to Stan who nodded. Jones looked out of the window.

"Stupid bastard still fiddlin' with that yacht, Tom?" asked Stan.

Jones nodded. "Be bloody glad to see the back of 'im next week."

"What'll we do without 'im?" demanded Stan in mock horror.

"Fuckin' manage, that's what!" volunteered Fred, speaking for the first time, unable to stand the philosophical attitude of his colleagues. "He's a pain in the bloody arse."

"Now Fred, calm down, he won't be here long."

"How d'you work that out?" asked Fred sharply, immediately interested.

Jones shrugged. "Stands to reason, see. Man like Stanier's too ambitious for the likes of Port'Ardur. You watch this connection with Sir Bloody Hector."

Jones turned away from the window and sat down. Fred got out a pack of cards.

Stanier completed mooring *Sea Dragon* and left her. High water had already passed and he noticed with annoyance that the caisson gates were still open. Of 'his staff' there was no sign. He walked along the quay to the lock head opposite to his brick caboose. Between him and his office yawned the offending gap. An apple core was moving slowly, almost imperceptibly out. He raised his voice and shouted.

"Office 'hoy!" There was no response.

Stanier flushed with annoyance. "Jones!" he roared in the sort of bellow that one expects from annoyed Master Mariners.

"Raise you," said Jones, "who's makin' that bleedin' noise?"

"Stanier," said Fred not looking up but staring gloomily at his hand.

"Shit!" said Jones getting up and laying a royal flush on the table. He went outside.

"Jones! What the hell are you playing at?" Stanier yelled across the entrance, ignoring the dozen or so loungers, rod fishermen and holiday-makers that turned, attracted by the Harbour Master's bawling.

"Sorry, Cap'n? What's up?" Jones was deliberately dense. Fred and Stan came out behind him. Fred said, *"Carry*'s coming up the bay."

"What's up?" yelled Stanier. "It's well after high water, that's what's up. How many times do I have to tell you that I want the dock impounded on top of the tide and this is the best tide this month and the bloody ebb's away! Well, don't just stand there, man. Close the damned gates!"

"Close the gates, Cap'n?" hedged Jones, aware that Stanier was a comfortable distance from him while they remained open.

"Yes damn it, close them!"

"But the *Car*—"

"Don't argue! Close the damned gates!" Stanier was practically beside himself, well aware that he was not coming off best and that there were nearly two dozen onlookers now, if one excepted the faces at the windows of The Feathers.

"Oh, fuck it," said Fred, striding over to the lever that controlled the gates.

"But Fred . . ." began Jones then shrugged. As Fred said, 'Fuck it.'

As the gates began to close, Stanier moved out along the catwalk so that when they met he strode rapidly across to where his staff stood. It was like Napoleon admonishing his marshals.

"We're pushing it a bit, sir," said Foster to Captain Macready.

Macready lowered his binoculars. "But we're alright," he

said reassuringly. "I've asked the chief for maximum full speed until I ring down."

Foster nodded. "I'll get the hands to stand-by then?"

"Very well, Mr Foster." Captain Macready raised his glasses again just to confirm matters.

Caryatid steamed up the bay, smoke belching from her funnel and a great bone in her teeth. The hands came up and lounged on the rail as they watched draw near the dear, familiar roofs of Porth Ardur nestling under the shadow of Mynydd Uchaf.

"He's in a hurry," said Chippy spitting over the rail.

"Ebb's away, Chips," said the Bosun knowledgeably, "and there's dancin' tonight.

Captain Macready rang 'Stop engines' just off the end of the mole. *Caryatid* slowed. "Hard a-port!" he snapped and the steamer began to turn, slowing all the while. As she opened up the dock entrance Macready swore. The gates were closed against him. Simultaneously the quartermaster shouted, "Gates are closed, sir!"

"Midships . . . steady." Macready put out his hand to yank the telegraphs to full astern. Instinctively he looked aft, anxiously noting that *Caryatid* was still moving quite rapidly ahead. Then he saw something that changed his mind.

"Steady up for the centre of the gates, quartermaster."

There was a silence then: "Steady for the centre of the gates, sir."

"Thank you." Macready felt quite light-headed. He quickly scanned the mole for Jones or his side kicks but then caught sight of them standing in a knot with Stanier. He rang 'Slow astern' dragging some of the way off *Caryatid*. On the foredeck anxious faces, Foster's among them, stared uncomprehendingly up at the bridge. The Mate started to come aft, remembering the strange mood he had found the Captain in earlier in the week.

"Have two fenders ready, Mr Foster," said Macready in a clear voice and the Mate turned forward. Macready rang the engines to 'Stop.'

On the mole Stanier's diatribe was never finished. It faded out as he realised that his three underlings were looking intently behind him. Something of very great interest was obviously distracting them. He turned round.

Caryatid was about fifty feet from the gates, creeping inexorably ahead. Stanier rushed forward onto the catwalk over the tops of the gates. One hand was raised like a policeman.

"It's past high water! The port's closed! You'll damage the gates! Go astern!" As he issued each of these peremptory instructions his voice rose so that by the last, already weakened by too much shouting, it cracked into a squeak.

There were now about forty people standing on the quay.

Stanier reached the centre of the gates at the precise instant that *Caryatid*'s stem touched them.

"Wouldn't crack a fuckin' egg," opined the seaman holding one hand fender over the starboard bow.

"Fuckin' beautiful," agreed the seaman holding a hand fender over the port bow. Beneath them Stanier looked up. Foster looked over, then embarrassed, he looked away again.

Stanier was aware that his nose was about twelve inches from the sheer black bar of *Caryatid*'s stem. Some agency was easing his legs apart with a far from erotic sensation.

He looked down. A gap of water showed between them. *Caryatid* was forcing the gates gently open. Stanier realised he had a foot on each caisson and that if he did not do something very quickly, he was going to fall into the dock. His decision was prompted more by an instinct for survival than by common sense, for the side he ended up on was that from which he had started some twenty minutes earlier.

As soon as Jones saw Stanier safe he flung over the lever and opened the gates

"Like fuckin' rape," said the seaman on the starboard bow, hauling his redundant fender inboard.

"Fuckin' beautiful," agreed his companion on the port bow.

Caryatid eased into her berth and Captain Macready rang 'Finished with engines'. He was just descending from the bridge when an anxious Bernard Foster appeared.

"Harbour Master to see you, sir."

Stanier pushed past Foster. He was red with fury at his public humiliation. Not only had he been made to look a fool, he had been compelled to walk the entire circuit of the dock, past his own grinning crew aboard *Sea Dragon* and a crowd that was beginning to attract attention itself, as crowds have a habit of doing.

"What the bloody hell kind of a display of seamanship do you call *that*, Macready!?" Stanier roared, practically foaming at the mouth. "You bloody stupid, incompetent fool!"

Macready smiled. "Would you mind stepping out on the boat deck a moment, Harbour Master?" The Captain of the *Caryatid* gestured Stanier to the teak door.

Stanier stumbled over the high coaming. "What the god-damned—?"

Macready followed him and gently pushed him round clear of the funnel ventilators. With the utmost gravity Macready raised his arm and pointed.

It was a gesture pregnant with confidence.

Stanier looked. Against the blue hills on the far side of the bay the end of the mole stood out. Rising from its extremity the signal mast and yard bore four black balls disposed in a square.

"The port's open, Harbour Master, you forgot to take down the signals . . ."

The Cruise of the Sea Dragon

Sir Hector's domestic staff arrived on Saturday evening. The knight bachelor and his guests were due for dinner the following evening. The meal was to be an informal buffet to which James Stanier and 'lady' were cordially invited. Stanier was not a man to be outdone in matters of protocol. He and Tegwyn had arranged that he should meet Sir Hector and his party and that she should arrive herself some ten minutes later.

Stanier was well satisfied with *Sea Dragon*. Her teak decks were spotlessly clean and all paint drops had been carefully scraped off. The white paint was pristine and the teak rails, doors and other brightwork shone with the incomparable sheen of fresh copal varnish. All visible brass was polished and Stanier himself had made some fancy rope-work in white cotton line for the accommodation ladder, learnt on his training ship a decade earlier. He had had the anchor crowns picked out in blue and the cable lengths over the toy windlass enamelled in white. All parcelling was finished at either end with four-strand turks' heads and any rope's end about the deck was cheesed. Captain Stanier was justifiably pleased with the appearance of his first command.

There was only one cloud on the horizon. He had been unable to purchase a mess jacket in Porth Ardur and, as Master of the *Sea Dragon*, did not wish to resort to a dinner jacket when dining with Sir Hector and his friends. However he had hit upon the expedient of dispatching Fred into the nearest major town, some thirty miles away, where telephoned enquiries had elicited the information that such items might be purchased.

Fred was expected back at any time and before proceeding ashore to his house Stanier had gone below to consult Sir Hector's steward on the identity of the expected guests.

He found the steward, who was a butler ashore. "Good evening, Horrocks, isn't it?"

Horrocks was a small, neat, competent man. "Yes sir, that is correct."

"Well, Horrocks, could you tell me exactly who to expect tomorrow?"

"Certainly, sir. Apart of course from Sir Hector there will be his associate, Mr Argyle. Mr Argyle is a ship-broker, sir, and will probably bring his secretary who is usually a Miss Dorothy Loring . . ." Irony was absent from Horrock's voice, though the merest inflection on the words carried a conviction more potent than crude explanation. ". . . I expect Mr Pomeroy will be of the party, he's an extremely wealthy young man who has invested heavily in Sir Hector's shipping company."

"And Mr Pomeroy's lady?" asked Stanier.

"I doubt it, sir. I do not believe there *is* a Mrs Pomeroy. Mr Pomeroy prefers to travel alone, sir. Mr Pomeroy is an Old Etonian, sir, and a former Guards officer."

"I see," said Stanier. "Anyone else?"

Horrocks shrugged. "It is possible Miss Caroline may

come, sir, she is a somewhat impulsive young woman . . ."

"Miss Caroline?"

"Sir Hector's daughter, sir."

"I was unaware that Sir Hector was married . . ."

"Sir Hector and Lady Blackadder are estranged, sir," explained Horrocks, in a tone that precluded further enquiries.

Fred resented his mission to such an extent that he got no further than the Station Bar, where he got so drunk that he missed the train. It was fortunate that in staggering home he met Jones who, quickly discovering that Fred had failed to collect Stanier's mess kit, was prescient enough to realise a contingency plan was required.

Jones left Fred to his fate and, mounting his bicycle, swiftly descended the hill to the harbour. He met Mackerel Jack at the gangway of *Caryatid*. Mackerel had the watch and was also known to Jones. The two men retired to the messroom for a conference on terms and when it was concluded, in the currency of pints of beer ultimately chargeable to Fred, they proceeded into the officers' accommodation.

The conspirators' biggest problem was the presence of Second Officer Charles Farthing, but they discovered him dozing on his settee and moved swiftly past his cabin door.

It was the work of a few minutes to slip the latch in the Captain's door and enter Macready's cabin. Twenty minutes after boarding *Caryatid* Thomas Jones was ashore again, cycling round to *Sea Dragon* with a bundle under his arm.

"Don't forget to square it with the steward," were his last words to Mackerel Jack.

"Don't forget the bloody beer," replied the seaman.

* * *

"So you'll be away next weekend, dear?" asked Gwendolen Macready.

"Er, yes, we've the big job to do at Ynyscraven and I don't anticipate finishing it before the following Monday . . . There, does that look better?" Macready stepped back and lowered paint pot and brush to the floor.

"Yes, that's very nice. Right then, I'll have the vicar organise the PCC meeting here, that'll ease the burden on his wife, she's not been at all well lately, d'you know Septimus . . ." But Septimus did not know, neither did he honestly care, he just kept thinking of Justine.

"There love, that's the best I can do for you." Justine tied the ribbon around the cardboard box. "Alright Betty, I'll lock up, hang on a minute, love . . ."

Betty Byford said her "Goodnight, see you on Monday," and left the shop. Tegwyn waited impatiently for her mother.

"I know you're itching to be off, dear, but I would be stupid if I didn't know the purpose of some of the things in there." Justine indicated the box under Tegwyn's arm. The little shop was stuffy. Motes danced in the slanting rays of late afternoon sunshine that poured in through its one window. Tegwyn tightened her arm possessively around the box. It contained a frothy confection of lingerie that she had not known her mother stocked. She flushed, feeling her cheeks burn.

"Are you sleeping with him, love?" asked Justine, realising that she had paid scant attention to her daughter in recent weeks and knowing the answer to her question before she asked it. Tegwyn was silent.

"Of course you are . . . well, don't say I didn't warn you about him when he drops you, and don't think I approve because I don't but I can't condemn you and don't want you hurt, love." Justine gently took the box from her daughter and laid it on the counter.

"You just be careful, my girl." She said the words in that low husky voice that men privileged to hear, never forgot. The two women looked at each other. Tears of happiness were welling in Tegwyn's eyes, tears of compassion in her mother's. The two clasped together, then Justine kissed her daughter's mouth and drew away. Tegwyn was very lovely. For the first time Justine experienced a real pang of painful jealousy: she envied her daughter's flesh, even the faint, betraying shadows beneath her eyes. Tegwyn submitted herself proudly to Justine's gaze. She had lost that slightly inferior feeling when in the very physical presence of her mother.

"Goodbye, Mother."

"Goodbye, *cariad*." Justine turned away. She felt like a relay runner who had just handed over the baton. There was nothing further for her but to slow down and pull off the track.

Captain James St John Stanier watched the Daimler pull up ('The car's nothing pretentious, old boy,' he could hear Sir Hector say). The chauffeur jumped out and opened the doors. From the back Sir Hector emerged followed by a small, stocky, grey-haired man of about fifty, presumably Argyle, thought Stanier. The stocky man handed out a youngish woman, little taller than himself, with dark hair and a compact figure.

"Miss Loring," explained a voice at his elbow. Stanier turned to find Horrocks. He nodded. Next out was a graceful blonde of about thirty who tossed her hair as she straightened up.

"Sir Hector's special guest, sir," said the *sotto voce* Horrocks. "I omitted to inform you earlier as one is never quite sure . . ." a gentle, dignified emphasis lay on the words 'special' and 'quite'.

"That's Mr Pomeroy."

Stanier looked at a foppish young man coming round the bonnet of the car.

"No Miss Caroline?"

"Not as yet, sir."

Sir Hector led them on board and made introductions.

Tegwyn arrived some twenty minutes later in a taxi. For Tegwyn to travel in a taxi was something of a treat but it was a comment on her self-confidence that she alighted from it as though the occurrence was not unusual. She was fortunate in having acquired a deportment peculiar to duchesses or exceptional dancers. Stanier was at the gangway to meet her. Any misgivings he might have had at her appearance were instantly dispelled, for she managed the gangway without those irritatingly superfluous giggles that women often use at such moments.

Neither was her Ardurian accent out of place when Stanier introduced her, for Argyle's Gaelic burr was matched by Miss Loring's unmistakable Cockney. The only person who showed any inclination to be stand-offish was Sir Hector's special guest, who was introduced as Samantha.

As Stanier relaxed with his third whisky he looked

happily around. Things were going very well, very well indeed.

Charlie Farthing saw the lights in *Sea Dragon*'s saloon. He slipped up to the bridge of the *Caryatid* and focussed the long glass on the windows. Charlie was bored, impatient and longing for Monday when *Caryatid* would head for Ynyscraven.

He was even more impatient when he at last took the glass from his eye, for the sight of laughing women and the lights catching the gentle swellings of silk covered breasts was having an effect upon his pulse rate.

It was even worse later. He had tried to turn in early but constant thoughts of Sonia, not all of them of the purest, had driven him out on deck to pace up and down. Here he had been subjected to the mirth of post-prandial diners taking their brandy on *Sea Dragon*'s open quarterdeck.

In the end Charlie gave up and went off to The Feathers, where he found Calico Jack. Rank was abolished and the two got drunk together, happily telling their most intimate secrets to each other until it began to dawn on Charlie that here, if Calico had his way, was his prospective father-in-law.

Sea Dragon sailed from Porth Ardur shortly before noon on the Monday morning. Her departure was watched by *Caryatid*'s crew who paused in the operation of taking on board the long five-inch wire for the lighthouse hoist.

Sir Hector and Argyle were sitting in the smoke room reading the papers but Pomeroy and the ladies were out on the quarterdeck, their hair rippled by the sea breeze and cardigans loosely about their shoulders.

There were one of two ribald remarks from *Caryatid*'s foredeck and a clenched fist was jerked in an obscene gesture which elicited a guffaw of laughter from the seamen, but Stanier did nothing to bring on his head the disapprobation of the watching 'experts'.

The woman called Samantha turned to Pomeroy and in a coolly arch voice asked "I expect you'd rather be over there amongst all those sailors, wouldn't you, darling?"

Tegwyn, only half aware that there was something different about the young man, turned to catch his reply.

"Only if you're going to be beastly for the whole trip, Sammy, then I'd rather."

"I expect you'll find something to tickle your Greek fancy . . ."

Pomeroy ignored her and smiled at Tegwyn. "I must say," he said, "that crêpe-de-chine blouse suits you admirably, Miss Morgan." He touched her arm. The gesture was one of extreme delicacy. Involuntarily, Tegwyn shuddered with pleasure. Pomeroy smiled again.

On her back in the heather Sonia stared skywards. The blue arch of the sky soared above her. No cloud was visible and she tried unsuccessfully to grasp what she was looking at. It was infinity, blue infinity and yet it was nothing, nothing at all.

She sighed languorously. The sky, the hugeness of it was like love . . . she fought off clichés which seemed to cheapen the sensation of being at one with that blueness. She felt the ground warm beneath her and breathed deeply, pressing the palms of her hands onto the roughness of the heather. Her breasts rose and fell in slow undulations.

She thought about Charlie and suddenly realised that all the time her subconscious was debating whether or not she would let him make love to her. Her breathing quickened and she opened her legs a little, trying hard to imagine what it was like . . .

A shadow fell suddenly across her face. She sat up guiltily, flushing at being discovered with her mind in such abandoned raptures and imagining her fantasy was written in letters upon her forehead. The kestrel, hovering between Sonia and the sun, side-slipped at the sudden movement.

Sonia clasped her knees and transferred her gaze to the sea. It stretched empty to the horizon. No, a small white dot was away to the north east. She lay back again. Small white dots were not the *Caryatid*.

Presently she rose. The light breeze that blew up on the spine of Ynyscraven moulded her blouse around her. Her nipples stood out, rigid against the material. The white speck that Sonia had seen was the westward steaming *Sea Dragon*.

The *Sea Dragon*'s cruise, like any voyage, soon settled down to a daily routine in which all aboard participated to a greater or lesser degree. Breakfast was not compulsory but Sir Hector expected all his guests to be present for morning coffee at which the social events of the day were discussed. They might land on an island or at a fishing village, anchor to sunbathe and swim, or steam as close inshore as Stanier dared, which was not very close since he was trained to keep a good offing.

The weather was kind. Day after day of light breezes and sunshine prevailed. Indolence and pleasure sailed with the passengers of the *Sea Dragon* against the deceptively picturesque backdrop of the Cambrian coast.

The party, which considered itself the ultimate in civilised sophistication during the day, occupied itself at night according to its inclinations. Sir Hector, a man of easy morals, was not a degenerate and although it was obvious that carnal liaisons were the main purpose of the cruise, they were required to be discreet.

Private opinions tended to be concealed and the party rubbed along without friction in an atmosphere in which the food, the wine, the weather and the delightful prospect of the seascape tended to enervate the participants. Even the arrival of Miss Caroline failed to upset the delicate balance of the yacht's ethos.

Miss Caroline joined when *Sea Dragon* put into a small port about fifty miles west of Porth Ardur. She was slender with bobbed hair and an air of restless energy that must have characterised her father at an earlier age. She was also slightly loud in her opinions and this might have ruined the equanimity of the party had she not been dropped by her latest boyfriend but a day earlier. This circumstance tended to render her less disruptive, and she fell into deep, meaningful silences that the others thankfully ignored.

To some extent, however, her presence was a problem. All the other members of the group had selected, and tacitly acknowledged, their sexual partners. Now Caroline by herself threatened to upset the equilibrium.

The party had devised a little ritual after dinner in which the partners left the company. The pecking order had been established the first night when Stanier had been aware of his responsibilities.

At about eleven o'clock he had excused himself: "Perhaps you would excuse me? I have to write up my night orders." Goodnights were exchanged and then, "Tegwyn, would you care to see the view from the bridge?" at which hint the two left. The others then stretched or drained their glasses or filled them for a night-cap, and the party dispersed.

When, the following night, the hour had approached eleven, Sir Hector had said, "I suppose, Captain, you have to write up your orders?" Stanier took the hint and the ritual was established.

But Caroline did not interfere with the arrangements, at least not at this juncture, for her self-esteem was undergoing an extensive rebuilding programme from which, her father privately assured Argyle, she would presently bounce back with disarming force.

Stanier was enjoying himself. It must be admitted he took to his job like a duck to water. If he erred on the side of caution his confidence increased daily until at the end of the first week his self-esteem had reached a new peak. His professionalism reasserted itself as the mainspring of his life and his interest in Tegwyn began its inevitable wane. There were other thoughts in his head besides the management of *Sea Dragon*. His spell as commander of the yacht brought realisation of the limitations of his post at Porth Ardur. In private conversation Sir Hector had repeatedly intimated an interest in Stanier's career that was fast becoming paternal. Argyle, a shrewd Gael, had quizzed him several times and given Stanier the impression he was undergoing an examination rather than an interview.

Finally Stanier was attracted by the person of Caroline, whose languid attitudes about the decks of *Sea Dragon* were a sharp contrast to Tegwyn's more obsessive nature. Stanier had enjoyed almost every one of his adolescent fantasies in actuality with Tegwyn. He had worked through the gamut of his imaginative lusts and it was beginning to dawn, at least on his subconscious, that he was drowning in the flesh of Tegwyn Morgan. By contrast Caroline was enigmatic and distant. She was also slightly romantic, at least to the pragmatic judgement of James St John Stanier.

After all, her father was an extremely wealthy man.

Poor Tegwyn was quite unaware of the gradual cooling of her lover. Every night with the faithful loyalty of the true mistress she adorned her body for him. Her allurements were always irresistible and she gave him physical love with an enthusiasm that could only come from a devotion that transcended the carnal.

So besotted had she become, and so romantic were her circumstances aboard *Sea Dragon*, that her happiness was undisturbed when Stanier came down late to her cabin. She believed his excuse that he had thought the yacht might be dragging her anchor and had found it necessary to check the position.

She did not know that Caroline had begun to bounce back.

Stanier had been en route to Tegwyn's cabin as was his usual practice when a figure waylaid him from the shadow of the engine room ventilator.

"Good evening, Caroline," he had said, instantly recognising the girl since the moon was full and shone from a sky devoid of even a wisp of cloud.

"Good evening, Captain. It's a beautiful night."

"Yes indeed. I wish you wouldn't be so formal. My name's James."

"Would you be offended if I called you Jimmy?" Stanier detested the idea but found himself saying, "Of course not."

She moved over to the rail then leaning back on it, faced him.

"My father's interested in you. Says you've a ruthless streak. I should say he was probably considering taking you for a partner. He's acutely conscious that he's already outlived his own father. I was supposed to be a son." She turned and gazed out over the moonlit sea. The lights of a little town were going out one by one. The mountains rising behind looked as they might have done a millennium earlier.

"Come here beside me, Jimmy." He moved over and leant beside her.

"I expect that he will be planning how to get you and me together. As you are, at present, occupied you'll get an invitation to Laycocks, that's our house. Probably for Christmas if not before."

Stanier was stunned into silence.

"Haven't you anything to say, Jimmy?"

Stanier shook his head. "Not really, I'm a little dazed, that's all . . ." Pictures of Stanier as a successful ship-owner swam into his imagination.

"You'll be expected to marry me, of course, having done a voyage in command of one of Daddy's ships."

Stanier's heart leapt. Then he could really call himself 'Captain' and perhaps, or was this going too far, perhaps there might yet be a knighthood?

He looked sideways at Caroline. Marriage?

She turned and looked back at him.

"Well?"

"D'*you* want to marry *me*, Caroline?"

She smiled, a cold, resolved, Saxon smile.

"As you were gentleman enough to ask me I'll give it my consideration. Good night, Captain."

The result of this conversation made no difference to the behaviour of either Stanier or Caroline. She waited on events and he waited for her reply, wondering whether he had made a fool of himself, or whether, quite by accident, he might be on the verge of a successful liaison. In the meantime he continued to satisfy Tegwyn, such is the fecundity of youth. It was almost a week after their departure from Porth Ardur when Sir Hector suggested a visit to Ynyscraven. *Sea Dragon* was well to the westward and it was late on Sunday evening when the blue painted anchor dropped from her gleaming bow.

She shared the anchorage with the steam vessel *Caryatid*.

The Ravens of Dungarth

The island of Ynyscraven lies in the Silurian Strait like a giant, elongated 'Q'. Millions of years before man's antecedents emerged from the primeval slime, geological changes had wrought it of a hump of granite with a covering of oil-bearing shale. Most of the shale had weathered away except at the southern end of the island. The northern extremity was high and fairly steep-to, a broken escarpment plunging into the sea and giving the lighthouse a tiny plateau to cling to. Thousands of screaming sea-birds, from auks to shags, nested here.

The higher spine of the island was mainly covered with heather or bracken, though areas of grass and gorse provided rough pasture for sheep and the hardy ponies that constituted the island's most prestigious 'export'.

The land sloped slightly to the settled southern end where, with the granite disappearing under the more dramatically eroded shale, it became an untidy victim to the ravages of the Atlantic. Here the tail of the 'Q' extended south and east in a long vicious reef that at low water had the appearance of a row of slavering fangs as the ocean sucked and swirled white about them.

This reef was appropriately known as the Hound's Teeth

and although dangerous, for the tide set across the jumble of rocks on both ebb and flood, its presence formed a lagoon-like anchorage within which ships of a considerable tonnage could lie in comfort and ride out any gales that blew from the prevailing wind directions of south-west to north-west. At the easternmost extremity of the reef, where Ynyscraven finally gave up its struggle with the sea and fell away to deep water, a bell buoy clanged its dolorous warning.

The noise of the Hound Buoy was the first indication to Justine that she was nearing the island. Despite the relative calm of the sea, the fishing vessel *Plover* was scarcely the *Mauretania* and Justine's passage from Aberogg had been decidedly uncomfortable. It had not been helped by the fact that she had not eaten for many hours. So excited was she that the thought of stopping to consume food was repugnant to her. Almost as soon as Tegwyn had left the shop and long before *Caryatid* had even had steam raised in her boilers, Justine had reached the station and taken a train on her circuitous route to Aberogg.

The *Plover* was on a fortnightly contract to take mail and provisions to the island and bring off sheep, ponies and passengers. There were no cabins for the latter, who had to take pot luck in the tiny messroom with such of the three crew who happened to be below. Justine's imposing appearance and friendly manner had of course charmed the three fishermen, who offered her every comfort their little ship could muster.

Nevertheless she was thankful when the *Plover* rubbed alongside the tiny stone jetty and she could take her trembling limbs ashore. The *Plover*'s skipper deputed his 'boy', a fair giant of about twenty-five, to shoulder her suitcase and walk up the steep path to the reeve's house.

Justine was utterly enchanted with the house in its little coombe. A small, neat lawn was overhung by trees that sheltered in the diminutive valley, and the smell of soft earth and flowers greeted her.

Inside the house she met the reeve and his wife. They appeared to be somewhat embarrassed at her arrival and for one awful moment Justine thought that the conspiracy had been uncovered.

"Mrs Morgan, how nice to meet you. I am-er-well, it is a little awkward-um—"

"Mrs Morgan, what my husband is trying to say is that only this morning we received a message from our son that he wished to see us urgently. Captain Macready mentioned to us that you were a friend of his and his wife's and we wished you to stay with us. As a result my husband has let the two guest cottages . . ." The reeve's wife spread her hands, "You see our problem."

"Well in that case, perhaps I ought to return . . ."

"Oh good heavens no!" continued the woman. "What we wondered was whether you would consider . . . well, whether you would mind looking after the house for us? You see, we've no idea what our son wants, except that it's important, neither do we like leaving the house empty as we've a daily maid, the daughter of one of our shepherds, she's a bit careless without supervision . . ."

Justine was, under the circumstances, hardly likely to refuse.

"No, of course, I shall be delighted. I am flattered that you trust me . . ."

The reeve's wife made a deprecating gesture. "You are a friend of Captain Macready's; that alone is recommendation enough and now that we've met you, well . . . the arrangement seems satisfactory." They smiled at each other.

"Besides," added the reeve, "you can't run away from Ynyscraven, even if you wanted to." They all laughed, Justine with genuine mirth.

So, for a little while, Justine Morgan became mistress of the island of Ynyscraven.

Justine did not expect to see either Macready or *Caryatid* until Monday evening at the earliest. She therefore had slightly less than twenty-four hours to settle in. After the reeve and his wife had left and she had made the acquaintance of the maid, a simple red-faced child called, inappropriately, Faith, Justine explored the house.

It was double fronted and slate roofed. On either side of the entrance hall large reception rooms were sparsely but elegantly furnished. The floors were of stained boards with rich Indian rugs upon them. In one room a wall of bookshelves dominated the room; the other was a dining room with a long mahogany table. The stairs led to a passage that went across the back of the house with three bedrooms opening off it. Each had a double bed, a chair and a washstand with basin and ewer.

At the rear of the house a jumble of kitchen, outhouses and stables gave way to the sheer rise of the rock wall that terminated the little coombe, so that one might have stood not twenty feet from the back of the house and thrown a stone down one of the chimneys.

The coombe faced east, losing the heat of the day early

and soon in shadow. As the cool of a summer evening began to steal across the patch of grass, Justine ventured forth to inspect her domain. She also thought she might see the anchorage from the end of the garden.

She discovered the wicket gate and passed through it, recognising the path up which she had followed the fisherman earlier in the day. Retracing her steps a few yards she discovered a vantage point from which the whole bay lay below her.

"Are you looking for the *Caryatid*?" The voice made her jump. She looked round. A girl in an Aran sweater with russet hair and green eyes was standing behind her. "You made me jump!" laughed Justine, still surprised.

"Are you waiting for the *Caryatid*?" the girl persisted.

"Well yes, as it happens, I am." It was useless pretending for she and Macready were bound to be seen together. The girl came and stood next to her.

"She's expected up at the north end of the island tomorrow."

"Oh I see," Justine felt inadequate; this girl, appearing out of nowhere, seemed omniscient. "How do you know?"

"I was up at the lighthouse this afternoon. The keepers told me. Are you staying at the reeve's house?"

"Yes I am. Do you live on the island?"

"Yes. My name's Sonia." The girl turned and extended her hand. The two women faced each other and Justine found herself thinking of Tegwyn. This girl, of an age with her daughter and nothing like as beautiful, seemed much less vulnerable. They shook hands awkwardly and Sonia asked, "Are you in love with someone aboard the *Caryatid*?"

Justine laughed, flashing her teeth in a smile that caught up her interlocutor so that Sonia too laughed. "What on earth makes you ask that?"

Sonia shrugged. "Why else are you here?"

"For a holiday, perhaps?" suggested Justine.

"You are far too beautiful to be on holiday alone," said the girl with a directness that Justine found disarming. "Besides, I'll soon find out. I know everything that happens on Ynyscraven." She looked wistfully northwards to where a spur of cliff formed a small headland.

Justine felt the chill of night approaching and shivered involuntarily. She was about to turn away when Sonia spoke again in a lower, more confidential tone.

"I too am waiting for the *Caryatid*."

"Are you in love with someone on board?" Justine asked. The girl nodded.

"I suppose that makes us sort of sisters," she replied.

Justine chuckled. For a second the two stood silently then Justine had an idea. "As you know all about the island you'll know I'm alone."

"In the reeve's house, yes, I know that."

"Would you join me for something to eat?" Justine was suddenly ravenous after her self-imposed fast. "You can tell me all about Ynyscraven, the real Ynyscraven. I don't want to feel like a visitor while I'm here."

Sonia looked at the dark, ripe beauty of the older woman. Justine would never be that, she thought. "Your hair is as black as a raven's wing," she said suddenly.

Justine moved her hand in an involuntary gesture to her head.

"I wonder if that is significant . . ." Sonia's words faded

away as though she were contemplating some secret problem.

"Will you come to the house . . . say in half an hour?"

"Of course. One never refuses regal invitations." Sonia turned abruptly away, leaving Justine completely confused. The girl's remark about her hair had been odd enough. Was this last a piece of insolence? If so it had been delivered in a strangely level way. Justine turned and walked back to the house. Below her the anchorage submitted to the shadow of the night.

The maid Faith was dismissed as soon as she and Justine had organised a fire in the sitting-room grate, found a cold shoulder of lamb and a jug of cider. Justine lit the oil lamps, pulled up a chair to the warmth of the fire and waited for Sonia. Around her the cold granite of the house was so still that she could hear the blood rushing in her ears.

When Sonia arrived Justine carved the meat and the two women sat at a small polished table. The oil lamp caught the girl's green eyes and Justine was surprised at the sudden beauty they lent to her face.

"Do you always talk in riddles?" she asked at last.

"I'm sorry, I didn't know I did . . . oh, you mean what I said about regal commands?"

"Yes, that, and something about the colour of my hair being significant."

"It's not dyed, is it?" Sonia was sharply inquisitive. She repented instantly. "I'm sorry, that must have sounded very rude but it wouldn't be significant if it was dyed."

Justine was about to deny that it was, then realised that women who deny things with vehemence are often thought of as lying. She put down her knife and fork and put her hands up behind her head.

Her hair tumbled about her shoulders, the lamp catching the blue lights in it. "There," she said. "Is that as black as your raven's wing?"

Sonia rose and came round the table. Her fingers scarcely touched the tumbled mass. "Yes, it is," she said, sitting down again.

Justine tossed her head and flicked her hair behind her shoulders.

"Now you tell me all about it."

Sonia put down her knife and fork. "It would be easy to tell you if I knew why you have come to Ynyscraven. You have come here to love someone, haven't you? I bet I know who it is. As the reeve's left you in the house alone I'll guess: you're a friend of Captain Macready, he and the reeve are very thick . . . am I right?"

"Perhaps," said Justine, colouring. "Love seems much on your mind."

"Yes. Would you mind if I came and asked you things; not now, perhaps, but later?"

"Have you no family?"

"Not really, my mother's a little distant."

"If I can help, of course." Justine replied, wondering what, in this enchanted place, constituted distance.

"Thank you. Now let me tell you about the island. It belongs to the Earl of Dungarth. The Earl traces his line back to the Conqueror and it is said that the first of them came here just after the Conquest. At that time the island was independent. It seems to have held off the Saxons, for it had a Celtic monastery and a king. The first Earl had had the island included in his fief by the King and came to take possession of it, but his landing was disputed down in the bay where you came ashore. There was a fight and the king of Ynyscraven died, but the invaders were driven off for a while. The next east wind brought them back again. This time, the story goes, the Earl approached the beach under full sail and the wind was a gale. The defenders were well back and confident that the Earl's ships would be dashed to pieces. But they reckoned without knowing the spirit of the Earl. He ordered all his warriors to lie down while he took the helm of his ship and his lieutenant the helm of the other. Sorry, am I boring you?"

"No, my dear, I am fascinated. You mean all this happened just below where we were this afternoon?"

Sonia nodded, lowering her glass of cider. "Well, the two ships drove straight up the beach, broached-to in the breakers, and as they rolled over, the Earl led his warriors ashore. The islanders were broken and fled, only a few remaining in the king's hall which was supposed to have been on the site of this house.

"The king had a queen who was a great beauty, a woman celebrated by poets for her raven hair, whose reputation is supposed to have inflamed the Earl and led to him begging the island as part of his fief from the Conqueror in the first place, and also, of course, sharpening his desire to capture the island. She retired to an old hill fort, or dun, up on the high ground. It's near the lighthouse and you can still see the remains of it today. It's on a bit of a headland, or garth. It was called the 'fort on the point' or Dungarth."

"Ah, I see, go on."

"Well, the Earl had overrun the island and did not wish

the queen to hold out, merely to surrender without further bloodshed, so he cut off the landward side and summoned her to give up. The story goes that she appeared on the rampart and taunted him and he was further inflamed by her beauty and courage. He gave her until dawn the following day to change her mind and when she had not done so he attacked. His men overran the dun without opposition and when they got inside a great flock of ravens rose from the ground. But there were no warriors, no Queen, nothing."

"And the Queen, what happened to her?"

Sonia shrugged. "History won't tell. Legend says she will return one day, bringing a new race of rulers to the island."

"And d'you think that's likely . . . I mean that the queen will return?"

"It's possible, in this island you can believe anything like that might happen; the islanders still call an easterly wind an invader's wind, yet few of them know why. I thought you might be the Queen, for you were somehow, I don't know, the way I have always imagined the Queen might have been, a real woman . . . Oh you mustn't laugh at me! If I'd known you would laugh I would never have told you!" Sonia was furious but Justine reached out a hand and restrained her.

"My dear, I believe your story may well be true." Seeing the look in Sonia's face Justine regretted the sudden loss of rapport with the girl. Very gently she said, "I will tell you that here, on Ynyscraven, I feel a strange peace. You are right about my purpose here. Why should I conceal it? What happens here will make me like a queen. No my dear, I was simply laughing at myself and the irony if I, at my age, were to conceive a child, never mind a race of kings."

Sonia breathed a sigh of relief, then had another idea. "Have you a daughter then, of child-bearing age?"

This time the smile disappeared entirely from Justine's face.

The two women talked a little more. Justine confided in her, surprising herself that she could, and wanted to, talk to this strange, fey creature. At last the girl rose.

"It is late," she said. "As you are alone I'll light you up to your room, I know the house and can find my way back. Nobody locks their doors at night so I can slip away." Sonia picked up the lamp and led Justine into the hall.

Inside Justine's bedroom Sonia put down the lamp on the washstand. She moved the jug and ewer out of the way and put a mirror on the marble. Then she pulled up a chair. "There you are," she said, indicating the chair.

Justine sat down and picked up her hair brush. She was about to say goodnight when the girl took the brush gently from her hand and began to brush Justine's black tresses in long sensuous sweeps. For a minute Justine was embarrassed, then she closed her eyes. It had been a long day and the sensation was delicious. She thought of her bedroom in Porth Ardur and the lonely ministrations she had submitted herself to.

For several minutes neither said anything. Then Sonia spoke. "My father, who ruined my mother by seducing her, was a Slav count. Sometimes my mother calls me her 'petite vicomtesse.' I suppose it is alright for a vicomtesse to dress the hair of a queen."

"I have no objection," answered Justine in that low, sensual voice that she could not help using at such times.

Sonia saw the scarlet ribbon lying on the bed and caught

up the hair in a thick tail behind Justine's head. She gently patted it. "There, the raven's wings are folded . . ."

Slowly Justine rose from the chair and her skirt slipped to the floor. She peeled her blouse back from her shoulders. "Good night, my dear," she said, gently dismissing Sonia.

"Good night," whispered the girl.

Different Ships, Different Longsplices

Caryatid anchored off Ynyscraven Lighthouse on Monday evening. Charlie operated the semaphore arms and Captain Macready, together with his Chief Mate Foster, went ashore. They were met at the landing by the keepers and Macready and Foster briefed the latter on the job the ship's crew intended doing. An hour later *Caryatid* steamed into the anchorage at the southern end of Ynyscraven and brought up to her anchor. The final preparations for the rigging of the new hoist wire having been made, Captain Macready gave his ship's company a watch ashore.

At the gangway door Foster watched the last grinning fireman into the boat and waved the coxswain away. "Back at midnight, lads," he called after them as with a roar of its engine the boat turned away from *Caryatid*'s side.

Foster met the boat when it returned and Captain Macready came down to leave the ship. "Farthing coming?" asked the Captain.

"Here sir," puffed Charlie, hurrying along.

"Er, Bernard," began Macready rather bashfully, "I've been invited to stay ashore, send a boat in at eight o'clock, will you?"

"Yes, of course, sir. Where will you be, at the reeve's house?"

Macready had not the foggiest idea where he would be except that it would be in the arms of Justine. He nearly forgot himself and answered facetiously. In the end he guessed. "Yes, yes that's right . . . ah, here comes the boat."

"Back at midnight, Charlie," said Foster to the second mate.

Charlie just grinned. He had four hours before midnight.

"She's in, she's in!" Justine looked up from her book. Sonia was running across the grass towards the house, her hair loose behind her. "The *Caryatid*'s just anchored," she explained, bursting breathlessly in. Justine rose, her heart thumping like a hammer. Sonia's eyes were shining like sunstruck spray. "Come *on!*" She led the way into the hall.

"Where are we going?" asked Justine bemusedly, following Sonia up the stairs.

She followed the girl into the main bedroom. From the window the view commanded the last ten yards of the path from the landing before it forked.

"We wait here until the crew have gone past. Then the officers will come up."

"So you're waiting for one of the officers?"

"Yes!" answered Sonia, standing beside the window, concealed from outside by the curtain. Justine frowned, suddenly moral. "You're *not* having an affair with Bernard Foster, are you?" she asked incredulously.

"Who's Bernard Foster? No, Charlie is *my* darling!" They both laughed. The garden was already in shadow. Night rolled up from the east in a cloudless sky. A gaggle of heads appeared; untidily, noisily and thirstily *Caryatid*'s crew filed up the path beside the reeve's house treading a path once used by Celtic monks.

"Oh, we don't consider *them* invaders," explained Sonia, uncannily reading Justine's mind. "They're rather sweet really. There's one old chap that's madly in love with my mother. He's a fireman, they are old friends, it's really quite touching."

"What, that old people should like each other's company?"

"No, that they should get on so well. I don't expect he'd want to know her if he knew she was the daughter of an Earl."

"So you are . . . ?"

"The bastard of a philandering Slav count and begot upon the body of—"

"No, no I didn't mean—"

"You meant to ask if I was related to an Earl. Well, Mother was the last Earl's sister. When she became pregnant by a Slave emigré she was disowned by her family, I don't know why, for the males made a profession of getting bastards off anybody who would oblige. The old Earl died when I was about three and his son, my cousin, took pity on us. He gave us the cottage on Ynyscraven. Here they come."

The figures of the Captain and Charlie approached the crest of the path.

The two women went downstairs and out across the lawn. There the men saw them. It struck Macready then that this was neither the time nor the place for further dissembling and that the next few days could not be concealed from the world, at least the tiny world of Ynyscraven, without blighting the pleasure of them.

"My dear . . ." he said, striding through the wicket gate with extended arms.

Justine drew him inside the house.

On the grass Charlie and Sonia buried their tongues in each other's mouths and ground their impatient bodies together. Charlie had scarcely noticed the Captain's disappearance or with whom he had disappeared.

After a little Sonia pulled away. "Before we go any further, and," she flashed him a smile of pleasure at his presence, "before Mother disappears to the Craven Arms, we had better go and introduce you to her."

They walked across the turf and out through the gate, leaving the house silent behind them.

"Before we get there, Charlie, I need to tell you something of my mother . . ." Sonia told him her mother's sad history. "Please don't take too much notice if she's a little odd," she concluded.

Inside the reeve's house Captain Macready was slowly being enchanted. The idea of spending this idyll in a house of their own far exceeded his wildest imaginings. It was as though some sympathetic angel watched over their forbidden love, nurturing it tenderly even down to the details. That Faith was simple and accepted the Captain's presence without demur only served to heighten the lovers' intense awareness of each separate moment they were together. They did not hasten to bed as young people might have done, they savoured their intimacy, pretending it was a normal life they were leading, guessing they might have to live on the memory of these stolen days for a long, long time.

When at last their bodies melted together they found that each had fulfilled its promise for the other and their hopes and imaginings had not been in vain.

Sonia and her mother lived in a stone cottage on the southern extremity of Ynyscraven. Ducking under the low doorway, Charlie found himself in a long room with a fireplace in the centre of the rear wall. There were no windows in any side other than the south wall through which they had entered. One other door, of recent creation, had been knocked in the east wall and gave onto a sort of lean-to conservatory. A few pots and pans were hung over the fireplace, which was occupied by a wood-burning range and an overmantel burdened down by artefacts, objects and beachcombed rubbish. Remaining wall space was filled with weirdly executed paintings and crude shelves of books, many of which were quite ancient, their leather bindings clearly suffering from the effects of Ynyscraven's damp. Furniture was sparse. At each end was a bed and washstand with a goatskin rug indicating a minimal concession to comfort. In the centre, occupying the greater part of the cottage, ran an enormously long refectory table which had a number of ill assorted chairs tucked under it, groaning under a burden of clothing, bits of wood and miscellania. Unwashed crockery littered the table, along with some sheets of paper bearing indecipherable scribbles.

"Mother's an artist . . ." explained Sonia, as she led the wondering Charlie through into the conservatory.

"Hullo, Mother," she said. "This is Charlie. We're very fond of each other."

Charlie had seen her before without really absorbing

details. She was working on a panel less odd than the work in the main room. She turned and stared at him.

Sonia's mother was in fact not yet fifty. She had a thin, weathered, striated appearance, like sea-eroded iron in which the weaker metal has oxidised and left a grain-like pattern of tough, durable material that gave the impression of greater age. Her face was oval and drawn, her mouth no more than a pale gash beneath a nose that clearly indicated a fondness for drink. Her hair was lank and straight. She was at once old and not so old. Feeble and strangely strong.

"Fond?" she asked in a voice that was surprisingly and undeniably refined. "Fond?" she repeated rising to survey Charlie. She wore about her neck a skein of dull stones and beads that looked like sea-tumbled pebbles. Her dress was a once-fashionable black crêpe garment that hung about her like a black shift. Beneath it she apparently wore little else for the thin material lifted over the points of her breasts, a fact of which Calico Jack had not been unaware. They were oddly incongruous compared to her slim hips and the thinness of her wrists and ankles.

"So she's fond of you, eh?"

"And I of her, ma'am," began Charlie.

"And you'll be wanting to seduce her, I'll warrant; you young men are all the same."

"Mother!"

"You be quiet, my dear. I'll trouble you to hold your tongue until I've finished with this fellow." She wagged a paintbrush under Charlie's nose until he had to move his face back to avoid having his nostrils painfully penetrated.

"Now you listen to me. I'm not having you mess about with my daughter unless you're decent. My family's been a victim to whoredom and whore-masters for generations; Sonia's different. She's an island bird that'll never leave Ynyscraven. There are spirits of ruined, raped women all over this rock, hundreds of 'em. Widows, mothers, sisters, wives. All the dead come here to keen over men lost on the rocks in shipwrecks, in rapine and bloody murder . . ." There was quite a lot more, but Charlie could not make head or tail of it and eventually stopped listening. Instead he looked politely at the panel on which the old woman had been working. He recognised it at once as an inn sign for the Craven Arms.

Eventually the old woman fell silent.

"They are the Craven Arms, are they?" asked Charlie changing the subject.

The woman looked at the panel. "Yes," she said slowly. "Three ravens sable upon a ground blanc . . . the 'C' is a phonetic addition to the island's name. It is added to the word to make it easier for persons unused to the true tongue to cope with. Sonia, light the lamps inside and tell the young man the history of the island." Sonia smiled at Charlie and returned into the cottage. Charlie was about to follow but the woman detained him. "Young man, do you love my daughter?"

Charlie looked down at her. It was growing dark and alone in the glass room he felt oddly frightened, as if she possessed some power that drew strength from her feebleness compared with his youthful vigour; as though her knowledge and experience outweighed all his physical advantages. Her eyes held his and he saw now where Sonia inherited her green irises. Yet Sonia's lacked the fire that burned fever-bright within her mother's. Charlie was suddenly afraid of the tremendous power in this woman's brain that blazed out through her eyes, a power of knowledge that grasped portents and formed oracles.

Was it thus that Cassandra entered the house of Agamemnon?

"Do you love her?" the woman hissed at him, the urgency of her question slicing through the air between them so that the reflex answer that he hastily uttered was true.

"Yes!"

The woman shot out a hand and touched his face. The fingers were dry yet sensitive. Charlie was later to see her touch pebbles and sea-smoothed driftwood in this way, as if learning their nature and shape, like a blind person.

At last she seemed satisfied.

"Then you shall have her."

There was a pause. Charlie was shaking, so tense was the atmosphere. "Young man, beware the invader's wind, for I smell it coming and with it the scent of death . . . now go into the house and Sonia will tell you the history of Ynyscraven and of the ravens of Dungarth."

"Mother likes you," said Sonia, leaning her head on Charlie's shoulder. The two of them were slowly descending the path to the landing. Above and behind them they could hear the approach of *Caryatid*'s watch ashore, a drunken, joyous riot that spilled out of the dark night and down the cliff like a freshet.

Charlie felt the yielding waist and turned her, crushing her suppleness to the hardening urgency of his own body. Around them the rocky crannies of Ynyscraven gave off the sweet scent of growing ferns.

*   *   *

Back in his bunk aboard *Caryatid*, Charlie pondered on the events of the evening. Coming down the path Sonia had told him the rest of her mother's history. There was little in her appearance or her behaviour to give the slightest clue as to her blue blood. Perhaps that was explained away by her madness or her eccentricity. No, there was more to the older woman than the eccentricity produced by aristocratic genetics. Had Charlie glimpsed a soul in some kind of torment within the crackling fire of those green eyes? Then another thought struck him. A disquieting, sinister thought that reeked of the old, cynical, pre-Porth Ardur Charlie. Was this old woman the obverse of the romantic coin of the island? Was she the toad under the stone? Or a witch?

Charlie inevitably thought of Sonia, steeped as she was in the history of this granite and shale heap of inhospitable rock. Was she touched with the same poison? Was it poison, isolation or the island that had turned the old woman's mind, or perhaps the other suffering?

Charlie did not even know the nature of the old woman's madness except that when he had pressed Sonia, she had shrugged and fallen silent. He drifted into sleep regretting that one could obtain a First Mate's Certificate without the slightest knowledge of psychology.

Sonia returned to the cottage. Her mother was still about, decanting gorse wine from a jug. She poured a beaker for her daughter and regarded the girl.

"You could do worse, *ma petite vicomtesse*," she said at last. "He does not have the look of a libertine." Sonia said nothing, used to her mother's moods and knowing when to keep silent.

151

"I suppose you must have a man?" Sonia held her tongue. She lowered her eyes in a tiny, affirmative gesture, blushing and betraying herself more than at any time up on the spine of Ynyscraven.

The old woman rocked on her chair. "Yes," she hissed at last, "that is our tragedy . . . we must have our men."

She took a deep draught of the wine and staggered to her feet. Sonia helped her gently to the bed. She felt her mother's shoulders heaving with sobs.

Not mad, Sonia thought, just smashed to pieces.

Captain Macready woke the following morning to the sight of sunlight flooding horizontally into the bedroom and the sound of birdsong.

He remembered the night and looked at Justine. She lay on her back, one arm upflung behind her head. Around her face cascaded her black hair, one lock of which had fallen across her cheek, giving her a youthfully carefree appearance. Sleep was kind to her, smoothing the lines upon her face so that her lashes lay like a young bride's, trembling slightly with the dreams behind them.

Septimus smiled a smile of adoration. There was no cheap male triumph in his face. He wore the look of an angel, albeit a damned angel.

He knew he would not sleep again and rose carefully from the bed, shivering slightly as his feet touched the polished boards of the floor. He padded over to the window splendidly aware of his own nakedness, scratching the hair mat over his chest. At the window the sun hit him, not three degrees above the horizon, well north of east at this season, blazing

its burning welcome to a magnificent day. Macready shut
his eyes, drew a deep breath in through his nostrils and
stretched the sleep out of his middle-aged body. Then he
slid up the sash window and looked out.

"God bless my soul!"

On the lawn below him a naked woman was bent over
picking mushrooms. At the squeal of the window she had
stopped, though remaining doubled up. Her flanks and legs
were thin, lank hair hung from her shoulders and pendulous
breasts sagged towards the ground. Macready felt breath on
his shoulder.

"What is it?" Justine, heavy with sleep stood beside him.
She too was naked.

The three stood looking at each other. In the garden,
Sonia's mother straightened up, a strange wan creature,
witch-like with a basket on her arm.

Instinctively Macready put his arm around Justine, pulling
her closer to him so that they stood framed in the window.
For a long time they stood thus, an incongruous tableau, each
waiting for something to break the odd spell that seemed
wound about them.

Macready felt a sudden surge of guilt, caught like this.
Justine, closer to truth, felt a twinge of pity for the older
woman whose identity she guessed. In the garden Sonia's
mother felt her mind spin. The man and the woman were
not the reeve and his wife, they were out of place, spectral
and beautiful. The man's face was familiar . . . she fought
off a fog that seemed to threaten her sight . . . they looked
so happy . . . one flesh . . .

The old woman inclined her head and dropped into a
curtsey. It was a ridiculous attitude and Septimus opened

his mouth to snort at it indignantly. But Justine was too quick for him. She put her hand over his mouth.

"No, my darling, you don't understand." Macready turned to look at her. He bent to kiss her and she slid her hand down over his belly. He began to kiss her neck, arousingly. She yielded, turning her head again to the garden. The old woman was bowing herself backwards down the garden, as if from a throne.

Justine smiled to herself and let Macready slide inside her.

Two hours later Macready stood, brass-bound and break-fasted, on the bridge of *Caryatid*. It was in truth a magnificent morning. Hardly a breath of air ruffled the surface of the sea so that the cry of the sea birds came to his ears clear and unmuted. The cliffs at the northern end of the island loomed forbidding above the ship's bow. He rang 'Stop' on the telegraph and crossed the bridge. He was manoeuvring *Caryatid* much closer in than was customary.

"Hard a starboard!" The quartermaster answered and Macready pulled the two telegraph handles back to 'Half Astern'. Below the bells jingled then answered on the bridge. *Caryatid* began to tremble. He rang the port engine to 'Stop' and watched astern as the ship turned.

When the *Caryatid* had completed her turn to her Master's satisfaction he ordered, 'Midships!'

Ringing the port engine full astern to deaden the swing he called out to Foster forward: "Leggo!"

With a splash and a roar of veering cable the starboard bower anchor dropped from the hawse pipe as *Caryatid* gathered sternway.

Macready watched the stern. He had to drive *Caryatid* into the gut between the main cliffs and the off-lying rocks where the heavy hoist wire was secured. He had also to keep control of her or – he did not think about what might happen. He rang 'Stop' on both engines. The marble green-white of the stern-wash died away and the hiss of its fading convolutions moved past the bridge. He waved.

The motor boat which had been sent in ahead to place seamen on two selected rocks, surged forward, closing the counter. A roar from her engine and she spun, heading ashore towing the brown snake of a coir mooring line from the starboard quarter. "Hold on forrard!" called Macready to the Mate.

Caryatid stretched her cable and the boat came back for a line from the other quarter. Within a few minutes she was moored with her stern well into the gut. From there her deck machinery could assist replacing the heavy hoist wire.

Captain Macready leaned out of the wheelhouse window, "Alright, Bernard. She'll do there, let's get the lads going, there's a lot to do."

There certainly was a great deal to do. Charlie soon found that Bernard had not been exaggerating when he said the work was gruelling. Although a simple operation in theory, the practical problems involved seemed legion. The distances, heights, weights and power requirements seemed to dwarf the *Caryatid*'s limited resources of machinery and manpower. It reminded Charlie of one of those lectures at the Board of Trade, where marvels are done on a blackboard and every sailor worth his salt knows the practical hitches involved render the whole exercise futile. What he had not realised that here, in this forgotten, taken-for-granted little service, such problems were met head-on and overcome.

Charlie's admiration for Bernard Foster increased enormously. The Mate seemed to be everywhere. Skidding down the hoist wire in a box loosening shackles, easing back on the great tackles that took the wire's tension from its securing screws prior to letting it go, scrambling over rocks checking on the grouting in the eyes that secured the end of the wire . . . the list of the Mate's activities seemed endless. Charlie did what he could, chiefly from the boats, but he was certainly a tired man as on each successive evening he trooped ashore behind the *Caryatid*'s crew as they made for the path leading upwards to the Craven Arms.

The routine was soon established and pints of gleaming beer were already set up on the bar when, on the second evening of her stay at Ynyscraven, *Caryatid*'s crew burst like a discharge of grape-shot into the open hall of the pub.

The majority of the greasers, firemen and seamen rolled ashore to roister and drink. And drink they did, threatening to deplete the Arms' supply before the *Plover* was due to replenish it. They sang, danced and yarned, they boasted and argued and at the end of each evening they staggered, slithered or were dragged down the shaly path to the landing. Each morning the boat came in for the Captain and, minutes later, *Caryatid* weighed from the anchorage and steamed the couple of miles to the lighthouse where her men, fighting off hangovers, sweated the beer out of themselves until the steamer again moved south for her night anchorage and another watch ashore.

Without doubt it was not the exhausted seamen who presided over the drunken revels. The elderly fireman Calico Jack seemed to have taken on a new lease of energy since the ship began working at Ynyscraven. The old madwoman who kept him company was usually already in the Arms when the crew arrived and in that self-mocking, amusing way seamen have, the crowd seemed to gather round the old couple as though they formed a court.

The old woman always wore her fur coat but, despite the efforts of *Caryatid*'s less gentlemanly crew members, none found out whether or not she was naked beneath it. She hardly spoke and the men soon took her presence for granted.

One night, tired with effort and too much drink the conversation began to plumb the depths of philosophy in an ill-informed, maudlin way.

Asked for his opinion Calico Jack, who was nodding gently to himself, threw up his head and called defiantly: "Love! Love is what makes the world go round!"

There were cheers. "That's bleedin' original," said someone. But Jack was not to be gainsaid.

"Love will make a man do mad things!" There was a chorus of assent from the crowd. Most were thinking of some riotous night in Santos, Sydney or Yokohama where the sense their mothers had given them succumbed to their fathers' legacy of lust.

"I mind a bosun once," began Jack and there were shushes of silence around the table. "I mind a bosun once who staked all on love and was ruined by it."

"How was that then, Calico?"

"Shut yer face an' you'll find out, won't yer," added a shipmate helpfully.

"I was on a fleet oiler once, would you believe we burned coal in our own boiled bloody daft Admiralty." Jack quaffed his pint and drained it.

"Buy 'im another, look you . . ."

Calico Jack sipped from his refilled glass. "This bosun you see, 'e fell in love with a young seaman who was, it has to be admitted, a fine-lookin' fellow. All the officers called him Billy Budd after some book or other. Well, you see, this bosun was very unpopular because he shopped an old queen of a fireman what'd made passes at this young lad and the fireman, who was harmless anyway, got into trouble. Anyway, none of the crew liked the bosun because the loss of the fireman meant no one got drinks bought for them anymore." Calico Jack swallowed a mouthful of beer.

"One day this seaman, Billy Budd, comes into the messroom with a letter. Says, 'What'll I do about this, boys?' an' shows us like. Well, the letter was one of them love letters, fairly dripping with passion, see. We all has a laugh, see, then notices the seaman's cut up about it. Well 'e would be, wouldn't he? I mean the bosun's the bosun and can make life pretty bad for a fellow.

"Anyway the letter said that if this lad liked the bosun, would he hang his towel out through his port-hole the next morning."

An appreciative ripple ran through the *Caryatid*'s crew. Even those who had heard the story before, or those who guessed at the ending, leaned forward eagerly.

"Next mornin' all the crowd are having tea on deck when

along comes the bosun. Young Billy sidles up to him and gives him his mug of tea, but don't say a word, see. Bosun takes his tea and walks kind of slowly over to the rail. Puts his foot on lower rail, casual like and leans his elbows on the cappin'. Everybody's watching, see. Bosun looks over the rail, very casual like. Sees fifty-seven towels all hanging out of portholes . . ." Laughter exploded round the room. The barman joined in the guffaws and screeches of delight at Calico Jack's story.

Eventually it died away.

"But it ruined the bosun, see. Eight years he'd been on that ship, an' a good bosun . . . drunk too much after that and went over the side not six months later. Terribly destructive thing, love . . ."

The old woman beside Calico Jack reached out a hand and gripped his arm. The two smiled at each other. "All right, mother?" said Calico Jack solicitously.

Every night Macready and Charlie walked up the hill together. "Mr Foster's doing all the watches," explained Charlie on the third night as they paced slowly up the hill.

"Good man, Mr Foster, good man."

"Yes, indeed, sir."

They walked on, the cool evening damp of the island settling round them like a cloak. Macready writhed internally. In a few minutes they would reach the wicket gate where Justine and Sonia were usually chatting. The women seemed to get on so well while their two lovers, rank-bound and stilted, came up together yet worlds apart. In the end Macready decided to chance the young man's scorn.

"I'm a married man, Mr Farthing. I'm trusting your

discretion not to mention these dinners I'm having with-er-h'm Mrs . . ." He mumbled the name which came as a poor contrast to the emphasis he had laid on 'dinners'. Charlie smiled to himself. Bloody long dinners that lasted until eight the next morning. They could see the two women now.

"Not a word, Captain Macready. She's a fine-looking woman."

Macready basked in the young man's approval, but was wise enough to hold his tongue from further chatter.

Every evening Justine had a simple meal prepared for the Captain. It was his task to clear it away while she slipped out and prepared for their night of bliss. When she was ready she called him in that low mellifluous voice of hers, so that his name echoed through the dark, still house.

The bedroom was always perfumed with fresh flowers new cut from the reeve's garden, the curtains always drawn and a low-burning oil lamp always threw the room into sensuous chiaroscuro.

Charlie and Sonia did not experience the sense of urgency and desperation that influenced Justine and the Captain. They suffered the pangs of youth. Eagerness and inexperience in such circumstances are often our first introduction to the dichotomous nature of life. The ambivalence of the situation seems to demand a decision by each or both of the parties. Made together in favour of succumbing to the natural urges the couple can experience the joys of coitus, and, unprepared, risk the consequences. Made independently either rape ensues or deep wounds are left on one or other. However, a degree of maidenly modesty veiling healthy curiosity is usually enough to curb outright male lust and encourage it to follow less consequential activities.

Not that Charlie was totally without experience with women. But the mechanics of distant couplings seemed very remote from this turmoil he was experiencing in his manly bosom with Sonia. She coyly assuaged his more urgent needs and he knew the scent and feel of her breasts, withholding a final violation of her deepest intimacy only because she promised him heaven at a later date.

In the meantime they walked and talked, watching the last embers of each succeeding day flare out their last to the west-north-west of the island.

"Tomorrow, Charlie, I promise you . . . everything."

"Why not tonight, Sonia? I love you . . . I never want to leave you . . . you've nothing to fear . . . I promise . . . Sonia, I *want* to marry you." She silenced him with a kiss and dragged him down into the damp heather.

Charlie lay on his back and Sonia lay on his chest. Her breath was warm on his face. "It's special for a girl, Charlie, the first time. I just want it all to be right." She kissed him again. He reached for her breasts.

"No, Charlie, lie down." She pushed him firmly back, then in a swift movement moved her hand to his belt. For a minute Charlie was too annoyed with the rebuff to react. When he did so it was too late.

He felt her cool hand extract his latent member. It burned to a rigidity that took her breath away. "Tomorrow," she whispered to him later as he lay gasping on the ground.

Charlie worked at the lighthouse the following day in high good humour. He stripped to the waist in the boats, bronzing himself in Sonia's honour. The new wire was hoisted and stretched. Foster was down reshackling the new securing eyes for the ancilliary wires onto the heavy main one. The sun burned and again there was no wind.

In the reeve's house Justine had finished lunch and had selected a book from the library to read on the lawn when she heard a voice in the hall.

"Who is it?" she called.

"Me. Sonia."

"Come in, then." The girl was hesitant, standing diffidently by the door.

"Thank you, it's a beautiful day, isn't it?"

Justine smiled, recollecting the girl had said something about being able to ask her anything.

"It is, my dear, but that wasn't what you came here to ask, was it?"

"No. Is the maid about?"

"She's washing up, come into the library, we won't be disturbed."

"Justine?"

Justine turned, caught in the act of opening the door. "Yes?"

"You won't laugh about what I've come to ask?"

"Of course not. Come on in."

The two women passed into the library and the door closed.

Justine took Macready's arm as usual when the Captain reached the wicket gate. They walked slowly over the lawn towards the house. Justine watched Sonia lead Charlie up the side path towards the pub.

"Not many more evenings like this, my dear," said Macready gloomily, then receiving no reply asked, "What is it?"

Justine was waving to Sonia who looked over her shoulder and waved back.

"Sonia."

"What about Sonia? What's she carrying that bunch of campion for?"

"She's going to her wedding, Septimus."

"I don't understand . . ."

"It doesn't matter, love, come inside."

Sonia led Charlie up through the old monastery gate and on to the high path. They strode purposefully past the pub and the cluster of dwellings that constituted Main Street. Charlie's questions were silenced and it was all he could do, after his day's work, to keep up with his guide. On their left a magnificent sunset was building up, gilding high cirrus clouds so that they looked like golden horse tails flickering across the sky.

After half an hour's relentless walk, when Charlie was very close to losing his equanimity, Sonia slowed her pace and dropped back alongside him.

She took his hand. "Remember what I told you about the Ravens of Dungarth, Charlie?"

"Yes, of course."

Sonia pointed. Ahead of him Charlie could see a low ridge set hard-edged against the flaming sky. There was something commandingly artificial about the ridge. It curved away towards the edge of the cliff.

"Is this the place?"

"Yes," she whispered. "This is Dun-Garth. Come on."

They walked slowly now up the glacis, over ground that the Norman Earl and his war-band must have passed over nine centuries earlier, to breast the final ridge.

Before them in an irregular circle ran the remains of the rampart. Apart from the isthmus upon which they had approached, the cliffs fell away sheer to the Atlantic. There was no escaping from the place except by the narrow neck of land. In the centre of the bare circle stood a sarsen stone. Sonia led Charlie towards it. At its base they sat down. No word passed between them as, hand in hand, they simply watched the last of the daylight bleed out of the western sky. The campion in Sonia's hand wilted.

There was hardly any wind down on the sea, but up on the cliff top there was just sufficient to set up a low moan around the tip of the sarsen stone. It mingled with the moans of the two lovers at its foot.

Just before midnight, Calico Jack decided to overstay his leave. He had tottered into the hutch that, equipped with a stone trough, served the Craven Arms for a urinal and spewed the contents of his stomach up. He felt his head clear and moved to re-enter the pub when the old woman approached him. She had followed him from the bar, and now stood in his way. There was light enough for him to see her as she slowly opened her fur coat. Calico Jack blinked at the barely discernible breasts and the dark triangle below them.

"Come on Jack, come to my house, I'm in need of a man."

* * *

As a young woman Sonia's mother had succumbed to the plausible nonsense spouted by a young, very handsome Slav count. He had been in town for the season and decided to seduce the prettiest woman under his host's roof.

His victim had yielded almost from the first, but the realisation of the true nature of what most called 'love' had both repelled and fascinated her. The physical pain she experienced that first time had combined with a revulsion for the way her 'lover' had so roughly handled her to leave her with a feeling of antipathy for men. When, nine months later, she had borne Sonia, her mind had been affected, a condition that was scarcely helped by her family's reaction.

Her banishment to Ynyscraven, however, had been the saving of something of her shattered life, for here she had been able to find herself. She had taken up painting, wild-tortured work at one with the landscape she found herself in. She had steeped herself and her daughter in the island and everything about it, earning a precarious living and receiving a small allowance from the present Earl.

But though disliking the sex, she still occasionally sought out the company of men. It was difficult to discern the precise nature of her obsession unless it was to return to her youth, to try again and discover if love, as she had been conditioned to think of it, was possible, or whether it was all a terrible, terrible deception. She had dreaded the time when Sonia would come to her and say she was leaving with a young man. And now it had happened.

He had seemed a pleasant young man, without the blandishments of her Slav count and the thought of her daughter being truly loved . . . she shook off the image but it returned to haunt her. What had she missed, what had she missed?

Calico Jack walked beside her, stumbling on the uneven path. He banged his head on the lintel as she led him inside her cottage and lit a lamp.

Jack leaned against the door and blinked. His experienced eye located the bed. The old woman turned and slid the fur coat onto the floor. Matter-of-factly Calico Jack peeled the cotton cap from his head and the shirt from his torso. The remnants of a fine physique appeared. The old woman watched as his spindle shanks stepped out of the dungaree trousers.

Victor of many a brothel sortie, drunk or sober, Calico Jack did not fail now. His was not the clumsy eagerness of Charlie, nor the yet sprightly love of Septimus, his was the tired desire of one human's company for another. Perhaps Calico Jack was the greatest lover of the three, for when he drifted into sleep the old woman cradled his bald head on her shoulder, crooned endearments into his unhearing ear and dreamed of glittering ballrooms and the bustles that women wore a million years ago.

Charlie and Sonia lay till a midnight chill drove them from Dun-Garth. Ambling contentedly south, wordless and wondering, they came to the ruins of the old Celtic monastery. Beneath an arch and remnant of roof they made love again before falling asleep.

Hours later a wraith of fog licked them from their hole and, running and jumping to restore circulation, they burst into the cottage in search of a hot drink.

Sonia's mother was not there.

"Gathering mushrooms, I expect," explained Sonia, brushing her hair from her mouth and smiling happily at Charlie who never took his eyes from her. She handed him a steaming mug and came round the table to sit on his lap.

Captain Macready rose from the bed, aware that the fog was present before he reached the window. He threw up the window and sniffed the air.

"Not too bad," he muttered. "It'll clear by nine or so, must be able to see about – Good God!"

"What is it, Septimus?" called Justine languidly from the bed.

"I'm not sure."

Macready could see the lawn below, though the hedge and wicket gate were lost to view in the white mist. Out of the fog, bent over, were two apparitions. Calico Jack and Sonia's mother picked mushrooms like two superannuated water babies, naked and grotesque, yet oddly appropriate on this strange island.

"They're rock sprites," said Justine beside him, the sheet drawn about her against the damp chill. There was bubbling laughter in her voice. "If you watch them they'll fade into the background."

The male goblin straightened, looking up and saw the two lovers in the window.

"Mornin', Captain," said Calico Jack, cool as the fog, as if he was meeting Macready on the quay at Porth Ardur. The woman looked up, then she moved, almost swiftly, to stand beside the man. The two couples stood looking at each other for a few seconds then Calico Jack winked and resumed picking mushrooms, moving away into the fog. The old woman lingered a moment then smiled. She too moved off into the fog. But she did not retreat.

Charlie was about to leave the cottage when Sonia's mother returned with Calico Jack. He retired into the house astonished at the two basket-bearing figures that shambled unconcernedly into the parlour. Sonia flickered him a warning glance and equally insouciantly made more tea.

"Good morning, Mr Farthing," said Calico, stepping into his dungarees and accepting the mug from Sonia. Still naked the old woman cracked four herring gull eggs into a bowl and began to whip an omelette into which she dropped the chopped mushrooms.

Charlie and Calico Jack started down to the boat with a breakfast inside them. "I remember a time in BA when a mate and myself knocked off a mother and her daughter. *They* made us breakfast as well . . ."

Calico broke the spell for Charlie. He suddenly remembered he had overstayed his leave.

They met Captain Macready at the wicket gate. Justine was kissing him goodbye. She was wrapped in a peignoir.

"Morning, Captain," repeated Calico, winking again, conspiratorily.

"Morning, Evans, and you too, Mr Farthing . . . goodbye, my dear—" Red-faced, Macready tore himself out of Justine's arms. Behind him he could hear her low chuckle. The three men strode down the path in silence. The fog thickened as they descended to the beach. In the white silence they could hear men's voices, then the chug of the motor boat's engine. Macready stopped. Out of deference the other two stopped as well.

"I'm displeased by your behaviour, both of you, particularly yours, Mr Farthing, you should know better as an officer. Evans I'd expect it of, but not you."

Charlie hung his head in genuine embarrassment. He felt terrible, respecting old Macready as he did. He burned with shame at the thought of what he and Sonia had been doing, as if this dressing down made it all cheap and like some one-night stand with a whore in, where was it? Buenos Aires?

"As, however, we are all gentlemen of the world this matter will go no further unless Mr Foster brings you up, Mr Farthing, or the Chief brings you up, Evans, in which case I shall have no alternative but to do something. D'you understand?" They both mumbled their thanks. The boat engine was loud now. Then it shut off and there was the scrunch of bows on shingle and the shout of the bowman leaping ashore.

"Now, gentlemen, you go on ahead and pretend to hide under the canopy. I'll follow. One word of any of this and—" Macready left the threat hanging in mid air. He was himself aware that he was on very thin ice. Relieved, Calico Jack and Charlie turned gratefully away, loping downwards with the air of schoolboys out of bounds.

Breaking Strain

Charlie did not get away with his night adrift. Calico Jack did. He stood so many watches for firemen living in Porth Ardur that no one really questioned his absence. For Charlie it was different.

Caryatid did not move from the anchorage until about noon when the fog finally lifted. During the forenoon Bernard Foster came quietly into Charlie's room and sat himself down. Charlie was dozing on his bunk. Foster lit his pipe and put both his feet up on the settee.

"Charlie, I'm rather disappointed in you." He puffed and then lit another match.

Charlie sat up, flushing.

"Sorry?"

Foster looked up at him through a dense cloud of tobacco smoke. "I know you're over the moon with this girl, but Charlie, I don't expect the Second Mate to come back with a screw-loose fireman after a night on the loose."

Charlie swung his legs over the bunk.

"Look, Bernard, I'm sorry I overstayed my leave. It won't happen again and I realise I'm totally in the wrong, but before we go any further I've not been having a bag-off with a whore. Sonia and I intend to get married.

170

Didn't you go a bit off the rails when you were courting Anthea?"

Foster was silent, laying a smokescreen between himself and the aggressively defensive Charlie. Had he? To tell the truth he couldn't remember. He got up, fanning the smoke away. "Alright, Charlie, drop it, but don't do it again." He paused, waiting for some reaction. "And just to rub it in *I'm* going ashore tonight. It's your watch aboard."

Charlie flopped back on his bunk. Christ! He'd really asked for that!

That evening Foster came into Charlie's cabin and threw him the store-room keys. "The old man's gone in, I'll take the dinghy." Foster left. Charlie felt like hell about the whole world.

Half an hour later he was aware of a familiar voice calling his name. He raced on deck and peered over the side. There, sitting in the rowing dinghy that they had been using at the lighthouse, sat Sonia. She spun the boat and brought it alongside. Making fast the line Charlie threw down, she was soon standing beside him.

"That Mr Foster met me on the path, said I'd find a boat and could get out to see you if I liked. Here I am. Oh! He said something about he'd done some remembering but that didn't make it right . . . and you'd still got to do your watch. No, he said 'bloody watch', that's right." She smiled. He took her hand and led her along the alley-way.

Then he locked his cabin door.

The following evening *Sea Dragon* anchored in company with the *Caryatid*. The fog had not returned and as the shadow of the island fell over the anchorage it became the

171

warmest, stillest night of all. Aboard *Caryatid* the grumbling watch regarded the *Sea Dragon* with ill-concealed distaste.

"Bleedin' gin palace."

"Jus' a floating brothel."

"It's the rich that gets the pleasure . . ."

Sir Hector Blackadder had decided to have a formal dinner. He liked to alternate a formal dinner with a buffet but the anchorage was beautiful and Stanier had suggested the occasion. That Stanier wished to show off to *Caryatid*'s Master, never entered Sir Hector's mind; that Captain Macready was enjoying the flesh of Tegwyn's mother never entered Stanier's.

Dressed in his mess kit, feeling every inch the sailor, Stanier knocked discreetly on Miss Caroline's stateroom door.

"Who is it?"

"Jimmy," he winced at the name.

"Come in."

She was dressed in black, plainly, almost severely. Her bobbed hair and voguish looks combined with her slender figure to give her a boyish appearance. She was a stick compared to Tegwyn, and yet . . . Stanier felt slightly uncomfortable as she watched him, resenting the fact that he was not quite in control of the situation and yet enjoying it.

"Well?"

"I wondered if you had an answer for me?" he asked.

She came nearer and he was suddenly aware of the way she moved. Willowy she might be, but there was a compelling power, a confident sensuality about her that he found overpowering.

She stopped just in front of him. Stanier was aware that her hard breasts barely lifted the material of her dress but she leaned backwards on her thighs, gently pushing her pelvis forward against his. She smiled into his face.

"Your answer is ready, but I'm not ready to give it. Go and have your Celtic tart for a bit longer . . ." She trailed off, poking his pelvis twice more and then turning and wiggling her backside at him in an unbelievably provocative dismissal.

Stanier sat between Tegwyn and Miss Loring. Opposite was Caroline, who seemed to be watching him with a sardonic smile on her face the entire evening. She certainly discomfited poor Tegwyn, opposite whom sat Pomeroy. Samantha and Sir Hector sat facing each other while Argyle regarded Miss Loring on Caroline's right.

The saloon was warm and the cool gaze of Caroline sent Stanier's blood pressure sky high. He tried making conversation but somehow the heat seemed to enervate the whole company. Nevertheless the food was excellent and it kept the group occupied. Sweat stood out on Stanier's brow and his collar felt suffocatingly tight. He could stand it no longer and reached into the mess jacket pocket for a handkerchief.

He pulled out Justine's panties.

A cascade of brief lace dangled from his wrist as he passed it over his brow. It was only as its scent of lavender wafted past his nose that Stanier noticed.

Caroline's grin spread and Pomeroy gave an excited sort of whimper. At these two spontaneous changes of expression directed to her left, Tegwyn turned to look at Stanier. Her mouth dropped open at the same instant that Stanier realised what he was doing. He hurriedly dropped his hand and attempted to crush the garment back into his pocket.

Tegwyn was too quick for him. She snatched the panties from his hand and, with cast down eyes spread them on her lap. She recognised them instantly. Her mother bought them from a Bond Street representative who called once a year and sold her a few very exclusive items for certain ladies of Porth Ardur.

If Caroline was expecting a gaffe from Tegwyn she was disappointed. A girl who can lose her footing in a quickstep and recover it without tripping her partner can handle the discovery of her mother's panties in the pocket of her lover.

Disappointed, Caroline rose to lead the ladies out onto the quarterdeck.

In all justice to James St John Stanier it has to be admitted that on this occasion he was a victim of circumstances over which he had had very little control. However he was ready to protest his innocence and anxious to do so before Tegwyn caused a row. He therefore initiated the bedtime ritual with almost indecent haste. Tegwyn was not slow to take the hint, eager to accuse Stanier of unspeakable things. Caroline watched their flushed faces disappear. She crossed to Pomeroy who was, as far as she knew, the only other person who had really seen what happened.

"Did that amuse you, Pom?"

"A little, although I'm not sure what annoyed Tegwyn so."

Caroline chuckled. "It's an odd name. Coarse really."

"But she's very beautiful," said Pomeroy musingly.

"Pom! I'm surprised at you!"

"Oh Caro, for heaven's sake. You've been listening to that silly cat Samantha again. She thinks that anyone who doesn't fall into bed with her must be queer."

"Have you ever been to bed with a woman, Pom?" Pomeroy was silent. "Haven't you?"

"Once." He said flatly. There was a bitter defeat in his voice.

"And didn't you like it?"

Again there was a long silence. Caroline waited expectantly.

"She didn't like me. And I had to pay her for it."

"Poor Pom." There was an unexpected sympathy in Caroline's voice.

Pomeroy sniffed and straightened up. "That's enough of confessions for one night. I'm for bed." He sounded so artificial. Caroline thought, he's really quite brave.

Pomeroy slipped into his stateroom and quickly undressed. He slipped into silk pyjamas and a silk robe. Then, lighting a cigarette he slithered across to the bulkhead and lifted down the mirror. The noise of rowdy voices from the next stateroom was dying down. He put his eye to the hole.

His heart beat faster.

He had a view of the low bunk and of Tegwyn's upper body. Her dress was off and Stanier was slavering all over her belly. He ignored the yacht's master and watched the girl's face. Her head was thrown back so that the line of her throat formed a curve as eloquent as a line by Botticelli, thought Pomeroy. Her eyes were closed but he could see the sheen of tears drying across her cheeks. Falling from her cast-back head onto the bedclothes, the blue lights dancing in its sheen, Tegwyn's hair bobbed with the quick jerking of her body.

Pomeroy did not sense the other person in his cabin until he felt breath on his neck. He whirled to face Caroline.

"Pom!" she said in mock indignation. "You voyeur!"

Pomeroy's heart was thumping crazily. He was aware that Caroline had changed into pyjamas like himself but was nonplussed at her appearance in his cabin.

Gently she pushed him out of the way and put her eye to the hole.

He watched as her lips curved in a smile. "Mmmmm, he's not bad. *Quelle technique . . .*"

Pomeroy suddenly recovered himself.

"Not him, Caro, not that fool, her!"

Caroline took her eye away and turned to look at Pomeroy. "You mean you've been watching her?"

Pomeroy nodded unhappily. "She's the most beautiful thing I've ever set eyes on," he said wretchedly. "I have collected the most exquisite *objets d'art* and never seen anything to match her."

Caroline turned and took one more look through the hole. She began to feel indignation, jealousy even.

"Dammit, Pom, I came down here tonight to see if I could convert you."

Pomeroy stood with his mouth hanging open. Caroline suddenly felt very foolish. "And, by the way, don't call Captain Stanier a fool, he's going to be my husband."

Pomeroy's jaw dropped further.

Caroline bit her lip. "If you mention one word of that

before I do, I'll let everyone know what you're up to." She turned and left the stateroom.

Behind her, hands shaking, Pomeroy replaced the mirror.

"What d'you think of him then, Argyle?" Sir Hector lit a final cigar and poured a last large brandy.

"He seems suitable enough, Hector." The Gael scratched his nose. "He's determined and I'd agree fairly ruthless but he's had no business training. Although he's intelligent enough to pick a lot up I still canna understand why you didna choose someone fra' yer ain circle."

Sir Hector shrugged. "You must allow me a little sentiment. I've no son and I doubt that I've long to go. Ah, stop that snorting, I just met him and took an instant liking to the lad. I'd be surprised if I liked my own son as much, particularly bearing in mind his mother."

"Och mon, yer ower hard on Ellen, she's a sick woman."

"Sick woman or not, Ian, I'd sooner have Stanier as a son than any lad of hers."

Argyle chuckled.

"What's amusing you?"

"I was jus' thinkin' that mebbe ye've a better son in Miss Caroline . . ."

"Happen I have, my bonny friend, in which case they'll get on fine together."

Sir Hector Blackadder rose and went to bed, happy that the matter was settled. Argyle lingered a little longer. Then he too rose and went out onto the starlit quarterdeck.

"Samantha, Hector's away down for a wee bit o' shut-eye."

The lissome blonde straightened up from the rail. "Och aye, Rob Roy," she said rudely, "I'll away and rub his sick leg."

From the depths of a steamer chair Miss Loring giggled. Ian Argyle looked at her. Women, he thought. Pity you couldn't set 'em off against the income tax.

An Invader's Wind

Caryatid lay at her anchor off the northern end of Ynyscraven. From her stern several fishing lines reached down into the limpid water. They were desultorily jerked to animate the feathers far below in the hope of attracting mackerel. It was the seamen's holiday, for the previous day the hoist had been completed and tested. Today the second engineer and a couple of greasers sweated up in the engine house overhauling 'all that shit and split pins', as Mackerel Jack put it.

Further forward Captain Macready sat at his desk. With a flourish he signed the report that informed the Commissioner's Secretary that the hoist wire and engine at Ynyscraven had been completely renewed and overhauled as necessary. It gave him some satisfaction, a job well done never failed to do that for the Captain, but he reflected sadly that the idyll that he and Justine had enjoyed was nearly over.

He rubbed a finger round the inside of his collar. It was hot as the hobs of hell. He ruefully thought of Justine lazing the day away in the garden. The thought was disquieting, he got up and peered out of the port hole. The gentlest of zephyrs was rippling catspaws across the blue surface of the sea.

179

Easterly, thought the Captain inconsequentially.

Sonia's mother sensed the coming of the wind in the pre-ternatural stillness of the dawn. There were no mushrooms on the lawn of the reeve's house. She shuddered with more than the coolness of the air upon her bare flesh.

Sonia was up when her mother returned to the cottage. The old woman was wild-eyed and haggard.

"What's the matter, Mother?"

"The wind, Sonia. The invader's wind!"

The girl walked outside the cottage and sniffed the air. It was still as as a dark pool. She shrugged and went back inside the cottage. Later Sonia walked down to the reeve's house. Justine lay in a deck chair reading. "Hullo, love," she said as Sonia plumped down on the grass beside her.

"Hullo. Justine, I think they've nearly finished at the lighthouse. What'll happen to you when they sail?"

Justine smiled sadly. "I don't know, love. I'll go back to Porth Ardur of course, carry on as normal . . ." her voice trailed off.

"Will you still see the Captain?" The girl's voice was candid, open. It was a sharp contrast to the dissembling tone of Porth Ardur gossips, Justine reflected.

"Yes, we'll still dance together, I suppose."

"Would you like to stay here on Ynyscraven, I mean forever?"

Justine laughed again, a high clear laugh. "As a fairy tale, yes, but it is impossible. I have to live on something, I've a business to run."

"Your daughter could do that."

"That's true," said Justine, a faint spark of excitement

lighting in her brain. It was instantly extinguished by more practical considerations.

Aboard *Sea Dragon* the holiday party lounged, swam and drank Pimm's No. 1 cup. Samantha, long and cool, lay draped like a pair of silk stockings over a steamer chair. More compact and less comfortable, Dorothy Loring sat sweating slightly, sipping an excessive amount of Pimm's under the mistaken impression that it would quench her thirst.

Stanier had been summoned to Sir Hector's stateroom where the two men were joined by Argyle. Certain business propositions were put to Stanier. They followed the outline already sketched out for him by Caroline. Nevertheless Stanier was out of his mind with excitement at the golden road the two men laid before him. By noon the several large whiskies that Sir Hector had poured into him and the back slapping and shower of 'My boy's' that he had received from the millionaire had served to render him somewhat injudicious.

When the yacht's bosun reported the freshening easterly wind he dismissed the matter. It was only a force three and would die with the sun.

By afternoon it was cool enough to drive the languid Samantha from her steamer chair.

Tegwyn had woken alone and spent sometime staring at the deck-head above her. She thought over the events of the evening before and was, for the first time, ashamed of submitting to Stanier. There had been something different about him last night. He had lacked a little of that exclusive attention to herself that had so attracted her vanity at first. And the argument left a dirty taste in her mouth.

Come to think of it, he had been perceptibly cooling for some time. Tegwyn sat up, suddenly furious. She remembered several little incidents; glances; secret, covert gestures. Her rival's face blazed suddenly before her.

Caroline!

Tegwyn leapt from her bunk like a tigress. She tore the nightdress from her shoulders spitting little oaths from twisted lips. Struggling into some clothes she caught sight of herself in the mirror of the dressing table. A wild-eyed, half-hysterical Celt. God, how those stuffed shirts would laugh at her if she went out like that to row with James.

She bit her lip. Then she remembered her mother's warning. In another minute she had collapsed on the stool and her head fell forward among the powder, the hair brushes and the scent bottles.

She did not hear the gentle knocking on the door.

"May I come in?" Pomeroy entered the stateroom. He was shaking and did not trust his legs. He sat quickly on the bunk. At the sudden movement Tegwyn sat up and spun round. "Mr Pomeroy!"

"Please do not distress yourself, Miss Tegwyn."

"But I—"

Pomeroy could not stop himself now. He had screwed himself up to such a pitch that having come so far he felt he could not retreat.

"Miss Tegwyn, please listen to me. I want to be your friend. I know Stanier is a rogue, I've seen so many of his arrogant type at school and in business. They stop at nothing to satisfy their ambitions. They hurt anyone who is in their way." Tegwyn had stopped crying. She was repairing the damage to her pride. She felt Pomeroy's voice caress her in an oddly soothing way. As if he understood how abused she had suddenly, revoltingly, felt.

"I've admired you from the very beginning of this cruise. I know nothing about women except that you are the most exquisite I've ever seen." Pomeroy looked down at his carefully manicured hands. "I love to possess beautiful things, to display them, just to touch and handle them." There was crooning adoration in his voice now. It was utterly seductive, Tegwyn thought, as she looked at Pomeroy's tear-filled eyes. He was awaiting her derision as he must have received the scorn of many, both men and women.

"I'm a very rich man," he whispered as though it made a difference.

Tegwyn reached out and touched his forehead.

Late in the afternoon, scending before a following sea, the *Plover* ran in to the jetty at Ynyscraven. The reeve and his wife disembarked. The *Plover* also brought a cargo of much needed beer for the Craven Arms. A real hooley was planned for *Caryatid*'s last evening.

When the engineers completed work, *Caryatid* weighed her anchor and steamed down to the southern anchorage. On her bridge Foster was remonstrating with Macready.

"I'll be frank, sir, this wind'll not die with the sun. I'm not happy about lying the night here."

Macready said nothing. He knew that Foster was right but every nerve in his body screamed out to see Justine once more, to say his real goodbye, to mark the end of his idyll.

"You may be right, Bernard, but I don't think it'll be too bad a blow at this time of the year. Anyway, the lads are expecting a final swan song at the Arms tonight and I don't want to disappoint them."

"Shore leave to finish sharp at midnight then, sir?"

"Yes."

Foster went off mumbling about standing offshore with a drunken crew. Macready felt a pang of foreboding then dismissed it. He *had* to see Justine.

Foster went down to Charlie's cabin after the ship had anchored. The Second Mate had just come off the bridge and was changing.

"Look, Charlie, I'm sorry but I want to keep you on board tonight – no, don't argue. I don't know what's got into the Old Man but he insists on giving shore leave and I'm bloody sure we'll have a gale here by midnight."

Charlie swallowed his disappointment. Bernard had been very good to him. He owed the Mate something, even if it was only moral support.

"You'll be coming back to Ynyscraven, Charlie, although the Old Man's acting as though he isn't."

"Okay, Bernard."

Up at the reeve's house Justine was welcoming the owners back. She was as charming as she could be under the circumstances but her mood revived when the reeve's wife suggested she and the Captain, as they were such good friends joined her and her husband for a sort of valedictory dinner. Of course Justine could stay longer, but if she didn't want to

. . . well, she was very welcome. Justine smiled her thanks. Later she went out to meet Macready a little further down the path than was usual, and out of sight of the house.

Against his better judgement Foster passed word for a watch ashore. A great gaggle of *Caryatid*'s crew struggled up the path, eyes eager for the inside of the Arms. Leading them strode Calico Jack, buoyant with the promise of a final tryst. Justine watched them pass then slipped out through the wicket gate. She saw nothing of Sonia until she had met the Captain and the pair were returning to the house, a discreet distance separating them, their voices in low and earnest conversation.

"Charlie not coming, Captain?" Sonia asked, abruptly breaking into the couple's deliberations.

"Eh?" Macready looked up. "Oh, it's you, my dear. I-er-don't know. He was not in the boat."

"Oh," said the girl and walking past them began to run down the hill.

The *Plover* was still lying at the landing jetty. She waved at the skipper.

"Are you sailing?"

"Ah'm not stayin' here," he nodded at the eastern sky.

"Can you pop me aboard *Caryatid?*"

"I'd pop you in the club," said a voice at her elbow and the skipper's grinning son helped her aboard.

"Sonia!" exclaimed Charlie when he saw her in the cabin doorway. They embraced, only to be interrupted by a knocking on the open door. They turned to find Bernard Foster. He looked irritable.

185

"I'm sorry, Mr Foster, I came on impulse, it's not Charlie's fault." She smiled at him.

"Alright, but you must leave the instant I say. When I send the boat in for the crew. Alright?"

"Alright, thanks."

Foster pulled the door closed after him. Yes, he did remember what it was like. And they faded so soon, these flowers.

Bernard Foster went up to the bridge. A quartermaster was polishing brass. He dogged his cigarette out. "That's alright, Jones, don't worry."

Foster peered out of the wheelhouse windows. The sea was getting up, following the increase of the wind. "About force four to five," volunteered the quartermaster.

"Mmmmm," agreed the mate.

Not too bad, yet.

Aboard *Sea Dragon* the dining table pitched gently as the yacht became wind-rode. Stanier seemed not to notice it, but emptied his glass. At any rate no one remarked upon it as Sir Hector outlined his future plans to Pomeroy, Argyle and the newly accepted Stanier.

The women shuddered at the chill and retired into the smoke room where they chatted desultorily.

At the reeve's house the dinner was a contrast in couples. Justine and Macready made the best of it but they were clearly frustrated from expressing their innermost thoughts to each other.

Across the table the reeve and his wife were excitedly

talking of the news their son had brought them. He had just made a great deal of money on a stock exchange deal and was in a position to buy them a house ashore. Because of his age and rheumatism the reeve was very tempted to take up his son's offer. His wife seemed delighted at the prospect of seeing her grandchildren regularly.

"Of course there'll be the question of a successor for you here, though," said the Captain.

"Oh yes. That'll be the prerogative of his Lordship, of course. He may ask me to nominate someone suitable."

"Tell me," said Justine, "tell me, do you have any cottages free at the moment? I was thinking of renting one on a more or less permanent basis."

Beside her Macready held his breath. The evening was suddenly rosy again. Justine, Justine, is there no end to your sweetness?

Sonia sat alone in Charlie's cabin brushing her hair with her hand. Charlie was on the bridge, summoned by Bernard.

"It's backed nor'east and still freshening; once the wind-sea alters direction this anchorage'll be untenable. Get yourself ashore and round up the crew. And be quick about it!"

"Aye, aye, sir." Charlie was off. He was suddenly alerted to potential danger.

Charlie burst into the reeve's house unannounced, Sonia at his heels. Macready knew instantly what was happening. A wind came in with the second mate that had the whip of malice in it.

Charlie, breathless, opened his mouth to speak.

"It's alright, Mr Farthing, I'm coming." Sudden guilt seized the Captain as he turned to say his farewells. All he could impart to Justine was a look. Less even than he had thought he would manage that evening.

They were dancing and singing in the Craven Arms. The place was thick with the smoke of forty-odd cigarettes, loud with raucous shouts and noisy oaths. The whine of the accordion was drowned beneath the stamp of feet on the flagstones.

With a whoop Calico Jack leapt into the centre of the floor and whirled his ancient partner after him. The dance had no name beyond being the vertical expression of a horizontal desire. It reached a crescendo of noise and sweaty effort and Calico Jack stopped abruptly, jerking his partner to a halt.

The company fell silent as Sonia's mother slipped the old fur coat from her thin shoulders and stood naked before the ship's company.

The door crashed open and a wind like a knife whipped into the bar. Charlie stood in the doorway.

"Caryatids out, down to the boat, move, come on, get some ginger into it!" He strode into the bar, thrusting men to their feet, trying desperately to infect these half-drunk bodies with his own sense of urgency.

"Come on! COME ON!"

Calico Jack pulled the fur coat back over the old woman's shoulders and smiled at her. She did not smile back.

The *Caryatid*'s crew stumbled out into the screaming darkness and Charlie drove them sheep-like down the hill.

*   *   *

Charlie never remembered how they got aboard the *Caryatid*. He remembered Sonia grabbing his neck and kissing him even as he thrust a greaser forwards. He remembered pulling a steward away from the edge of the precipitous drop that flanked one section of the path.

He remembered too the lights of *Caryatid* looming over them. Foster had got her underway to make a lee for the boat. Captain Macready was the last man to ascend the ladder. At the top he turned and shouted to Charlie.

"Mr Farthing, take the boat across to that yacht. Tell Stanier to get the hell out of this anchorage!"

"Aye, aye, sir."

The boat turned away, swooping and dipping across the seas that now roared up out of the gathering gloom. Their sides were streaked with spume and their crests reared into breaking foam only to be whipped to shreds by the cutting wind. Charlie was soaked with the first sheet of spray that the boat flung up.

His leap across to the *Sea Dragon* was afterwards described with great admiration in the *Caryatid*'s mess deck by the boat's crew. Charlie burst into the smoke room where the women languidly lay about drinking. At his sudden, soaking appearance they squealed and started.

"Where's Stanier?" The reaction was blank. He strode wetly across the carpet and flung open the dining saloon door.

"What the hell d'you think—?" Stanier and Sir Hector rose protesting.

"Stanier! Get under way at once, man. There's a rising gale and you're on a lee shore!"

"How dare you, burst in here and—" Charlie waved Sir Hector to silence. He realised Stanier was half drunk.

Taking three strides over to the semi-recumbent form, Charlie grabbed his lapels and shook him. "Stanier, get under WAY!"

Stanier shook his head. "I've sheen you before. You're a damned insholent puppy from that bloody *Carya* . . ." he stumbled over the name. "Gerroff," he tried plucking Charlie's fingers from his jacket. "I . . . I'm a Master Mariner, you damned scum."

"You'll be bugger-all if you don't get off your arse!" Charlie dragged Stanier to his feet. The Harbour Master stood swaying. Charlie fetched him a swipe across his face.

"LEE SHORE!" he shouted at Stanier, seeing the beginnings of alarm awaken in the puffily handsome features swaying before him.

Abruptly, frustratedly, Charlie walked out of the saloon.

"Playing sailor boys?" remarked Samantha from the depths of a leather armchair, then the intruder was gone into the windy gloom outside.

Pomeroy caught him as he stood poised to leap into the launch.

"Have we to move?"

Charlie turned. At last! Someone with a shred of sense aboard this useless toy boat. "Yes! Get your anchor up and steam into it. Get Stanier to steam into the wind, d'you understand?" Pomeroy nodded. Spray soaked the pair of them as it lifted over *Sea Dragon*'s handsomely flared bow.

Charlie returned to *Caryatid*.

Darkness had almost descended onto the scene. The faintest glimmer of day threw up the loom of the island astern of them, then that too vanished. But the island remained outlined at its base where the waves dashed themselves to pieces in a roar that increased minute by minute.

High above the anchorage on the turn in the path which commanded a view of the bay, a little knot of figures gathered. The reeve accompanied Justine, and Sonia joined them, peering intently down into the darkness.

They watched as *Caryatid*'s lights swung beam on to the wind and she raced sideways towards the rocks. "Picking up the launch . . ." explained the reeve, sucking in his breath. "My God but I hope Macready knows what he's doing . . ."

They watched as steam clouds caught the deck lights and the glimmer of figures on the boat-deck showed where furious activity was in progress.

The launch rose to the dripping boat deck as Macready fought *Caryatid* head to wind. Seamen rushed forward with lines to secure the boat. Foster stood, bawling orders, a black shiny figure in his oilskins. The launch swung inboard and down onto the chocks. Charlie scrambled out.

Up on the bridge he reported to the Captain. "Stanier's pissed, sir. I tried to tell them they're in danger. One of the men seemed to understand." Macready looked across to where *Sea Dragon* still rode pitching to her anchor. At full speed ahead *Caryatid* was only passing her slowly. He rang 'Half Ahead' to keep the yacht under observation. A sea crashed over the *Caryatid*'s bow, deluging the foredeck with white water that glowed wickedly in the darkness. The foremast stood out of the swirl like a tree in a flooded field.

191

Caryatid shook herself, rose, and poured the unwanted water out over the side at the after end of the deck. Then she thumped into the next sea. It too thundered aft, with all the screaming demons of hell riding upon its crest. The wheelhouse windows shuddered at the impact of the gust. They were armoured glass.

Beyond the next two or three approaching seas visibility was negligible. Spume and spray smoked across the torn surface of the blackness, here and there a riven crest shredded away before it was half formed.

"Force Ten," muttered Foster more to himself than anyone else. In the chartroom the barometer needle twitched as the next gust hit them.

"Only whores, thieves and sailors'd work on a night like this," remarked the bosun to the carpenter as they each sucked a mug of tea in their messroom.

Aboard *Sea Dragon* Stanier staggered up to the little bridge. It was only when he got there he realised the danger the yacht was in. Because it was still a flood tide some local anomaly of the stream running north eastwards through the Hound's Teeth caused a deadening of the sea where *Sea Dragon* lay. But when the ebb got away . . . Stanier shuddered, suddenly remembering Farthing's words: *'You'll have bugger-all if you don't get off your arse!'* Christ! Panic suddenly gripped his guts, shook his stomach and he spewed abruptly, violently, over the deck. His head cleared; he must make an effort. HE MUST. All his future lay before him, a mistake now . . . if James St John Stanier never knew humility this was his first taste of it.

He reached for the engine room telephone.

At that instant the anchor cable caught on an outlying projection of the Hound's Teeth. It sawed across the granite and snapped.

Sea Dragon fell into the trough of the sea. She began to drive inexorably to leeward and the waiting cliffs of Ynyscraven.

Aft in the smoke room the men joined the ladies. There was some idle chatter and mention of 'interesting visitors' and 'lee shores'. Caroline went forward to the wheelhouse. Half way along the alley-way she was thrown headlong as *Sea Dragon* slewed round.

Samantha's chair fell over and she was deposited, a leg-waving heap of frills, upon the thick carpet. Miss Loring began to scream. Argyle hit her. Sir Hector banged his head and out in the screaming darkness Pomeroy tried to get forward to see what was the matter. A wave washed him aft but, with a superhuman effort he made the wheelhouse door and opened it.

Pomeroy skidded in the vomit. Stanier was heaving the wheel over. From below came the rumble of a diesel starting. The aspirated air hissed from the funnel and the engine fired. Stanier breathed a sigh of relief. Soon, soon *Sea Dragon had* to turn . . .

The *Caryatid*'s officers watched as the *Sea Dragon* drove down wind. She rolled abominably so that they could see her boot topping in contrast with her white sides.

After a minute or so Macready said flatly, "She's had it."

No one disagreed with him.

Down in the boiler room of the *Caryatid*, Calico Jack plied his shovel and raked ash. With the nimbleness of years he countered the pitch of the ship. Turn, shovel, turn, fling. He stopped, wiped his gleaming brow and clanged the boiler door shut with his foot. A sudden heaviness seized him. A pain in his chest opened before him like a huge red flower. He plunged into it and its bloody petals folded round him.

High above the two struggling ships, barely heard in the wind's howl, a not so very old woman screamed. The sound was caught by the cliffs in the diminuendo of swift descent.

Sea Dragon began to gather headway.

Before he could get her to answer her helm the motor yacht drove southwards, still rolling across the wind but gathering the momentum needed for her rudder to bite.

She began to turn . . .

"She's turning," yelled Stanier at the white faced Pomeroy.

Sea Dragon began to bring her head to the east.

Then the Hound's Teeth found her bottom.

Aftermath

The rocket blazed up into the night and hung like a ruby star before falling seawards slowly.

There was nothing those aboard *Caryatid* could do until daylight.

"They'll just have to hang on." Macready spoke for them all. *Caryatid* was having her own problems keeping head to sea. The sudden collapse of one of the firemen had caused a temporary loss of steam and Macready had endured a quarter of an hour of extreme anxiety before he had conned the old ship back onto a safe heading.

"It's Evans, sir," reported Foster. "He's had what looks like a heart attack."

"Which Evans, Bernard?" asked Macready patiently, never taking his eyes from the next sea rising massively ahead of his little – oh so little – ship.

"Calico Jack, Captain, we've got him out of the boiler room but he's quite dead."

"I'm sorry about that." Macready watched the sea. "Starboard, midships, steadeeeeee." The sea exploded over the bow and the whole ship trembled.

"What's the light-bearing now, Mr Farthing?"

"Two five eight, sir."

"Magnetic or True?"

"True, sir."

"Good. I wonder if there's any chance of some tea?"

Sea Dragon drove onto the rocks as each succeeding sea raised her up and smashed her down again. She lay on her beam ends, her steel hull screaming a protest as the Hound's Teeth ripped at her guts and the sea, like some monstrous tongue, ground her down on the granite molars.

Aboard her all was terror and confusion. There were no lights and loose gear flew about indiscriminately. Water sloshed up and down alley-ways and passengers and crew scrabbled mercilessly at one another. Stanier did what he could. The other anchor was let go to try and prevent the yacht from driving further up the reef, he sent off the rockets and an SOS on the radio, but a sea-drenched aerial about a fathom from the surface of the waves was of little use.

It was Pomeroy who organised them. Despised Pomeroy who at last found some shred of use from an education that had otherwise blighted his life. Calm, unhurried, he organised the crew and passengers into groups to check on lifesaving appliances and the chances of organising some food and keeping warm. Anything to pass the night. When Stanier thought of the same thing he found Pomeroy had beaten him to it.

Pomeroy earned the grudging admiration of even Samantha when the whole group, sheltered in the main alley-way, each adorned in a bulky lifejacket, were sipping rum toddy.

Up in the wheelhouse Sir Hector stood watching his yacht disintegrate.

"Will she hold till daylight?" He turned to look at Stanier.

The yacht's young master was ashen-faced. He had no experience to base his answer on. Would she? *Sea Dragon* gave a sickening lurch as a huge sea broke over her and the Hound's Teeth.

"My God—" Sir Hector slipped in the slick of vomit that now smeared the greater part of the *Sea Dragon*'s wheelhouse deck. He fell with a crash, his head striking the wheel mounting. Blood spurted and he rolled concussed into the lee corner as Stanier stood stock still, bracing himself for the onslaught of the next wave which, by its delay, he knew instinctively was enormous.

The sea which hit *Sea Dragon* rolled roaring up the reef, hummocking itself into a furious entity baulked by the granite barrier. Its outriders ran left and right into a hundred gullies and fissures, boiling with energy. As the impeding rocks sapped the momentum below, its crest rushed on, driven forward by its impetus yet undermined of its own support. As it toppled over and collapsed in a moil of spent energy it burst into the yacht. Her boats were swept away by the funnel as it imploded, vanishing into the night. The cowl vents disappeared and ton after ton of salt water roared down into the alley-way. Bodies were washed screaming and kicking up and down like flotsam.

Eventually the water subsided and *Sea Dragon* seemed to have settled, to be moving less. The waves seemed less powerful.

Stanier moved across to Sir Hector.

Sir Hector Blackadder was dead. Stanier turned away, his stomach heaving again. He stumbled aft, making for the alley-way where he knew the others were.

Pomeroy had got them on their feet and was tallying them.

Horrocks was missing, so too were Tegwyn and Samantha. Caroline pointed aft. The door to the saloon and smoke room was smashed. Caroline struggled towards it, Pomeroy and Stanier followed.

Water impeded their movements, difficult enough with the vessel lying on her beam ends. They found Tegwyn in the corner of the smoke room, an armchair on top of her. The two men pulled it off. She lay like a dropped marionette. Even in distress Pomeroy drew in his breath at her beauty. Stanier felt sudden revulsion at the incongruity of her sprawled body. The two men exchanged glances then Pomeroy, his face white with strain, lowered his head onto her bosom.

"She's alive, and only unconscious." Grunting with effort they dragged Tegwyn into a sitting position. Pomeroy found a bottle of cognac and forced it between her lips.

Stanier regarded the open door to the quarterdeck. No glass remained in it. Was that where Samantha and Horrocks had gone? They found Horrocks by accident. A lurch of the *Sea Dragon* swung open a water closet door. Inside lay Horrocks, driven into a foetal curve around the porcelain pan, his head and hand cut and his dignity disposed of, but alive. They dragged him out into the alley-way where the others huddled. Of Samantha there was no sign.

"She's easier now, skipper," said the bosun. Stanier nodded silently, wiping the rime of white saliva from the corners of his mouth. He did not even notice the man's use of the fishing boat term.

"Anyone else hurt?" he managed at last.

A few cuts and several bruises were displayed. Miss Loring hid her head. Caroline was bent over her.

"What's the matter with her?" asked Stanier.

Caroline looked up. "Poor Dot's lost two of her front teeth." Miss Loring wailed pitifully.

Stanier suddenly remembered the corpse in the wheelhouse.

"Where's Argyle?"

"Here, laddie." The Gael looked much older than he had a few hours earlier. Stanier took him up to the wheelhouse.

"Oh my God!" said Argyle bending over his friend. "If ah wasna' a hard heided business mon ah'd swear he'd a premonition o' his death."

"We'll have to tell Caroline."

"Tell Caroline? Oh, sweet Christ!"

The girl came forward and bent over her father, cradling his head in her arms.

Argyle plucked Stanier's sleeve and they descended to the alley-way.

"Captain," said Pomeroy at last. "What are our chances?"

Stanier bowed under the responsibility. Why the hell did they keep asking bloody silly questions? Then he recollected himself. Dammit, he *was* master. A picture of the ever confident Macready in this situation sent the blood to his head. Macready!

"I hope *Caryatid*'ll get a boat to us in the morning. In the meantime we must make the best of this." A thought dawned on him. "The ebb tide's away, that's why we're no longer pounding. We'll be high and dry at daylight."

An hour before daylight the wind began to veer. On

Caryatid's bridge a monotonous routine of position fixing and course checking had culminated in the information that in something under six and a half hours the steamer had made four miles offing from the island. Everyone on board was dog tired.

Macready turned from the window. "Bernard?"

"Sir?"

"This wind's sou'east, it's low water. There'll be the beginnings of a lee in the anchorage at Ynyscraven. If we aren't there at daylight we'll have precious little chance of getting those poor bastards off that yacht once the flood makes."

"No, sir."

"We are going to have to turn round. Go down and let everyone know they're to hang on. Don't forget the engine room. Do it personally."

"Aye, aye, sir."

Charlie watched Foster go below. The man had not rested for hours, constantly patrolling the ship to check on damage, closures, personnel.

When the Mate returned to the bridge, Macready seemed to gather himself, draw in his breath and with it the whole wheelhouse seemed to contract ready for some muscular spasm.

The Captain was the lonely lord now, staring out into the furious night, perhaps two hundred crew and their dependants waiting on his judgement and his alone.

Macready watched the sea. *Caryatid* plunged through an enormous wave and Macready banged the telegraphs to 'Full Ahead'. *Caryatid* gathered speed, hoisting the next wave over her battered foredeck so that, with the increased impetus, it hit the bridge front with a shuddering thump and exploded over the wings in a white hiss. *Caryatid*'s bow lurched out of the wave and hung over the trough, then she plunged downwards, pounding into the next sea and flinging that too over her funnel. Then her motion eased. Behind the big, cumulative waves came the lull.

"Hard a-starboard!"

"Hard a-starboard, sir." Charlie watched the wheelspokes spin in the dim light of the binnacle. "Wheel's hard a-starboard, sir." *Caryatid* began her turn.

The reeve's house became a kind of headquarters for the island's insomniacs that night. Sonia was there with Justine and half a dozen other people. The off-duty keepers from the lighthouse had struggled down across the wind-torn island to assist as they could when they had seen the red flare go skywards from the *Sea Dragon*. For the first time the name of the yacht that had been lying in the bay was mentioned. When Justine heard it confirmed that it was, in fact, Sir Hector Blackadder's yacht, fear for her daughter overwhelmed her. It was fear laced with guilt and a deep Celtic submission to divine retribution that lit her beautiful eyes with sorrow. She felt now the inevitability of the train of events, how the idyll with Septimus must be paid for in the same total currency with which it had been enjoyed.

At dawn one of the shepherds came down from the high ground with the news that he thought the *Caryatid* was approaching the island. There was a disbelieving exodus from the reeve's house. Wearing sheepskins Justine and Sonia held hands against the wind and struggled out to the cliff path. Justine shrieked her fears for her daughter into the gale and Sonia squeezed her hand in comprehension.

The gale was easing as it veered. For a while they could see nothing in the grey murk. As the sky lightened they made out the white, broken shape of the *Sea Dragon* lying on the black rocks below them and out to their right.

"There she is!" shouted Sonia, pointing. Justine's heart beat wildly at the scene. The waves still marched into the anchorage in long lines, streaked with white. Their crests still crashed remorselessly upon the granite bulk of the island and if they did so with less venom than earlier, it took a seaman of Macready's experience to detect the difference. To the two women the anchorage still looked a fearsome place. Then they saw the steamer. *Caryatid* seemed to race towards the island, scending in the following sea. The black smoke from her funnel blew forward, advancing before her as the wind whipped it along the sea surface mixing its sulphurous stink with the clean white spume.

"He's either very brave or mad, your captain," shouted Sonia, squeezing Justine's hand again reassuringly.

"What's he going to do?" asked the elder woman, scarcely able to believe her beloved Septimus was, like Lancelot, coming to the rescue. "He's coming straight at the cliffs!"

Sonia shrugged. "I don't know."

They watched *Caryatid* drive into the anchorage past *Sea Dragon*. They were unaware that Macready's sea-sense told him that with a veering wind there *must* be a point just under the lee of the Hound's Teeth that would allow him to launch a boat.

Charlie walked along the boat deck as the hands swung the launch out-board. Mackerel Jack and his crew looked apprehensive. Charlie stared out over the port side. The cliffs of Ynyscraven were looming inexorably closer. He could see lights still in the windows of the reeve's house and there, on the path . . . was that a patch of russet?

Caryatid forged ahead even with stopped engines. Macready shook his head to clear the fatigue from his brain. He had to get this manoeuvre right. Sensing the moment was correct he slammed the starboard engine telegraph to 'Full Ahead' and blew the whistle, yelling out "Hard a-port!"

At the signal the carpenter forward let go the port anchor and on the boat-deck the launch started its jerky descent to the roaring sea.

Justine watched spellbound while Sonia jumped up and down, so great was the tension. *Caryatid* turned, almost snatched herself round as her anchor cable bit into the hawse-pipe and smoke rose blue from her elm-block capstan brakes. She hung a moment broadside to the wind and sea, rolled down, up and down again.

"Hooks!" roared Foster as the boat was slipped into the wave, then *Caryatid* rolled again, away from the boat.

Charlie gasped as the engine coughed and fired. The boat shot from the lee of the steamer as *Caryatid* snubbed her cable head to wind and began to heave it in again.

Minutes later Charlie was scrambling ashore on the landward end of the Hound's Teeth where the wind effect was lost and the sea, emasculated by the reef, was no more than a surging nuisance to a fit man.

Up on the cliff Sonia saw who it was that scrambled ashore and turned to Justine with shining eyes. "Charlie's there, Justine! Charlie's there!"

She put her arm round Justine for the older woman was

crying, partly from relief, partly from love and partly from a terrible apprehension.

Under normal circumstances none of the passengers and few of the crew of the *Sea Dragon* would have undertaken that 'walk' ashore to safety. It was a nightmare journey of stumbling and wallowing in rock pools a fathom deep; of scrambling cut and bruised over granite and shale fissured by the sea and sharp with shell-fish. Oar weed tore at their legs and the trembling rocks shook with the impact of the sea not a dozen yards away from them. But the launch picked them up and landed them at last on the store jetty. Up at the reeve's house they were dried out and fed and made to get some rest. About mid-afternoon, the wind having gone to the south and moderated still further, *Caryatid* finally anchored safely and the survivors trooped out to be accommodated aboard the ship.

Charlie and Mackerel Jack and the boat's crew made no attempt to regain the ship after rescuing the *Sea Dragon*'s people until *Caryatid* returned. Macready had been specific upon this point, ordering Charlie to sacrifice the boat rather than run the further risk of attempting a recovery in a place not of his, Macready's, choosing.

It was evening when the survivors were all on board and Captain Macready, tired though he was, ordered the ship under way for Porth Ardur. Clear of the island he rang down 'Slow Ahead'.

"We'll arrive at daybreak," he explained.

Such was the combination of guilt and dread in the soul of Justine Morgan that to find Tegwyn alive was nearly as much of a shock as if she had received what she conceived to be her inevitable deserts. Her solicitude for her bruised and battered daughter was fulsome by way of compensation; though whether to propitiate the deities or ease her own conscience was uncertain. In her relief Justine was magnificent in bringing comfort to all the survivors of the *Sea Dragon* and, as their ministering angel, it did not seem unnatural that she should take passage with them in *Caryatid*.

Aboard the steamer Justine stayed close to her daughter who, still in a state of shock, did not seem surprised to find her mother suddenly on the scene of disaster. The survivors were accommodated in the officers' saloon and Justine herself asked no questions when a smooth, oiled, yet pleasantly attentive young man paid court to Tegwyn. Justine kept well out of Macready's way and was content to be on his ship and making herself useful.

Caroline had said very little to Stanier during the entire incident of the grounding. Aboard *Caryatid*, however, she drew Argyle aside and talked at some length with him. About ten o'clock that night, as *Caryatid* wallowed along at slow speed, she sought Stanier out.

He too had kept himself to himself after the disaster. His world lay in ruins about his feet. His pride and aspirations, so readily buoyed up, so recently at a zenith of scarcely-imagined promise, lay dashed to fragments upon the evil line of the Hound's Teeth.

He leant on the rail gazing astern where the swells dipped and lifted, still angry but dying as the wind dropped away.

"Hullo, Jimmy," said Caroline gently.

"Caroline?" There was a catch in his voice that betrayed him. Was it grief or self-pity?

"Oh, Caro, your father . . . I . . ." he began to weep. She held out her arms.

"Come, come, Jimmy, don't say the witch Tegwyn has unmanned you completely."

He looked at her. There was no grief in her face. He sniffed inelegantly. She kissed him full on the lips. After a little he responded as she summoned his virility from its own tight coil of misery.

"Oh, Jimmy, life has to go on, you know, it has to go on and we can make it change direction."

James St John Stanier, late master of the motor yacht *Sea Dragon*, ground his hips into the pelvis of the daughter, the wicked daughter, of the late and unlamented Sir Hector Blackadder.

Tegwyn and Stanier never said another word to each other. It was as though that final wave that had crashed aboard *Sea Dragon* had extinguished forever the fierce heat of their affair. The lovely Tegwyn, who had bruised a rib in her headlong, water-propelled flight along the alley-way, gave herself willingly to the ministrations of her mother and the gentle Pomeroy. She accepted his proposal before *Caryatid* turned the point and brought the grey-green mountain of Mynydd Uchaf ahead.

Return of the Argonauts

Long before Mr Marconi harnessed them, radio waves were crackling through the ether. It was by some telepathic link utilising this phenomenon that news of *Caryatid*'s doings always seemed to arrive in Porth Ardur ahead of the ship.

It is true that Macready sent in a message via the Coast Guard, but it was brief and without details. Afterwards there were many who swore they knew that *Caryatid* was coming in with survivors before she had even left Ynyscraven.

Gwendolen Macready spent the evening during which Tegwyn Morgan was accepting Pomeroy's proposal of marriage and Stanier was accepting Caroline's proposal of God knows what, in organising the church hall for the reception of the victims of shipwreck. She mobilised half the women-folk of the town into a sort of trench kitchen which had enough blankets, soup and tea for a small brigade of the regular army, and was on the quay when *Caryatid* berthed. It was the first time in ten years that she had been this near the ship. It was not, of course, to meet her husband that she stood thus in the windy morning, but to organise the unfortunate in their misery. She saw the huddle of figures waiting for the gangway to give them access to *terra firma* and among them she saw Justine Morgan.

Now Gwendolen had absolutely no knowledge of how Justine had got aboard the *Caryatid*, nor is it certain that, although she knew Mrs Morgan's shop had been closed for some days and that Mrs Morgan was not on the guest list of the *Sea Dragon* while her daughter was, her brain went through any logical process of deduction at the moment when she saw Justine. But like St Paul on the road to Damascus she suddenly knew. Knew everything. Her intuition flashed, long held suspicions, idle gossip, her own feeling of justified martyrdom, all suddenly crystallised into certainty.

But being who she was, she first had work to do.

The survivors allowed themselves to be marshalled into the church hall and kitted out in badly fitting clothes. Tegwyn and Justine slipped quietly home. After receiving dry gear, Stanier and Caroline drove to the house in Glendŵr Avenue while the others made their way to the Station Hotel and those of the crew who had not already done so and lived locally, also drifted home.

That night Caroline permitted Stanier to sleep with her, but only after he had resigned as Harbour Master of Porth Ardur.

Captain Macready was very tired when he eventually got home. Already the mental exertions of the rescue had reduced a guilt he might otherwise have felt on first encountering his wife after a week in another's arms. His exhaustion was too obvious for Gwendolen to take advantage of, and in any case she was too cautious a person to mistime a scene in which the full savour of her martyrdom could be enjoyed. Wronged women not only have justice on their side, but can also choose when to gratify the last shreds of departing pride.

Pomeroy called on Justine and Tegwyn before his train left the following morning.

"Will you come up to town soon, my dear?" he asked Tegwyn. "Your trousseau will receive my personal attention. You will lack nothing a truly feminine heart could desire." He smiled, a degree of confidence in his bearing that had not been there before the night *Sea Dragon* pounded herself to pieces upon the Hound's Teeth.

"Yes, of course. Mother has decided to sell the shop if she can find a cottage on Ynyscraven."

Pomeroy turned towards Justine in surprise. "You want to return to that Godforsaken rock, Mrs Morgan?"

Justine smiled at him. "If I can be sure that you'll take care of Tegwyn."

Pomeroy returned her smile. "I shall do more than that. I shall adore her as my dearest treasure." He paused. "And Mrs Morgan, I would be pleased to help financially with the cottage."

Justine looked at him. There was no diffidence about him, no embarrassment. He was a rich man, a rich and confident man, and Tegwyn was smiling delightedly.

There was little more to say after that fulsome speech.

In the train, Argyle travelled up to town with Miss Loring and Caroline. Pomeroy joined them before the train pulled out of Porth Ardur but said little during the journey. Dorothy Loring hid her face in a scarf and felt wretched. She would never, ever travel again. It might broaden the mind but it had ruined her looks. Argyle was aggressively articulate though, half whispering when he remembered, half shouting when he forgot, remonstrating with a cool, determined Caroline.

"But in heaven's name *why*, Caroline? The man's bluidy nearly responsible for the death of us all. He's certainly morally responsible for the death of your father. What possible asset will he be now to Blackadder Holdings and the Cambrian Steam Navigation Company?"

"Don't be a fool, Ian. Who's morally responsible for my mother's health, or lack of it? D'you think I mourn the old tyrant? Oh, I know you liked him and I know others admired him, but I could never forgive him for those painted trollops with the airs of duchesses that he used to tow around."

"But Caroline, your ain Stanier's nae different."

"My Stanier's *very* different. I'll be pulling the strings, don't you worry, but out front, where Cambrian and Blackadder need a good, impressive public image, that's where Jimmy Stanier will be." Caroline licked her lips. Besides, he was not without certain technical accomplishments.

Argyle sat back with a sigh. "Och dammit! I ken well your father liked him . . ."

Caroline seized the point. "Exactly! If he fooled Father he can fool the world." She paused. "How d'you like the name 'Argyle and Blackadder', Ian?"

"What exactly are you planning?" Argyle asked, his interest rekindled and redirected.

Caroline smiled as the train plunged into a tunnel.

On Ynyscraven Sonia had watched *Caryatid* fade into the distance. She returned sadly to the cottage and wondered why her mother was still absent. It was not unusual for her mother to be missing, but there was a vague worry forming in the back of her mind.

Next day the body of Samantha came ashore in the little cove beneath the coombe. The long blonde hair floated like weed about the once lovely, disdainful face A herring gull had already found her eyes but even in disfigured death she still possessed something of that lissome beauty that had attracted the experienced attention of Sir Hector Blackadder. Sonia saw the body as they brought it up for burial. The reeve, as the island's coroner, forwarded a report for the formal inquiry at Porth Ardur. They never found Sonia's mother, despite an island-wide search. Sonia felt sad at the death of the old woman, little grief but a deep sense of pity and relief at the mercy of death for the old and shattered soul.

Out on the Hound's Teeth the first gales of September churned the white plating of *Sea Dragon* into a rusting mass of red oxidisation. The wreck slowly yet inexorably lost the appearance of a ship. By Christmas she looked as if she had once been a lean-to stable made of rusty iron. She had become merely another victim of the iron-bound coast of Ynyscraven.

By the spring, the reeve had made definite plans to leave the island. He spoke to Sonia about the possibility of sharing her cottage with another lady.

Sonia had asked who, and the reeve had replied that he had received a request from Mrs Morgan of Porth Ardur for the first vacant cottage. Sonia eagerly jumped at the idea.

"I would love to have her here," she replied, her eyes catching fire, "at least until I'm married."

Justine arrived in the *Plover* a month later. Sonia was delighted to see her. She looked older, less buoyant. She had slipped the wrong side of middle age during the winter, but she was still a handsome woman.

"The *Plover*'s crew are talking of the Earl coming down soon to appoint a new reeve," she told Sonia. "D'you think Charlie would be interested?"

"Charlie?" Sonia was thunderstruck. "Why-I-er-good heavens I never thought . . ."

"You'll have to talk it over with him next time *Caryatid* comes here."

"Oh, what an idea, Justine. That would be marvellous . . . I never thought of that."

Charlie had no idea of the plans being hatched for him on Ynyscraven. He was content to visit the island as often as *Caryatid* called and to plan for a future of bliss with the lovely Sonia. He had attended the inquiry into the loss of the *Sea Dragon* and the consequent deaths. Oddly it was his and Macready's evidence that saved Stanier's professional certificate. Partly out of guilt, partly out of truth, Macready testified that the gale had been exceptionally fierce, arrived with no warning and been devastating in its effect. He explained the ease with which *Caryatid*, a steamer with steam constantly on her boilers and manned professionally could weigh her anchor faster than a motor yacht. He ignored Stanier's pained look, aware that he had it in his power to destroy the younger man. Charlie did not volunteer the information that Stanier was drunk and was not asked. As a consequence the stranding was adjudged 'an accident' and the deaths recorded as by 'misadventure'. Poor Calico Jack's was recorded as due to a coronary thrombosis and his shipmates mourned his loss as only sailors can. They bemoaned the hardship that now compelled one of their number to turn-to early and prepare *Caryatid*'s boilers for sea.

No one saw the going of Stanier. He passed quietly from the scene, regretted only by the wives who had found in him an ally against the smoking funnel of the *Caryatid*.

Charlie heard later that on the recommendation of Captain Macready, Thomas Jones was appointed temporary harbour master of Porth Ardur and that either Stan or Fred were often to be seen mowing the Captain's lawn or weeding his herbaceous borders.

It was only after the inquiry that Gwendolen Macready felt the moment ripe for her outburst. She sat knitting by the fire. The chimney smoked into the room as a gust of wind blew down it. Opposite, her husband sat dozing, unaware that the smell reminded Gwendolen of an *auto da fé*.

"Septimus," she said.

He woke. "Uh?" he stretched. "What is it?"

"Now that all the unpleasantness of the inquests is over I can talk to you about your behaviour recently." Macready jerked awake. "Don't argue with me. I've been aware for some time that what went on between you and that Mrs Morgan was very unpleasant for me, has made me the laughing stock of the town . . . please don't deny it. I've been in correspondence with the reeve's wife and reading between the lines . . . well, it's not very pleasant is it? I

believe that Mrs Morgan's gone to live permanently on the
island and I suppose that means that you'll be . . . that you
and she . . ."

Gwendolen had prepared all the speech down to the last
detail but now, in her moment of agony she could not betray
her dignity to utter crudities. She faltered.

Macready, who had listened open-mouthed, urged her
mentally on. Go on, he thought, say it.

". . . you'll be seeing her there." Gwendolen managed at
last.

Macready sat up, carefully choosing his words, making
his case as plaintive as possible. "I did not mean to cause
you any pain, my dear, but we've never been very close
in bed."

"Septimus! You really are disgusting! Now listen to me.
I intend to remain your wife and continue as I always have
in this town." She gave a heroic little sniff that Macready
found quite incongruously appealing, reminding him of a
certain cast of her head that once, long years ago, he had
found attractive. He stifled a smile.

"I shall expect the highest standards of propriety from
you while you are here. If I do not receive them I shall
make a fuss." She uttered this with an air of quite terrifying
finality. She had fired her broadside and Macready knew
the ammunition in it was enough, at least in Gwendolen's
opinion, to destroy him. By 'fuss' Gwendolen intimated
in her euphemistic way that she would institute divorce
proceedings. It would hurt her, he mused, far more than
it would hurt him. But he must capitulate, touched as
much with pity as guilt. "I am truly sorry, my dear, to
distress you."

He hung his head like a chastised schoolboy.

Gwendolen sniffed, the gleam of triumph in her eyes. "That's all there is to say on the subject. If you keep your side of the bargain I shall not mention the matter again." Macready sank back in his chair. Across the infinite divide of the hearth rug his marriage held together on agreement. Like the perfect railway lines it so resembled.

On her side of the hearth Gwendolen stilled her beating heart. Now she could really organise the town with her husband to loyally back her, not questioning any decision she might make in wielding his not inconsiderable influence. She had received his proxy and was ready once again to enter the lists around the parish pump from where his actions had besmirched her right to champion just causes.

Gwendolen Macready felt the exquisite agony of burning at a self-ignited stake.

Justine looked up from the table where she had been reading. Sonia lay asleep on her bed. Justine wondered about Tegwyn, whom she had last seen wrapped in silk and furs like a movie star, looking lovelier and happier than ever. She put down her book and walked quietly over to gaze down at the girl. The russet hair spilled out across the pillow, the darker lashes lay closed on the high, Slavic cheekbones

Beneath her blouse the girl's breasts rose and fell rythmically. Justine regarded her for a long time, then she bent and pulled a blanket up over the recumbent form. Returning to the table she blew out the light.

A full, yellow moon sent its beams into the old cottage. The wind moaned softly in the chimney. Justine slipped out of her clothes and into bed. She lay on her back staring out of the window. She wondered if she too, like Sonia's mother, would go mad in this eldritch place.

Caryatid steamed south west. Astern the blue hummock of Mynydd Uchaf faded into the distance. The sea sparkled blue and banks of cumulo-nimbus rose ahead, their heads shearing off into anvils.

Captain Septimus Macready paced his bridge. His brass-bound uniform caught the sunlight, twinkling with pride. Macready thought of Stanier and wondered where he had got to. He remembered the ugly scene when Stanier had accused him of being a charlatan. He chuckled to himself.

He, Captain Septimus Macready, was the real sailor, Stanier a mere stuffed shirt gigolo! He alone remained the pre-eminent nautical figure in Porth Ardur. Why, thought the Captain sniffing the briny air happily, had he not left one wife sitting by her hearth fire in Porth Ardur? And was he not even now steaming towards another waiting patiently for him upon his own enchanted isle?

THE CRUISE OF THE
COMMISSIONER

THE CRUISE OF THE COMMISSIONER

Richard Woodman

PAN BOOKS

CONTENTS

To Brian Davies,
who first showed me the Celtic coast.

A Cloud on the Horizon

"**B**ullshit!" exclaimed the Chief Engineer with such violence that small crumbs of toast shot across the white napery of the saloon table and struck Mr Farthing sitting opposite; the First Mate was drawn reluctantly into the argument.

"Take it easy, Chief," the Mate said, placing a protective hand over his cup of tea.

"You keep out of this! This is an engineering matter and nothing to do with you damned deck ornaments," expostulated the Chief Engineer, turning once more on the Second Engineer who was fighting a gallant rearguard action in the face of superior rank. Mr Farthing rose from the saloon table leaving the two engineers to savage each other in the technical language of their race. As he passed the partially open door of the saloon pantry he saw the face of the Steward and gave him a wink.

Caught eavesdropping, the Steward flushed then quickly covered his embarrassment by saying, "At least it ain't oil and water having a go, sir."

"No indeed," replied Charlie Farthing, lifting his uniform cap from the row of hooks in the alleyway.

"Well, it makes a change, like," breathed the Steward to the Mate's retreating back, retiring to his interminable task of washing up.

After initialling the muster book left upon his desk by the quartermaster, Charlie Farthing put on his cap and went on deck to view the cause of this disruption to the normally peaceful saloon of the SS *Caryatid*. The Steward's remark about the

1

incompatibility of oil and water, that is to say the engineering and deck departments, was a gross and unwarranted slander. For most of the time, that is. Mr Farthing liked to think the ship was run harmoniously. That, after all, was the chief part of his own job and much of its success rested upon the maintenance of a smooth routine. Intrusions like the steamroller were inimical to smooth routines.

And there it was, sitting upon the deck just forward of the *Caryatid*'s single hatch where, under normal circumstances, she would have half a dozen brightly painted buoys ready to be deployed at sea, replacing the rusty and weedy seamarks which had done their stint of warning mariners off the dangers of the Celtic coast. Mr Farthing regarded the thing with some distaste. It gleamed with the gloss of paint, its boiler and housing fir green, its heavy iron wheels bright scarlet; the pipework polished and proclaiming pristine newness. Mr Farthing walked round it, testing the securing chains with his feet. Its immobility reminded him of Gulliver lashed down upon the Lilliputian beach.

"All right, sir?" The Bosun appeared from the port side, similarly fascinated by the unusual deck cargo.

"Yes, seems fine, Bosun. I don't think she'll go anywhere."

"Not till we discharge her, anyways."

"Quite," responded Mr Farthing, unable to resist slapping the boiler of the monstrous machine.

"Any heavier and it'd have put the old lady down by the 'ead, sir."

"Yes. Have the lads had breakfast?"

"Just finishin'. I'll start singing up about ten and she'll be all ready for the tide."

"Grand," said Mr Farthing. "High water's at a quarter-past and we'll have to follow *her* out." He nodded across the small dock which formed the inner harbour of Porth Ardur, drawing the Bosun's eyes to the *Kurnow*. The Bosun spat skilfully over the side. Mr Farthing smiled to himself. The fact that the Bosun's brother was carpenter aboard the *Kurnow* did nothing to ameliorate the hostility between the two ships.

The *Caryatid* was a lighthouse tender owned by the Commissioners for Celtic Lighthouses, a practical, no-nonsense ship whose crew basked in the self-confidence of the supremely able. The *Caryatid*'s appearance bore witness to the fact: a working foredeck from which rose a heavy mast and derrick together with enough wire and manila hemp to do credit to a windjammer and a boat deck chock-full of boats. A tall buff funnel stood among its harem of boiler-room ventilators abaft the varnished teak bridge with its wheelhouse and chartroom. True, there was a touch of elegance aft, a long raking counter that boasted some gold leaf around the ship's name, but by and large the overall impression was one of rugged utility, a proud maid-of-all-work.

By contrast the *Kurnow* was a debutante; a flighty, flush-decked, turbine-powered steamer with the grandiloquent title of 'Royal Mail Ship'. Her task, daily in the summer and weekly (weather permitting) during the winter months, was the conveyance of the mails, supplies and holidaymakers to Ynys Meini. The Island of Stones was the largest of the Bishop's Islands, an extensive archipelago off the Celtic coast. The new service inaugurated by the *Kurnow* two summers previously had so boosted the number of the islands' tourists that the steamroller was now considered indispensable in the construction of a proper road across Ynys Meini. It was therefore a matter of the profoundest satisfaction to the crew of the *Caryatid* that they, and only they, were capable of delivering it to the island. The *Kurnow* had no such heavy lifting gear as *Caryatid* possessed, and the deficiency marked her for a flibberty-gibbet.

"Aye, pity she's leaving on the same tide," the Bosun mused.

"There's one glimmer of light on the horizon," Mr Farthing said, catching the Bosun's drift. The Bosun looked up at the Mate, a glint of suspicion forming in his eyes. "What's that?"

"She's under orders to vacate the berth before the next high water at Ynys Meini and make way for us."

"About bloody time," remarked the Bosun, expectorating a second time over the side. "And we'll get a night alongside."

3

"And you and the lads will get your run ashore," confirmed the Mate, suppressing a smile.

"About bloody time too," said the Bosun, repeating himself as evidence of satisfaction. "So we'll discharge this thing next morning, on the low water, is that it?" It was the Bosun's turn to slap the steamroller.

"That's it. The quay and deck will be about level then and the ship will be sitting on the bottom."

The Bosun tore his mind away from the prospect of a night at the Mermaid's Tale and scratched his head.

"Aye, sir. It's botherin' me how we're goin' to get this bloody thing up the quay. My brother tells me there'll be no driver until yon hooker takes the road-makin' gang out, and that ain't tile next month. If it's left on the quay it'll block the bloody place."

"Ah," said Mr Farthing, thinking of the row which, for all he knew, still raged in the saloon. "That's what the Chief is concerned about. He and the Second were at it hammer and tongs over breakfast, deciding which of them was the better qualified to drive it. We just have to land it safely on the quay and then the spanner-tappers can sort it out."

A slow smile spread across the Bosun's face. "Well now . . . I think," the Bosun said after a brief, thoughtful pause, "I'd rather see the Second do it, sir. I've never seen the Chief so much as go down the engine room in the seven years he's been here—"

"Now, now, Bose," said the Mate grinning, checking the Bosun's assault on the wardroom officers, "that's an exaggeration and you know it. He's got a Chief Engineer's certificate, he should be able to manage this thing." Once again the steamroller received a pat upon its rotund boiler.

"I sailed with a skipper once, Mr Farthing, on the old *Loch Killossan* it were, an' the old bugger had never been on a royal yard, not even to overhaul buntlines when he was a 'prentice boy."

"So?" said the slightly nettled Mate, losing the thread of the Bosun's argument.

"He put the old barque on the Pratas Reef off Hong Kong. I tell you no good'll come of it if the Chief drives this bloody monster." The Bosun sent a third gobbet of spittle over the side in an impressive arc.

Both men looked up at the tall funnel that rose from the forward end of the heavy machine. A few clouds drifted across the blue sky high above it, like prophetic smoke. When Charlie Farthing went to say something about the weather he found the Bosun had gone.

Mr Farthing met Captain Macready as that worthy came aboard at precisely ten o'clock, resplendent in his uniform and brass-bound cap. "Good morning sir," the Mate, said saluting. "Steam's raised and we're just singling up. The *Kurnow*'s on the move."

"Morning, Mr Farthing," Macready responded, acknowledging the salute then looking across the dock at the *Kurnow*. Her screws suddenly churned a welter of white water under her cruiser stern. Macready dismissed her with a glance then looked up at the sky. "Fine morning. All right, Mr Farthing, all hands to stations for leaving harbour. We'll get going. Deck cargo secure?"

"Yes, sir."

The passage to Ynys Meini passed without event. The stern of the *Kurnow* disappeared out of sight ahead of them, leaving them alone on the ocean as the coast dropped astern and even the dominating height of Mynydd Uchaf faded into a blue cone before dropping over the rim of the world behind them. Although a few clouds drifted across the blue sky, the sea sparkled under sunshine pocked with the clouds' shadows so that the occasional transformation of the day made men look up, only to resume their work as they passed into sunlight again. Such a contrast gave them an appreciation of the privilege they enjoyed. An ebb tide gave the old steamer and her incongruous deck cargo a favourable shove, while the presence of the steamroller prevented any distraction, such as the proper business of the lighthouse tender, from spoiling the even routine of the day's passage.

"Like a regular cruise, it is, Chippy," the Bosun remarked

to the Carpenter, "Jus' as if we was off on holiday ourselves, like."

The Carpenter, a man of taciturn disposition emitted a grunt which the Bosun, from long association with his fellow petty-officer, knew to be wholehearted and enthusiastic agreement. Then he said something, so unusual an occurrence that the Bosun, not expecting any articulated comment, had to ask him to repeat it.

"I said, bit of a swell comin' in off the Atlantic," the Carpenter said, adding for fulsome measure, "must be a blow to the westward."

"Aye," agreed the Bosun who had not really remarked the low undulations that ribbed the vastness of the sea and were barely noticeable on the *Caryatid*'s deck, "you're right."

Up on the bridge the low swell was distinctly visible. Its period was so long that the *Caryatid* merely rose and fell as each undulation passed beneath her, hardly dipping her bow or raising her stern as she did so. But the parallel lines of each successive and advancing swell could be seen like faintly drawn shadows lying across the ship's line of advance.

Captain Macready sniffed the air and screwed up his eyes. Far, far ahead of them, beyond the as yet invisible archipelago of the Bishop's Islands, beyond the fluffy white of the passing cumulus clouds, a faint muzzing above the horizon was the first indication of high cirrus.

"Bit of a swell building up, sir," said Mr Farthing, coming up on the bridge alongside Macready.

"Aye, Mr Farthing. The dog before its master."

By the late afternoon the blue hummocks of the islands rose over the horizon and an hour and a half later, as the sun westered, *Caryatid* steamed up the Sound, with Ynys Meini to starboard and the smaller island named after St Illtyd to port. Slowly, around a low hill on the Island of Stones, the little town of Porth Neigwl opened to view. Macready rang the engine room telegraphs with a clanging of bells and *Caryatid* slowed. Both Master and Mate trained their glasses on the huddle of houses and the granite breakwater.

"*Kurnow*'s still alongside," observed Captain Macready, and Mr Farthing grunted agreement. "I suppose they're going to drive the road over the spine of the island from the town," Macready ruminated as both men continued their conversation with their binoculars to their eyes.

"That's what I heard, sir," Mr Farthing agreed. "Apparently someone's bought the old castle with a view to turning it into an hotel and the road to link it with Porth Neigwl and the fishermen's cottages on the north side."

Captain Macreday rang the engines to dead slow. Up on the bridge they could hear the faint jangling of the telegraph bells down below in the engine room. As the engineers reacted, they swung their own telegraph and the bridge bells rang, the telegraph indictors swinging to conform with the bridge levers. *Caryatid*'s speed dropped to a gentle forward motion which barely disturbed the surface of the sea as Macready ordered, "Hard a-starboard!"

"Hard a-starboard, sir," the quartermaster in the wheelhouse replied, following this a few seconds later with: "Wheel's hard a-starboard." *Caryatid*'s head began to swing against the jumble of rocks, skerries, islets and the larger islands which made up the archipelago. Forward the solitary figure of the Carpenter emerged onto the foredeck and, with two heavy clunks, dropped the slips from both anchor cables.

"Both anchors cleared away," he called and Mr Farthing waved acknowledgement.

"Midships . . . Steady . . . Steady as she goes . . ." Helm order and response followed in disciplined measure. "Starboard anchor and three shackles in the hawse pipe, Mr Farthing."

"Starboard and three in the pipe." Charlie Farthing slid with practised ease down the ladder to the boat deck, his feet never touching a step, his hands running down the brass handrails with a faint but audible squeak. From the boat deck he dropped to the foredeck and next appeared to Captain Macready, watching from the bridge, as he clambered over the wires and bottle-screws securing the steamroller.

Macready rang the engines to stop. The rumble of the ship's propulsion ceased as she ghosted to the marks which Macready had for years used to find a patch of sedimentary ooze of which he appeared particularly fond. Here he knew his anchors would hold and the crew, if they were inclined, might find the odd sole. As the square church tower came into line with the gable end of the Mermaid's Tale, Macready jangled the telegraphs and *Caryatid* began to shake. Water boiled green and white under her stern as the screws went into reverse. Slowly the marbled water surged forward, indicating all forward motion was off the vessel and she had begun to move astern. Macready stopped the engines, the rumbling and shaking ceased and all that could be heard was the seething of the whorls of disturbed water as it ran along the ship's side below the bridge.

Raising his right arm, Macready dropped it sharply. Mr Farthing, now watching his commander from forward, nodded to the Carpenter and that worthy swung the brake off the starboard capstan. In a cloud of rusty dust and with a roar that broke the tranquillity and sent a dozen quietly soaring gulls sheering away, *Caryatid*'s starboard anchor dropped from the hawse-pipe and plunged into the water with a splash, dragging forty-five fathoms of heavy stud-link cable behind it. Mr Farthing hung over the side, closely observing the lead of the cable as the ship continued to drop astern and the cable drew ahead. He watched as it came taut, dragging the anchor so that the flukes turned, dug deeply into the mud on the bottom, and checked the sternway of the ship. A moment later the cable slackened as the catenary pulled *Caryatid* forward again, and she brought up securely to her anchor.

"Secure, Chippy," he said, turning to the waiting Carpenter then, turning to face the bridge, he held both forearms in a crossed stance. "All brought up," he called and Macready waved his acknowledgement. The Captain took off his uniform cap and ducked into the wheelhouse. "Finished with the wheel, Quartermaster, until that hooker has sailed." Macready jerked his head in the direction of the distant *Kurnow* alongside the only berth Porth Neigwl boasted on the granite pier-cum-breakwater.

"Aye, aye, sir."

Macready scribbled the time of anchoring in the rough log, then stood in the wheelhouse looking down at the steamroller. He was still staring at it when Mr Farthing joined him. "That thing," said Macready as though all his contemplation had produced the remark, "is going to clog up the pier," he observed, "unless there's someone here who can drive it."

"The matter's in hand, sir," Mr Farthing explained. "I understand that although there's no driver available until next month, the Chief has plans to drive it away, clear of the berth."

"Oh good," Macready said, bestirring himself and turning to go below. "I'd hate to mess up the *Kurnow*'s delivery of beer and cigarettes." Mr Farthing smiled dutifully at the Captain's little joke. "The Chief's organizing it, you say?" he asked, pausing at the head of the companionway.

"Well, yes, sir," responded Mr Farthing, thinking of the row in the saloon that morning.

"Ahhh, well then . . ." said Macready enigmatically, drawing the syllables out so that they seemed to contain immense and prescient foreknowledge.

When, to derisory cheers from *Caryatid*'s crew lining her rail, the *Kurnow* sailed and *Caryatid* was able to inch into the now vacant berth before the tide had ebbed too far, the lighthouse tender weighed her anchor and slid quietly alongside. As Mr Farthing had indicated to the Bosun earlier that day, the monstrous machine dominating the ship's foredeck would be discharged the following morning at local low water. By a curious anomaly, when it was high water at Porth Ardur, it was almost low water at Porth Neigwl. The curious run of the tidal streams made possible the schedule of the *Kurnow* and meant that the matter of the steamroller's delivery, which could not of course be undertaken in the hours of darkness, would take place at about eleven o'clock next morning when the granite pier and steel deck were as level as would be possible.

As the sun set amid a tangle of cirrus that confirmed Captain Macready's prediction of a coming gale, a festive mood settled upon the steamer. Showers were much in demand, steam and pink flesh filled the lower alleyways while above the hiss of spraying water a gently obscene banter marked a keying up of spirits, such was the spirit of anticipation abroad in the *Caryatid*. Of course the men whose duty confined them to the

ship were disconsolate. They sat about the messroom still in
their working clothes, brewing tea and rolling cigarettes with
the resigned air of men contemplating several years isolated
on desert islands.

It had been some months since *Caryatid* had last anchored in
the islands (and some years since she had last laid alongside),
allowing her people a run ashore in Porth Neigwl. Her crew
were supremely good seamen. They did not have to stay at
sea for months to prove it and many had already trod the
path of distant, deep-water voyages in their impetuous youths.
Service aboard the vessels run by the Commissioners for Celtic
Lighthouses was appropriate for men of mature years with
wives, families and commitments. But they still managed to
view their forthcoming hours of freedom with an air of hungry
enthusiasm that belied the fact that only that morning they had
left their own domestic hearths. In its post-tourist, autumnal
evening, Porth Neigwl waited like an unsuspecting maid.

At seven o'clock, Mr Farthing summoned the Bosun.

"Red and white watches ashore, Bose. All hands back on
board by midnight."

The Bosun's "aye, aye, sir" was flung over his retreating
shoulder as he hopped blithely over the sea-step at the end
of the officers' alleyway. A second later his stentorian bellow
hollered the order down the companionway to the messdeck
below, then the Bosun headed for the gangway. The Bosun's
voice had not ceased to echo off the steel bulkheads before
there was the clattering of boots on ladders, the liberated
whoops and hoots that only shore-bound sailors can make and
only ship-bound watch-keepers recall, filled the air. Three
minutes later, the silent resentment of the confined blue watch
settled back upon the ship.

Mr Farthing decided to go ashore and went along to the
wardroom to see if any company could be found. The Chief
and Second Engineers were standing before the fireplace that
the Commissioners for Celtic Lighthouses seemed, somewhat
incongruously, to consider an indispensible furnishing to an
officers' wardroom.

"Now look here, Roberts," the Chief was saying, wagging a

finger ominously at a man with whom he had sailed for years, with whom he was frequently drunk in the Conservative Club in Porth Ardur and who was commonly called Gwyn, "for the last time, I'm making this an order. If I so much as *see* you on the bloody pier tomorrow, I'll have the Old Man suspend you from duty!"

The Second Engineer, his face an empurpled mask of truculence, opened his mouth to speak, thought better of it and looked vainly round for support. The Second Mate, a sallow young man by the name of Wentworth, who miserably filled the evening duty as the watchkeeping officer, avoided Robert's eyes and buried himself deeper in a paperback novel, the cover of which featured a remarkably voluptuous corpse draped half dressed across an iron bedstead. The Third Engineer, who shared the watch with Wentworth, pretended no interest in the word "suspension" which might earn him at least a temporary promotion and a weekly increase in pay of one shilling and sixpence for its duration, noisily turned the pages of the *Western Courier*. The Second's imploring glance then fell upon Mr Farthing as the Mate entered the wardroom from the adjacent saloon. Mr Farthing was about to say something to mollify the two men who must, judging from their colour, have given the matter of the steamroller little respite since breakfast. But the Chief was terrible in victory, sensing he had at last gained the upper hand and that Mr Farthing was best swept into his own camp.

"And furthermore, Mr Farthing," the Chief said, detaching himself from the fireplace and heading for the door, "I look to you to see the order carried out." Mr Farthing stepped aside as with awesome dignity the Chief Engineer strode from the wardroom.

The silence he left in his wake was punctured by Wentworth. "Do I assume," he said with airy facetiousness, "that the Chief Engineer will be driving the steamroller clear of the pier tomorrow morning?"

"You can sod off!" snapped Gwyn Roberts, his face furious with rage and humiliation. "I'm going ashore to get legless."

"Good idea," responded Mr Farthing. "Mind if I join you?"

*   *   *

Disappointment was the first emotion experienced by the Bosun and the lads as they tumbled ashore. At its landward end the granite pier swung through an angle of about sixty degrees and ran along the wall of a long stone building which had been built some time in the last century as a boathouse. The boathouse and its adjacent dwelling had been bought by a speculator and turned into a public house and hotel shortly after the turn of the century when the fashionable and artistic set were discovering Ynys Meini as the ideal place for bohemian holidays. The resulting 'hotel' had, however, only enjoyed two summers' popularity by this set of shocking young people before half its clientele, the male half, had found more permanent accommodation in the mud of Flanders. The only relic of these intellectual days was the name of the place, which reflected a literary hand in its punning name. The pun was the bane of the local school teacher, for almost every child on the island spelt 'tail' as though it were a story. After its failure as a hotel and before the renewed popularity of the island as a destination for more numerous holidaymakers of less flamboyant style, the building had become a common tavern. The converted boathouse, however, made an excellent public venue, particularly for the island's regular and sometimes hasty wedding breakfasts.

The Mermaid's Tale enjoyed great popularity among *Caryatid*'s crew largely on account of the fact that the bar sported two well-endowed blonde barmaids and rarely closed while a customer was left standing. It was also a place where reputations were made and lost, for both the young women were commonly held 'to do a turn'. Who had done what to whom was largely a matter of mystery, much talked of on hungover and work-ruined mornings after, and the matter is only mentioned because it explains the alacrity with which the Bosun led the men ashore that evening. Though many claimed to have benefited from the favours of one or other of these beauties, *Caryatid*'s Bosun was believed to have once bedded them both simultaneously, a fact which conferred upon him almost legendary status and greatly augmented his authority on the ship's foredeck. By association with him, men basked in the reflected glory of this stunning deed and while it was only mentioned in whispers among male-only gatherings in Porth Ardur, in Porth Neigwl there existed a greater liberty.

All of which explains the corporate disappointment when the human tide, fetching up against the door of The Mermaid's Tale, found it firmly closed against them.

"The bloody sign's gone too," the Bosun said to no-one and everyone as he sought to find some explanation in the indifferent heavens above. It was true.

The sign depicting the beautiful siren, winking one eye and beckoning enticingly with one promisory finger, was no longer there. Instead its iron bracket stuck out from the masonry with all the pointless uselessness of an unoccupied gibbet.

"And look at that!" All eyes, seeking in vain the fishy temptress, swivelled as one. There, on a freshly painted board bolted to the gable above, was a new legend: *The Mermaid Bakery.*

"Mermaid Bakery my arse," said the Bosun, speaking for them all, adding, with that limitless resource that is the foundation of all good seamanship, "right lads, follow me." And turning away he led them shoulder-hunched in their silent regret up the road toward the Anchor and Hope.

The Mate and Second Engineer made the same discovery half an hour later, though with less frenzy and more curiosity than the hands, for it was not their intended destination. They were both slightly abstracted. Charlie Farthing because he hated a run ashore anywhere other than on the island of Ynyscraven where his wife Sonia lived, regarding liberty spent elsewhere as a waste of time, and Gwyn Roberts because he was mortified by the threat of suspension that hung, like the sword of Damocles, above his head.

As they reached the bend in the quay, the Second had looked back. "It's so bloody narrow, Charlie, I don't suppose there'll be more than six inches either side of those damn great wheels."

"Eh?" Charlie said, not understanding the allusion, thinking as he was of Sonia and feeling his belly hollowing out for a pint, or something.

It was with something like relief that they discovered the transformation of the public house. It gave them a topic of conversation that united them, a neutral subject upon which they could venture opinions, though about which they knew absolutely nothing. They were still discussing the economics of running a public house and how it would be a fine way for a seafarer to end his days, when they pushed open the door of the Buccabu Light. It was not because the pub was named after the famous lighthouse whose maintenance was one of *Caryatid*'s principal tasks, that they drank there. It was simply because with the nicety of pragmatic diplomacy and by the usage of the Lighthouse Service, the officers of *Caryatid* traditionally drank in the Buccabu Light when in Porth Neigwl.

It was with mixed feelings that *Caryatid*'s people greeted the new day. For the majority of those who had enjoyed a run ashore the previous evening, the predominant sensation was one of cranial agony, an unpleasant feeling made worse by the sanctimonious self-righteousness of those who had had the duty watch. During breakfast on the messdeck, a story went round that the Bosun had attempted to assist the new deck boy to lose his virginity with the landlady of the Anchor and Hope. She was a widow with certain characteristics in sympathy with the granite landscape in which she had grown up, though these became less obvious as a jolly evening wore on, and she was certainly not without a degree of comeliness elsewhere about her person. The story varied in the telling. Some inclined to the version that the boy had proved his manhood, despite first having been compelled to swallow more beer than he could comfortably hold. This version was said to be verified by the sheepish look on the youth's pallid face. Others pointed to this as concrete evidence that the lad had failed and that the Bosun had had to complete the job himself. This was apparently proved by the Bosun's early turning-to on the foredeck where the seamen stumbled about easing the wires and bottlescrews which restrained the steamroller, and his zealous frenzy in drowning a conscience in work. Whatever the truth, neither party seemed inclined to reveal it.

In the saloon, the Chief presided over the breakfast

table, scarcely able to contain his excitement. Since Captain Macready rarely took breakfast, being conscious of his figure which it was necessary to maintain in as trim a state as possible in order to keep his place in Porth Ardur's ballroom dancing team, the Chief was able to bask in his seniority, throwing out good-natured remarks which arose from a good night's sleep, a clear conscience and a clear head. The Chief ignored the unpleasantness of yesterday and, as a consequence of this and the combination of a hangover, was ignored in turn by Mr Farthing and Mr Roberts. The Chief had risen at the uncustomary hour of six and turned out the hungover Donkey Man, instructing him to break up two bucketsful of bunker coal, ready to fuel the steamroller. Needless to say, the feckless Donkey Man had muttered something about there being all day to play bloody train drivers, and had turned in again.

Neither Mr Farthing nor Mr Roberts said anything to mute the Chief's self-esteem. They were too preoccupied with their own suffering, though their jaded countenances were taken as tokens of submission as they munched their respective ways desultorily through their breakfasts. At the head of the table the Chief Engineer completed his with a flourish of his napkin and rose with the energy of a second Napoleon flinging the Grand Army across the River Niemen.

"Right!" he exclaimed, rubbing his hands as he left the saloon.

The fact that the Donkey Man had gone back to sleep was the first thing that went wrong. Had the Chief Engineer possessed a shred of prescience, he might have seen in the sleeping man a providential warning of the chain of events which was to follow. Alas, the skills that form a man into a marine engineer are not normally those found in seers and mystics. The Chief did not recoil from the recumbent form when, in the absence of the broken coals, he went in search of their bearer only to find the Donkey Man much as he had been over three hours earlier.

A roaring bellow that resounded throughout the lower-deck accommodation brought the Donkey Man into the middle of the morning and full consciousness at a rush. The poor man had once been torpedoed and was in the alleyway with his life-preserver before he recollected himself. He was, however, soon in the stokehold with the Coal Trimmer, breaking nuggets of coal into small pieces while the Chief, in the boiler room next door, loudly organized two firemen into drawing out of the starboard boiler a quantity of red and glowing coals. These were soon on their way up the steel ladders and heading for the open air.

By the time the Chief and his acolytes emerged on deck, Mr Farthing, the Bosun and the hands had unlashed the steamroller, slung it and lifted it. By heaving on one derrick guy and slackening the other, they had slewed the heavy spar through an angle of some seventy degrees with the ease of long practice, treating the gleaming machine as if it had been a particularly heavy buoy. As the steamroller traversed the *Caryatid*'s deck, the ship, though hard aground on the soft mud of Porth Neigwl, nevertheless heeled a little. Moreover, as the steamroller's wheels touched the granite pier and its weight came off the heavy purchase, the old ship eased back to the vertical. The Chief was confronted by his charge sitting upon the pier, in the very act of being released from the chain slings by which it had been suspended from the purchase hook.

As the Chief Engineer emerged with his followers – the Donkey Man with two buckets of black lumps and the Trimmer with a third bucket of hot and burning coals – quite a crowd had assembled. From Captain Macready on the *Caryatid*'s bridge above, to the cook leaning out of the galley port slightly below the level of the pier, *Caryatid*'s crew waited like a jubilee throng anticipating the arrival of monarchy. The only exception was the Second Engineer who, in a mood of sullen obedience, was staring out over the opposite rail to the advancing bank of cloud coming from the west.

From this position he could just hear the Chief's voice raised in the giving of his commands. "Let's be having them live coals now . . . That's it . . . Now the rest, Donkey . . ."

Mr Roberts could also hear the squeals and laughs of schoolchildren, particularly when they heard a grown man called 'Donkey'. "Oh, bugger the bugger," Mr Roberts said and, struck by an idea, returned to his cabin.

By the time steam had been raised in the steamroller's boiler, the Chief was bathed in a lather of sweat and his white boiler suit was sullied by unaccustomed grime that the steamroller, immaculate in its newness, had maliciously produced from its inner recesses.

Many of the now not inconsiderable crowd, which had mustered to see the arrival of the steamroller, had not seen a steam engine before. In this category were a number of small boys who had been led down to the harbour with their classmates for educational purposes. They had broken away from the strictures of their crocodile and were clambering all over the steamroller even to the extent of pinching lumps of coal and hurling them at each other. That they would undoubtedly be caned for their behaviour only added to the fun and when their teacher, a plain but dutiful young woman, sought to bring them back into line, *Caryatid*'s watching seamen thought the day improving by the minute.

The Chief, intent on his fire and the quick raising of steam, merely swatted these boys when they became excessively importunate; otherwise he fiddled with the draught controller and tapped the pressure gauge, drawing from the observant Macready the murmured comment that, "It's not a bloody barometer that you've got to be tapping it like that, man."

At this point one of the boys became over-exuberant and both Chief and teacher grabbed him at the same instant. A moment later they were arguing with each other over the rights and wrongs of having a steamroller on the pier at the same time as a crowd of schoolchildren. This altercation was terminated by the late, but inevitable arrival of the law. The island's only constable had naturally felt it necessary to return home to collect his helmet, before proceeding to investigate the imminent affray then brewing on the pier. He led the heated teacher back to her charges who were now in impeccable formation, having long since spotted the approaching policeman.

Muttered approval of the lady's heaving bosom was generated along *Caryatid*'s rail and more than one suggestion was made to the Bosun and the Deck Boy in which the honour of the ship played a small part.

The intervention of the constable was signalled by a watery, but irrefutable hoot from the steamroller's whistle which terminated these speculations. Steam was almost raised and the spluttering whoop was greeted by a small cheer from the expectant throng. Several children jumped up and down in the excitement and one or two thought the entertainment over, and that they would soon be back in the classroom, victims of disillusion and disappointment.

The brief hoot also drew the Second Engineer back into the mainstream of human affairs. He watched from the concealment of a boiler room ventilator trunk, then moved nearer, as though drawn by the mounting pressure in the green boiler, to crouch furtively behind the boat-deck bulwark, peering through a panama lead.

When at long last the Chief gave a triumphant thumbs-up to the ship's company and was met by an ironic cheer, Mr Roberts could, had anyone taken any notice of him, have been seen with his camera, poised to take a shot of the departing steamroller.

The Chief was now in the throes of carrying out the preliminaries necessary to starting a steamroller moving. Draincocks dribbled, spluttered and then hissed satisfactorily, whereupon the sweating Donkey Man was ordered to shut them off. The Chief settled himself in the driver's seat and motioned the Donkey Man up behind him. Regarding his sins forgiven, egged on by the acclamations of his mates on board and the presence of the audience, the Donkey Man obliged. For the Chief, the presence of the Donkey Man was not so much an act of indulgence as a snubbing of the Second Engineer.

With a frown of concentration, the Chief let off the brake and opened the steam valve. Slowly the juggernaut eased forward to a tentative noise of enthusiastic approval. At this point two things happened. Mr Roberts defied the Chief's order and, unable to contain himself further, leapt onto the pier with his camera. The sudden movement caught the Chief's eye just as, with the steamroller trundling slowly forward, he turned to wave to the ship's company. His gratification was swiftly turned to anger at the Second Engineer's defiance. His bellow at Mr Roberts was drowned in the cheer raised by Mr Farthing, taken up loyally by the Bosun and all hands and augmented by squeals from the schoolchildren. Then the Donkey Man drew the Chief Engineer's attention to the fact that the steamroller occupied almost the entire width of the pier. Simultaneously, with eighteen turns of his steering wheel lock-to-lock, the Chief discovered that guiding the steamroller was a difficult task.

Sweating profusely despite the sudden chilly, rain-bearing wind that was freshening every moment, the Chief corrected the steamroller's slew. The green and gleaming machine lumbered along in a straight line and the Chief relaxed, feeling himself in control. Ahead of him ran the straight granite pier. He opened the throttle and the crowd moved back. With a delightfully sibilant hiss-hiss and the trembling rumble of its progress over the granite cobbles, the steamroller made its juggernaut progress towards the bend in the pier.

Having, as it were, seen the steamroller off on its regal progress, Mr Farthing went up to the bridge and joined Captain Macready on the starboard wing. From this vantage point both men had a grandstand view of what followed. Indeed the elevation alerted them to the possibility of disaster at least a minute before any indication of danger impinged itself upon the Chief's consciousness.

Caryatid's crew spilled down the gangway onto the pier, filling in the vacuum left by the departing steamroller like leaves that are sucked into the wake of a passing vehicle. Close behind the roller itself ran Mr Roberts, the Second Engineer, whose presence on the pier had been specifically proscribed by his superior.

"Oh dear," said Mr Farthing, aware that he too was in dereliction of his duty.

"I think," added Captain Macready, unaware of the situation of the Second Engineer and more concerned with the approaching bend, "that the Chief is about to experience a navigational hazard."

"Oh dear," repeated Charlie Farthing, grasping the significance of the Captain's remark and, with an intuitive leap, guessing why Gwyn Roberts was so attentively following the Chief.

As the juggernaut reached the bend the Chief shut in the steam slowly, grinning confidently at the Donkey Man whose face bore an expression of sudden apprehension.

"I should put a bit of brake on, Chief, if I were you."

"Nonsense, man," said the Chief, elated by their progress as he started to whirl the little steering wheel. The long boiler began to nose round the corner.

"A bit of brake, Chief!" The Donkey Man called, his voice raised in alarm.

It was now clear that the rate of the steamroller's turn did not conform to the geometry of the bend. The Chief whirled the wheel faster and, at the moment the Donkey Man decided to use his own initiative and leaned forward to apply the brake, the Chief leaned outboard to observe the progress of the heavy forward roller. In so doing he all but unseated the Donkey Man who, clutching for his life, narrowly avoided being dropped neatly under the huge, nearside rear wheel. He recovered just in time to watch the forward end of the steamroller penetrate the long stone wall of what had once been the dance hall of The Mermaid's Tale.

But it was no longer a dance hall. What the Chief had driven into and was now in the process of demolishing, was the flour store of the Mermaid Bakery. To the slightly distant observers on *Caryatid*'s bridge a silent explosion seemed to occur, a soundless release of elemental forces that was as delicate as the flap of a butterfly's wing. Great soft white clouds rose up in huge billows to be torn to leeward in the wind.

"Oh dear, oh dear," Mr Farthing said yet again, scarcely able to conceal his amusement. Aware of its impropriety he did his best, skewing a sideways look at Captain Macready whose face bore a look of resignation, like a man brought before a circumstance he had long foreseen. Mr Farthing looked again at the white cloud which was now beginning to subside. Figures moved within and around it. A gleeful covey of schoolboys leapt up and down and turned and smiled and shouted at each other. The *Caryatid*'s crew stood in a half moon of spectators, many rocking backwards and forwards with obvious laughter. The police constable advanced rapidly, withdrawing his notebook while Mr Roberts could be seen bent over his Kodak.

Then, like a supremely skilled actor making an entrance, upon the timing of which rested the credibility of the scene, the Chief emerged bellowing from the centre of the cloud. Brushing the policeman aside, he advanced on the Second, shouting incoherent abuse as the latter, still snapping and rewinding his Kodak, fell back before his enraged superior. As though at a signal, although it may have been at the policeman's protest at being manhandled, the Chief broke into a run, whereupon the Second went into full retreat. In a single body, those members of the *Caryatid*'s crew who had followed the steamroller's progress along the pier, turned and fled with the Second before the wrathful Chief, a flock of sheepdogs being chased by a single, mad white ram. Behind the Chief in feeble imitation, ran the constable.

"Oh Lord!" said Mr Farthing, who could now hear the words, "Sabotage . . . ! Your fault . . . ! Suspension . . . ! Bastard!" coming from the approaching Chief Engineer.

The proximity of the ship to the pier and the level nature of her deck enabled the athletic to dispense with the gangway and merely vault the bulwark rail. Bodies leapt inboard again, as though quickly taking up their original places as spectators before being seen as accessories to what promised to be further entertainment. Gwyn Roberts, encumbered by his camera and its precious evidence, was making for the gangway when he was caught by the Chief. The two engineers began an unseemly grapple for possession of the Kodak box camera and the hand of the constable was already reaching out for the Chief's collar when all was suddenly transformed.

At that moment Mr Farthing's admiration for Captain Macready increased. He had observed the Captain in a number of situations fraught with incipient disaster. In all of them he had remained calm, unruffled and supremely confident of his own abilities. This, however, was scarcely one in which Charlie Farthing would have expected *Caryatid*'s master to manifest any talent. But Mr Farthing was wrong.

In a monstrous bellow that put past muster anything the

21

breathless Chief could now produce, Captain Macready froze the little group on the pier. Even the police constable responded to the authority inherent in the stentorian monosyllable.

The Second recovered his camera with the thought of the price the negatives would fetch when offered to the *Western Courier*. Behind him the Chief stared mawkishly up at the bridge.

"Chief," called Captain Macready, dropping his tone without losing the attention of all within range, "how many times have I told you that many are called to drive, but only a few chosen to navigate?"

The New Commissioner

Far to the east there was no hint of a gale. The sun still shone, in tune with the mood of James St John Stanier as he sped along the streets of the capital in his chauffeur-driven limousine. He leaned back exuding satisfaction. It had been a good morning and, on his way to his inaugural meeting as a Commissioner of Celtic Lights, he anticipated a good afternoon. During the forenoon he had chaired a meeting at his offices at which a Member of Parliament and a peer of the realm had promised their support for a project to mine coal from an open cast site near Porth Ardur. The produce of the mine would be exported in the ships of the Cambrian Steam Navigation Company, of which Stanier was the chairman. After this, he had lunched well at his club and the excellent burgundy put him in an even more expansive mood, so much so that he had engaged the chauffeur in some casual small talk about the weather.

Being a stickler for punctuality, a characteristic developed during his early years at sea as a young officer in the legendary liners of the Isthmus and Occidental Steam Navigation Company, Stanier arrived at the porticoed entrance of the Commissioners' headquarters at exactly half past two. The imposing Georgian building, its red brick warm in the afternoon sunshine, added to the inner warmth induced by the burgundy. He had made it, by Jupiter! To have been elected a commissioner was the icing on the cake of his career. Ship-owning gave him kudos in the city even if they were not quite the sort of steamships owned and managed by the great I & O Line, and in its own way, the Cambrian

Steam Navigation Company now reflected much of what was practised in the I & O liners, not least among which was a strong reliance upon punctuality. But his appointment as a commissioner set him truly apart, a man of approved rectitude, a pillar of the establishment, a paradigm among his peers.

Only one small shadow marred Stanier's prospect of the afternoon and that was the question of his title. He had been appointed to the Board of the Commission for Celtic Lighthouses largely as a representative of shipowners' interests, but what chiefly recommended his candidacy was the fact that he was himself a master mariner. His fellow shipowners had therefore felt that he was uniquely qualified among them to do battle on their behalf, mostly it has to be said, in the matter of keeping their costs in the form of light levies to a minimum. The majority of the other commissioners were former shipmasters, but the Commission's constitution required that three of its Board came from the commercial world in order to maintain sensible control of its finances. In this way the running expenses of the Celtic Lighthouse Service were properly managed by a Board which constituted representatives of both paymasters and customers. It was an ancient body, with some odd rites, but it had worked well for 350 years, since its inception in the late seventeenth century.

It was Stanier's good fortune, therefore, that the resignation of one of the number of the commercial trio had left a timely vacancy and the outgoing Commissioner had nominated Stanier for election as his successor. Duly elected, Stanier had assumed his new dignity eagerly. However, while he was proud of his status as a master mariner, he felt privately most uncomfortable about using the formal title of 'captain'. He would have admitted this to no-one, not even his wife Caroline, but it had been Stanier's personal tragedy to have wrecked his first command, the steam yacht *Sea Dragon*, owned by the millionaire shipowner, Sir Hector Blackadder. A few years earlier, *Sea Dragon* had been driven ashore from her anchorage off the island of Ynyscraven, to have her bottom torn out on a reef known as the Hound's Teeth. Stanier still had the occasional nightmare about that terrible night, though, to any other person, his fortunes might have been said to have taken a decidedly upward turn as a result of it. Despite the fact that several people had been lost along with the yacht, including Sir Hector himself, James St John Stanier's career had risen from that dreadful and awesome moment, for he had married Sir Hector Blackadder's beautiful daughter Caroline and taken over much of the late Sir Hector's business interests, among which the most significant was the chairmanship of the Cambrian Steam Navigation Company. Caroline, sweet darling that she was, had suggested that he took command of one of the company's ships for two voyages, and the experience had largely buried the spectre of the loss of the *Sea Dragon*. This period of command had the salving effect of rehabilitating himself in his own mind. It was only at such awkward moments, as the present might prove to be, that he worried about the disaster and his use of the title of 'captain'.

He got out of the car and was immediately met by a commissionaire. The man was not only clearly expecting him, but solved his problem with almost providential tact.

"Good afternoon, Captain Stanier," the flunkey greeted him. "If you would be so kind as to follow me."

Stanier strode up the wide stairs behind the coat tails and lacquered shoes of the commissionaire, passing some fine ship models and beneath the glowering gaze of half a dozen full length portraits which, he might have observed, were he the observant type, reflected the change in male hair styles from the full-bottomed wig of the seventeenth century to the establishment short-back-and-sides of the present day. He might also have observed that one thing remained the same – the portly demeanour of his predecessors. They all seemed to be men stuffed full of good food and self-esteem and Stanier felt immediately at home with their painted images.

Three hours later, as the meeting drew towards its conclusion, Stanier was well content. He felt he had given the Board, the members of which had greeted him with affable cordiality, the benefit of good counsel. It was clear that the Board were not hostile to the general principle of economies and, Stanier thought, his advice in this area was both welcomed and would form the basis of an initiative. Stanier felt his heart-beat quicken. He was not an impulsive man, but it had occurred to him when he had accepted the appointment as Commissioner, that the post might give him the opportunity to get even – he eschewed the concept of revenge – with a man who had once got the better of him, Captain Septimus Macready. Stanier did not wish to get even with Macready because the master of the *Caryatid* had been involved with the tragedy of the *Sea Dragon*. Not a bit of it. The animosity felt by Stanier for Macready arose from some real humiliations Macready had subjected Stanier to when he, Stanier, had had his first shore appointment as harbour master of Porth Ardur. The two men had clashed then and Stanier was not one to let matters die away when fate gave him an opportunity. Indeed, Stanier regarded such a thing as signifying providential approval, but he could hardly have hoped such an opportunity would present itself at his very first attendance at the Commission's Board.

From the nature of the discussions that afternoon, Stanier had gleaned a desire on the part of the Commissioners that the scrapping of their oldest lighthouse tender, which happened to be the *Caryatid*, and the closure of the small establishment at Porth Ardur, could form the substance of his suggested initiative. He kept his voice subdued when the Chairman, Captain Sir Charles Mudge said, "You know Porth Ardur, Captain Stanier, do you not? Weren't you harbour master there for a while?"

"Yes, Sir Charles, I do know the place. I should guess the *Caryatid* to be reaching the end of her serviceable life, certainly . . ."

He proceeded cautiously, seemingly uneager, and when a fellow commissioner, Captain Blake, said in a tone that challenged contradiction: "Old Macready's a fine seaman, though. I'd hate to see him go," Stanier was quick to agree.

"A fine seaman, yes, undoubtedly, but he's not in the first flush of youth."

"Wasn't there some damned tittle-tattle about his having a floosie on that bloody island, what's it called? Ynys . . . Ynys—"

"Ynyscraven, Captain Jesmond." Sir Charles Mudge said

helping the oldest member of the Board to recollect an island graced with one of its lighthouses.

"Yes, yes, that's the place. Well, if he's got a bit of fluff tucked away, he can't be too damned old, can he?" The old sea dog laughed at his own humour to the general embarrassment of his fellows.

"Well, gentlemen, that's hardly germane," Mudge said, "and certainly we shall not record that in the minutes." He motioned to the assiduous clerk who, under the sombre shadow of the Secretary to the Board, nodded compliance.

"No, don't put it in the bloody minutes, of course not," persisted Jesmond, "but it's a consideration when thinking about a man, don't you think? It shows vigour, by God!"

"Well, that is true, of course," Stanier put in quickly, seizing the advantage the old fool had given him. "But I imagine moral turpitude is not to be condoned in the public service—"

"Quite so," agreed Blake and Sir Charles quickly.

Having achieved this moral ascendancy, Stanier drew in his breath and frowned, as though giving great consideration to what he was about to say, gaining the attention of all his fellow Board Members. "Of course, I suppose with the *Caryatid* ageing, her running costs are mounting to a prohibitive extent and therefore her demise would effect considerable savings. In addition, though I agree that Captain Macready is a fine seaman of the old school, indeed I had the pleasure of knowing him quite well during my brief stay at Porth Ardur, he does lack a master's certificate and this would provide a technical reason for premature retirement."

"Yes, that is a good point," agreed Sir Charles. "He was promoted under the old system of internal examination by the Board and while it has its merits, it exposes our people to charges of not being fully competent. One might run risks if the press got hold of such a thing nowadays."

"Damn the bloody press!" barked Jesmond. "If you want officers with master's certificates, you may have to pay 'em more, and then they'll have the same qualifications as ourselves! We'll have 'em up here arguing with us then! Unthinkable!"

"Most of the up and coming generation of officers in our

ships hold master's or mate's certificates, Captain Jesmond,"
Sir Charles Mudge said soothingly, "but Captain Stanier has a
moot point. The matter provides an excellent pretext, especially
as the only item under any other business also concerns the
worthy Captain Macready."

Stanier listened with supressed triumph as Mudge instructed
the Secretary to the Board to read out the letter of complaint
received from a certain Ifor Davies. In a sonorous voice that
lent a tragic air to Mr Davies's complaint, the Board were
informed that Mr Davies was the only baker on Ynys Meini
and that his bakery had been wrecked by the incompetence of
the crew of the Celtic Lighthouse Service Steamship *Caryatid*.
These men, having enjoyed a drinking spree the night before,
had wilfully driven a steamroller into his flour store. This
action had ruined his entire stock of flour which had only
just been shipped to Ynys Meini at great expense, expense
which had been secured against a bank loan raised at the
exhorbitant rate of two per cent per annum. Mr Davies had
lost business and now faced bankruptcy and the imminent
starvation of his wife and six children. The islanders were
faced with a crisis and to cap it all, this unprovoked incident
had culminated in Captain Macready making a public joke at
which his entire crew had laughed uproariously. In short, a
sum of compensation was sought.

"Doesn't sound like Macready to me," said Jesmond testily.

"Nor me," offered a heavily bearded Captain Gostling, who
stared at Stanier over half-moon glasses.

"Nor me," said Mudge, "but perhaps, with the benefit of
local knowledge, Captain Stanier can give us his opinion?"

Stanier leaned forward and pursed his lips as though reluc-
tant to gossip. "Well, Sir Charles, it is not entirely outside
the man's character. I recall him once driving the bow of
the *Caryatid* against the dock caisson and insisting the port
was open, even though the closed caisson indicated it clearly
wasn't—"

"High-handed, d'you mean?" asked Captain Blake.

"Not Macready," Gostling insisted, his face clearly expressing disbelief. "There must have been a reason for such a
thing."

Stanier shrugged. "I leave it for you to decide the man's motives, gentlemen," he concluded obscurely.

"Well, your loyalty to an old colleague does you credit, Stanier," Mudge pronounced approvingly, bringing a deep inner satisfaction to the dissembling Stanier who merely nodded graciously. It was not necessary to state that it was his own inefficiency that had caused the port signals to show Porth Ardur remained open to traffic.

Mudge laid the file down and went on. "Nonetheless, this chap Davies has a good claim against the Service, with unimpeachable witnesses which include both the local police constable and the schoolteacher. We shall have to pay him something by way of compensation. Captain Macready's ship's company have caused us to incur substantial unforseen expenses. It is not something to recommend them to us in a more general sense." Mudge paused. "I propose one of us chairs an enquiry aboard *Caryatid* at Porth Ardur to establish our side of the case. It will at least give Macready a chance to tell us his version. Mr Davies, I fear, may be a little self-raising in his claim." They dutifully laughed at Mudge's joke as he looked round the table.

"Captain Jesmond?"

The old man shook his head. "I'm damned if I'm going down there as the hangman, Charlie. Get the new boy to do it."

"Captain Blake?"

"I'm afraid my diary is full, Sir Charles. I agree with Jesmond. Captain Stanier seems the ideal candidate . . . It'll be good experience for him too." And so it went on until Mudge confirmed the matter.

"I agree then. You'll be the best man for the task, Stanier. You know the place better than most of us who have only visited on inspection cruises, you know the man, you know the local background. In fact Macready's probably lucky to have an old friend to attend to the business."

And thus, it being a tradition in the Celtic Lighthouse Service, Captain Sir Charles Mudge brought his polished wood gavel down three times on the table top, where an area of the glossy wood had been thus defaced by centuries of the practice, and the matter was concluded. The blows rang loud and triumphant in Captain Stanier's ears. It hardly seemed possible that the day had ended so well. His moment of uncertainty had been smoothed away; and he had been rewarded to an extent far beyond his most fanciful anticipation. The downfall of Captain Septimus Macready was in his hand.

He was filled with a boyish glee as his limousine sped towards his town flat.

Caroline Stanier received her husband with the customary Martini cocktail. He did not really enjoy Martini cocktails, but the ritual was but a prelude to a greater event, and this helped make the drink more palatable. Caroline had long ago recognised her handsome husband for a vain and biddable man and had engineered their marriage with a precision that in anyone else might have been called cold. Stanier himself, being a man of natural conceit with an early realisation that he was attractive to women, had largely taken their marriage as a matter of course. The business of satisfying women had been ingrained upon his not unwilling perception as a young officer in the I & O's liners. It was expected of them, a matter of duty. It never occurred to Stainer that Caroline had picked him up from the wreckage of his career and his first command from motives of her own. She had lost a father to whom she was close, and understandably he thought that she sought some consolation in the arms of a sympathetic lover. Their losses were, Stanier thought, the coincidental points of their lives. That Caroline also took a great interest in her late father's business enterprises pleased Stanier. She was intelligent, a modern and progressive woman, with whom he could discuss matters. Not that he ever actually sought her advice, of course, but Caroline would almost always have a gratifying grasp of a situation. Naturally she had never sought a seat on the Board of the Cambrian Steam Navigation Company, remaining content to let her adored husband guide its affairs.

Senior staff at the steamship company's office might be heard to venture a contrary opinion. They might, over a drink, even be persuaded to reveal that they considered Mrs Stanier more than an *éminence grise*, but this fact was not obvious, least of all to Stanier himself, and it was generally considered politic to say nothing. Mrs Stanier had quietly engineered the dismissal of at least two senior employees, both of whom she was rumoured to have been unusually fond of.

Within five minutes of his arrival home, Stanier had outlined the events of the day and was already basking in his wife's approval. He stood holding his glass, his arm resting on the marble overmantel. One leg was crossed elegantly over the other while she regarded him from a sofa, the long length of her lower leg tantalisingly exposed. She drove the sweet feelings of incipient revenge from his mind, forcing him to reiterate the deliberations he had had over his lunch with Lord Dungarth and Mr Duncan Smith, the member for Porth Ardur.

"They are much more important than silly old Macready and his little ship, my sweet,' Caroline prompted, setting down her cocktail glass, getting up and leaning against him. She kissed him on the cheek. He felt the warmth of her lean body against his own and marvelled, for the umpteenth time, that so boyish a form could so arouse him. She felt this and smiled, placing her hands on his hips and drawing him away from the fireplace.

"Caro—"

Her skirt fluttered about her ankles and she stepped out of it, lying back on the sofa already naked where he sought her as he dropped his trousers and helplessly thrust at her.

"Caro—"

"We're dining out tonight, my sweet," she said a few minutes later, sliding out from under him. Bending down she recovered her skirt and strode towards the bathroom.

"Oh? Who with?" he mumbled, still face down, kneeling where his rutting had left him.

"The Pomeroys," she said, pausing for a moment by the bathroom door.

"Oh no." He looked round at her frowning. "Why them?"

"Because Pom's got a lot of money and he's looking for a good investment."

"How d'you know he's looking for a good investment? I thought he put all his money into those ridiculous African heads."

"They aren't African, they're Tasmanian and while they may be ridiculous, they are also valued and sought after. As for what is ridiculous, my sweet, you are at the moment, with your shirt-tails hanging out and your dear little bottom showing. We've to be there by eight."

Stanier always felt ill at ease in the company of Mrs Pomeroy. Five years ago, when he had first gone west to Porth Ardur as an ambitious young harbour master, he had started a passionate affair with a certain Tegwyn Morgan. It had culminated when Sir Hector Blackadder, on appointing Stanier master of his yacht, invited him to bring along a 'companion'. He took Tegwyn but in the emotional aftermath of the shipwreck, Stanier had found their love played out, gone like the yacht herself. Instead he was infatuated with Caroline Blackadder while Tegwyn had formed an attachment to Sir Hector's guest, an odd character called Pomeroy. It was as though their affair had simply vanished, like the *Sea Dragon* herself.

Stanier always considered Tegwyn's relationship with Pomeroy as 'an attachment', partly because he could not really understand why she had ceased to fawn upon Stanier himself, but mainly because Pomeroy seemed such an unlikely husband for the stunningly beautiful country girl. An ex-Etonian Guards officer, Pomeroy was at best an epicure, a collector of art, a quiet and exquisite dandy, and at worst a suspect character, a rather dodgy queen. Stanier, of course, thought he recognised the type, but what he found even more disquieting and incomprehensible was the effect this attachment had had on Tegwyn. Pomeroy had accomplished a transformation not, like Professor Higgins, in the matter of her accent, for her Celtic lilt was charming, nor in her demeanour which was naturally proud and upright, but in her manners and her personal magnetism. A fiercely passionate woman, Pomeroy had made of her a society hostess of distinction and, in their apparently blissful happiness, he disarmed all but a hardened and prejudiced clique who clung to notions of his own perversity. The only remaining evidence of this was a lack of children, which was circumstantial enough.

Pomeroy had other interests. He collected rather more than carved Tasmanian heads. The Pomeroys' huge flat contained several reception rooms each given over to distinct areas of

Pomeroy's acquisitive interests. One, dominated by a Poussin but also containing a small work attributed to Vermeer, contained his older paintings; another held later works including a Renoir, a Georges Roualt and a Puvis de Chavannes. In yet a third, lit by subdued lighting and with walls of dark green, several large sculptures of the male nude stood like petrified guests left behind by some wicked fairy who had deprived them of their clothes at the same moment she had taken their lives. Finally, a fourth held Pomeroy's spectacular collection of ethnography, a subject in which he was becoming increasingly interested. At half past eight he was conducting his guests round his latest acquisitions, some strange wood carvings, he explained, fashioned by the extinct natives of Tasmania.

"It is strange, is it not, that these are almost all that is left of a people quite literally hunted down and shot like wild animals? Stranger too that they should end up here, in an apartment on the other side of the world."

"Very odd," agreed Stanier, though his wonder was a conclusion arrived at by a less philosophical route.

"What exactly are they, Pom?" Caroline asked, taking her host's arm in cosy intimacy.

"We don't know, Caroline; not exactly anyway. One can conjecture, of course, but without even so much as a single descendant to give us a clue, the nearest guess we can take has to be helped by matching them against what we know of mainland Australian Aboriginal culture—"

"And?"

"We are still none the wiser."

"I think they are just tree roots," said Tegwyn smiling archly, "but beautiful tree-roots—"

"Tegwyn discovered, due to her innate irreverence and philistinism, that if you blew through these holes which might represent eye sockets, you produce a most beautiful low note. Listen—"

And Pomeroy put the largest of these dark and grotesque objects to his mouth. The low sound vibrated in the room in a curiously soothing note of such low register that Caroline shuddered. "Oh, that sounds horrible—"

"Like the dying note of a race of people, I think," Pomeroy said with such seriousness that the fanciful image seemed stamped upon the strange artefacts. He laid the odd, twisted shape down again, adding, "full of a terrible and prophetic melancholy."

For a moment they stood, their drinks unsipped in the wake of the note, as though momentarily held in thrall by a strange, elusive magic. Then Stanier suddenly resented this lugubrious shadow thrown across his day.

"Well, Pomeroy, it's very interesting, but I've a proposition to discuss with you. I don't expect Caro mentioned it."

Pomeroy threw a quick, complicit glance towards Caroline who disguised the wry twist to her mouth with the rim of her glass.

"Come, Caro, let's leave the men to talk business for a moment, I'm sure you and I could use another drink." Tegwyn led Caroline out of the room and into the lounge. As Tegwyn poured them each another drink, Caroline said, "Jimmy's going down to Porth Ardur next week."

Tegwyn's eyes widened. "Oh? What on earth for?"

"Oh, some sort of enquiry to do with the Lighthouse Service. He went to his first board meeting as a Commissioner today. He's rather full of it all."

"I expect Pom's Tasmanian carvings left him rather cold then."

"I shouldn't wonder. They chilled me a bit too."

Tegwyn laughed. "I'll ask Jimmy about it over dinner," she said. "It'll make him feel better."

"That's very sweet of you," Caroline smiled, accepting the refilled glass.

"Will he mind?"

"Mind?" Caroline frowned. "What, you asking him?"

"No," Tegwyn laughed again, "mind going to Porth Ardur."

"Why should he mind?" Caroline asked sharply.

"Well, he must have some difficult memories . . . You know, the *Sea Dragon*—"

"And you, my dear," Caroline put in pointedly, adding wryly, "but Jimmy's made of stern stuff—"

"Oh, I didn't imply otherwise, I assure you, it's just that we all have a peculiar attachment to the place."

"I don't, I didn't grow up there!" Caroline said, suddenly almost hostile.

"No, my dear, but the place played its part in your life," Tegwyn riposted with a gently compelling firmness, quite unabashed. "Without Porth Ardur there would be no Jimmy—"

"What's that about Porth Ardur?" asked Stanier, blundering into the conversation as the two men rejoined their wives. But the question hung unanswered in the air as dinner was announced and after they had sat down Stanier gave voice to a more important preoccupation, grinning across at Caroline.

"Well, my dear," he declaimed, "old Pom's on board, aren't you, Pom?"

Pomeroy inclined his head. "So it seems, James, so it seems."

"You *have* had a good day then, James," said Tegwyn smiling at him.

"Absolutely," said Stanier, tucking in his napkin and picking up his soup spoon. "Absolutely."

The Enquiry

The letter announcing the holding of 'an enquiry into the late events occurring at Porth Neigwl' signed by the Secretary to the Commissioners for Celtic Lighthouses, was awaiting *Caryatid*'s return to her home port of Porth Ardur. The chilly formality of the tone taken by a man Macready regarded as a cold fish at the best of times, nevertheless sent a shiver of apprehension down his spine. For some time now, Captain Macready had been subject to slight feelings of disquiet whenever he was in Porth Ardur. He was no longer quite the master of his own destiny he had once been. Since his wife Gwendolyn discovered the existence of her husband's love affair with Justine Morgan, their marriage had become a neat, very civilised and mutual accommodation. With his former dancing partner Justine quietly installed upon the island of Ynsycraven, Macready could have been said to enjoy the best of both worlds, and he kept the agreement reached with his wife to the letter. He conferred upon her, undiminished, all the respectability and attentiveness that was her due as the wife of the commander of the lighthouse tender *Caryatid*, a position of considerable social prestige in Porth Ardur, establishing Gwendolyn as one of the principal wives of the town. But Macready had a conscience and he had once loved Gwendolyn, for all her subsequent frigidity. That he had later fallen for the voluptuous widow Morgan was both Macready's salvation and his tragedy, rescuing him from the bleak fidelity forced by sexual indifference upon decent middle-aged men, but saddling him with a deep and ineluctable guilt made worse by the reflection that circumstance and

36

passion meant that he could never repudiate Gwendolyn, nor fully acknowledge Justine. Somehow his presence in Port Ardur exposed Macready's conscience to moments of vulnerability. The news of the enquiry now dripped like acid into these cracks in his self-esteem.

He set the letter down on his desk. The so-called late events had turned out rather well, he thought. It was true that the Mermaid Bakery had suffered somewhat, but a hole in mortared granite was easy enough to repair and the broken slates which had skidded off the disturbed roof could be readily replaced from the quarry not half a mile from the little port. Most of the destruction had been wrought by the front roller, the collapsing masonry inflicting reciprocal but lesser marring of the runaway machine. As for the steamroller, the only damage was some scuffing of the paintwork on the boiler front and a rather heavier battering of the funnel. It was a pity that the Chief Engineer's ego was crushed, for it was in the nature of ships and ships' companies that while a man's successes might be recalled upon occasion, his humiliations and errors pass quickly into local legend. One was, it was frequently averred, only as good as one's last mistake, a circumstance compounded by the fact, Macready ruminated, that chief engineers tended to be odd individuals who believed that they were in fact the real commanders of ships. The argument that without them the ship would not work, failed to hold water. Macready naturally knew better. As a real commander he appreciated the value of the key individuals within his crew and knew that as much depended upon a cook as upon a chief engineer. A crew were hungry three times a day whether or not the engines worked. A good commander always knew his own reputation rested upon the quality of his ship's cook.

Conditioned by such considerations, Macready regarded professional matters with more detachment than the Chief who had, after detaching himself from the steamroller and the clutches of the local constabulary, retired to his cabin and locked the door. Macready disregarded this unfortunate petulance. He was confronted with the problem of removing the steamroller from its position perched half in and half out of the bakery and in this, in his opinion, his crew had excelled.

It is true he would have expected nothing else, for his officers and men regarded themselves as possessing infinite resource as seamen and what the gathering population of Porth Neigwl and the surrounding hinterland were coming to regard as a major disaster, had been swiftly rescued. In the wake of the disappearing Chief Engineer, the Second strode briskly, manning the beleaguered steamroller with commendable promptitude while Charlie Farthing, the Bosun and deck crew had rapidly laid out upon the quay a complicated array of blocks and tackles made up of two 120-fathom coils of four-inch manila hemp. The purpose of this had been to withdraw the roller from the flank of the bakery, since the precarious position of the machine no longer allowed the driving wheels to gain traction with the surface of the pier. The operation had attracted a larger crowd than its initial discharge from the ship and, in due course, even the schoolchildren returned, to be given a lecture by their teacher on the mechanical advantage the sailors would derive from their impressive arrangement of 'rope and pulleys'. The labouring seamen, making the final tucks in the long splices that joined the two coils of hemp, had been heard to correct this inaccuracy with the expression 'block and tackle', the latter word pronounced to rhyme with 'take-all', but this did not deter the schoolmistress. Afterwards several of the younger and more muscular sailors had attributed her interest not to the practical application of physics, but to their own physical attributes about the upper arms and shoulders which were, by any standards, impressive.

In due course, when these preparations were completed and *Caryatid* had provided a massive inertia against which even a steamroller might be pulled, the running part of the system had been taken to her powerful forward capstan. Then, with four turns of rope about its upright drum, the steamroller had been smoothly drawn from its lodgement in the Mermaid Bakery with less fuss than a tooth is pulled. Despite the ease with which this had been accomplished, it had roused a hearty cheer from the onlookers, which deeply gratified Captain Macready, Mr Farthing, the Second Engineer, the seamen and those members of *Caryatid*'s crew who took no active part in the operation, but whose membership of the crew entitled them to some reflected glory. The spontaneous sound of acknowledgement had brought no comfort to the mortified Chief Engineer. The Captain's insulting words still rang in his ears and the flour dust still lay heavily upon his person and all about his cabin. He was a grown man and could not weep. He had had only a dram or two in a bottle of whisky which he soon despatched, and could only counter the wretchedness of his humiliation by blaming all upon the treachery of his supposed friend and colleague, Gwyn Roberts, the Second Engineer.

Macready became aware of the Chief Engineer's self-imposed solitary confinement after the gale had come and gone, and *Caryatid* lay off Mitre Rock lighthouse, while a working party cleaned out the station's freshwater tanks. He realised he had not seen the Chief for several days and, upon enquiring his whereabouts from Mr Farthing, had been informed that the Chief had taken to his bed. Being a conscientious commander, Macready had visited the cabin and ordered the Chief to unlock the door, slipping inside while the curious Steward stood unhelpfully outside.

"Pull yourself together, man," Macready had advised, sniffing the stale air of the cabin, drawing back the chintz curtains at the cabin portlights and rounding upon the supine Chief as he lay under a blanket. "Get up at once!"

"There was no need for you to say what you did, Captain. It was an insult!"

"An insult, was it?" responded Macready, genuinely bemused. "And how long have we known each other, Chief? D'you think I'd deliberately *insult* a man who had kept up steam for me all these years? What d'you take me for, an ingrate? Why should I want to insult you in a moment of such difficulty? Damn it, Chief, I only invited you to laugh at yourself, to ease the tension. It was an old joke between us, man. The old oil and water joke." The Captain had paused, awaiting the impact of his words and the reaction they might provoke.

Nothing came from the shattered Chief beyond the muttered admission that, "I haven't been able to sleep since."

Macready had slapped his colleague on the leg and laughed.

"Come on, Chief, you know very well that if you can't take a joke you shouldn't have joined! I'll see you in the saloon at dinner." And with that Macready had left the man to shave off the growth of untidy stubble that had accentuated his pathetic state.

Now, recalling the whole incident under the reviving influence of the Secretary's letter, Macready's sense of disquiet grew. If the Chief chose, he might make matters awkward. The Captain sighed, slipping a raincoat over his uniform, for it was almost dark and drizzling outside. The rest of his mail he would leave until tomorrow. He needed the walk home to think matters over. One of the consequences of his arrangement with Gwendolyn was that she was no longer prepared to discuss with him the business of the Lighthouse Service. It was one small slice of freedom she had recovered from the partial deconstruction of their marriage.

As he walked into the wet evening, through the puddles of Porth Ardur's ill-lit streets, Macready considered the forthcoming enquiry. He guessed it owed its origin to a complaint from the owner of the Mermaid Bakery. Macready himself had advised the excitable man to make a claim, in the knowledge that the Lighthouse Service would have covered the carriage of the steamroller in one of its ships, even though the matter itself was a favour to the local authority on Ynys Meini. Macready was used to the grasping ways of islanders; the matter was of consuming local interest and the maximum would be made of it by Ifor Davies. He supposed the Commissioners had decided to carry out a full investigation at the request of their underwriters and satisfy themselves that the matter really was an accident.

Of that Macready had no doubt and this conclusion, reached as he opened his front garden gate, cleared his mind for his encounter with Gwendolyn.

For years the twin existences of Captain Septimus Macready and his wife had run, like railway lines, along equidistant parallel lines. The years when Macready had partnered Justine in the ballroom dancing championships had been oddly innocent, enabling him for a long time to rest content with the symmetry of his marriage and the voluptuous beauty of the woman with whom he most conspicuously appeared in public. Yet, when the inevitable happened and husband and wife had afterwards settled their differences, the railway lines remained, running straight and true towards the horizon, if at a wider gauge.

Septimus's infidelity had empowered his wife and diminished him when he was with her. It was a fair payment for the joy of loving Justine, but convention compensated this by making him spend more time with Gwendolyn than he ever could with Justine. It was this uneasy feeling, compounded of guilt and a mild discontent that he knew he had no right to feel, that assailed him in Porth Ardur. It reached its greatest intensity as he turned the key in the lock and prepared himself for the customary bland anodyne greeting to his wife.

Once this private and awkward formality was over it was customary for them to discuss any domestic matters that might require them to function together. There were few enough of these nowadays, Gwendolyn filling her life with worthy activities and needing only the periodic appearance of her husband to formally endorse her status. A church service, perhaps, a wedding, or the occasional meeting of the parochial church council might be advantageously attended in his company. Since she ran the house herself and a gardener-cum-handyman was sent up from the buoy-yard once a week, he really had little to attend to when ashore, a circumstance that nowadays irked him and left him fretting over the hours he was wasting away from Justine. But it was part of the bargain he had struck with Gwendolyn, part of the price he paid for continuing infidelity and acknowledgement of the debt he owed his wife for this freedom. Above all, *her* life was to be unmoved by his great love affair and for this reason he was astonished when she put on her glasses, picked up a letter and asked him to sit down.

"There is something I wish to discuss with you."

He did as he was told, swiftly dismissing the unbidden thought that this might at last be a request for a divorce. "What is it, m'dear?" he asked, helping himself to a small peg of whisky and sitting opposite to her.

"I have had a letter from a firm of solicitors representing the Ardurian Slate Company."

"What on earth do they want?" Macready asked, frowning

over his glass and thinking of the rundown slate quarry that ripped into the far flank of Mynydd Uchaf, the mountain that rose behind Port Ardur, the summit of which could be seen far out at sea.

"They have apparently been bought up by another company which intends to invest heavily in a new mine," Gwendolyn went on crisply.

"A mine?" Macready was confused, supposing his wife had mistakenly used the wrong noun.

"Yes, Septimus, a mine. Not a quarry. A mine. A coal mine."

"Oh no, not that old story about coal again—"

"Yes, and apparently it is no longer a story, it is a fact. For some time I have known of geologists working over by Kynedoch and according to this letter the Ardurian Slate Company in its revived form wishes to exploit the deposit."

A small chink of light was dawning upon Macready, sparked by Gwendolyn's mention of Kynedoch. Some eighteen months earlier an elderly but redoubtable widow who ran a farm just outside the village of Kynedoch, had died. Mrs Evans left an idiot son and the title deeds of the farm to the worthy Mrs Macready, who, seeing this as a further burden to her already saddened existence, accepted it as the Lord's will. A place was found for the son in a mental hospital and the two labourers who had helped Mrs Evans, both distant cousins of the widow, were kept on to run the farm. Maintenance of the rundown farmhouse, however, was quite beyond the resources generated by the place and, on the sole occasion he was consulted, Macready had recommended sale, albeit with modest financial provision being made for the two brothers. Gwendolyn had demurred, placing one further barrier between them. However, thanks to her restless energy, the energy taken up in other women by domestic preoccupations and the upbringing of children, Gwendolyn had had some impact on the output of the farm. By abandoning the upkeep of the farmhouse, marketing its produce more effectively and slightly increasing its output, she had provided for herself a small but gratifyingly independent income. Not an ungenerous man, this had pleased Macready. He did not wish to see Gwendolyn unhappy and rejoiced in her success. And what he now sensed Gwendolyn was about to reveal, filled him with a faint but brittle hope.

"Go on, m'dear."

"You are not a stupid man, Septimus," she said, lowering the letter and looking at him over her reading glasses. "You will already have guessed the farm lies over the coal deposit."

"So, what will you do? They are, I assume, making an offer."

"A very handsome offer, as it happens."

"Handsome enough to provide for the Evans brothers?"

"I shall ensure the Evans brothers are employed by the mining company." Gwendolyn's tone was brisk, efficient; her mind was made up.

"So you have decided to sell."

"In principle, yes. I shall try and get a little more, of course. They are obviously eager."

"Good." Macready forbore from pressing his wife further. If she had other plans, plans made possible by the sudden and unexpected results of the hitherto burdensome bequest, it would not do for him to upset them. He must wait; perhaps even play a conciliatory role, for he felt no animosity towards her, fully conceding that she was a wronged woman. "You were right not to sell earlier then, m'dear."

"Of course," she said, half smiling, sensing his weak position and in the full knowledge of her own empowerment. "Do put the kettle on, Septimus."

He rose obediently and, as he passed her, he tapped her affectionately upon the shoulder.

The enquiry was held ten days later. The *Caryatid* had spent a week at sea laying clean buoys off the Hellweather Bank and was berthed for the occasion. On his arrival back in port, Captain Macready received notice that it would be chaired by a Captain Stanier, newly appointed as Commissioner to the Board. Macready dismissed the idea that this was the same pompous fool who had once been harbour master of Porth Ardur and had lost Sir Hector Blackadder's steam yacht *Sea Dragon* on the Hound's Teeth. *That* Stanier he had last heard of as master of one of Cambrian Steam's contemptible old tramp steamers, renowned in the shipping world as being ageing rust buckets of the worst kind. He seemed to recall something that Justine had said, some gossip tittle-tattled from her daughter Tegwyn, that her former boyfriend had married well and left the sea, but then Macready had long ago written *that* Stanier off as a man who kept his brains in his scrotum. This Stanier, he thought, laying the letter down on his desk, would be a man of some distinction. After all, one did not become a Commissioner of Celtic Lighthouses without some standing in the world of shipping.

The following morning the after smoke room was prepared for the occasion. This occupied a fine varnished teak deckhouse situated on the after boat deck of the *Caryatid*. Inside, a table and chairs were secured by short chains to the carpeted deck. This bore some stains of salt and neglect, for it was often used as a store for deck brooms, buckets and holystones. As the deckhands barbarised the teak planking of the surrounding boat deck itself, the officers' Saloon Steward frantically dusted and polished the interior of the smoke room itself.

The place was usually kept locked, for officially it was provided for the private use of the Commissioners when they were afloat in *Caryatid*, giving them a discreet accommodation in which they could attend to those weighty matters upon which they brought their experience and wisdom to bear. In reality, however, the Commissioners rarely went afloat in anything other than their own yacht, the *Naiad*, a specially appointed lighthouse tender in which they inhabited a grand suite and in which they annually cruised the coast, inspecting the work of the many men in their service. In the Silurian Strait and the rim of the adjacent Atlantic, their numbers included the men who manned the Hellweather, Scarrick and St Kenelm's lightvessels, and the Buccabu, Mitre Rock, Quill Point, Goose Rock and Danholm lighthouses. In Port Ardur they comprised the supporting storemen and labourers of the buoy yard, who were supervised by the Area Clerk. The Area Clerk, Mr Dale, was, with the lightvessel skippers and senior keepers of the lighthouses, answerable in turn to Captain Macready, whose superintendence of these personnel was additional to his command of *Caryatid* and her company.

To say that Captain Macready viewed the arrival of the Commissioners either singly or *en masse* with trepidation, would be an exaggeration. He had seen Commissioners come and Commissioners go and they generally conceded most points to his own expertise and local knowledge. But they possessed a formidable statutory and collective power, so that any visitation exposed him to a potential and official criticism. Some, Macready had learned over the long years of his service, made a fetish of winkling out small and petty irregularities in a lighthouse keeper's dress, or the cleanliness of his bedsheets. While Macready knew he had nothing to fear from the annual inspection, his area being run to his own exactingly high standards, the irregular matter of the steamroller and its collision with the Mermaid Bakery might, he thought, ruffle the serenity of his life.

While Mr Farthing chivvied the crew to complete their deck scrubbing and brass polishing, Captain Macready briefed his chief witnesses in his cabin. Having shed their habitual boiler suits, the Chief and Second Engineers were unusually smart in their best doeskin reefer uniforms. They sat upon the Captain's settee attentively while he attempted to coach them.

"Now, gentlemen, it is some time since this unfortunate incident occurred and I think the lapse in time has healed those breaches that you might have felt towards each other, eh?" He waited a few seconds, expecting some reaction from the two engineer officers. The Second looked sideways at the Chief who maintained a silent impassivity which, Macready knew, had unfortunately characterised the relationship between the two men since the day of the incident. "Well, anyway, we none of us want this matter to be made more of than is necessary, do we? I have reported the matter as an accident and recommended the baker at Porth Neigwl recovers the cost of reconstructing his bakery wall. Have you anything to add?"

"No, sir," responded the Second. The Chief remained silent.

"Well, Chief?" Macready prompted.

"Whatever you say, sir."

"I do say, Chief," Macready rumbled ominously. Whatever

this Stanier fellow said or decided today, he would be on the train back to the capital tonight and Macready would revert to his position of primacy. He saw the Chief's bulk shift slightly in acknowledgement of the implicit threat. There was a knock at the door.

"Come in. Ah, Mr Farthing . . . News?"

"Old Dale's just waved the scarlet hanky, sir."

"Ah. Very good. Quartermaster all ready?"

"Everything's ready, sir."

Macready smiled. "Of course it is."

Mr Dale, the Area Clerk, had received a telephone call from his brother the stationmaster to let them know that their cousin the taxi driver had just picked up his important passenger from the train. Macready stood, gathering the file from his desk. "Very well, gentlemen. Let's go."

Realisation that it was the same Stanier hit Macready like a physical blow. He was obliged to salute the man, obliged to call him 'sir', obliged to mutter pleasantries as Stanier greeted him, his voice edged with sinister intent.

"So, Captain Macready, we meet again."

Stanier snubbed Macready's introduction of his officers and turned aft, looking disdainfully at the houses of Porth Ardur as they climbed up the lower slopes of Mynydd Uchaf. "Nothing much changes here, I see." The remark implied that while Porth Ardur stood still in its provincial slumber, Captain James St John Stanier had changed a great deal. Macready noticed it in his eyes where lurked a steely intent that Macready felt as keenly threatening as a knife blade. After pausing for a few moments looking past the ensign as it flapped in the breeze, Stanier turned sharply.

"Well, Macready, let's get down to business."

They shuffled into the smoke room and settled down round the table while the Saloon Steward served them coffee. Stanier had brought with him one of the clerks from headquarters. The man doled out papers, adding to the individual files each officer had prepared. Macready, discomfitted by Stanier's sudden appearance, felt his confidence ebb. There could be little doubt but that the man would seek revenge. He caught

Mr Farthing's eye. Charlie too was pale with apprehension and Macready looked away. He felt chastened, like a small boy caught scrumping. Then Stanier briskly swept them up in the business of the forenoon.

"Well, gentlemen, you have before you the signed deposition of a certain Mr Ifor Davies of the Mermaid Bakery, Porth Neigwl on the Island of Stones, otherwise known as Ynys Meini . . ." Stanier made the most of it. He read right through this outrageously inaccurate and exaggerated document. On completion he then read through the report submitted by Macready. A man of precise thought and instant decision, Macready's was a model of brevity, setting out the facts in chronological sequence. It took Stanier only a moment to read it and then he laid it down and leaned forward on his elbows.

"I find it difficult to square these two accounts, Captain Macready," Stanier said. "Yours is so lacking in detail as to suggest concealment of something."

Macready, who had by now recovered some of his composure, also leaned forward. He did not wish to appear truculent, merely to block each thrust of his enemy with a polite parry. "My account, Captain Stanier, gives you the facts without the embroidery of any speculation. It does not deny the central fact that, despite his best endeavours, the Chief Engineer was unable to turn the machine fast enough and unfortunately crashed through the wall of the Mermaid Bakery. Some loss of flour was inevitable, but I am certain that no-one has subsequently starved and I know that the *Kurnow* shipped extra flour from Beynon's Bakery here in Port Ardur the following day."

"Then you admit to carelessness?"

"In what way?"

"Why, you have just said that your Chief Engineer was unable to turn the machine fast enough. Now, Captain Macready," Stanier went on, ignoring the presence of the culpable officer sitting on Macready's right hand, "it occurs to me that either the corner was too sharp for the geometry of the steamroller's steering, or the machine was going too fast to allow the driver to turn the steering gear fast enough."

47

Here the accompanying clerk nodded, for it was really his idea that the error resulted from either of these two causes and that Stanier should open with this line of questioning.

"I do not dispute that, Captain Stanier." Macready turned to the Chief. "Do you wish to add anything, Chief?" he asked.

Reluctance showed in the Chief Engineer's expression. He coughed with embarrassment, but bravely admitted, "I had not allowed for the time it took to turn the steering wheel, sir. So yes, the steamroller was going too fast. I suppose to that extent I was careless."

"That is a handsome admission, Chief," Stanier said, smiling condescendingly, disarming the unfortunate engineer. "But I do not seek a scapegoat, merely to establish the facts." The Chief nodded and swallowed, relaxing a trifle. "But there is the matter of mitigation, is there not?"

Macready looked up as the Chief swung his uncomprehending face to Stanier. "Mitigation, sir?"

"Provocation really, Chief, wouldn't you say, eh?" It was clear to Macready that Stanier was prompting the Chief and a small ganglion of fear was unravelling itself in Macready's gut. A pregnant silence filled the room. Outside a sailor walked past carrying a tin of white paint. The officers present sat waiting for Stanier's next pronouncement, for they had nothing to contribute. Stanier drew in his breath, as though the act automatically drew after his inhalation, the gaze and attention of the *Caryatid*'s assembled officers.

"Oh, your loyalty does you credit, gentlemen. Yes, indeed. Loyalty is a characteristic I esteem highly, particularly when it is given to the Lighthouse Service where it belongs. Indeed your salaries place you under an obligation to render it to the Lighthouse Service. I therefore caution you against misplacing it, gentlemen. Do not misplace it." Stanier looked round the ring of faces. He smiled inwardly; he had their attention now. The briefest mention of salaries, the small, implied but deadly threat to their jobs would, he knew, open up the crack which existed between their corporate existence in their uniforms, and the wretched little lives that lived inside their pink skins. After the Service, loyalty went to the Captain and Stanier's insinuation was intended to prise it out, like an escargot from its shell.

"You know what I mean, gentlemen, don't you . . ." Stanier's tone hardened as his eyebrows came together into a forbidding frown. It was not a question.

"I think I know what you are trying to imply," Mr Farthing said suddenly, impetuously breaking the silence.

"Oh, and what is that?" snapped Stanier, leaning forward towards the Mate.

"Perhaps you would be kind enough to tell us, Captain Stanier," Macready interjected quickly, frowning at Farthing.

"Oh I will, Captain Macready. You see, it is the matter of the insult you shouted at the Chief Engineer, making him lose concentration. Such a provocation—"

"How would it make the Chief lose concentration?" responded Macready, "since he had already hit the bakery wall?"

"Then you at least admit that you insulted the Chief?" Stanier said, his eyebrows now each individually arched above triumphantly gleaming eyes.

"I merely made—"

"Did Captain Macready insult you, Chief?"

"Well—" The Chief was about to say 'not exactly' and admit he had made more of the Captain's joke than he intended, but he was unused to these formal and intimidating proceedings, and Stanier gave him no chance.

"I quite understand," Stanier went on, "your reluctance to implicate the Captain, Chief. It does you credit, it really does, but if that is what happened let's openly admit the matter—"

"Oh, this is preposterous." Charlie Farthing was on his feet. "We all know that Captain Macready made a joke, and the joke was made after the steamroller was embedded in the wall of the bakery. It upset the Chief, but it was not the cause of the accident. This whole thing's a farce—"

"Sit down, Mr Farthing, I'll ask for your contribution when I want it."

"No, I won't sit down, Captain Stanier. You are not impartial in this matter. See to it that your clerk writes down in the minuted proceedings of this enquiry that you have an old score to settle with Captain Macready, that you are not impartial and that you have sought to lead the witnesses in order to achieve some petty revenge—"

"Sit down, sir! You are talking nonsense!" Stanier roared.

"I will not sit down—"

"Sit down, Mr Farthing." Macready broke in and the Mate reluctantly obeyed.

"I shall not tolerate impertinence such as we have just witnessed, Captain Macready and I shall temporarily suspend these proceedings . . . Please clear this smoke room as I wish to consider matters."

Caryatid's officers trooped out onto the sunlit boat deck and Macready led them forward to his cabin.

"That was a bloody silly thing to do, Charlie," Macready began, but Charlie shook his head.

"You know the man, sir—"

"Is he the same bugger that used to be the harbour master?" the Chief asked.

"Of course he is," responded Farthing tartly. "He's not forgotten how things were between the Captain and himself if you have."

"Well I'm damned. I see his game now, the cheeky bugger." The Chief turned to Macready, flushing with embarrassment. "I'm sorry if I've caused you trouble, sir—"

"Just tell me one thing, Chief. Did you make a complaint against me behind my back?"

The Chief frowned. "Good heavens, no sir! Why should I be wanting to do that?"

"I've no idea. I just wanted to establish where the story of this shouted insult came from. I'm sorry if it upset you, and perhaps it was bad taste to have made fun of you at such a moment, but any malice in the occasion has been added by that bloody Ifor Davies at Porth Neigwl and he's only out for what he can get."

"Well, what's going to happen then, sir?" the Chief asked, his face anxious with honest concern.

"I don't know. A reprimand for me and Mr Farthing will get a black mark."

"I've some photos, sir," said the Second, speaking for the first time. "They show the whole thing, including the state of damage after the steamroller was pulled out."

"Why didn't you tell us before?" expostulated Macready.

"I didn't want to embarrass the Chief, sir."

Macready looked at the Chief Engineer. "What d'you say to showing them to his lordship, Chief?"

"I'd show him my fucking arse if I thought it would do any good, sir, so I would . . ."

And they were all laughing when Stanier's clerk summoned them back into the smoke room.

"It is my intention to recommend—"

"I'd like to stop you there, Captain Stanier," Macready said. "We have a sequence of photographs to show you which illustrate the problem we had . . ."

The black and white shots were deployed in front of Stanier who stared at them. "These do not show when Captain Macready shouted his insult—"

"Captain Macready did not insult me, sir," the Chief said. "He had a joke at my expense. Oil and water, you know the sort of thing. I admit to being annoyed at the time, but nothing more."

For the first time Macready saw the old Stanier, the blustering stuffed shirt with no wind in his sails, with no real confidence and less of a case.

"The whole thing was an accident," the Chief went on and Macready rejoiced as the old Chief finally emerged manfully from his humiliation. "We were doing the island a favour and unfortunately I misjudged the corner. You can see from the Second's last shot that the damage wasn't all that extensive. You can't trust those islanders. They think the rest of the world owes them a living, you know. They're notorious for trying anything to turn a buck to their advantage. Get three quotes for repairs from local builders and then another from Taylor here in Porth Ardur and I'll put money on the last being cheaper despite the need to travel offshore."

"Thank you, Chief," broke in Stanier, his voice cold. "When the Board needs your advice on such matters, I am sure it will ask for it. Very well, I shall now finally wind this enquiry up. I have noted all your remarks . . ." Stanier paused, allowing his clerk to nod in agreement. Stanier coughed self-importantly. "I have also noted the personal remarks levelled by Mr, er . . ."

"Farthing," prompted the Clerk.

"In their specifics, I hope, Captain Stanier," Farthing broke in, but Stanier ignored him and rumbled on to his conclusion.

"And these matters will be laid before the Board at next Tuesday's meeting."

Stanier rose and shuffled papers. Once again the officers trooped out, though Stanier called after Macready to remain a moment. While his clerk stuffed the files into a briefcase, Stanier drew Macready to the after end of the smoke room. Outside the glass-panelled doors a ladder led down onto the after deck and the mooring bitts, capstans and towing gear. Above the rail flew the defaced ensign of the Commissioners.

"It was not my intention to mention the past, Captain Macready. It's unfortunate young Farthing did so." Macready said nothing. 'Young' Farthing was not much younger than Stanier, but he forbore from correcting the Commissioner. "I don't think he's the sort of officer we want in the Lighthouse Service—"

"On the contrary, Captain Stanier, he is diligent, efficient and reliable."

"He had no right to say what he did. He has no evidence for it and in any case the matter is largely irrelevant. Between ourselves, Captain Macready, this ship's days are numbered. She is too old, too expensive and with additional costs like the one we have to address in the case of Mr Ifor Davies, a burden on the Service. She will not be replaced. Frankly I shall not be sorry. The Board is considering economies which will make her and all her company redundant." Stanier smiled at Macready. "Including Mr Farthing, Captain Macready, not to mention yourself."

After Stanier had gone, Macready stood for some time staring abstractedly after the departing taxi. He thought of a hundred things he should have said. He could, for instance, have reminded Stanier that the Commissioner only held his own master's certificate courtesy of Macready himself, but these considerations were moved by *l'esprit de l'escalier*. Macready was in a kind of numb shock. Although Stanier had unwittingly reunited the *Caryatid*'s officers, his news threatened to destroy their whole world.

An Agent of the Devil

In the fortnight following the enquiry, Captain Macready threw himself into his work in an attempt to shove out of his mind the news that Stanier's malice had insinuated into it. *Caryatid* loaded the gleaming red, black and chequered steel buoys from the buoy yard at Porth Ardur, deploying them at sea on their lonely stations and removing the rusty, weedy and barnacle-encrusted units they replaced. Charlie Farthing in his sea-boots waded among heaps of scraped mussels and oarweed, heaving and veering heavy chain moorings and the huge, cast-iron sinkers that anchored these remote aids to navigation to their lonely stations. *Caryatid* anchored off various lighthouses and worked her boats back and forth, pumping oil and water into the reservoirs and tanks attached to each of the tall stone towers. They spent a week, as they did every month, steaming round the entire Sea Area, changing the crews of the lightvessels and lighthouses and on one occasion they towed a lightvessel to a dry-dock on the north-west coast, enjoying a run ashore, roistering like deep-sea men amid the purlieus of the great port.

Macready even took the ship to an anchorage off Ynyscraven more times than were strictly necessary in order that he could enjoy the company of Justine to whom, in the end, he confided the dreadful news. Long years of widowhood and a positive disposition enabled Justine to console herself with her situation. She had found in Sonia Farthing, Charlie's wife and her next-door neighbour, a true friend and this deep attachment in some way consoled them for the separation from their men they both endured. Furthermore, Sonia's total and

53

committed love of the island helped to reconcile Justine to her own fate. However, in the news that Macready now brought to her, Justine perceived the possibility of a brighter future.

"But if Gwendolyn was made financially independent by the sale of her farm, Septimus, and you were to retire, we could be happy here."

"I should leave Gwendolyn, you mean?" he asked, sitting up and throwing his legs over the edge of the bed.

"Of course. Without a ship you will have to settle somewhere. Frankly, my love," she said, putting her arms about him and leaning her head upon his naked back, "once *Caryatid* has gone—"

"I know, I know," he interrupted irritably, "I shall amount to nothing in Porth Ardur."

"Women will envy Gwendolyn her full independence. She will have the sympathy due wronged women and she will be able to do what she likes. Let Stanier have his petty way. A man who nurses all that venom will never be happy. Think what *we* stand to gain ourselves – an end to these dawn partings."

Macready shook his head, gently detaching himself from her embrace. "There is not only us to be considered, my darling." He paused and pulled his shirt over his head. "What about the crew and all their families? A few of the older men will want to retire, of course, but the younger ones will have nothing."

"What about this new mine—"

"Oh, Justine, no self-respecting seaman wants to work in a mine, even an open-cast mine. Anyway, what about Charlie and Sonia?"

"Ah, now there there is a ray of hope. The Reeve really is retiring, he's not well again and this time he has decided to go. Lord Dungarth is due here any day to see the poor old boy. Sonia wants Charlie to take the job."

"Give up the sea, you mean?" Macready scraped at his chin, the rasps of his razor punctuating his words.

"Well, yes." He turned and stared at Justine who lay back on her pillow, one arm behind her head. Her hair spilled about her face and her breasts lay exposed. Macready swallowed and turned back to the mirror, wiping his face and reaching for his collar and tie.

"That would be a pity, but Stanier's knife will be out for Charlie, and Wentworth the Second Mate mentioned he had heard Charlie muttering about resignation." Macready hated upheaval. Evolution was acceptable, natural, but the work of maintaining navigational aids had a timeless quality. The philosophy of dependability rested upon the very principle of constancy. All things had a season; in due course it was right that he should retire. Charlie Farthing had first come to *Caryatid* as Second Mate and had now risen to the position of Chief Mate. In due course, when he himself retired, Charlie would in all probability become the ship's commander. That would be in the fullness of time, but for them both to go within a short period, precipitated by the nastiness of Captain Stanier, flew in the face of logic. Stanier, Macready recalled again, would not now have his master's certificate at all if Macready had not given favourable evidence at the enquiry into the loss of the *Sea Dragon*. It disgusted Macready that Stanier could forget the matter.

"So you are going to fight?"

Macready pulled on his reefer jacket. "I am going to fight for the ship's sake." He paused, bending over her, his eyes softening as she reached up and touched his smooth cheek.

"And you?" Justine asked huskily. "What will you do for yourself?"

"Think of you," he said enigmatically, kissing her and leaving.

Macready met Charlie Farthing on the cliff path down to the beach. After each wished the other a good morning and exchanged a brief remark about the weather, which promised a fine day, they walked for a moment in silence. When they came to the bend in the path from which the ground dropped almost sheer, both men spontaneously paused. From this point the ship, lying peacefully in the anchorage, came into view. They could see the distant activity on the boat deck as Wentworth prepared to lower the starboard motor boat which was to come in and fetch them.

"I, er . . . I hear you have been considering resignation, Charlie."

"Well, sir, I don't think I have done myself any favours and with Stanier newly appointed to the Board, the situation will only get worse. Stanier's that sort of bastard. Besides, I'd like to spend more time with Sonia and, well, there's a possibility that the Reeve's job will fall vacant at last."

"Yes, I heard about it. It's what you've been waiting for, isn't it?"

"Well yes. There was mention of it some time ago. We more or less married with the prospect of my living here and becoming Reeve."

Below, the faint smack of the boat hitting the water came to them and Macready began to walk again. Timed properly, both boat and passengers should reach the beach at the same time. For a little while the two men walked in silence, then Macready said, "Charlie, there's something you should be aware of, but I don't want a word of it made known to another soul. D'you understand?"

"I understand, sir, but is it about the ship being scrapped?"

"You know?" Macready was surprised and stopped abruptly.

"Whispers, scuttlebutt, gossip." They began walking again. "Don't ask me how these things come up, sir, maybe Stanier mentioned something, he spent the night at the Station Hotel. The Bosun's sister waits at the breakfast tables there."

"Ahhh. Yes, and the Clerk . . . He'd want to impress the Clerk, wouldn't he now."

"Exactly."

"But it's not just scrap *Caryatid*, Charlie, it's get rid of the ship altogether. There'd be no replacement. The Area would be taken over and run as a sub-Area from Cavehaven. The *Waterwitch* would cover the Silurian Strait."

Mr Farthing shook his head as they reached the beach and trudged over the shingle. "That must remain confidential," Macready insisted.

"Of course, sir."

The whispers reached Mrs Macready at about the same time. Oddly it was she who was to first learn more than anyone else, for one evening she received an unexpected telephone call from a man announcing himself as David Smith. It took her a moment to realise she was speaking to the local Member of Parliament and a moment later she found she had accepted an invitation to dine with him. She was never quite certain why she so easily agreed, except that she was left a little breathless by the fact that he had called her at all.

"I am holding a constituency surgery in Porth Ardur on Thursday, Mrs Macready, and shall be staying at the Station Hotel that night. Would you be kind enough to dine with me? I have a most important matter to discuss with you in confidence and I should appreciate your not mentioning the matter to a soul until after we have spoken. I don't want to say too much over the telephone either, if you don't mind, but I'm sure you can guess what it's about. Say half past seven? Good. Thank you so much. I look forward to meeting you. Good evening."

And he was gone, leaving Gwendolyn staring at the wallpaper in the hall with a heart beating as though she had just been requested to attend the palace for an audience with the king. For a moment she dithered uncertainly about the purpose of the call, then her natural good sense reasserted itself.

It was the mine, of course.

But then it might also be the ship . . .

Yes, that was it, it *was* the ship! The rumours were true! David Smith MP, who had never so much as visited Porth Ardur in his life before, as far as Gwendolyn Macready knew, was going to do something about the ship. Smith was, Gwendolyn knew, a junior minister, but for precisely what, she could not recall. Yes, she could, he was in the Ministry of Power and that swung her thinking back in favour of the mine. But the certainty, as soon as it had taken root, was deracinated by the man's insistence upon secrecy. No, it was almost certain that he was acting as local MP and therefore it would be the ship . . .

And thus vacillating, Gwendolyn Macready found herself caught up in a heady, speculative night of fitful sleep such as she had not known since she had first set eyes upon the handsome person of the twenty-year-old Septimus Macready.

On Thursday afternoon Gwendolyn took a bath. It was her habit to do this every afternoon, but on this particular occasion she took longer than usual. She had not stopped turning matters over in her mind and, as soon as she had erected a careful argument in favour of the mine being Mr Smith's motivation, it would tumble down. She would chastise herself that she was selfishly pandering to the private fantasies of enrichment that had haunted her since she received that first intimation that the Ardurian Slate Company wished to purchase her farm. It had therefore to be the ship and this was always the eventual and final conclusion which, once reached, allowed her to sleep or get on with the ironing or whatever chore, committee meeting or visit next demanded her attention.

But she bathed and dressed with care for, despite her complex private distaste of intimacy, Gwendolyn Macready remained a woman susceptible to the honour done to her of a private dinner at the invitation of the local MP. There was a seductive hint of intrigue about the matter, not dissimilar to the scenarios painted by the novels she enjoyed reading. No one could guess how the girl that still lurked behind the public face of Mrs Macready still longed for what she had thought a marriage offered. Besides, she had not yet quite lost her looks, she thought, as she reached for her lipstick with a flutter of her heart. She rarely wore lipstick and the idea of putting it on for what she had become to consider a confidential, if not a secret assignation, a meeting with a strange man, gave her an unexpected and delicious frisson of excitement.

David Smith proved to be a short, stocky man. This pleased Gwendolyn as she caught sight of them both shaking hands in a full-length mirror in the dining room of the Station Hotel. She disliked craning up at tall men. She had chosen a maroon silk dress which fell from her shoulders in a modest simplicity which disguised her lack of height. Smith smoothly announced how delighted he was to meet her and how utterly charming she looked. Despite her naturally dismissive reaction to such blandishments, she was unable to suppress a treacherous quiver as he motioned her to sit, nor for a vain moment at least, to pretend she did not need reading glasses to decipher the menu.

When they had ordered and were taking their first sips of

Chablis, Gwendolyn took stock of her host. He was a little younger than herself, she thought, though his brilliantined hair was thinning rapidly. He wore a dark, double-breasted suit and his shoes, she had already noticed, were neat, black and glossily polished. He wore a signet ring with, she thought, a seal set in it and his plain white shirt was tied with a striped tie that could have been regimental.

They ate their first course talking inconsequentially, establishing an atmosphere of relaxed understanding. Gwendolyn learned that Smith was indeed in Porth Ardur on constituency business, but his actual reasons for meeting with her were rather complicated and he would come to them in a minute. He did indeed hold a junior portfolio in the Ministry of Power, but again, this was not quite relevant to what he wished to discuss with her. She also learned that he knew she was married to the commander of the local lighthouse tender, and, as the main course was served and Smith tasted the newly opened bottle of Burgundy, Gwendolyn realised that although she had been in Smith's company for forty minutes, she was still none the wiser as to his motivation.

Smith on the other hand had learned that Mrs Macready was a cool and intelligent woman, that she was guarded in her admissions and therefore possessed a degree of discretion. Although she seemed essentially a self-effacing person, he detected a desire, perhaps even a positive ambition, to be effectual. She was also, he knew, susceptible to a little attentiveness, though wise to overt flattery. This was all very pleasing. As for her lingering sexuality, this did not interest Smith.

By the time the waiter left them to their main courses, he had established that she understood the need for absolute confidentiality.

"You see, Mrs Macready, one of the problems often encountered in democratic government when one seeks to encourage the march of beneficial progress and economic growth, is the hostility of people who perceive only part of an initiative. It is a natural reaction to resent change, of course, it unsettles us, it threatens us, but so often we end up by missing great opportunities! It therefore becomes necessary for people in government like myself to act in a . . ." he paused and pulled a face as if it pained him to use the expression, "well, semi-secret way in order to lay the groundwork so that matters can, when the time comes to reveal them, proceed smoothly. The unfortunate thing is," Smith said, leaning forward and topping up Gwendolyn's wine glass, "it looks as though one is acting furtively, whereas in fact one is only acting sensibly, d'you see? With an absolute economy of effort and, of course, the much more important consideration, an economy of resources."

He smiled charmingly and, with an expansive gesture, added the non sequitur, "You know this is awfully pleasant. I really am delighted to meet you, you know," and he looked into her eyes for a fraction of a second longer than she could bear and she felt a stupidly girlish flush creep across her cheeks.

"Now," he went on briskly as though not noticing her reaction, "to specifics. I am aware that you have already been approached with a view to selling your farm. Oh," he added hurriedly as she paused, her fork halfway to her mouth, "please do not worry, I am not here to influence the asking price." He laughed. "That's the last thing a Tory would do! No, no, Mrs Macready, I am certain you will sell and that's the important thing, because the coalfield is huge and the economic benefits to the locality are in proportion. Those accruing to the nation, in terms of exported coal, cannot be overlooked and will also be considerable. Of course," Smith went seamlessly on, his mellifluous tone actually soothing in its urbanity, "one fully understands the concern of many who regard an open-cast mine as an eyesore but, you know, there is a certain abstract beauty in the concept of a mine which yields up great wealth to those whose labour extracts it."

Gwendolyn, who could see no circumstances mitigating the sheer ugliness of an open-cast mine even in the abstract, found herself unable to formulate any dissent as Smith went on.

"Having thus established the beneficial mine, we next have to consider the matter of exporting its produce. Now Porth Ardur is, in a sense, ideally placed. It is close to the mine, requiring only a short run of railway track to connect the two facilities, but it does possess one disadvantage."

Smith laid down his knife and fork and dabbed his lips with

his napkin. "To be truthful, it is a small disadvantage and one easily overcome with some local encouragement and this is the nub of why I have sought you out tonight, Mrs Macready. You see, I believe you are a considerable influence for good in the town, indeed people speak highly of you in that context, and to occupy so high a place in the public's opinion is, I assure you, no mean achievement. There's many a politician who would envy you, I do assure you." Smith laughed, laid down his napkin and refilled Gwendolyn's glass again.

"The long and the short of it is that your assistance is required to further the scheme."

"In what way, Mr Smith?" Gwendolyn was becoming impatient, sensing a slight prevarication on Smith's part.

"In the matter of the port, Mrs Macready. You see, strictly between ourselves, a decision has been made by the Commissioners for Celtic Lighthouses that their entire operational facility in Porth Ardur is unnecessary. It is their intention to scrap your husband's old ship and to run everything from Cavehaven. I believe there is another ship, a newer ship there—"

"The *Waterwitch*," Gwendolyn muttered almost automatically, appalled at this revelation. The smooth and handsome MP suddenly assumed the awful proportions of an agent of the devil. She began to see all the threads of her speculations converging, and running into an awful knot. The first tentative whispers of the old ship's redundancy were now more than confirmed; she was horrified, aware of the impact such a decision would have upon the population of Porth Ardur, not to mention herself. The little town was bound to the sea, derived its very name from it. Some held that it was from its strand that King Arthur's body had been taken on its last voyage to the mystical land of Lyonesse. But such considerations were swept from her mind by the necessity to pay attention to Smith's words.

". . . Now this gives us the opportunity to redevelop the port and to use it for the export of the coal produced by the mine and we would like you to make it your business to emphasise the manifold opportunities this will give the town. I shall, of course, keep you personally fully informed of all contiguous developments. In return I would appreciate your reciprocal confidences. I do not expect this to be easy, but it will help if you will let us know any specific concerns in order that these can be addressed and disarmed." Smith paused to drain and refill his own glass. "I am sure that your own private transactions will proceed smoothly. I don't have to emphasise the fact that without your land none of this can go ahead."

She recalled little else of the evening. She had been a little tiddly, she recalled the following morning. The most surprising thing about the evening was the way both her guesses at the MP's intentions had proved correct. That they were inter-related she had never even considered.

It was not until the following morning that she sat quietly and reviewed the events of the previous evening. As she ordered her own thoughts, dragging them out, as it were, from the weighty, persuasive weight of her host's, she realised that not only had Smith tried to bribe her but he had already, unknowingly succeeded. Earlier that week she had written to propose a settlement value upon the farm. It would, she knew now, be accepted. Far from thinking she might have asked double, she realised she had no weapon to bring against the monster, that the one thing she might have done, refused to sell the farm, would now prove well nigh impossible, for in addition she had taken the Evans brothers into her confidence and explained the provision she intended making for them. And to cap it all, in her confusion she had failed to ask Smith, who would have given her anything she wanted last night, for the two men to be employed in the mine. Perhaps there was still time for that, but then, what was she thinking? She did not want the mine at all now!

She rose, wringing her hands in an agony of confused frustration. The whole matter could have pivoted on her decision! For a moment she had unknowingly held all the key cards to the situation and she had flung all that advantage away! It did not console her to reflect she could not have possibly known all the facts any earlier and had acted in good faith. None of these considerations would carry much weight in Porth Ardur once the word was out that Mrs Macready had dined with David Smith and had consequently sold the farm, allowing the mining to begin. When news broke that the Lighthouse Service were pulling out and her husband was going to retire, the fat would be truly in the fire! My God, she could never hold her head up in Porth Ardur again!

Thus preoccupied, Gwendolyn Macready spent a day in disshevelled consternation, impatiently awaiting the return of her errant husband who, for once, she longed to see.

It was a black night of lashing rain and gusting wind as Macready brought *Caryatid* in through the open dock caisson and laid her gently alongside the berth. For the first time for many years he felt a reluctance to go home. It was nearly midnight, he was depressed, dog-tired and wanted to turn into his bunk. He was no longer young and the wearying thought of having to trudge home up the long hill depressed him still further. He longed to be sleeping with Justine, to end the seemingly endless calls of duty and obligation, to give up, concede the game to Stanier and his ilk, to retire to Ynyscraven and the idyll he knew existed there.

It was so bloody unfair. Charlie was going to do just that, and Charlie was half his age! Charlie had yet to endure the tedium, isolation and responsibility of command. Charlie, damn him, was taking the easy way, running up the providential ladder while he, Septimus Macready, once the happiest of men, slid down the snake of despair.

"Orders, sir?" Charlie knocked at the cabin door.

"Steam for fourteen hundred. Discharge all the dirty buoys and get the clean ones aboard. I'm sleeping at home tonight."

"Aye, aye, sir," acknowledged Mr Farthing, surprised that the Captain had thought the routine matter worth mentioning.

"And you've not changed your mind?"

"No, sir. I've the letter ready for the post."

"Well, I'll miss you, Charlie, when the time comes." Macready turned and smiled at his young second-in-command.

"I'll miss you too, sir."

"I don't know who they'll send as a replacement . . ." the Captain lowered his voice, "if they even bother."

On that lugubrious note Macready quit the ship. He looked

back at her once. The cluster of lights, palely illuminating the long column of her buff funnel seemed so much a part of Porth Ardur that he wondered what the place would be like without her. It did not occur to him that most of the inhabitants of the port saw the same view without the ship and that only he, and those of his crew that drifted up the hill towards Acacia Avenue, only ever saw it with their ship looking like a permanent fixture.

He knew the moment he saw Gwendolyn that something was wrong. He had only ever once before seen her in so untidy and neglected a state, when she had been sick with a serious bout of fever which turned out to be appendicitis.

"What on earth is the matter, m'dear?"

"Oh, Septimus, it's just too awful to tell you—" She threw herself at him and he found himself embracing her and muttering silly words of comfort such as he had not done for many years as she mumbled against his chest an incomprehensible catalogue of apparently dire and terrible events. In the end he succeeded in quietening her, got her to sit, made a pot of tea and joined her.

"Now, Gwendolyn, just explain to me what this is all about."

It was about half past two in the morning when she had finished telling him and he had completed all the questions her occasionally disjointed account provoked. For a long time he sat staring at the floor, with his wife watching him. "What on earth are we going to do, Septimus?" she whispered at last, unable to endure the silence a moment longer.

He drew in his breath and looked up. "Well, my dear, we must do something, that much is clear. But I don't know what." His remark to Justine that he would fight for his ship's company had been outflanked by Gwendolyn's precipitate sale of the farm and now sounded mere boyish hubris.

"There must be some way—"

"I think we shall have to accept the inevitable," he said. "We cannot fight it, although I should like to minimise the effect it will have upon the ship's company. But if the festering Commissioners have decided *Caryatid*'s to go, we are quite powerless to stand in their way. What we have to do is to see if there is some way we can soften the blow to Porth Ardur."

"What about *us*, Septimus? I am totally compromised."

"Yes. I suppose you are. Even though you acted quite innocently, people won't give you the benefit of any doubt. On the other hand you will have received a good price for the farm, and can perhaps move away as soon as possible."

"And you, you'll go to that woman the moment I'm out of here."

"Once you are out of here, Gwendolyn, I shall have no reason for being here myself."

"Oh, this is awful!"

"It is not so very awful. Most of Porth Ardur are aware of our situation. It would be more open, more honest, to acknowledge it. You will be quite comfortably provided for. You will have the money from the farm, your father's old investment income, half my pension—"

"I don't want half your confounded pension!"

"Don't be foolish, Gwendolyn. You may need half my pension."

"I suppose you and your tart are going to live on love! At your age, it's preposterous!"

"She isn't a tart," responded Macready, too tired to rise to Gwendolyn's taunting. "She's had her own fair share of bad luck, having to bring up Tegwyn on her own and all that."

"I've been thoroughly humiliated," Gwendolyn said bitterly, but her husband was no longer listening. Something had just occurred to him. Something Stanier had said.

"I suppose it is a coincidence that the scrapping of *Caryatid*, the closure of the buoy yard and the opening of the port to the export of coal from a brand new mine is all happening at once."

"What d'you mean?"

"Only that nothing happens here for a century and then all hell breaks loose." He paused. "Tell me, d'you think Smith was acting in his capacity as MP, trying to do whatever he said for his constituents and the local economy, or was he acting on his own behalf?"

Gwendolyn shrugged. "How should I know? He's too shrewd to let much slip by accident."

"I wonder," mused Captain Macready. "I just wonder . . . It's all too damned pat for my liking."

Captain Stanier apologised for his late arrival at the club. "Bloody meeting was interminable, David, but," he took the whisky and soda off the salver the club waiter proffered, "we've got what we wanted: closure of the whole bloody caboodle."

"Well done," replied the MP, laying his broadsheet newspaper down with a rustle. "I knew the old buggers would, the economies are too persuasive and with threats to their jolly cruises in the offing, no sacrifice is too great, eh?"

"No," Stanier agreed enthusiastically, unsure whether or not Smith was guying him. Personally he was looking forward to the annual inspection cruise of the Commissioners enormously, but it was clear Smith, pragmatic politician that he was, was not in favour. Stanier recalled a remark made by his wife only the previous evening when he was discussing the forthcoming Board meeting with her.

"Let's not lose sight of the fact, David, that whatever you think of the inspection cruise as a waste of public money, it does have a value."

"Oh, all that nonsense about direct contact between the Board and the shop floor, or is it the deck? Well, that's gilding a rather tarnished lily when you consider the enormous cost of the *Naiad*, isn't it?"

"No, no," said Stanier, glad to have caught out the nimble-minded politician for once, "I mean it gives *us* a priceless chance to prove beyond doubt the rightness of our proposed course of action in respect of *Caryatid* and the whole old-fashioned set-up of Porth Ardur—"

"It does?" Smith frowned, uncomprehending.

"Of course!" Stanier hissed, looking round as adjacent newspapers rustled their disapproval at the animation of their conversation. "We can simply damn the whole thing by turning in a negative inspection report!"

"Could you actually carry that off? Mrs Macready impressed

me as one of those delightfully anachronistic characters that believe in probity and rectitude. It's as amusing as finding a dinosaur these cynical days, but I suppose it's what one expects in so appalling a backwater as Porth Ardur. If she's formidable I have no reason to suspect her husband isn't equally as straightforward. I daresay he runs – what do you call it? – a taut ship."

"Oh, we'll catch him, don't you worry. There were half-a-dozen things wrong with his ship when I visited her the other day; besides, the Board approved a letter of reprimand to him only this afternoon. That'll catch him flat aback for a start, and we've had a letter of resignation from his Chief Officer which I have managed to influence the Board to accept. Life will be pretty unsettling for the old stick-in-the-mud, what with one thing and another, so things are definitely going our way!" Stanier swallowed his drink and clicked his fingers for the waiter. "Another one before we dine, David?"

"Why not," Smith agreed, smiling.

"Perhaps we shall find a dinosaur in the mine," laughed Stanier, and it took Smith some seconds to see the lame joke.

"Oh yes. Perhaps we shall."

Macready was stung almost as much by the news of Charlie Farthing's resignation as by the letter of reprimand. He was unable to shake off the feeling that a conspiracy lurked behind the threatened changes to his home port, but he was completely at a loss as to how to discover the truth, still less what he could possibly do once he had done so. There was no *deus ex machina* to come to his aid and the letter of reprimand seemed, as indeed it was intended, to signal the end of the epoch over which Captain Septimus Macready had presided.

Changed Circumstances

Tegwyn Pomeroy set the glass beside Lord Craven and settled herself on the chair next to him.

"Pom won't be long—"

"I didn't come to see Pom. I haven't seen a Tasmanian wind devil in months and I certainly don't want to see his, the bloody things give me the creeps. No, I came to see you."

"Me?"

"Yes, Teggy, don't be all bloody coy, you know that if you weren't spoken for, I'd propose instant marriage—"

"Don't be silly, Roger."

"I'm not, but I'll spare us both and come to the point. I want your advice." The son and heir to Lord Dungarth, owner of the distant island of Ynyscraven, deliberately closed his eyes to slits and stared at Mrs Pomeroy. "Damn it, though, you're the most beautiful creature."

"Shut up and say what you came to say before I throw you out."

"Well, I have really, Teggy," his lordship said, rolling his eyes, "but I do want your advice."

"What about?"

"In a word, Ynyscraven."

"What about Ynyscraven?"

"Well, I hate the place. Far too quiet for me. Pa loves it, though he used to pretend it was hell when he took us down there for holidays. Anyway, to the point . . . Oh, Teggy, *do* come and live with me. I adore you to distraction—"

"Anyway, what, Roger?" Tegwyn said severely.

"Anyway, my darling and cruel heart, the bloody old Reeve

has finally decided to chuck his hand in. Now, I know your ma lives there in sin with some bloody old sailor . . ." Craven held his hand up to silence Tegwyn's protest with a laugh. "Pa's getting too old to take much of an interest and he wants me to look after it. Frankly the place could drift away on the tide, but I suppose I've got to show an interest so, what I want to know is, how suitable is this fellow Farthing? I gather your ma knows his wife or something like that."

"Yes, she does. Sonia's lived on the island—"

"Oh, I remember her. Pretty thing with red hair. Had a mad artist for a mother, didn't she. I remember when I was a kid being down there one summer. She wanted to see my winkle—"

"And I expect you obliged," remarked Tegwyn laughing.

"I expect I did. A gentleman always does what a lady asks. No chance of you asking I suppose?"

"I'm not a lady. Go on anyway."

"Must I?"

"Yes."

"Well, I've nothing more to add really. If this cove Farthing's competent and wants the job he can bloody well have it. I wouldn't want to be cooped up on the damned place. It's always raining and when it isn't, the island's covered in fog," His lordship exaggerated petulantly.

"He and Sonia would be ideal for the job, Roger. There was some talk of them taking over, oh, about three years ago, but it all fell through when the Reeve and his wife changed their minds about leaving. Sonia's a dear, she really is."

"I'm not certain I can trust part of the Craven fortune to a woman who's keen on looking at strange men's winkles."

"Try. You might be surprised."

"I shall remind her of the occasion when I go down there."

"Are you visiting Ynyscraven?"

"Got to really, under the circumstances," his lordship said gloomily, adding in a brighter tone, "I'm sailing down there, so I needn't stay long and don't have to wait for that horrible little *Plover* to take me over from Aberogg."

"You're sailing there in your own yacht, then?"

Craven nodded. "Yup. The lovely *Lyonesse*. Want to come?"

Tegwyn shivered and shook her head, recalling the awful hours aboard the wrecked *Sea Dragon*. "I should simply hate it."

They heard the door and a few minutes later Pomeroy entered the room. "Ah Craven, good evening. Are you tormenting Tegwyn again?"

"I keep trying to seduce her, Pom, but she's depressingly faithful. I even offered to show her my winkle but she declined."

"I've told you before she's a woman of discernment and taste. Tell me, have you come across any more of those Tasmanian carvings?" Pomeroy smiled up at Tegwyn as she put a glass into his hand.

"No. What d'you want more of the things for? They give me the willies."

Pomeroy said nothing, but smiled as he sipped his cocktail. "I bumped into Stanier today," he said, addressing Tegwyn. "He was full of himself, as usual."

"I really don't know why you encourage him, Pom."

Pomeroy shrugged. He had known Caroline since she was a girl, but his real motive for the friendship with the Staniers was more obscure. He used Tegwyn's reaction to the occasional encounter with her former lover as a barometer of her own affection for himself. Perhaps, he thought, he ought to shift his focus to Lord Craven. The dilettante art dealer might prove more dangerous than Pomeroy supposed.

"Who?" asked Lord Craven.

"I don't think you know him, Roger," Pomeroy said. "He and Tegwyn used to know each other."

"We were lovers," Tegwyn admitted candidly, "before I met Pom."

"What's the lucky devil got that I haven't?"

"Charm," riposted Tegwyn swiftly.

"Oh, *touché*, darling," laughed Craven. "Is he the fellow who married Caro Blackadder?"

"The same," said Pomeroy.

"Well, he might have charm, but he certainly has no taste. She's clever, but cold. It must be rather like making love to liquid carbon dioxide; you get burnt, but the experience freezes you."

"She's a very clever woman," Pomeroy said. "Uses her divine Jimmy up front, and pulls the strings from behind. He's a marionette."

"Yes, I know the cove. He's a club member; isn't he Chairman of the Cambrian Steam Navigation Company? Pater had some dealings with him. Tried to get one of his ships to run to Ynyscraven to increase the visitors, but the ship was put on another service to those islands to the north, what are they called, Teggy?"

"Ynys Meini and the Bishop's Islands. You mean the *Kurnow* then. She runs out of Porth Ardur. I didn't know Cambrian Steam owned her, I thought—"

"Oh, it's some sort of fiddle," said Craven, running his left hand through his long flax hair and throwing one leg over the arm of his chair. "The *Kurnow*'s registered as a single ship in a discreet company, but she's beneficially owned by Stanier's lot . . . What used to be Blackadder Holdings. I'd forgotten you came from Porth Ardur. Funny little place. I'm intending to call in with *Lyonesse* next month. Pity old Pom's not interested in shipping, isn't it, Pom?"

"I never want to see another ship in my life," Pomeroy admitted. "Surviving one shipwreck is enough for one lifetime."

"Ah, but you floated out of it with Teggy, now didn't you, eh?"

"Now you're being impertinent, Roger, and I shall not be able to ask you to dine with us."

"Oh, damn you, Pom, for an old spoilsport," Craven said with a good-natured laugh, hauling himself out of his chair. "In that case I shall have to dine at the club."

After he had seen Lord Craven out, Pomeroy returned to his wife. "You know, for all his light-hearted banter, I really believe he would take you from me if you ever gave him the chance," he said.

She smiled up and stretched her arm out towards him. "I know, darling," Tegwyn said smiling, "but I have no intention of ever giving him the chance."

* * *

The club seemed to Lord Craven more than usually boring. An hour later he was seated alone, toying with a lamb cutlet and musing over the unkindness of a fate that allowed an old queen like Pomeroy to possess as lovely a wife as Tegwyn. The vivacious and spontaneous charm of her transcended anything he ever came across in the young women paraded by their greedy mothers for his own delectation. It was true Lord Craven kept a mistress in a small flat in the northern suburbs, but Nancy was a convenience, a good-time girl four years older than his lordship, who knew her fate even before she let his lordship into her bed. One day she would be dropped, but he would never quite forget her and, she knew in due course, he would be kind-hearted enough to make a small provision for her out of his fortune.

Musing on whether or not to stay in the club, seek out Nancy's bed, or wander to the family's town house, Craven was startled from his reverie by a greeting.

"May I join you, Lord Craven?"

Looking up, Craven evinced surprise. "Good God, it's Stanier, isn't it?"

"Indeed it is, my lord. May I . . . ?" Stanier had the opposite chair half drawn out.

"Well yes. Yes, by all means." Craven watched Stanier settle himself, trying to imagine him and Tegwyn making love.

"I wanted a word with you, Lord Craven—"

"Oh," Craven said, surprised, as if Stanier had divined the impiety of his thoughts. "What on earth about?"

"Your father once approached one of my companies with a view to our mail ship visiting Ynyscraven. We declined at the time, didn't have the capacity, d'you see, but I anticipate we might be able to accommodate his lordship in the near future. I'd not like to let an opportunity slip."

"It's rather small beer for a chap of your, er, what-d'you-ma-call-it? – expanding enterprise, isn't it?"

"Oh, you've heard about Porth Ardur." Stanier chuckled and sat back as the waiter handed him a menu and he quickly ordered. Craven thought it odd that not only Stanier but Porth Ardur had cropped up either in the flesh or in conversation twice in one evening and leaned forward, filling Stanier's glass from his own bottle.

"Oh, I heard something," Craven admitted vaguely.

"From your father, I suppose."

"Yes," lied Craven. "But he wasn't very specific. Pater's got this dreadful habit of thinking I'm about to take over everything before he's dead. Reads too much Shakespeare, I guess."

His casually confidential tone fooled Stanier, who leaned forward, dropping his voice. "Well, we're going to open a new export trade in coal from Porth Ardur. As you probably know I've recently been appointed a Commissioner of Celtic Lights and this has helped. We're taking over the whole port . . ."

Craven spotted the lack of logic in the use of the pronoun and rightly concluded Stanier was drunk. "You mean 'we' as in Cambrian Steam, rather than the Lighthouse Authority, I take it?"

"Absolutely, old man. There won't be any Lighthouse Authority presence in Porth Ardur by the end of the year. It'll all be down to Old King Coal."

"And where's this coal coming from? The nearest deep mine is thirty miles away and most of its output goes into power stations."

"The coal, old man, will come out of the ground about five miles from the dock at Porth Ardur. New. Open cast. Hardly an overhead in sight. Stacks of it. Coal I mean. Piece of bloody wonderful cake."

Craven frowned. "I've seen no new flotation on the stock market."

"Didn't need one. Old company own a quarry almost on the spot. It produces nothing now, only ever had a small vestigial strata of slate. Most of it's now covering the roofs of Porth Ardur. But the Ardurian Slate Company actually owned a substantial part of Mynydd Uchaf which, though it has no slate, covers a great deposit of coal."

"I know the mountain," Craven muttered, more to himself than to Stanier.

"The slate company cost us a mere one hundred pounds! Of course the purchase of two adjacent farms has set us back a bit more, but very little in real terms. It's an absolutely sure-fire project. We just can't go wrong."

"Who's in with you?" asked Craven, with just that tone of breathless excitement that persuaded Stanier he too might be fired with investment fever.

"Oh, Dickie Angerstein and Julius Throgmore, along with David Smith—"

"The local MP?" Craven said surprised.

"Yes, but he's a sleeper, so that's confidential, old boy."

"Of course, of course," soothed Craven. "By God, Stanier, you don't let the grass grow under your feet, do you?"

Stanier's smile was almost sickening. "Nice of you to say so. What's more, the exporting company will be Cambrian Steam."

"So you've got the whole thing sewn up. Well, well, nice work if you can get it, as the Yanks say." Craven watched Stanier tuck into his meal. "And you're a Commissioner of Lights too, eh. Haven't you got the annual inspection cruise coming up soon?" Craven deftly turned the subject and Stanier, his mouth full, nodded. "I thought so," Craven went on. "Pater was saying something about it. He used to go down to Ynyscraven about this time of the year so that when the Commissioners arrived to inspect the lighthouse, he'd get an invitation to dinner aboard the lighthouse yacht. He used to say the Commissioners kept a better table than anyone else he knew and the only way to get at least one good meal on the island was to waylay them! I wouldn't be surprised if he tried the trick again this year; he's been reviving some of the worst habits of his youth as he enters his second childhood."

"Well, old boy . . ."

"For heaven's sake, do call me Roger."

"Well, Roger, oh, please call me St John . . ."

"I thought your name was Jimmy."

"Ah, that's what my wife calls me," Stanier said with a hint of sheepishness.

"Ah yes, Caro . . ."

"You know her?"

"Not in the biblical sense, but yes, I am acquainted with her. Pater used to be quite friendly with her father. He had some investments with the old boy some time ago. He was killed when his yacht ran aground and broke up. All the fault of the yacht skipper, I believe . . . You all right, Jimmy? Had a bit much of the old pig-swill, have you?"

Justine finished reading the letter out loud. It was Tegwyn's habit to write a fortnightly letter to her mother. These were more often than not filled with news and gossip about Tegwyn's new circle of friends, distant characters known to Justine only through Tegwyn's correspondence, but Tegwyn took her duty seriously and, when news of so overwhelming a nature cropped up, intimately affecting the place where her mother lived, she passed it on quickly.

Of course, Tegwyn's emphasis was quite different. First came the news of Craven's intention to ask Charlie and Sonia to take over from the Reeve. This was followed by the possibility of an increase in the island's tourist trade if a new ferry service was opened up. It was only then that Tegwyn informed her mother of the dissolution of the lighthouse depot at Porth Ardur. Both women saw the opportunity this might provide for Captain Macready to retire to the island. Tegwyn, long uneasy about her mother's current circumstances, wished only for her happiness as she grew older. Mother and daughter were very close, the long years of Justine's widowhood having dominated Tegwyn's childhood and adolescence.

It was a quite incidental postscript that mentioned the involvement of Mr David Smith MP, for Tegwyn hardly thought it worth adding until she suddenly recalled that, in the days when the voluptuous Mrs Morgan ran a small lingerie shop, it had received a visit from a young, prospective Tory candidate. Mr Smith had been canvassing and, in the hope of securing Mrs Morgan's vote, had bought some feminine items from her. They had afterwards laughed over the matter, since Betty Byford, Justine's assistant, had sworn they were for himself, not the wife he vaguely alluded to.

It was fortuitous, too, that Lord Craven had discovered another Tasmanian wind mask and, opportunist that he was, had called upon Tegwyn late one afternoon, long before her husband was expected home, to leave the hideous thing for

Pomeroy to see. He also brought her a present of red jade, a small figure of the sea-goddess Kuanyin which, he assured her, 'is at least five hundred years old'.

Craven, besotted by Tegwyn, used the news gleaned from his encounter with the bibulous Stanier, in tandem with his gift, to increase his standing in Tegwyn's eyes. To be in her presence was delightful enough, but his lordship enjoyed even further excitement at the prospect of seducing her. She had, after all, fallen for a twerp like Stanier and lived in some state and, as far as he could see, perfect harmony with her odd, strangely likeable but undeniably queer husband. Pomeroy *must* have acquired her on some sort of a rebound, Craven believed. Some time soon, he concluded, Tegwyn's natural desires would manifest themselves and he wanted to be the fortunate fellow who benefited from their re-emergence. He was therefore generous and attentive in dispensing as much gossip as Tegwyn's feminine curiosity wished for.

It was not long before the intelligence had been passed by Justine to Captain Septimus Macready.

"I knew it!" exclaimed Macready, his eyes alight. "The bastard! The festering bastard!"

"Septimus!" Justine had upbraided him. "Is there anything you can do?" she asked.

He shrugged his broad shoulders and looked at her. "D'you want me to do anything? I thought you wanted me to ditch Gwendolyn and come and live here in quiet retirement."

"Of course that is what I want, my darling, but—"

"But what?"

"Life is never quite that simple, is it? You'll spend the rest of your life with a bad conscience on two accounts – your wife and your ship. One we could live with, but two . . ." she shook her head, tears filling her eyes, "I'm not so sure."

Macready took her in his arms. "The course of true love never runs smooth," he observed. "Shakespeare was right, the canny old devil. We are a pair of star-crossed lovers, all right."

"You could expose Stanier. I mean his conduct is improper, so is that of the MP . . ." She told Macready of her past meeting with David Smith and the conviction of Betty Byford that the prospective MP had purchased a basque, two garters and some stockings for himself. Their laughter rescued them from depression and when Macready left her, he had decided to write in confidence to Captain Jesmond. Justine's tale had reminded him of an incident in his own past. It had been a very long time ago, he thought with a chuckle as he walked briskly down the path towards his rendezvous with Mr Farthing.

He saw Charlie blow the rain off the end of his nose as both men began the descent to the beach and the motor boat.

"Not so pleasant this morning, sir."

"No. Remind's me of the morning we nearly lost old Jessie Jesmond. Have I told you the yarn, Charlie?"

"I don't believe you have, sir."

"Oh, it was when I was mate of the old *Naiad*. Lovely old ship with a clipper bow, counter stern and auxiliary sails. We used to set them to steady the ship when the Board were dining. Old Jesmond refused to have fiddles set up on their table in bad weather and it was our job to keep the ship as steady as possible!" Macready chuckled. "Silly buggers used to lose tons of glass and crockery and the pattern of the saloon carpet used to receive regular additions, but we'd get a message, brought up by one of their stewards, congratulating us on our fine seamanship if the losses were below a certain number of plates and glasses for the state of the sea!"

Charlie shook his head in wonder.

"Anyway, one day we were off the Buccabu light and the weather was terrible," Macready went on. "Rain and wind and plenty of both. Jesmond insisted on landing to inspect the place even though it was not just dangerous, but quite impossible. Old Captain Voss, whom you won't remember but who was the best seaman I've ever known, was in command of *Naiad* and took me to one side. 'I can manoeuvre to lower a boat and pick you up,' he said. 'I want you to take the Commissioners in and give that fool Jesmond the fright of his bloody life. Can you do it?' So off I went. None of the other Commissioners wanted to go but once Jesmond had announced they were off, it was a matter of honour. They all mustered on the boat deck, putting on their life-preservers and going a pale shade of green. You know what the Buccabu reef is like, there's a powerful eddy on the last two hours of the ebb just off the southern rocks and outside it, about fifty yards away, are those standing waves you got caught in once, d'you recall?"

"How could I forget?"

"Anyway, I primed the boat's crew and while we were getting ready, Voss had the signaller send a semaphore message to the keepers not to leave the security of the tower to rig the landing. Voss made a superb lee and we got the boat away, even though there was a hell of a sea running. Then we were on our own and it wasn't long before we were off the reef. It was almost low water, but even so the rise and fall of the swell was completely inundating the main rock at times. I thought the sight would put Jesmond off, but not a bit of it. He had commanded a wool-clipper and liked us all to know he was a real hard case. He used to tell a tale about amputating a seaman's crushed hand when off Kerguelen and I've no doubt it was true.

"Anyway, at this point the entrance door to the Buccabu tower, which, as you know, is about thirty feet above the rock, opens up and we could see two of the keepers staring at us.

"'Mr Macready,' Jesmond sings out, 'there are no keepers rigging the landing!' 'No, sir,' I replied, 'it's too dangerous.' 'Well, we can't go alongside without the boat ropes being rigged for us,' he glared up at the two faces, 'and if they won't do it for us, we'll have to do it ourselves!'

"By now I realised it wasn't Jesmond who was going to get a fright, it was me! 'We can't do that, sir,' I shouted back above the roar of the wind and the breaking sea which was terrific. 'Look, it's like a bloody pond in there,' he bellowed, pointing, as you will have guessed, at that small area just off the landing steps that is cut to a smooth by the effect of the ebbing tide. A seal had popped his head up and was looking at us in disbelief. Anyway, I tried to explain to Jesmond that this was deceptive and the rise and fall of the breaking waves and swell made the whole thing so dangerous that we would assuredly smash the boat if we approached any closer. The next thing I knew he's kicked off his boots and dropped his hat in the lap of one of the other Commissioners who had been regarding this whole farce with faces stark with terror, and jumped over the side!

"He made two or three strokes towards the landing before the tide got him. The next minute I saw him dashed against one of the rocks. I ordered the coxswain to get out of the way and to take the boat out south of the standing waves and went in after the silly bugger. I knew there was no chance of plucking him out of the sea before we were clear of the overfalls and fortunately I managed to grab hold of him and get him over on his back. He was out cold with blood running all down his face, but by good fortune he went into the smooth and I could see he was breathing. I remember seeing the lighthouse go round me, though of course it was us spinning in the eddy, but it was growing smaller and the next thing we went through the overfalls. Those standing waves must be six or eight feet tall, I was nearly sick with going up and down; had my guts in the sky one moment and God knows where the next. Anyway, we broke out into the regular waves to the south which, though it was still blowing hard, seemed like heaven. Then the boat loomed up and fished us out after a bit of a struggle.

"Old Voss picked us up and we got Jesmond down aft into the Commissioners' quarters. I'd just got myself dry and into clean gear when I was called down there. Jesmond had come round by then, declined a hot bath and sent for me. The other Commissioners had retired to their bunks and Jesmond was alone, sitting in the smoke room dressed in a magnificent silk dressing gown, his feet in a bowl of steaming hot water, smoking a cigar and drinking a large peg of whisky.

"'Mr Macready,' he said, waving his cigar at his feet, 'this bowl of water is slopping all over the deck! Kindly set the auxiliary sails!' 'Aye, aye, sir,' I said and turned to leave when Jesmond called me back. 'Mr Macready,' he said, 'you were right and I was wrong. You saved my life. Don't come crawling to me with any trivial matter, but if there's ever anything I can do for you, don't hesitate to ask.'"

"And did you, sir?" Charlie asked. The two men stood on the tideline as the motor boat's forefoot scrunched on the shingle.

"No, never. Not until now, that is."

The Obscure Decisions of Fate

Macready's letter to Captain Jesmond reached its destination ten days later. It had had a curious genesis, originating in Stanier's bibulous admission, spurred on its way by Craven's self-centred lusty desire and, finally, by Tegwyn's familial duty. Idle gossip was in this way passed through the due processes of human motivation and analysis, augmented and presented to Captain Jesmond as matters of established fact. It was not so much that Macready had penned the letter with such certainty that the allegation was laid out in cold accusation, but the power of the allusion was taken as implicit by the reader. Captain Jesmond, who in his younger days had dismissed as mere cowardice the caution of a professional, was no less a man of certainty in his later days. Age had cemented the vigour of his prejudices and his powers of judgement were swift and stubborn.

Captain Jesmond dived into the maelstrom of capitalism with as little fear as he once, long ago, braved the broad bosom of the Atlantic. Besides, he could not abide Stanier. The one almost objective faculty the old man still possessed undiminished by a hard life and rooted dislike, was his ability to tell a good seaman from a bad one. Stanier was not merely a bad seaman, he was a sham, a phoney, a man whom Jesmond could not even countenance as a master mariner, and admitted to the councils of the Commissioners only as a shipowner. And for Jesmond, who had grown up in the days when a sailing ship was not romantic but back-breakingly hard work and a constant concern for the man who occupied the berth of master, a shipowner represented the most extreme form of capitalist.

Politically, Jesmond occupied that strange no man's land of a man who automatically and naturally assumed the mantle of tyrant whenever he was afloat, but who, in the more reasonable atmosphere of a drawing room, was the mildest of socialists, genuinely believing in the dignity of labour, but admitting the depravity of sailors and the divinely appointed divisions of rank. This came with a degree of contempt for money, which he regarded only as an adjunct to survival, not a reason for living. As any man knows who has driven a sailing ship round Cape Horn in all weathers, there are other things in life. With this philosophy, Captain Jesmond nevertheless dutifully turned in a handsome profit for his owner and kept his crew in thrall, admired by both for his fair dealing, but disliking both parties himself, for their ignorance and weaknesses.

As well as intensely disliking Stanier, the old man greatly liked Macready; Macready was a similar soul to himself, not so much a seaman, as a man of the sea. It was therefore with a mounting sense of wrathful indignation that Jesmond read Macready's letter. Detained in his bed by rheumatics, the old shipmaster had been unable to attend the Board meeting at which the Commissioners had approved the entire shutting down of the buoy yard at Porth Ardur. Unfortunately, since he never read minutes, Macready's letter first acquainted him with what he considered as a perfidious act.

A telephone call to Mudge confirmed matters and his protest found only a partial sympathy. "The motion was carried by a majority," Mudge explained, "and though I was against it, I was the only one. Even if you had been there, Jesmond, we should have been overwhelmed."

"Damn it, Charlie, get rid of *Caryatid* by all means, old ships must go when they're ripe, but the whole of our depot at Porth Ardur . . . what's the point of scrapping that as well?"

"Economics. We can run matters just as well from Cavehaven; the place isn't tidal, *Waterwitch* is only five years old and the buoy yard there is a more up-to-date facility than the old place at Porth Ardur."

"Yes, but the bloody *Waterwitch* will have to steam a lot more miles to get up into the Silurian Strait on a regular basis."

"She doesn't steam anywhere, Jesmond, she *motors*. She's a motor ship and her bunkering costs are a fraction of *Caryatid*'s. To be frank, we should have thought of all this years ago. It's no consolation to have this young jackanapes Stanier pointing out so obvious a matter to us. It's rather embarrassing."

"He's doing it all in his own interests, you know, Charlie. You're being made more of a fool than you know."

"What d'you mean?"

"You wait and see."

Jesmond came off the telephone chuckling. He was not going to reveal all and risk a tip-off being passed to Stanier, to rob himself of a dramatic moment at next month's Board meeting. Jesmond felt an anticipatory surge of blood in his old arteries. By God, he would show the young whipper-snapper that he could not abuse his position as a Commissioner of Celtic Lights! It was an almost sacred trust and safe in the hands of men like Jesmond, but the influence of a self-seeking worm like Stanier, a man who could buy the services of a Member of Parliament and wreck a whole community with his greed could not, *must not*, be allowed to get away with it! Such modern notions, Jesmond told himself, had no place within an ancient organisation dedicated to the sole purpose of serving the mariner where constancy, probity and, above all, reliability were the watchwords!

As he laboriously ascended the staircase at the Commissioners' Headquarters on the day of the next Board Meeting, Captain Jesmond felt his old heart thumping with suppressed excitement as much as the effort of climbing. He fetched his seat with a sigh and glanced round the assembled members. There was an empty seat.

"Captain Stanier sends his apologies, Sir Charles," intoned the Secretary. "He is unavoidably delayed in the West Country."

It was a second before anyone present noticed the empurpled visage of Captain Jesmond. Only when he kicked his legs in a fury of frustration at the choking in his throat, did they sense something was wrong with the eccentric old man. His eyes had begun to start from his skull and then, with what seemed an impertinent and final act, his tongue stuck out at them. For horrified moments they all stared at the appalling sight and then Jesmond ceased to twitch.

In a rictus of startled horror Jesmond's head lolled sideways. He slowly fell from his chair onto the carpet, stone dead.

The signal arrived while *Caryatid* was at sea. The ship was ordered to haul her ensign down to half mast in honour of the deceased Commissioner. Macready, watching from the bridge as the quartermaster dropped the ensign its own depth below the truck of the staff, saw his own hopes descend with it. Turning forward he stared at the horizon. He wished a good gale would stir itself up and blow like blue blazes for a bloody week so that he could anchor *Caryatid* under the lee of Ynyscraven and he could disappear into the Craven Arms and get very, very drunk. But the day was fine and there was work to be done lifting and cleaning the fairway buoy at Aberogg, removing a sick man from the St Kenelm lightvessel and attending a fishing boat aground near Port Mary. Fat chance he had of drowning his sorrows! No, life went on and he had a job to do. Until they took it away from him, that was.

Gwendolyn Macready's hand shook as she accepted the cheque. Her mouth was dry and the fur cape she had set her severe black suit off with seemed to be generating a tremendous heat. The partial shadowing of her face afforded by the hat's veil helped her dissimulate a little, but she was desperately uncomfortable and ill at ease.

"Five thousand is a most handsome settlement, Mrs Macready," Mr Robertson, her solicitor, was saying. "Why, at two and half per cent per annum the income will be most useful."

"Yes, yes, Mr Robertson, I am sure you are right . . ." But Gwendolyn was not sure at all. She could have stopped the sale, could have put the brake on the whole thing, if she had had the moral strength, but once the neighbouring farm had been sold – at half the price per acre she herself had been offered, Robertson had informed her – the mine was inevitable. A patch of land isolated by an open-cast mine would have been of depreciating value and fallen to this modern, unavoidable economic siege as surely as Monday followed Sunday. She would have ended up with nothing, not even the means of providing for the Evans brothers whom, she had been told only that morning, were quite unsuitable for even a labouring task on the mine.

"They are starting work almost immediately, I understand," Robertson said matter-of-factly. "A shipment of plant is expected within a day or two and then, well, a new era of prosperity for us all I hope." He looked at his watch. It was almost one, time for Mr Robertson to make his daily journey the hundred yards to the Tory Club.

Gwendolyn rose. She held out a gloved hand and shook Robertson's pudgy paw. "Mr Robertson," she said formally.

"It is always a pleasure to do business with you, Mrs Macready. I should deposit that cheque without delay, if I were you."

In the street the sea-breeze cooled her. She hesitated a moment and then walked quickly, almost furtively to her bank. Passing under its sign, the red Pendragon, she felt like a traitor. No native of Porth Ardur, she had nevertheless come to love the place for it had, in its way, provided her with all the consolations absent from her marriage. To her surprise she found the manager himself waiting for her.

"Robertson telephoned, Mrs Macready. I have delayed my lunch—"

"That is very good of you, Mr Sinclair." She followed the manager into his office and sat down.

"Not at all, Mrs Macready. I did not suppose you would wish one of my tellers to become acquainted with the details of your recent business," Sinclair said, sitting opposite her, behind the rampart of his desk.

"No. That is most thoughtful of you." Gwendolyn found herself flushing again. She most certainly did not want Porth Ardur to know that she had been enriched by five thousand pounds. The sum, already shrinking in her own imagination, would conjure up fabulous wealth in that of the less fortunate. She pulled herself together and sought to regain the upper hand.

"Mr Sinclair, Mr Robertson said that a two and a half per cent investment would yield a reasonable sum. Is there not a better rate to be obtained somewhere?"

"Of course, Mrs Macready. There is always a better rate, depending upon the risk you wish to take. One could, if one was brave enough, attempt to secure twenty per cent, but one would have to accept the fact that there would be grave risks. One might lose that part of the capital sum one had put at risk. On the other hand, one can spread an investment in a portfolio, risking a little while holding some in a cast-iron fund with a low yield. The remainder one can juggle with, using one's fiscal judgement; it can be quite absorbing and many people actually enjoy playing the stock market. There are also," went on Sinclair, waxing as lyrical as it is possible for a bank manager, "means by which we, the bank that is, can act as your agent and broker, taking a small commission on your profits. In addition," he learned forward confidentially, "you can attend to matters on your own behalf and I am quite willing to come to a private arrangement to act as your adviser, if you so wish."

"Thank you, Mr Sinclair," Gwendolyn said, feeling better at this small revelation of parochial venality. She took the cheque from her bag and passed it across Sinclair's desk.

He took it and stared at it for moment, then looked up smiling. "You are fortunate, Mrs Macready. Most people have to work for their money. Some of us are lucky enough to possess money which can work for us."

Sinclair's smile, Gwendolyn thought, possessed no charm and she wanted time to think. "I should like to place it in a safe deposit account at your best rate of interest for the time being," she said. "I shall return to settle matters with you in a week's time, when I have made up my mind." She stood up.

"Of course, Mrs Macready, that is most sensible. You will want to discuss the matter with your husband, I am sure."

Walking home it occurred to her that she did not want to discuss matters with Septimus in the least. Whatever her previous misgivings, the deed was done and the money was hers. For a wicked moment Gwendolyn was overcome with a wave of pure, almost terrifying elation. It caught her so suddenly that she felt her knees buckle and had to pause, leaning against a lamp-post until she had mastered the emotion. When it came down to practicalities, she had a decision to make between two choices: invest sensibly or speculate?

For a moment she vacillated, suddenly wanting to see the reassuring bulk of her husband, and looked down into the harbour in sudden expectation, but the dock was empty of all but a few fishing trawlers. Then her resolve hardened again. No, he had repudiated her and it was her turn to repudiate him. The money was hers by due process of law; she had no need to be ashamed; she would put it to good use but she must not be like the woman with the talents, hiding them under a bushel. First, as Sinclair had pointed out, it had to be made to work.

She drew in a deep breath and stared at the horizon. The sun sparkled on the sea and in the very far distance she could make out, blue as a bruise, the undulating line of the southern shore of the strait. Between lay the small, blue-grey silhouette of a ship. It was not *Caryatid*, that much she knew, and was probably a tramp passing along to one of the several ports to the eastwards of Porth Ardur.

Mrs Macready was proved wrong. Next morning the strange ship filled the enclosed dock in Porth Ardur and with her derricks swung out over the quay, disgorged some of the contents of her hold. The caravans, huge diggers and crane-grabs that were deposited so surprisingly, were accompanied by several score of rough-looking men who, having fired up these monstrous items of industrial plant, either drove them away, or swaggered off in their wake, winking at the young women of Porth Ardur as they marched in a loose and insolent column, like an impromptu army of invasion.

The men who worked on the docks reported the ship as being the SS *Lancelot*, belonging to the Cambrian Steam Navigation Company. They had had little notice of her arrival since their trade union had been hurriedly locked into discussing more important matters. Quite by chance one of the shop stewards had discovered the port had changed hands over the previous weekend and the dockers were eager to enter negotiations with the new owners. These turned out to be a company called Celtic Ports Limited and the Chairman and chief negotiator was a man called Stanier. People remembered him in Porth Ardur for being not only their harbour master, but the man who had taken on Captain Septimus Macready of the Celtic Lighthouse Service. The name of his company seemed somehow to defy that of the lighthouse authority which was not without its enemies in Porth Ardur. Most of these comprised the casual labour erratically employed on the other side of the enclosed dock, who regarded everyone paid by the Commissioners for Celtic Lights as having well-paid sinecures for life.

In fact, many more of the townsfolk, those not intimately concerned with ships and especially the women of the town, remembered Stanier for his brave stand against Captain Macready and his filthy old ship whose black funnel-smoke besmirched their weekly washing. Among these people, the intelligence that *Caryatid* was to be scrapped caused unalloyed joy. To this good news could now be added more, for Stanier's company had offered Porth Ardur's small group of dockers a deal promising them a great future centred on a regular sailing by a Cambrian steamship. Moreover, until the new tips were constructed, the first cargoes would have to be handloaded. This would provide a great deal of manual work.

"What happens when the tips are finished?" one man had queried from the back of the hall in which the meeting had taken place.

"By that time," Stanier had said, "the local economy will have picked up and our predictions show that a general import-export trade resourced from locally generated and regenerated trades will create a highly viable environment from which you will all be able to derive great benefit."

"And what does all that mean?" the hectoring went on, though others in the hall were hushing the man to silence.

"It means more ships, more work and more money, my lads." A modest cheer greeted this news. Stanier held up his hands for silence. "Moreover," he went on, "we are a highly progressive organisation. We want to end the pointless and mutually destructive confrontation of capital and labour. The Celtic Ports Company wishes you all to participate in its success by becoming stakeholders. Your labour is as important as the capital invested by shareholders. We promise we will share our profits equitably with all of you who chose to work for us. Therefore, in addition to your contracted wage, we will pay you an annual bonus . . ."

Stanier sat down to the gratifying ring of genuine, heartfelt applause. He began to believe he had written the speech himself.

The SS *Lancelot* had sailed by the time Macready next brought *Caryatid* into Porth Ardur, but she left in her departing wake air thick with rumour and speculation. News had yet to break formally about the full dissolution of the Lighthouse Authority's depot, for Macready had not divulged it for fear of it causing too much trouble both on board *Caryatid* and ashore. He expected the matter would be revealed by the Commissioners themselves when they arrived in *Naiad* for their annual inspection. He therefore bent his neck to the haughty impositions of fate and awaited the dreadful moment. Meanwhile, as the weeks passed, the turf on the lower slopes of Mynydd Uchaf was torn up; the gangs of navvies laboured on the embankments of the new railway; granite boulders rent from the higher slopes of the mountain were crushed and spread along the levelled stretches and new tarred sleepers were placed in position, to be, in due course, overlaid by steel rails which gleamed like spear shafts, as they ran from the heart of Mynydd Uchaf straight into Porth Ardur. Amid all this seething change, the public houses of Porth Ardur benefited from the thirsty influx of navvies, while fights occasionally erupted between them and the young men who had expected jobs on the new mine and whose girlfriends were proving faithlessly fickle. About now the first unexpected conceptions were reported.

It was a kind of madness that settled on Porth Ardur. Captain Macready continued his business as though nothing was wrong, while his wife had privately turned her life upside down by investing heavily in the new companies which seemed to be running the town. Sinclair confessed he had himself ventured some capital and viewed Mrs Macready's decision with huge enthusiasm. The promised return was forecast as seventeen per cent and Gwendolyn would have been personally satisfied with half, but she was suddenly intoxicated with the prospect of so large a return that she happily agreed to allow Sinclair to handle the matter for her, his commission notwithstanding. She told her husband nothing of all this, beyond admitting that she had been pleased with the sale of the farm.

"I hope you got at least two thousand," Macready had observed.

"I got a little more than that, dear," Gwendolyn had replied, a self-satisfied little smirk playing around her lips, and Macready, pleased that she appeared happy with the transaction, decided to leave her to enjoy her triumph.

"I am pleased to hear it," he said, picking up the day's newspaper. Had Gwendolyn not had her own preoccupations, she would have noticed that something had knocked much of the stuffing out of Septimus Macready.

Lord Craven was not a wicked man, but indolence and intelligence had combined to make of him a mischievous one. His father, bowed with age and the growing uncertainties of keeping together a small, though undeniably aristocratic fortune, had done his heir the disservice of not soon enough involving the young man in his family's affairs. It is difficult for a man who has sired a son and seen him grow from infancy to manhood, to define the precise moment of maturity that permits admission of confidences and the discussion of private affairs. Sadly, Lord Dungarth's countess had died while the boy was still in preparatory school, so his lordship, who exercised his paternal responsibilities through the assorted agencies of schoolmasters and his Steward, was apt to regard his heir as locked into a permanent state of adolescent rebellion. Equally sadly, idleness had produced in Lord Craven a predisposition to act the fool in his father's presence. It might have been helpful to both of them, had they been sailing together for, notwithstanding Nancy and Tegwyn, Lord Craven's real passion was exercised in his ketch *Lyonesse*, while his father had once been a notable yachtsman and beaten the old king himself.

However, shortly after Parliament was prorogued that summer, Lord Dungarth ran into his son in the hall of their town house and the two men were more or less forced to dine in each other's company at their mutual club. Here, to Craven's dismay but his father's evident pleasure, they ran into Stanier. The conversation soon concentrated upon the possibility of a new steamer service to Ynyscraven and, as the matter now seemed certain, Craven sat back and let the other two formulate a loose, promisory agreement. As he smoked his cigar, Craven felt a great longing to see Tegwyn, but, just as he was seeking a convenient moment to extricate himself from his father's society, another man joined them. He was clearly known to both Lord Dungarth and Stanier, though Craven, beyond acknowledging a vague familiarity from newspaper pictures, failed to put a name to the man's face. Since no-one introduced them, on the pretext of visiting the lavatory Craven buttonholed one of the club stewards.

"That is Mr David Smith, m'lord, Junior Minister in the Ministry of Power and member for, er, I beg your lordship's pardon, but I cannot quite recall which constituency Mr Smith represents."

"No matter, Hopkins. I don't know how you manage to remember us as well as you do. Thank you."

As he returned to the table, Craven heard Stanier mention that he must leave and pick up his wife who was dining with the Pomeroys. The thought of Tegwyn stirred Craven with itchings of illicit desire.

"Should catch a nightcap," Stanier was saying. "Anyone coming?" he added expansively.

"Is Pomeroy that art collector fellow?" Lord Dungarth asked.

"Yes, Lord Dungarth. A true connoisseur—"

"D'you know him, Roger?" the Earl asked, turning to his son for the first time for over an hour.

"Quite well, Pater. He's interested in Tasmanian wind masks. Odious things. Why, are you still trying to get rid of that alleged Canaletto?"

"Taxes, my boy, damned taxes. Anyway, what d'you mean, *alleged* Canaletto. The picture has as good a pedigree as yourself."

"Well, that's very reassuring, Pater, I'm sure, but why don't you give me the thing to auction instead of trying to con Pomeroy?"

"No harm in asking him though, is there?" Dungarth turned to Stanier. "Will he think we're intruding, Stanier?"

"I shouldn't think so," Stanier said, pulling out his watch and looking at it. "It's not quite nine yet."

"Let's all go then . . ."

And during this impromptu attempt by Lord Dungarth to sell a bad Canaletto, Mr David Smith MP first met Mr Pomeroy, though no-one at the time thought the casual encounter of any consequence whatsoever.

The final meeting of the Commissioners of Celtic Lighthouses before their annual inspection cruise was marked by one of the institution's traditions, specifically the formality observed when one of its members died.

Death was not actually admitted; the deceased was ritually said to have 'slipped his moorings and passed the last bar', a pronouncement made by the senior Commissioner, in the present case Sir Charles Mudge, while all those present sat, as though under the low deckheads of an ancient man-of-war, with their hats on. Sir Charles turned an old minute glass and all watched the grains of sand run from the top of the chamber to the bottom, a microcosmic representation of life itself. At the expiry of the minute, although all had been staring at the glass, its end was signalled by Sir Charles striking his gavel on the bruised table. The assembly then whipped off their hats and inclined their heads, immediately after which they rose and continued in conversation, as though nothing untoward had taken place, while wine and biscuits were brought in to symbolise the continuity of life and the stern business of the Lighthouse Authority.

This odd ceremony, seen for the first time by Captain Stanier, was also witnessed by a Captain Bernard Foster. Not being a Commissioner, Foster merely stood respectfully beside the table, his uniform hat tucked beneath his arm, watching in some wonderment what he had only hitherto heard of, despite his many years in the Commissioners' service. Once Macready's Chief Mate aboard *Caryatid*, Foster had risen to command the Commissioners' motor yacht, the *Naiad*. Properly, so prestigious a duty should have fallen upon the shoulders of the

Senior Master, Captain Macready, but at the time the post fell vacant, Macready had no desire to leave Porth Ardur, *Caryatid*, or the isle of Ynyscraven.

When sufficient wine and biscuits had been consumed to persuade all present that they were still physically in the temporal world and capable of digestion, Sir Charles Mudge called them to order.

"Now, gentlemen, we are of course also to consider our various duties during the forthcoming Commissioners' Cruise of Inspection. Captain Foster is here to outline our itinerary . . ."

An hour or so later the Board rose for lunch. All were acquainted with their proposed duties and the only matter they unfortunately had to leave until they reassembled at the end of the summer, was the election of a replacement for old Captain Jesmond.

From Captain Stanier's point of view, Foster had quite unintentionally done him an immense favour, for the cruise concluded in the Silurian Strait. This would give Stanier time to consolidate his position among the Board members and divine the best way of administering the *coup de grâce* to Septimus Macready. It would be like training for a race, gradually working up to a peak of performance, something upon which he could concentrate all his faculties. Stanier was confident, now that all was in place, that any small matters of business that cropped up in his absence could be handled by Caroline in concert with David Smith.

The first coal was gouged from the flank of Mynydd Uchaf the same day. A month later heaps of it were growing along the quayside of the enclosed dock at Porth Ardur. In a high wind the dust blew back over the town, besmirching the washing hung in gay lines to catch the breeze. The protesting women were hushed to silence by their menfolk who were anticipating good rates of pay as soon as the measuring clerks reckoned 10,000 tons was ready for shipping. After the first cargo had been cleared, the prefabricated coal tips would be erected, for the incoming cargo steamer would discharge the sections before loading the coal. The new port manager assured them that the inconvenience was only temporary.

Coal and Coalitions

Disillusion came upon the townsfolk of Porth Ardur like the dawn, beginning with a first vague suggestion, sensed more than actually perceived by a few souls. Later, as convictions hardened, the matter became more certain, a twilit realisation, and while it was some time before real evidence rose like the sun itself, there remained a few weeks before the full extent of the deception was known and understood by all. Many men and women relinquish their dreams as reluctantly as they relinquish their beds, belatedly confronting the realities that daylight inevitably brings.

The first few weeks of intense and profitable labour promised much. Coal seemed to tumble down from Mynydd Uchaf in such quantities that chapel preachers quit their promises of hell fire to the eager, promiscuous and pregnant young women of Porth Ardur, choosing instead to descant upon the bounty of the Almighty, the dignity of work and the eternal benefits accruing to the charitable. The visible heaps of coal were scooped up by grabs operated from the derricks of the first pair of the Cambrian Steam Navigation Company's ships, the *Bedivere* and the returning *Lancelot*. As the second cargo was loaded, the tipping towers were speedily erected. Two of these curious structures of steel and wood, each intended to service the fore and after hatches of the visiting steamships, reared up to dominate the dock, throwing their austere shadows over the town and signalling the march of industrial progress to those far out at sea.

"Bloody ugly things," Captain Macready pronounced as he made his approach, ringing the engine-room telegraph and reducing *Caryatid*'s speed as he prepared to swing round the end of the lighthouse pier and pass the open caisson into the enclosed dock.

Once the railway lines were connected, the laden coal trucks ceased depositing their cargoes on the quay and the great heaps of coal vanished forever. The waiting housewives sighed with relief, for now the coal was stockpiled at the mine where a mechanical loading system had become operational. This flung ton after ton of coal into the trucks just before the arrival of the ship was telegraphed. The trucks were then marshalled in sidings and trundled directly into the tipping towers where, one at a time, each was raised on the platform by a single operator, and up-ended. With a roar each truck flung its contents into a chute which was skilfully directed by a system of wires and pulleys, into the open hatches of the waiting steamship below.

In a stiff south-westerly breeze the dust produced swept in concentrated swathes directly across the backyards huddling behind the houses of Sudan and Egypt Road, soiling the washing hung out there. But, it was generally acknowledged, though it was a shame for the inhabitants of Sudan and Egypt Road, it could be avoided if they simply postponed their washing until the steamship had sailed. As for the rest, only the *Caryatid* still besmirched the sheets and pillow cases hung up behind the houses of Kitchener, Khartoum, Askari and Omdurman Roads, and she would soon be a thing of the past. Most people agreed that things were generally looking up.

Of course, once the tipping towers were established, the vast numbers of men employed to load the *Lancelot* and *Bedivere* were laid off. It would only be temporary, of course; once the generation of other trades got under way, the import and export of general cargo would mushroom and they would all have their jobs back. It was just a matter of time.

"Pie in the sky," one or two disenchanted souls muttered into their beer, pointing out that in addition to job losses on the docks, no more than two men had been employed as security guards at the mine. The remaining work at the mine was taken by the residue of the navvies who had arrived by ship to establish the eyesore in the first place. Most of them had now departed, no-one quite knew where, but those that remained were attracting an increasing hostility from the townsmen. The first marriage between a local girl and one of their number had very nearly been disrupted by the bride's brother who had had, it was generally acknowledged, more than he could comfortably drink. He had lost his job on the docks the previous day and the charitable considered this misfortune as his motive in mobilising his mates. Violence was fortunately averted at the last moment. Just as the vigilantes, led by the bride's brother and who had naturally boycotted the wedding, arrived at the church, the guard of honour appeared.

The happy couple emerged under an arch of turfing spades whose polished and honed blades gleamed in the fitful sunlight as the score of navvies waved them above their grinning colleague. The bride's brother, swearing vengeance, wisely ordered a retreat to The Feathers from where the landlord had trouble evicting them some three hours later.

Two weeks afterwards a more effective counter-blow was brewing in the sculleries of Sudan Road amid the damp washing now festooned indoors. It had been precipitated by a single, significant event. When the newlyweds returned from a brief honeymoon the bride bore a black eye.

"She fell out of bed," her husband explained in The Feathers, laughing, as his colleagues laughed with him.

Some thirty miles to the south-south-west of the island of Ynyscraven, the ketch *Lyonesse* was on a broad reach, scudding along under the impulse of a fresh breeze, swooping and diving over the low swell. At the helm sat Lord Craven, his blond hair dishevelled by the wind, an expression of complete satisfaction upon his face. Seen thus for the first time, an observer, had one been present, would have found it impossible to reconcile the same young man with the indolent spark formerly drifting round the capital, squandering time and money. A sailing yacht possesses the quality, for those who seek it, of putting constant demands upon her crew. One cannot dodge tasks without compromising one's very existence and Craven found this knife-edge life so exhilarating, so contrasting with his normal aimless existence, that he usually sailed single-handed. Not for the first time he toyed with the idea of simply taking it up permanently and sailing off around the world.

It was such a sunny day that he could easily persuade himself that he was off the Azores, heading west for the Indies. An hour ago a school of bottle-nosed dolphins had raced in from the starboard side and frolicked under the *Lyonesse*'s spoon bow for ten or fifteen minutes, adding to this illusion. But such a passage would be a long one on his own, and he was still troubled by the image of Tegwyn Pomeroy. What a delight it would be to have her here!

The last time Craven had seen Tegwyn had been on the occasion he had accompanied his father, Stanier and David Smith to the Pomeroys' apartment. It was clear the visit had been an intrusion. Pomeroy was not interested in the Canaletto. Craven had not for a moment supposed he would be. Pomeroy's taste for Tasmanian wind masks might have been reprehensible, but he was not foolish enough to believe Dungarth had a Canaletto worth buying. Still, Pomeroy's desire to show off the bloody wind masks in which Smith had shown a surprising and, Craven suspected, impulsive interest, had given him a moment with Tegwyn while his father paid Caroline Stanier flattering compliments.

"Sorry about this descent, Teggy," he had said. "This time it really wasn't my idea."

"You're just awful," she had said, but she had smiled when she said it, and he cherished the smile now. Had there been a hint of weary resignation in her face? He was sure he had noticed something like sadness in her expression. At this point a herring gull swept alongside him and, soaring close by for a moment, suddenly emitted such a raucous cry that it sounded like the gods laughing derisively at him. Craven chuckled at himself. What a self-deluding fool he was; if Tegwyn seemed weary it was due to their ill-mannered intrusion and not boredom with Pomeroy. An hour later Craven was frantically tucking a reef in his mainsail as a dark cloud began to brew to windward.

Lyonesse lay down under the assult when the squall hit her. It came with heavy rain which knocked the sea flat and the ketch seethed through the suddenly dark and cold sea. Dolphins and gulls had vanished and Craven strained at the tiller as the weather helm increased. Twenty minutes later the yacht emerged into sunshine as the cloud drove downwind. He shook his head, sending the raindrops flying and stared ahead. Craven caught his first sight of the Buccabu lighthouse as it broke the sharp line of the horizon.

Captain Macready spread his legs against *Caryatid*'s lazy roll and looked through his glasses at the Buccabu lighthouse at the same time, but from the opposite direction. He briefly recalled telling Charlie Farthing the story of Captain Jesmond and then dismissed the memory. Why on earth did his mind keep coming back to the mad old shipmaster? Jesmond was dead, and with him went the only hope Septimus Macready had of averting what he had come to think of as a great tragedy. That he had a central role in this drama was a natural assumption by the man who was, after all, the commander of *Caryatid*, the guardian of the ship's soul, the man whose will transformed her inert form into a moving entity and made of her a useful, almost sentient thing. It was something that one could only explain to another commander; a chief engineer for instance, was incapable of comprehending such a thing. It was something of this that had prompted the remark he had made to the Chief as the steamroller ploughed into the Mermaid Bakery.

Macready reached for the brass handle of the engine-room telegraph, wondering if that public display of hubris had precipitated the intervention of the fates. The notion perplexed and unnerved him.

He swung the handle to Stand-by, and then, a few minutes later, to Half Ahead.

"Starboard easy, Quartermaster . . ."

Macready raised his glasses again and shook off the metaphysical nonsense. He was depressed because he had lost Charlie. The mate had packed his traps and left the ship two days earlier, just before they had sailed from Porth Ardur on their present tour of sea-duty. He would have liked to have taken Charlie out to Ynyscraven aboard *Caryatid*, but the ship was not due at the island's lighthouse for a fortnight and, in any case, strictly speaking it would be contrary to service regulations.

His new mate, Mr Watson, was a decent and experienced officer, the temporarily promoted Second Officer of *Waterwitch*, who came aboard in the full knowledge that it would not be long before he returned to his old ship and reverted to his former rank. Macready manoeuvred *Caryatid* into a position to lower her boat and effect the relief of the keepers of the Buccabu light. When the boat returned the senior keeper coming off duty reported to Macready on *Caryatid*'s bridge.

"All well on the Buccabu light, Mister?" Macready asked formally, acknowledging the man's salute.

"Fine, Captain, except that the station could do with some oil fuel. We're well below half-tanks."

"Yes, I've seen the figures," Macready replied, indicating the board on the after bulkhead upon which the fuel and water states of all the lightvessels and lighthouses in the Area were recorded.

"I was just thinking that, as it's a nice day," the keeper hinted, "you might consider making a delivery."

Macready sighed. He had the St Kenelm lightvessel to relieve before dark and she was very low on oil fuel *and* fresh water. "We'll be back in a week," he said. "You go off and enjoy your leave. The station will be full up by the time you come back."

"Very well, Captain."

It was the first time in his career as a shipmaster that Septimus Macready simply could not be bothered. Nor did he feel guilty about it.

Charlie Farthing *was* feeling guilty. Arriving after a long and tedious train journey at Aberogg, a journey which had followed the anti-climactic business of leaving the service of the Commissioners for Celtic Lights and amounted to a tedious hour or so of paperwork in Mr Dale's office and an uncomfortable night in the Station Hotel. Now he was consequently experiencing an undeniable sensation of freedom. An efficient and conscientious officer, Charlie had always carried out his duties assiduously. Since his marriage, however, his life had been full of compromises. He saw too little of his beloved wife who had refused to move from Ynyscraven to Porth Ardur. Yet *Caryatid*'s routines were based upon the assumption that their ship's company were domiciled in their base port and the Commissioners for Celtic Lights were parsimonious with both the officers' salaries and their leave. His original expectation of soon becoming the Reeve of Ynyscraven, which had initially suggested that his continued employment aboard *Caryatid* would be short-lived, had not materialised. Charlie and his wife had had to bite the bitter bullet of separation. The course of true love, as Septimus Macready had sagely quoted to Justine some weeks earlier, never did run smooth.

But now, poised thus between one existence which was doomed, and another which was full of sweet promise, Charlie Farthing felt an intense surge of joy and unsullied happiness.

This received a blow when he discovered the island's supply ship, a small coaster named *Plover*, leaning against the small quay wall of Aberogg with engine trouble. All passages, it was announced on a blackboard lying against the wheelhouse, were postponed for at least five days.

"Bugger!" said Charlie, wondering if he could afford the lodgings and deciding that he was hot and thirsty. He headed for the open door of a public house on the quay named after the Buccabu Lighthouse above which hung a painted representation of the light tower offshore. It was an understandably popular name for public houses.

It was about this time that Lord Craven and *Lyonesse* swept past the lonely tower. A keeper on the gallery waved at the passing yacht; Craven waved back. Once clear of the reef, he ducked down into the chart space and picked up the dividers. Ahead of him opened the Silurian Strait; on the port bow the etched outline of Ynyscraven, to starboard and nearer, just past the great headland known to countless generations of seaman as Landfall Point, nestled the small, tidal port of Aberogg. He stepped off the distances and consulted the tidal atlas. He could just make Aberogg before dark. What was more, he could carry the flood and get alongside on top of the tide to enjoy a pint of ale and a star-gazey pie at the Buccabu Light.

"Right," he said out loud, climbing back out into the cockpit, "from the Buccabu Light to the Buccabu Light. That'll do us, won't it?" and he patted the tiller as he cast off the lashing and took it again. "Yes,' he added, speaking for the yacht, "that'll do us very well indeed."

The following morning Charlie woke with a slightly sore head and the feeling that all was not well. Confused for a second by his unfamiliar surroundings, he staggered to the window and remembered everything: he was marooned in Aberogg for at least four more days and with a rather depressingly finite sum of money. Across the estuary he could see the pine-clad hills rise rapidly to the scree-covered slopes of Cefn Mawr. The long ridge lay like a great sleeping dinosaur along the far side of the estuary of the River Ogg. It was low water, but the tide had turned. The silver stream running between gleaming sandbanks was imperceptibly swelling, inching out laterally over the sands upon which the oystercatchers fed. Immediately below the window of Mrs Gatcombe's guest house spread the quay with its litter of fish crates among which strutting gulls industriously foraged. The masts and superstructure of the immobilised *Plover* kept company with three smaller fishing vessels. More gulls wheeled and shrieked, perching and launching themselves in an endless circuit of flight and rest on the masts and dan-buoy spars of the fishing boats. Charlie yawned. How the hell was he going to spend the long hours of the day?

Shaving and dressing, he partook of one of Mrs Gatcombe's full breakfasts. The mass of eggs, bacon, mushrooms, tomatoes, black pudding and sausage, accompanied by buttered toast and a pot of tea, put him in better humour. At about nine o'clock he strode out onto the quay and, in the manner of seamen, started at one end and conducted a private review of the craft moored alongside. He passed the *Plover*, from the engine room of which came the dull ring of a hammer but which was otherwise deserted, and stared with a modicum of interest at the fishing boats. It was then that he spied the two masts of the ketch. The main mast towered over the quay and Charlie strode to the edge of the coping to stare down upon the deck of the elegant, teak-decked yacht.

The doghouse hatch was open and the smell of bacon wafted

up into the clear morning air. He caught a glimpse of someone moving about below and felt himself impertinent in thus staring, as it were, into another's private life. He walked idly away and for an hour lost himself in a second-hand bookshop near the church. After impulsively spending a pound on a slim, illustrated volume entitled *The Raptors of the Celtic Uplands*, Charlie drifted into the church, read all the tablets erected to the various worthies of Aberogg over the previous three centuries and then emerged into the sunshine again, just as the clock in the tower above his head struck half past ten.

He toyed with the idea of getting a message through to Sonia, but the difficulties of obtaining a telephone connection with Ynyscraven discouraged him. Besides, as yet he had no clear idea when he would arrive. It was this thought that drove him back to the quay. Perhaps someone would be more forthcoming with information about the *Plover*. All Mrs Gatcombe had been able to tell him was that the coaster would leave when the engine was repaired. This might be good news for her, but it was small comfort to Charlie.

The tide was making swiftly now, and had already reached the grounded keels of the vessels alongside the quay. The white-hulled ketch, whose name he could see was *Lyonesse*, was no longer deserted. One of the crew was up forward fiddling with the halliards at the base of the mainmast and looking up along the mast. Charlie saw a tall, slim, blond-haired young man a few years younger than himself. He followed the young man's glance aloft and at once located the fouled halliard.

"It's caught round a shackle pin at the hounds," he said.

"Ah, yes," said the young man, "I see it now, it's a bit difficult against the sky. You're a lot nearer."

"If you pass me a boat-hook I reckon I can clear it from here."

"Right. Thanks."

It was the matter of only a moment's effort to clear the halliard and, as he passed the boat-hook back, Charlie said, "If you turned the shackle the other way, that pin wouldn't foul the halliard."

The young man looked at Charlie and then at the shackle. "I don't suppose . . . No, silly of me."

"D'you want a hand? I've nothing better to do."

"I'm single-handed, so it's a bit awkward on my own."

"Have you got a bosun's chair? I'll hoist you up if you like."

The offer was accepted and Charlie clambered down on the yacht's deck while the young man disappeared below, to reappear a moment later with a short plank slung in a rope bridle. "You know about boats, I suppose, being from round here?" the younger man asked.

"Oh, I'm not from round here, but yes, I know a bit about boats," Charlie replied, smiling. "Have you got a spike? I'll slacken the bottle-screw."

As Charlie eased the tension in the shroud, the young man shackled the chair onto the main halliard and slipped his legs inside the rope. When Charlie was ready he sat on the plank as Charlie took the weight up on the halliard and then hauled him aloft. Ten minutes later, the job was done, the bosun's chair was thrown back down the fore hatch and the young man turned to Charlie.

"Thanks very much."

"That's all right. I'll be off then."

"Stay and have a cup of tea. I've another hour before the tide floats me off. If you're not in a hurry, that is."

"No," Charlie admitted ruefully, "I'm killing time. I'd be delighted to accept."

"Right. I'll put the kettle on. Come below."

"I'll just set up the shroud again," Charlie said, gesturing at the slack bottle-screw.

"Right. Thanks."

Going below, where the gas burner hissed under the copper kettle, Charlie passed the spike back to its owner. Taking it in his left hand the young man held out the right. "I'm Roger Craven."

"Charlie Farthing."

For a moment Lord Craven stared at his new acquaintance. "Did you say Charlie *Farthing*?"

"Yes," said Charlie, frowning, then he in turn recognised his host's surname. "Did you say *Craven*? Are you Lord Craven?"

Craven laughed. "Yes, I am, but don't let that worry you. Please call me Roger."

"I, er, I . . ." Charlie bumbled awkwardly. He could cope with knowing a peer by his Christian name, but when the chap was his prospective employer matters were less straightforward.

"Oh look," said Craven, "please feel free to dispense with formalities. I understand now why you're at a loose end. I heard when I got here last night that the *Plover* had coughed a head gasket or something technical. I had a star-gazey pie in the Buccabu Light," he added.

"I'm sorry, I didn't see you. I was drowning my sorrows there."

"Well, it doesn't matter, it was pretty crowded. The important thing is that you are here now and as one good turn deserves another, I can run you across to Ynyscraven when we float."

"That would be marvellous."

"Well, it gives us a chance to become better acquainted."

"Yes . . ."

Craven grinned as he put leaves in the teapot and poured in the boiling water from the kettle. He sensed Farthing's awkwardness and, having taken an instant liking to Charlie, sought to prevent the instinctive barriers of social diffidence from choking all prospects of friendship. "Make yourself at home, Charlie. Sit down."

Charlie squeezed along the settee and leaned his elbows on the fiddled tables. He recalled Macready's story of the old *Naiad*, Captain Jesmond and the lack of table fiddles.

"You're married to Sonia, aren't you?" Craven asked.

"Yes."

"When I was a small boy I used to spend some of my summer holidays on Ynyscraven. She was the first girl I ever tried to show my penis to. She had the good sense to decline the offer." Craven laughed with such self-deprecating enthusiasm that it broke Charlie's reserve.

"I'm glad to hear it," he responded quickly. "It might have put mine in the shade!"

They laughed together as Craven stirred quantities of sugar into the brew. "You come highly recommended," he said as their laughter subsided.

"I do?" Charlie frowned.

"D'you know Tegwyn Pomeroy?"

"Justine's daughter; yes. Not very well, but I know of her. My wife's a close friend of her mother."

"A sort of surrogate daughter, I hear."

"Well, I don't know about that—"

"I tell you what, Charlie," said Lord Craven, leaning across the table on his elbows and betraying the consequences of the loneliness inherent in sailing single-handed, "I'm absolutely enchanted by Tegwyn Pomeroy."

The effect of the deliberation in the sculleries and back kitchens of Sudan Road took some time to implement and a little longer to take effect. A reign of terror needs teeth to frighten and while no actual bodily malice was intended by the conspirators, its fortuitous appearance was not unwelcome to them.

The plan was as ancient as tragedy itself but, thought up as it was by women for whom its application was unlikely, the convincing of their younger, unattached sisters, daughters, nieces and cousins was a difficult matter. It is never easy to ask others to selflessly sacrifice what one has access to oneself. That those asked to give it up lacked the legal title that those who would continue to enjoy it possessed, did not help, for into the cogent arguments of logic was poured the bile of emotion. Once the plan of the matrons of Sudan Road was made known, it gained support not only with their sisters in Egypt, Khartoum, Kitchener and Omdurman Roads, but found allies up the hill towards the headier altitudes of Aspen Way and Acacia Avenue.

The transformation of this alliance into reality required several hundred private battles, battles held behind closed doors, when menfolk were at work, in the pub, or the lavatory. The arguments were hissed insistently between mothers and daughters. Tales of unnaturalness and beastliness, long known among the women to haunt the dark imaginings of men, gained new credibility and were added to whispers of bigamous conduct and the general infamy of foreigners. All boiled down to the Lysistratan admonition: 'Don't give the buggers the slightest chance to impregnate you!'

There were mild threats added to this instruction which were largely toothless until the unfortunate young woman who had been the first to marry one of the navvies, was found dead in a ditch. She had a deep head wound, and while the police were quite unable to find sufficient evidence that her husband was in any way responsible, for he had a cast-iron and apparently genuine alibi, the power of circumstantial evidence fanned by oblique suggestion and pure invented fiction was immense. Although a post-mortem showed her to have consumed a considerable quantity of raw potato spirit and an adjacent rock still bore traces of her blood, it was clear other marks upon her fair body were due to the intimate attentions of her husband. Mention was made of her earlier black eye. Morally, even the police considered a degree of guilt lay at her husband's door. Enough was known of his brutality to add weight to the story and lend it all the force of absolute truth.

The news passed quickly among the women, young and old. There was no need of more; chastity clamped its firm grip on Porth Ardur as formerly as the thighs of its peccant women had held the loins of their lovers.

The Inspection

It was long after midnight when Captain Foster dropped anchor off Ynyscraven and waited while *Naiad* brought up to her anchor. It had been a tediously long day. That morning *Naiad* had lain off Porth Neigwl and, in defiance of Foster's carefully planned itinerary, Captain Stanier had persuaded Sir Charles Mudge, who was naturally inclined to leave the matter alone, to call upon Mr Ifor Davis of the Mermaid Bakery.

"It will demonstrate that we care about what happened, Sir Charles. To simply sail into the bay then out again might put us in a bad light," Stanier had argued.

The Commissioners therefore left in their barge after breakfast next morning and landed ahead of the *Kurnow* which had just berthed and whose crew lined the rail and cat-called *Naiad*'s seamen and their strange passengers. The group of Commissioners, attired in formal blazers and flannels, and wearing straw boaters, moved through the disembarking crowd of visitors led by Captain Stanier who testily waved the mass of peasantry out of his way with his walking cane.

The repairs to the bakery had been completed long ago, but when he learned of the strangers standing outside his property, Mr Davis joined them, the marks of his honest trade covering his person.

Half an hour later as they returned to their barge, the Commissioners were soothed by Mr Davis's complimentary remarks. They were, he had assured them, gentlemen with whom it was a pleasure to do business. The only drawback to this effusion were the two floury loaves of fresh bread which Davis pressed upon them. Sir Charles insisted that Stanier

106

accepted these on behalf of them all. Relinquishing the two loaves as quickly as possible to the boat's crew, Stanier brushed down his blazer while the barge headed back towards *Naiad*.

"Lucky Macready hasn't got a photograph of you, Stanier," Sir Charles joked, causing a ripple of amusement among his fellow Commissioners. Stanier mustered a thin smile, harbouring increased resentment towards the man he now considered an implacable enemy.

The delay had cost them the tide at Mitre Rock. Foster was adamant that they were too late, the schedule was tight enough. To land too near high water was highly dangerous. A few years ago a keeper had been carried to his death with only a couple of inches of water sweeping the flat plateau upon which the tower was built. The thin layer of weed which covered it dried out within minutes of its exposure by a falling tide, but once wet it was as slippery as ice. They would have to steam instead directly to the St Kenelm's lightvessel, carry out the inspection there and then return to Mitre Rock and land after high water, as the tide fell away. It would mean additional fuel costs, but that could not be helped. They would just be that much later anchoring that night at Ynyscraven.

"You will have to eat dinner under way, gentlemen," Foster explained, "rather than in the security of the anchorage."

"That doesn't matter," Stanier said.

"Not to you, Stanier, maybe," grumbled Sir Charles Mudge, "but I've eaten too many meals at sea. A dinner in tranquil waters is always welcome."

"Oh, I'm sure, Sir Charles—"

"You're always *sure*, Stanier, that's your bloody trouble," grumbled Sir Charles. "By the way, what happened to that fresh bread?"

"I, er, I've no idea, Sir Charles, I passed it to the boat's crew."

"That's the last we'll see of that, then. I think I could swallow a whisky and soda."

Stanier felt better after the inspection of the St Kenelm's lightvessel. Sir Charles had deputed Stanier, Blake and Gostling to carry out the duty.

"No point in arriving mob-handed, damn it," he had decided, calling for another whisky and soda.

The inspecting party arrived back with Stanier in gleeful mood. They had discovered what he reported to Sir Charles as 'irregularities'. These turned out to be a seaman with hair of excessive length, the master's top reefer button undone, an ullage in the station's rum bottle for which there was no documented reason, a spillage of oil in the oil store and a coil of fire hose stretched along the deck, rather than nestling coiled in its box.

The Master accepted the hair length of his crew member as being a little untidy, but he was unable to explain the lack of rum, viewing the revelation with some surprise, even though the bottle was locked in his cabin. He hung his head shamefully at the oil spillage, but explained that they had washed the decks down in honour of the occasion with the fire hose and it was against regulations to stow damp hoses.

Stanier pooh-poohed all these excuses and inscribed the station's deficiency in the station order book. This leather-bound document dated back 128 years, recording every visit of the Commissioners since the establishment of the station. In all that time Stanier's opprobrious comments were only matched on two previous occasions. When the unfortunate skipper read what Stanier had written on the Commissioners' behalf, he was mortified. He was most personally hurt by the comment that he himself 'seemed incapable of wearing the service uniform correctly'.

It was only on the way back to *Naiad* that the bearded Gostling turned to Blake and asked, "Isn't there some tradition that if a lightvessel skipper has been in the rank for more than twenty years he's allowed to leave his top reefer button undone?"

Blake frowned and nodded sleepily. "Yes, yes, I think there is, old boy."

Both men looked at Stanier who stood staring astern with a stopwatch in his hand. He was timing the light and fog signal that now suddenly blasted its diaphone through the clear air of the afternoon.

"Are they all right, Stanier?" asked Blake.

"They'll time them from the ship too," Gostling said. "Sit down, Stanier. No point in keeping a kennel of dogs and doing all the barking ourselves now, is there?"

"Well, there wouldn't be if they were reliable," Stanier said obscurely, "but that fog signal's slow."

As Stanier climbed up to *Naiad*'s bridge after the barge had been recovered he had intended to complain the fog signal was slightly slow, but was met by Foster reporting it correct.

"I made it a little slow, Captain Foster," Stanier said sharply.

"The barge makes eight knots under full power, Captain Stanier," Foster said.

"I don't follow you."

"Eight knots introduces a period of delay between the arrival of the first signal and the second due to the increased distance the sound has to travel to reach you in the barge as you speed away from it."

"I see . . . Oh yes, of course, you mentioned that to me before." Stanier flushed, irritated.

"I did, sir, yes. And the position of the lightvessel is correct. We have just verified it."

"I see."

"I believe your steward is serving tea, Captain Stanier, if you'll excuse me, we have to set course back for Mitre Rock."

Stanier fulminated under Foster's withering politeness. As he reached the after smoke room Gostling met him with a broad grin. "Got caught with that old time and distance nonsense again, did we, Stanier?" Gostling's laughter followed him below to his cabin. Caught or not, Stanier told himself, that fog signal was slow and Foster was covering for his colleague. The truth was that Macready's Area was a bloody mess!

On the bridge Captain Foster handed over *Naiad* to his Second Officer and went into the radio room. He switched on the transmitter and let it warm up. When, on pressing the handset, the tell-tale neon attached to the aerial glowed bright orange, he began to call *Caryatid* on 2241 kilocycles.

"*Caryatid, Caryatid*, this is *Naiad*, come in, please. Over."

Unsurprisingly, with the whole Board of Commissioners in

his Area, Macready's radio watch was efficient and the response of his ship almost immediate.

"*Naiad*, this is *Caryatid*. All attention. Over."

"Request Captain to Captain. Over."

"Very good, sir. Stand by one." There was a pause, then Macready's deep bass boomed over the airwaves, making Foster smile. "*Caryatid* to *Naiad*. Macready here."

"Hullo, Septimus, Bernard here, who was that on the blower? Over."

"My new Mate, young Watson on loan from *Waterwitch*. Charlie's gone, settling at last on Ynyscraven. We've had the bad news. Over."

"Yes, we heard, sorry about that. I've got some more for you. We've just cleared the Kenelm. I think there's an anchor problem. Over." It was a euphemism, just in case one of the Commissioners rumbled their conversation.

"Oh, right. Thanks, Bernard. Not much of one I hope. Over."

"Middling, I'd say. Over.

"Got it. See you off the island. Over and out."

"*Naiad* out."

"Bugger," swore Macready as he emerged back on the bridge and met Mr Watson.

"Something the matter, sir?"

"Yes. Bloody St Kenelm's off station."

"Oh, shit."

"We must have dragged her when we were oiling the other day."

"Yes, quite possibly."

Macready reproached himself. He had not bothered to make a final check. It was unforgivable. The problem was he found his mind wandering these days. It was too stuffed full of uncertainties.

The Commissioners' inspection of Mitre Rock was similar to that of the lightvessel. It was sunset as they completed it and they decided to let the keepers light up before they concluded their business. The lighthouse was actually in first-class order, but a pedant seeking for dust could find it if he put his mind to the task and Stanier was in a bristlingly pedantic frame of mind.

On their departure, above the Commissioners' signatures, the order book bore in Stanier's handwriting the comment that 'this station is covered in dust . . .'

It was a quite unnecessary sophistry, for in fact one of the keepers provided Stanier with exactly what he wanted, a direct accusation aimed at Macready. When asked if anyone had any complaints, the man stepped forward and said he had been denied compassionate leave when his wife had been expecting a baby.

"The regulations state compassionate leave is automatic, sir, if due notice is given, and I got a doctor's letter to be sent to Porth Ardur with all the details."

"And?" prompted Gostling.

"I got a message that my wife had gone into labour, sir—"

"At the time expected?" asked Blake.

"No sir, a week early. But it was our first, sir, so it wasn't *that* unexpected."

"Go on. You were out here, I suppose?"

"No sir, I was on the Buccabu light then, sir, last March it were, sir, I've only been here since the twelfth of May, sir, haven't I, Chief?"

The senior keeper confirmed the fact and the supplicant continued. "As soon as I got the signal, sir, I asked the Senior to call up *Caryatid* and let Captain Macready know. The message I got back was in the negative, sir." The keeper drew himself up and added, "And I wish to make a formal complaint, sir."

"Of course, my man," said Stanier, taking his name and entering it into his notebook. He suppressed any sense of triumph with great care, but his heart was singing.

It was almost completely dark by the time the barge edged its way out of the gut between the dark fangs of the complex geological formation that made up Mitre Rock. Foster was fuming at the delay, but was mollified when at last the barge emerged and headed back to the ship, a touch of phosphorescence in her bow wave. Then they had had a five-hour passage to Ynyscraven.

It was now gone 0200 and by the time the Carpenter called from the forecastle that the anchor had brought the ship up, Foster was drooping with fatigue. He would have to be up by

0700. No wonder old Septimus had declined the command. It might be the most prestigious in the Service, but it was also the most wearying!

Foster was in fact woken shortly before 0600 by the Commissioner's senior steward, Sudbrook.

"I'm sorry to bother you, sir, but it's Captain Stanier."

"What?" said Foster, trying to clear his head of the fog of sleep. "What's the matter with him? Is he ill?"

"Oh no, sir," the Steward said, smiling. "He's asking where the *Caryatid* is, sir."

"He's *what*?" Foster's tone of incredulity startled Sudbrook. "Did you wake me to ask that?"

"Yes, sir. Captain Stanier told me to call you and ask you where the *Caryatid* is."

"Look, Sudbrook, go and tell Captain Stanier to . . . *Oh, blast it!*" Foster threw aside his bedding and got up.

Sudbrook fell back. "I'm sorry, sir—"

"Oh, it's not your fault, Sudbrook."

"I think Captain Stanier expected to find *Caryatid* at anchor in the bay, sir."

So did Foster, knowing of old Macready's arrangement with his lovely mistress, but if *Caryatid* was late arriving it did not matter. Her inspection was not scheduled until the afternoon and Macready was quite capable of arriving at the very last moment. Besides, inspection or not, the business of the Lighthouse Authority came first and Foster guessed that at that very moment, *Caryatid* was probably alongside the St Kenelm lightvessel, weighing the huge anchor which had dragged from its officially assigned position. Foster knew Macready well enough to know not even his mistress would divert him from his duty.

Foster shaved and dressed and then went aft. On the quarterdeck Captain Stanier was pacing up and down in a silk dressing gown with a telescope under his arm. To the south and west, the cliffs of Ynyscraven beetled down upon them. Although it was broad daylight, the two lighthouses at each end of the island were still flashing. Then, as if acknowledging Foster's appearance on the *Naiad*'s quarterdeck, they went out.

"I understand, Captain Stanier, you wish to know where the *Caryatid* is?"

"Indeed I do, Captain Foster. She is due to be inspected today."

"She is due to be inspected this afternoon, to be precise, Captain Stanier. I am confident that, unless some duty has unavoidably delayed her, Captain Macready will honour his obligation and turn up on time."

"I hope you are not being insolent, Captain Foster."

"So do I, Captain Stanier, but I resent being woken unnecessarily."

"That *is* insolent, Captain Foster," said Stanier, raising the telescope to his eye and laying it upon a yacht anchored close in, under the cliffs, not far from where a slim silver freshet fell down the precipitous rock.

"Then please feel free to report it to Captain Sir Charles Mudge."

"Oh, I shall, Captain Foster, I shall," remarked Stanier, still staring through his glass as Foster turned on his heel and angrily stumped forward.

Lord Craven woke to the steady roar of a boat engine passing close. A moment later he was almost tossed from his bunk as the Commissioners' barge surged past and *Lyonesse* rolled deeply in her wake. Indignantly he leapt into the cockpit stark naked waving his fist at the barge's stern.

"What's the bloody idea, you damned idiots!"

No-one in the boat noticed him, they were all deafened by the roaring engine and looking forward as they approached the beach where a uniformed keeper, the Senior from the south light, stood waiting to meet them.

Swearing fluently, Craven went below and put the kettle on. He knew the boat, and the ship lying offshore. Stanier would have been in the barge, of that there was little doubt and he would get even with Stanier later. He sat in the cockpit and drank his tea. Afterwards he jumped over the side and swam four times round *Lyonesse*, then hauled himself back on board by way of the bobstay. He had been invited to lunch with Sonia and Charlie Farthing and was looking forward to the occasion.

He really felt the chance meeting with Charlie was fated far more than fortuitous.

They had enjoyed an exciting passage across from Aberogg, a brisk sail during which Charlie had demonstrated his ability as a yachtsman.

"You're a natural," Craven had said admiringly, "we must do this again. D'you think your wife will come with us?"

"Not if you ask her to cook, she won't," Charlie had laughed.

"I wouldn't dream of such a thing. I enjoy cooking myself. It's the only chance I get. We could sail round the island."

"She'd love that."

"We must do it then."

"Give me a day or two to settle in, then. How long are you staying?

"How long's a piece of string?"

"Ahhh," Charlie had laughed again, "*that* long."

"You're implying the length of string on Ynyscraven may be considerable."

"No. Only that anything on Ynyscraven tends to be more complicated than one imagines."

Charlie watched the motor barge leave *Naiad*'s side from the window of his bedroom. It gave him a queer, disjointed sense of *déjà vu*. It was the wrong ship and he had no need to rush down any more and catch a boat, yet the sight was tinged with a strange sadness. He must have sighed audibly, for Sonia called from the bed.

"Are you all right, Charlie?"

"Of course I am," he said, turning.

She let her gaze trail down him. "Come here."

"Is it better than Roger Craven's?" he asked smiling, feeling it had a sense of its own importance.

"I never saw Roger Craven's. That one," she said, kicking aside the bedding and spreading herself, "is just fine."

As Charlie and Sonia drove each other to their climaxes, Captain Macready, with the St Kenelm lightvessel grinding the fenders between herself and the *Caryatid* to a flattened disfigurement, nudged the inert craft a few hundred feet back to the westward.

On the monkey island above his head Watson and the Second Mate wielded their sextants and sought the crucial angles on the distant land that would refix the correct position for the lightvessel's anchor. The offending killick swung beneath the bluff bow of the lightvessel, a clod of shell-encrusted mud clinging to its flukes. Patiently a seaman on *Caryatid*'s foredeck played a hose on the anchor disturbing clods of the mud, which fell away with loud plops as Macready neared the correct position.

"Left-hand angle coming on, sir," called Watson.

"Right-hand angle almost there, sir," added Wentworth.

Macready rang the ship's engines to stop and she lost way.

"On, sir!"

"On, sir!"

Macready gave a double ring for full astern. "Let go!" Macready roared and the lightvessel's anchor dropped from the hawse pipe with a roar and clatter of veering cable.

Twenty minutes later *Caryatid* and the St Kenelm lightvessel lay back to a scope of ninety fathoms of heavy cable. Shortly afterwards *Caryatid* detached herself from the lightvessel's side and headed south, bound for Ynyscraven at full speed.

"Oh well," mused Macready who really could not give a damn what the Commissioners said about a ship they had already condemned to the scrapyard, "better late than never."

He suddenly felt exposed and alone.

Having inspected the south lighthouse, the Commissioners bumped across Ynyscraven to and from the north light by tractor. To be accurate, they were actually accommodated in a small trailer which towed behind the tractor, an odd cargo with their sticks and straw hats who recovered their joint composure after a short stay at the Craven Arms where they were served by Sonia. It was clear they would have stayed and lunched at the inn had it not been for Captain Stanier who was anxious to get back to *Naiad*, to prepare himself for the afternoon.

They trooped out and made for the path to the beach while Sonia gave Charlie the all clear. He had no desire to run into his recent employers, but watched them retire down the cliff path.

"I recognised Stanier," Sonia said, clasping her husband's

arm and laying her head upon his shoulder. "But I don't think he recognised me."

At the bend in the path the group met a solitary figure coming up from the beach. They saw the Commissioners halt and Stanier addressed the blond-headed young man.

"Here comes our lunch guest," said Charlie.

At the bend in the path overlooking the bay, Craven almost bumped into the gaggle of dusty and oddly assorted gentlemen confronting him.

"Good heavens, Lord Craven . . ." Stanier held out his hand.

Craven ignored Stanier's outstretched hand and regarded the lot of them with an extreme air of truculence, his hands upon his hips. "Don't you buggers have any consideration for others?" he asked accusingly.

Stanier's face crumpled into a sheepish grin. "Craven, I don't think you've met Sir Charles Mud—"

"Met him? I don't need an introduction, the bugger tossed me out of my bunk this morning! What speed does that barge of yours do, Stanier?"

"About, er, eight knots . . ." responded the flustered Stanier, embarrassed at having revealed his acquaintance with this rude young man and confused as to Craven's line of reasoning.

"Eight?" roared Craven. "Eight? You shouldn't exceed four in Ynyscraven road—"

"Excuse me, young man, but there's no speed limit in the anchorage—" put in Gostling.

"There is now," Craven said. "Four knots!"

"What authority do you invoke?" asked Gostling.

"By mine, you damned fools. Don't you know who you chucked out of his bunk this morning? Stanier'll tell you. Good day to you!"

And Lord Craven all but ran until he was round the corner, out of sight of the blazered gentlemen, where he collapsed laughing. He was still chuckling when he reached the Farthings' cottage. Soon the walls of the place rang with it, so much so that Justine came in from next door, joined in when she heard the reason for their mirth and stayed for lunch.

As for the senior Commissioners, they agreed the young man

must have been drunk and, metaphorically pulling their tattered dignity about them, they continued their descent to the beach.

"You and that young fellow seemed to be acquainted, Stanier," Sir Charles Mudge said.

"I am acquainted with him, Sir Charles, somewhat regrettably, I think," Stanier added awkwardly.

"Well, who the devil is he?" asked Blake.

"Lord Roger Craven, heir to the Earl of Dungarth, the owner of this island."

"Then the bugger *can* make a local bye-law governing a speed limit within the island's inshore waters," observed Captain Blake, addressing Gostling who was famous among them for his recondite grasp of the most arcane facts of maritime law.

"Oh yes, yes indeed. And by ancient statute he still has the right to hang pirates caught in waters under his jurisdiction."

"Well, we're not pirates," said Stanier, attracting glances of withering contempt from his fellow Commissioners.

When they reached the beach the motor barge was awaiting them. Stanier suddenly recollected the business of the afternoon. Apart from Lord Craven's white ketch and the black, white and buff splendour of *Naiad*, the bay was still empty.

The lighthouse tender *Caryatid* steamed into the anchorage of Ynyscraven at 1355, just as the Commissioners emerged onto *Naiad*'s quarterdeck after their lunch. As they went forward to board the barge, Sir Charles Mudge went up onto the bridge.

"Ah, Captain Foster, please extend dinner invitations to Lord Craven and . . . what's the official name of the chap who helps run the tractor up to the lighthouses?"

"The Reeve, Sir Charles."

"That's the fellow. I suppose he's married?"

"He certainly was when I was last here."

"Very well, we'd better include his wife. And get Macready and his Chief Engineer over here . . . Oh, and I suppose you'd better come."

"Thank you, Sir Charles," Foster said dryly, adding, "that leaves the Reeve's wife rather on her own, Sir Charles."

"Any bright ideas?"

"There's a rather attractive widow, er, Captain Macready

knows her quite well. I'm sure he'd be pleased to act as escort, or, if you wished, I could ask her."

"If you can rustle up another lady, that'll be fine. Oh, and Craven's on his yacht, I understand. Must be that ketch inshore. I haven't seen another boat about."

"I'll see to it, Sir Charles."

"Very well. Now let's go and give poor old Macready the bad news."

Foster was about to say that Macready already knew, but decided against it. Idly he watched the barge leave *Naiad's* side then quickly went to his cabin, wrote several notes and, after instructing his Second Officer what to do with them, he folded himself in his armchair and went to sleep.

Aboard *Caryatid* the Commissioners rooted into every compartment in the ship. They were attended by Macready and his senior officers who picked up various key personnel as they progressed, such as the Second Engineer at the engine-room door, the Bosun in the hold and the Carpenter forward in the stores. By now Mudge and his colleagues were so used to Stanier fussing and complaining about every misplaced item, every smear of grease and scar of rust, that they discounted most of his diatribe as he tut-tutted his way through the ship. For those personally responsible for these various workaday blemishes that inevitably marred an old ship like *Caryatid*, this tooth-sucking disapproval was demoralising in the extreme. Finally, when Stanier, leading the posse like a bloodhound, discovered a small pile of paint scrapings and a scraper leaning against a bulkhead, he pointed and asked what on earth these things meant.

"I've a seaman working on scraping this bulkhead, sir," said Watson.

"But this is an inspection, Mister. All this stuff should be squared away before we come aboard."

"I'm sorry, sir, I had intended this should be finished, but it isn't and I thought it better to continue the work until it is."

"Then where is the man now?" Stanier persisted with warped logic.

"I expect he's taken himself off until you gentlemen have all passed through, sir."

"You mean you don't know where the dickens he is, Mister?"

"Not exactly," admitted Watson, wearying of the farce.

"An officer who doesn't know exactly where his men are is incompetent."

"Let's move on," said Sir Charles, taking Stanier's elbow.

"Incompetent, Mister, d'you hear me . . ."

The inspection completed its round of the ship on the bridge. Here Sir Charles took the *Caryatid*'s order book from Stanier's hands and wrote briefly in it before handing it to Macready. "I regret having to write what I have, Captain Macready, but . . ." Mudge shrugged, "these things cannot be avoided."

Taking the book Macready read the senior Commissioner's remarks and then repeated them out loud.

"*The final inspection of the S.S.* Caryatid *took place off the island of Ynyscraven. The ship was found in good, serviceable order, reflecting credit on Captain Macready, his officers and ratings. The vessel has acquitted herself very well during her long years of service and has always maintained the high standards of the Celtic Lighthouse Service.* Thank you, Sir Charles."

"Sorry, Macready. You'll retire with the ship, of course. We've no plans to replace her, I'm afraid. *Waterwitch* will take over her work."

"And the base at Porth Ardur, Sir Charles?"

Mudge shook his head. "We're shutting up the whole shop. You'll get your orders in the next few days. But it seemed proper that I should let you know officially."

"That's kind of you, Sir Charles."

"It's unfortunate, Captain Macready, but duty compels me to raise the matter of a formal complaint laid against you by Assistant Keeper Macleod on the Mitre Rock light. He was formerly on the Buccabu—"

"I take it this is about his aborted compassionate leave, Captain Stanier," Macready broke in.

"Er, yes."

"The night his wife went into labour, it was blowing a sou'

westerly nine. The following day it had veered westerly and increased to storm force ten. It dropped to an eight the next day, backed sou' westerly and blew like that for a week. By the time the sea conditions enabled us anywhere near the Buccabu reef, Macleod was due for normal leave. We took him off as a matter of routine. I think even the good Lord Himself would have found walking on the water difficult that particular night, Captain Stanier. That is the reason why Junior Keeper Macleod could not be with his wife the night her baby was born."

"Well, that settles that matter then," said Sir Charles hurriedly. "I think it's time we returned to *Naiad*."

The Commissioners' barge ran alongside *Naiad* and they disembarked. On deck a fuming and frustrated Stanier ran into the Second Mate who was about to leave with the letters of invitation. From the casual conversation of Sir Charles and Captain Gostling, Stanier had heard Macready's name mentioned as a dinner guest.

"D'you have an invitation there for Captain Macready?"

"Yes sir, and his Chief Engineer. They're the last to be delivered. I was waiting for you to finish your inspection before taking them across to *Caryatid*."

Stanier smiled. "Don't bother. They won't have the opportunity. Give them to me." He took the two envelopes and, stuffing them into his pocket, motioned the Second Mate to follow him up to *Naiad*'s bridge.

"I want you to send *Caryatid* a signal," Stanier said, waiting while the young officer reached for the message pad. "*Prefix: priority, stop,*" he dictated. "*Proceed and verify position of St Kenelm lightvessel, stop. Reported off station, stop.* That's all, get that transmitted right away."

The Second Mate looked from the message to Stanier. "We haven't received . . . I'll send it by semaphore, sir."

"At once, Mister!" Stanier commanded, waiting while the Second Mate called up the *Caryatid*. When the answering flutter of red and yellow flags indicated her readiness to receive, he went aft chuckling to himself.

"What's *Caryatid* signalling about?" Sir Charles asked as

he took tea on the quarterdeck, having noticed the flutter of the flags.

"Oh, something's out of position, Sir Charles, I guess he's sending his apologies about dinner tonight."

"You were damned hard on him, Stanier."

"Got to maintain standards, Sir Charles, you know that. It's not our business to go about making ourselves popular," and he swung the older man away from the fluttering flags for fear he might actually read the message. "And it's particularly important," he added with a flash of uncharacteristic genius, "to keep up the pressure, particularly as we enter this period of change."

"Well, you do have a point there, I suppose, Stanier."

"Thank you, Sir Charles."

After the Commissioners had gone, Macready stared across the water until their barge had disappeared behind the low hull of *Naiad*. He felt a profound sense of anti-climax. Although he had long known the truth, it hurt him to have been officially told the news of *Caryatid*'s demise under the cliffs of Ynyscraven. It was for him a place invested with enormous charm, a personal private place with which the Commissioners had only the most tenuous connection. The lighthouses were not *theirs*, they belonged, morally at least, to their keepers and the officers and men of the *Caryatid* who collectively maintained them with devotion for the benefit of the passing mariner. Those remote, unknown ships, bound outward or inward, each upon her own lawful occasions, moved him with their innate dignity. Yes, it was the essential dignity of ships with which he, Septimus Macready, identified. They inherently possessed something majestic, even, he ruefully admitted, the rust buckets owned by Cambrian Steam. He had not thought of it quite like that before. Perhaps it was only at this moment of realisation that his long connection with ships was coming to an end, that he was capable of formulating such a thought, but he felt it justified his hubris.

No-one saw the solitary tear that rolled down his cheek. He dashed it to one side as *Naiad* began semaphoring.

Invitations to Dinner and Other Intrigues

Captain Foster's invitations to dine aboard *Naiad* arrived at the Farthings' cottage as they finished lunch. It had been a happily relaxed occasion, with Lord Craven obviously charmed by Justine. She in turn enjoyed the young man's attentiveness. Even the intrusion of *Naiad*'s Second Officer failed to puncture the mood and he was invited to enjoy a glass of wine, happy to have found the elusive Lord Craven in the company of the new Reeve.

"Well, well," said Craven on reading the note. "I clearly did not insult them enough."

"Perhaps they want you to revise the speed limit," Charlie said laughing.

"I'm sorry about that," said the *Naiad*'s Second Mate. "I was in the boat this morning. They were muttering about your rights to impose it on the way back to the ship."

"If you can prove them to be pirates, I think I can hang them, too," Craven said, smiling.

"Yes," agreed the officer, "I overheard them mention that too."

"I'm glad they know about it."

"Well," said Justine, "it would certainly solve some of our problems."

"I don't think we've a tree tall enough on the island," chuckled Craven.

"Oh, there are some lovely old oaks in the coombe," protested Sonia, who would defend all criticisms of Ynyscraven.

"Well, we could always use the gallery rails of the lighthouses and string 'em up like pheasants after a shoot," suggested Charlie.

"What a delicious prospect," Craven agreed.

"I must go," said *Naiad*'s Second Officer, tossing off his glass.

"Just one thing," Charlie had said as the officer rose to leave. "I'd be obliged if you didn't let on to anyone that the new Reeve is a former officer in the Lighthouse Service."

"No, of course not," the fellow said, grinning conspiratorially.

"My God!" exclaimed Craven, slapping his forehead in mock horror after the officer's departure, "what the dickens will I wear? I suppose they'll all be dolled up in mess kit or something?" he looked enquiringly at Charlie.

"Yes, I'm afraid so."

"I've a plain reefer on board, but I'm damned if I'm going to wear that. What are you ladies going to wear?" he asked, winking at Charlie and precipitating a discussion that rambled on for almost half an hour during which Charlie and Craven made serious inroads into another bottle of Sonia's excellent gorse wine.

Justine felt strangely excited. Although she loved her new life on the island, she was undeniably attracted by the touch of glamour suggested by a formal dinner in the splendid surroundings she had heard prevailed aboard the Commissioners' yacht. As a former ballroom dancer she had a love of clothes and display, small vices she had no chance of indulging on Ynyscraven. Of course, she would have to be circumspect regarding Captain Macready, for in the invitation the tactful Foster had indicated Macready would be present, but he had underlined the fact that she was to be partnered by Foster himself. By such a diplomatic device, Foster could rob the occasion of any whiff of scandal. Justine chided herself; she had always thought of Bernard Foster as a dull man!

When the lunch party broke up amid yawns and protestations that it might be a good idea to lie down for an hour or two, Sonia cast a look out through the window as she began to carry the dirty dishes to the sink.

"*Caryatid*'s steaming away," she said, staring through the glass. "I wonder why."

Justine and Charlie crowded round her. The old ship was half a mile north of the anchorage, running up the eastern shore of the island, the white vee of her wash and the coiling black smoke that she trailed astern showing she was already at full speed. Clearly she was not just popping up to the north light.

"Any idea, Charlie?" Justine asked, her low voice vibrant with emotion.

Charlie frowned. "No."

He paused and Justine said, "If they're off somewhere, Septimus won't be there this evening."

"But you said Bernard Foster said he would be," Sonia put in.

"It must be an emergency," said Justine, used to disappointment.

"The weather's good," mused Charlie.

"Someone sick?" suggested Craven.

Charlie nodded. "Yes, it could be that."

"Well, there must be a logical reason," Craven said, uncertain exactly why the departure of *Caryatid* should so interest these people until he recalled they were islanders, and obsessed with the small things that loomed large in their lives. "It doesn't really affect us—"

"It affects me, Roger," Justine began.

"Oh yes. You and the Captain. I'd forgotten. I'm sorry . . . But look," Craven added brightly, "you can come as my guest."

"Officially, I'm already going as Captain Foster's."

"Captain Foster—" frowned Craven.

"The commander of *Naiad*," Charlie explained quickly, something occurring to him. "This could be deliberate, you know."

"You mean a snub to Septimus?" Justine asked.

"Stanier could have a hand in it," Charlie suggested.

Macready strode his bridge in a towering rage. He did not often lose his temper, but to be kicked out of the anchorage of Ynyscraven was a further affront and he wanted to believe that Stanier was behind the alleged signal claiming the St Kenelm lightvessel was out of position. But the knowledge that he attended to the very matter only hours earlier that same day and restored the lightvessel to her precise position, did nothing for Macready's equanimity. The fact was that once a lightvessel's mooring anchor had been broken out of the ground it was sometimes difficult to rebed it. Even digging it into the bottom by running the *Caryatid*'s engine astern at the end of a generous scope of cable might not entirely bury the anchor securely. It was therefore *just* possible that after they had left this morning, the strength of the tide had moved the lightvessel again. The uncertainty nagged at Macready, increasing his fury, until Mr Watson, his own competence affected by the apparent failure of the morning's operation, asked to have a word with him.

"What the devil is it, Mister?" growled Macready, following the Mate out onto the bridge wing out of earshot of the Quartermaster on the wheel.

"I took the liberty of going through to Porth Ardur on the radio, sir, by way of the coastguard."

"What?" Macready frowned. Strictly speaking, Watson had exceeded his authority in making a radio transmission through the coastguard without the permission of *Caryatid*'s master. But Macready sensed the moment was inappropriate for raising any objection. Besides, he had a vague feeling that he knew why Watson had done it and that he should have thought of it himself.

"The Nelson spirit, sir," Watson said by way of exculpation.

"Go on, Mr Watson," prompted Macready, feeling his temper subside.

"I asked the coastguard to query the time and origin of the signal that reported the St Kenelm out of position. He said he had not received one, so I asked him to check with Mr Dale at the base. Since we know that it was *Naiad* that discovered the matter yesterday and by so small an amount that a passing ship would only have thought it meant the lightvessel had a lot of cable out and not reported it, we could not get this report, if it existed, confused with another—"

"Yes, yes, I understand. Go on."

"Well, that's it really, sir . . ." said Watson.

He was a nice lad, Macready thought, he had used his initiative, but he was not of Charlie's calibre. "So what you're saying is that no-one, not the coastguard nor Mr Dale, has received a message stating the St Kenelm was out of position. Have I got that right?"

"Yes, sir. Didn't I make that clear?"

"Not entirely," Macready said dryly.

"Sorry, sir. You see it occurred to me that it was a bit odd that *Naiad* knew but that we didn't. Then I thought that with the Commissioners onboard, their bloody radio watches will be closed up all the time and nothing would please them more than to intercept a message for us and pass it on."

"Makes them look smart, eh?" Macready ruminated.

"Just so, sir."

Macready stood for a moment, then with a, "Thank you, Mr Watson, thank you very much," he headed for the radio room.

Captain Foster woke from his snooze and, after a quick wash and a brush of his teeth, felt himself a new man. He strolled out of his cabin and onto *Naiad*'s bridge. One of the few compensations of commanding her, he reflected, was that occasionally the day's work finished early and one had only to attend a dinner by way of duty. And then he recalled Justine. He had met her, of course, known her quite well when she and Macready had been ballroom dancing partners in Porth Ardur. A sexually unadventurous man, Foster was scrupulously loyal to his wife, but even he used to marvel at Justine's bosom, the complementary waspishness of her waist and the fine line of her legs. Though always slightly overblown for his own taste, it was impossible for any man not to be affected by Justine Morgan. The prospect of being in her company this evening gave him a small, delightful sense of anticipation. That he would be able to gently guy his former commander, only increased this rather unfamiliarly lubricious sense of anticipation. He emerged onto the port bridge wing smiling, sucking in fresh air with the enthusiasm of a man who takes some joy in his life.

The Second Mate straightened up from the rail. "Afternoon, sir."

"Afternoon." Foster stared round the anchorage. "Where's *Caryatid*?" he asked suddenly.

"Oh, she got under weigh, sir. Apparently a report had come in that the St Kenelm lightvessel was off station."

Foster frowned. "Oh . . . have you a copy?" He wanted to check the time of origin. If the report had originated before he had passed word to Macready yesterday then Macready was on a fool's errand and was reacting for nothing.

"Oh, there's no copy, sir. Captain Stanier passed the message."

"Stanier? Where did he get it?"

The Second Officer shrugged. "I have no idea, sir, I only—"

"Yes, yes, I understand—"

"Sir?" Both men turned as the quartermaster called from the wheelhouse door. "I've Captain Macready on the radio."

"Very well." Foster ducked back into the wheelhouse and passed quickly through to the wireless office.

"*Naiad* to *Caryatid*, Foster here. Over."

"Bernard, I'm going back to the St Kenelm. Received a message from your ship that she was off station. There's no corroboration that it was reported by any other ship. You'll appreciate my position. Can you confirm accuracy of origin, please? Over."

"Yes. I suspect mischief, Septimus. Report originates from, er, a Sea Dragon. Said dragon knew nothing of our conversation of yesterday. Over."

The veiled reference to Stanier concealed in Foster's reference to his first, wrecked command, was what Macready already suspected. Now Foster also confirmed it had nothing to do with what he and his officers had found out and passed covertly to Macready the previous day.

"Do you concur that a whiff of malice is involved?" Macready asked. "Over."

Foster did not want to make much of the matter. If the Commissioners had their radio receiver on and were listening to some light music, they would pick up his transmissions on almost any frequency as they blasted out from *Naiad*'s aerial.

"More than a whiff. Over."

"Perhaps one too many to dinner tonight, eh? Over." Macready was being persistent, Foster thought.

"Something of that order. Over and out."

"Wait one, Bernard. Anyone going that I know? Over."

"Affirmative. Don't worry. I'll look after it."

"I trust you, Bernard. Over and out."

"Thank you. *Naiad* out."

The decision of what Justine and Sonia were to wear was influenced by the necessity for them to clamber aboard the Commissioners' barge. This ruled out long dresses, but both looked, as Charlie remarked with ironic gallantry, 'a huge credit to the fashion houses of Ynyscraven'.

Their embarkation was facilitated by a small brow the barge crew lowered and there was no lack of strong arms to see them to the padded settles that lined the luxurious cuddy of the barge. On her return to *Naiad*, the barge ran carefully alongside *Lyonesse* where Lord Craven awaited them.

"I hope I shall not out-peacock you, ladies," his lordship said, stepping down and ducking under the cuddy.

"Oh, my word!" exclaimed Justine while Sonia giggled.

It was not that Lord Craven's attire was gaudy, for his resources were limited, but it was scarcely suitable dress for a formal dinner. He was in the habit of keeping an old set of cricket whites aboard *Lyonesse* which, with the addition of a tie or cravat and his blazer, could quickly provide him with the sort of dress in which he could attend a party. However, his lordship had eschewed the blazer and wore about his neck what appeared to be a bright scarlet sail tie knotted unconventionally in a loose and vapid bow. His shirt sleeves were rolled up and about his waist was a gaudy roll of yellow and black silk which Charlie guessed was Craven's personal yacht-racing flag, though in fact it was his father's. This improvised cummerbund gave the outfit a piratical, rather than a formal air, and this impression was heightened by his lordship's lack of footware.

"Please do not tread on my toes this evening," he said.

"D'you mean metaphorically as well as literally?" Charlie asked as the barge chugged across the bay at a steady four knots.

"Are you meditating mischief?" Sonia asked.

"I'm *always* meditating mischief, Mrs Farthing." Craven laughed as the barge drew alongside *Naiad*'s accommodation ladder.

Caroline Stanier sat back in the taxi and lit a cigarette as the damp and crowded pavements of the capital flashed past. She was too self-possessed a woman to betray any sign of self-satisfaction, but she was confident her dinner with David Smith would go well, for she had done the groundwork too carefully. Her dinner partner was, she was compelled to concede, a man who, when he wished, could deploy a compelling charm. Moreover, though she admitted it only in the deepest recesses of her heart, she found him more than a little attractive. He exuded a powerful air of success, of being a man capable of thrusting himself at the very heart of things, unlike her poor, dear, silly and quite stupid Jimmy.

At the thought of her husband she exhaled cigarette smoke through slightly viciously pursed lips. Sometimes the thought of him . . . Well, she had privately sworn not to dwell on such matters. He was useful . . .

No. He *had been* useful, Caroline mused, leaning forward, stubbing her cigarette out and calling to the driver, "Set me down here, please!"

Tegwyn and her husband dined at home. She was aware that all was not well with Pomeroy. He was occasionally susceptible to prolonged bouts of silent introspection which customarily ended in the purchase of an *objet d'art*, after which he became his old, considerate and attentive self again.

"Darling," Tegwyn said gently, tentatively seeking to prod Pomeroy into a more sociable frame of mind by inducing him to consider a purchase, "did you ever actually *see* the Canaletto Lord Dungarth is offering for sale?"

"Mmm?" Pomeroy looked up abstractedly. "What did you say?"

Tegwyn repeated her question and Pomeroy stirred himself. "No, no I didn't, but it's almost certainly not by Canaletto," he said kindly. "Frankly it isn't worth bothering with."

"Oh, I just thought that you might be considering another purchase."

"No, no I wasn't." He smiled wanly at her. "Look, my dear, I'm sorry if I'm a bit withdrawn. Truth is, I feel a bit off colour."

"Why don't you go to bed?" Tegwyn looked at her watch. "It's already quite late."

Pomeroy shook his head, looking at his own watch. "No," he said with what appeared to be sudden resolution, "I think I need some fresh air. Mind if I take a turn round the square?"

"Not at all," she replied brightening and smiling back at him. "I'll probably be in bed when you get back."

"Sweet dreams, my dear."

And Tegwyn held up her face for Pomeroy to kiss as he went out.

The Commissioners' dinner ended convivially. It had not been an unpleasant evening at all. Justine, although intensely disappointed at Macready's absence, found herself reconciled by the splendour of her surroundings. The opulent dining room fitted for the exclusive use of the Commissioners, occupied the beam of *Naiad*, a grand, rococo room which seemed out of place aboard ship and oddly at variance with the black and gold of the Commissioners bedecked in their evening finery. Sir Charles Mudge wore the ribbon and star of his order, while Gostling and Blake sported miniature medals and decorations, evidence of gallantry in the late war.

To have had Macready present but tantalisingly remote, separated by not only the conventions of staid morality, but those of the Commissioners' pomp, would have been well nigh intolerable, Justine thought. Dear Septimus would have been ponderously awkward in such surroundings, though Bernard Foster, who had greeted her with a kiss, had, it seemed, come into his own. Slowly Justine saw her lover's absence as perhaps a blessing in disguise.

She found herself seated between Captains Gostling and Blake, both of whom were overwhelmed by her and vied with each other in the extravagance of their flattery. Thus distracted, mellowed by wine and sated by rich food, Justine found she enjoyed being the cynosure of all eyes. Even the smoothly confident ogling of James Stanier only added to her pleasure and she purred under the compliments showered upon her by the two shipmasters.

Sonia, between Blake and Sir Charles Mudge, was less well equipped than her older friend to enjoy such an occasion. Island-born and island-bred, Sonia claimed the paternity of a

Russian *émigré* nobleman, but in her case nurture rather than nature dominated her personality. Untutored in the matter of small talk, she was a young woman of simple pleasures. The gilt and pastel decoration, the false, fluted columns and brocade drapery seemed quite ridiculously superfluous. There was, she thus concluded, a tedium about the evening, set, as it was, amid the pomps and etiquette of a strict formality.

Charlie had had a difficult moment, for Stanier had inevitably recognised him. While the party was still being introduced, Stanier confronted him.

"What the hell are *you* doing here?" he had hissed into Charlie's face.

Though somewhat affronted, Charlie had responded with considerable dignity. "I am now the Reeve of this island. You invited me." And with that Stanier had to be content, though it was clear that, completing the circle between Foster and Charlie, Stanier found himself isolated, disdaining to talk to Charlie and ignored by Gostling who was too occupied in fawning over Justine's bosom.

To his own left, Charlie became absorbed in conversation with Mudge and his lordship who, by virtue of his rank sat on Mudge's right. Craven had apparently been forgiven his morning impertinence, for no allusions were made to the encounter and it was as if it had never occurred. The eccentricities of his dress were similarly accepted without comment. Mudge, moreover, seemed equally unaffected by the identity of Mr Farthing as the recently resigned chief mate of *Caryatid*, courteously acknowledging that Charlie was free to decide these matters for himself.

"My wife was born on Ynyscraven, d'you see, Sir Charles," he explained, "so it seemed the most logical thing to do."

"Quite so, Mr Farthing. I drink to your good fortune."

"You've lost a good man, Sir Charles," remarked Craven, smiling at Charlie, "but that's my gain, wouldn't you say?"

Mudge sighed. "It is going to be our misfortune to lose a good many more, Lord Craven, once we close down the operation at Porth Ardur."

"Well, I must confess I'm surprised, Sir Charles. But I'm sure you know your own business best and my own nautical experience is confined to that of a common yachtsman. However, I have always considered the Silurian Strait, with its strong tides, to be one of the most dangerous places, fully justifying the retention of its own tender. Yet along the extent of its shores lie some of the country's most important harbours and it will always support a lively trade."

"It's economics—" Stanier leaned across and tried to break in.

"It's a matter of economics," Sir Charles remarked, ignoring Stanier, "and the fact that *Caryatid*'s an old ship."

They then became absorbed in an analysis of the pros and contras pertaining to the provision of seamarks in the Silurian Strait. From time to time, Charlie contributed a technical detail, but mostly he was content to listen, exchanging the occasional, furtive wink with Sonia.

It was after they left the table and retired to the smoke room on the upper deck above that the first sign of awkwardness occurred. There was no provision for the ladies to withdraw, so they moved *en masse* and, while those who wished to smoke stepped out onto the now moonlit quarterdeck, the ladies and their eager admirers remained inside the warmly lit, oak-panelled smoke-room, sipping their liqueurs.

The movement broke up the symmetry of the seating arrangements. Blake and Gostling had exhausted their vocabulary of superlatives and the predatory Stanier, fuelled by a swiftly swallowed cognac, moved in upon Justine, seating himself beside her and handing her a brandy. She looked in vain for Foster, but Sir Charles Mudge had buttonholed him. He cast a despairing glance towards Justine, but she smiled back reassuringly and turned to the importunate Stanier as he bent over her décolletage.

"I am delighted to see you again, my dear Mrs Morgan," he said, as if addressing a woman of equal age to himself instead of the mother of his former mistress. "The last time we met was in most unfortunate circumstances."

"You have done very well for yourself, James," she said coolly. "I understand from Tegwyn that you and Caroline sometimes visit her and her husband."

"Yes indeed. I wouldn't say we were intimate any longer—"

"That's just as well, seeing that you are married to Caroline," Justine said sharply, her antennae warning her that Stanier was drunk and had his own, sinister agenda.

"Marriage is just a convention, Mrs Morgan. I should like you to know that is how I view it."

"And why should you like me to know that?" she asked quietly.

"Because," Stanier said, dropping his voice and hurrying on as the knot of men clustered about Sonia burst into cheery laughter, "because I enjoyed your daughter and she enjoyed me," he breathed, "and because I wish to pleasure her mother."

It took a moment for Justine to grasp the extent of the man's meaning and when she did, she had lost the reflexive urge to strike his face, remembering her surroundings. Instead she took another tack. Keeping her voice deliberately, even seductively low, she leaned slightly towards Stanier, dangerously closing the distance between his nose and her breasts.

"Oh James, is that why you banished poor Septimus?" And when he nodded, she added breathlessly, "I scarcely dared hope so. You see, James, dear . . ." and here she put her warm palm upon his left thigh, "I am almost ashamed to say so, but I was always a little jealous of Tegwyn . . ."

She saw the gleam of triumph in Stanier's eyes. "My dear . . ." he breathed, so close to her that she smelled the alcohol on his breath.

"But what about Caroline?" she whispered.

Stanier, not the brightest of men sober, frowned. "What about her?"

"You threw Tegwyn over for Caroline. I imagine she is wonderful in bed."

Stanier shook his head and Justine saw a slight welling in his eyes. "She's cold, so cold—"

"My poor, poor boy," Justine said, almost moved now she had touched the core of Stanier's unhappiness.

"Don't monopolise Mrs Morgan, Stanier!"

Justine and Stanier both looked up as Craven bent over them. "Would you take the night air with me, Justine?" Craven asked, offering his arm.

"Of course. Excuse me, James," Justine said, rising as Stanier fell back in confusion.

As they emerged on the quarterdeck, Justine said, "Thank heavens you arrived when you did, I was on the verge of humiliating that creature."

"Well, I felt *he* needed *his* toes trodden on," Craven said. They chuckled, then Craven asked urbanely, "D'you find it odd that he was once your daughter's lover?"

"Well, he had a certain charm when he arrived in Porth Ardur all that time ago and my daughter's head was easily turned."

"I'm in love with Tegwyn, you know," Craven admitted simply.

"Good heavens!" Justine exclaimed, genuinely surprised, stopping and staring at him. "I had no idea."

"She can't be happy with Pomeroy."

"Why not?"

"Because she can't. He's a queen . . ."

David Smith threw away the butt of the cigar and put both hands in his pockets. His dinner with Caroline had been most enjoyable and they had concluded their business to a nicety. It was stimulating working with someone who was as straight-forward as Caroline Stanier. If more women were like her, Smith thought, there would be fewer of them having nervous breakdowns.

The frisson that business stirred in him also aroused other passions and when he had said goodnight to Caroline, he had decided the night remained young and he was ripe for adventure. As he turned into the square a clock somewhere nearby chimed midnight: he had been walking for about three quarters of an hour. For a moment he stopped to consider the wisdom of his intentions. It was late and he did not want scandal. It was one of the joys of working with Caroline. Her sense of discretion was almost painfully watertight. He wondered if she ever submitted to the sheer abandon of passion and decided it was unlikely. He was too little of an expert in the ways of women to wonder whether the quality was unique to her, or was to be found in a particular type. Anyway, her example was admirable. He must be careful, he warned himself, and hesitated.

But it was at this moment that he caught sight of a familiar and half-expected figure. Smith started forward again and quickly overtook the idling Pomeroy.

Captain Macready stood on for the St Kenelm lightvessel and, having taken a further check on its position, headed *Caryatid* for Porth Ardur. He knew it was the next port of call for the *Naiad* and anticipated that Sir Charles would make an announcement to the staff of the base and buoy yard about their imminent and collective redundancy.

For himself, the sheer stupid malice of Stanier stripped away the last shreds of his own sentimentality. He trusted Foster to watch over Justine and entertained no doubts as to her own loyalty. He was in a sense also glad that he had not had to pay court aboard *Naiad* that night. And he was touchingly sorry for old Mudge and the others. It was odd that they allowed themselves to be bamboozled by the likes of Stanier, but Macready had always remained uninterested in the higher politics of the Lighthouse Service. They somehow seemed too remote from the everyday realities he had to deal with.

As the shipowners' representative Stanier, Macready assumed, would naturally possess enormous clout at the Board. Nor would it help that while Mudge, Blake and Gostling were former shipmasters, they were all so much older than the ambitious Stanier.

"Damn the man!" Macready thought as he settled himself to sleep. "Damn him to perdition."

The barge rumbled across the anchorage towards *Lyonesse* at four knots. To starboard the great dark bulk of the island reared up into the night sky silhouetted against the moonlight. To the south the lighthouse gleamed dully, the light bright within the lantern. They could see the great lens revolving and the three fingers of gathered and concentrated brilliance revolve above their heads, periodically sweeping them. From a distance the group of three flashes would show to any passing ship every twenty seconds. Over to their left a low swell broke upon the extension of the island's shore, the rocks of the Hound's Teeth. At low water a few rusty remains of what had once been the engine of the motor yacht *Sea Dragon* could still be seen.

Yawning, the Coxswain conned the boat alongside the ketch.

"Are you sure . . . ?" Craven said, bending over Justine.

"Quite," she reassured him.

Craven hopped nimbly across the narrow gap onto the yacht's deck. "Good night and thank you, Coxswain."

"Pleasure, m'lord," said the young seamen grinning, delighted to have his overtime acknowledged. The barge drew away from the pale waving figure and headed towards the beach in silence.

It was unfortunate that Stanier insisted on accompanying them. Both Charlie and Craven had tried to dissuade him, but he had followed them down into the boat and now sat slumped opposite Justine. She found herself silently praying that he would fall asleep in the short period it took to close the shingle beach, but as the barge slowed and the crew prepared the wooden brow he stirred.

"Now, m'dear."

"I'm really quite all right, James," Justine said, making one last attempt to dissuade Stanier from rising.

"No, no, we must see our guests safely ashore . . ."

But once on the beach, Stanier began to walk up towards the path with them.

"Charlie," Justine hissed, "please try and get rid of him."

"Yes, of course. Walk on with Sonia," Charlie said quickly and turned, confronting Stanier. "Look, Captain Stanier, it's very kind of you, but I see no point in you coming any further. You don't want to keep the boat's crew up too long, I'm sure."

"I'll see Mrs Morgan home, damn it. It's no business of yours . . ." Stanier tried to push past Charlie, but Charlie kept moving in front of him, conscious that the ladies were beating a hasty retreat.

"Look, I'd hate to seem ungrateful after your splendid hospitality tonight, Stanier, but actually it is. You see, I'm the Reeve and, it may come as something of a surprise, but I combine the powers of police, magistracy and, er, the keeper of the Bridewell. I don't think the Commissioners would really appreciate having to bail you out tomorrow morning, do you?"

"You cheeky bugger! Are you threatening me?"

"No, Stanier," Charlie said with weary resignation, "I'm

actually cautioning you. In my judgement, you are drunk and potentially disorderly."

Stanier's blow caught Charlie squarely and he felt his head snap back, but the effort cost Stanier his balance and he staggered forward, so that Charlie, recovering, caught Stanier's chin with his knee. The Commissioner fell with a scrunch on the shingle and lay groaning.

"Bowman!" Charlie called. "I think Captain Stanier could to with a hand."

The seaman loomed out of the darkness and swore. "There's always one of them," he said as both men got hold of Stanier and began to half drag him down the beach.

"Yes," said Charlie between clenched teeth as they man-handled Stanier towards the boat, "isn't there just."

By the time he reached the cottage the women had lit the lamps and were pouring tea.

"Oh Charlie!" Sonia exclaimed, "what on earth happened?"

"You've a black eye, I think," explained Justine when she saw Charlie's lack of comprehension.

"Well, it was worth it," Charlie said grinning. "I think I came off best."

Porth Ardur

It was afterwards said that the air had been full of portents, for those who knew how to recognise such things. At the time, however, the first of these was remarked upon as being funny, an event of appealing poetic justice with more than a hint of irony in it.

It was a meteorological curiosity of the Silurian Strait that, if the centre of a depression passed eastwards between fifty and sixty miles to the south, and that this coincided with a spring ebb tide, an exceptionally strong easterly gale was induced in the Strait itself. Fortunately the conditions necessary for this phenomena synchronised relatively rarely, since the prevailing wind over the whole area blew in from the Atlantic from the west, or south-west, but when it happened, a strong easterly came as a highly disruptive event. Lying in the direct path of such a wind was the island of Ynyscraven, where an easterly gale was still known as 'an invader's wind', since such a gale had long ago brought the first conquerors to subjugate the indigenous Celtic inhabitants.

However, any meteorological analysis after the event shortly to be described would fail to associate this initial easterly breeze with any depression anywhere. Indeed it was this completely anomalous origin which gave this wind and the consequent incident the quality of a portent, like the quick, fleeting appearance of a scouting patrol, far ahead of the assault of the main war host.

Captain Macready had berthed *Caryatid* alongside that part of the lighthouse pier that lay inside the enclosed dock. On the opposite, landward side reared the monstrous coal-tipping towers, beneath which lay the dingy chocolate brown hull of the Cambrian Steam Navigation Company's 5,000-ton tramp steamer *Galahad*. Squeezed in ahead of the tramp, lay the *Kurnow* loading her passengers and cargo for the Bishop's Islands. Advertisements on the quay announced a new, twice-weekly service to Ynyscraven. Passengers could land upon this 'wonderfully remote, romantic island and meet the isolated inhabitants who carried on a tranquil way of life undisturbed by the worries of modern life'. Though not bound for the island this morning, bookings were available for the Friday service. At present only half a dozen people had shown any curiosity about the 'isolated inhabitants', while the local opinion in Porth Ardur was that the enterprise would founder, as seemed to be happening to so much of the promised expansion of Porth Ardur.

At high water the following morning, the caisson was drawn back and *Kurnow* slipped out to sea while into the already crowded dock edged the *Naiad*. Foster brought her in and laid her neatly alongside *Caryatid*, making the huge frattan fenders between the two vessels creak. Lying secured some four feet apart, a distance soon bridged by a short brow, the two lighthouse tenders made a curious sight, almost completely filling the dock. A moment or two later a bag of mail was brought aboard *Naiad*, passed over from *Caryatid*, most of which was for the Commissioners and included a note for Stanier.

At exactly half past nine o'clock that Thursday morning, saluted off *Naiad* by her officers and led by Sir Charles Mudge, the Commissioners for Celtic Lighthouses crossed the deck of *Caryatid*, where a similar side party led by First Mate Watson formally acknowledged their passage with their own salutes. Above their heads and at the sterns of the two ships, the flags strained at their halliards in a freshening easterly breeze.

Once ashore by way of *Caryatid*'s own brow and in the rear of which marched Macready and Foster, the little procession turned right and made for the whitewashed buoy yard. Here Mr Dale, immaculate in striped trousers, dark jacket and Eton collar, had assembled the entire workforce. In a huddle surrounding Mr Dale, as though unused to the bruising effects of fresh air, were the wages clerks, the stores clerk and his two storemen, Miss Gaynor Penfold the shorthand typist, and Cyrus Jones, a former seaman who had lost an arm in an accident on the foredeck of *Caryatid* and was employed as a telephone operator and messenger. In a darker, more truculent phalanx, stood the blacksmith, the carpenter and his two mates, the three stone-masons, two painters and two dozen workmen who by their labour attended to the harsher end of the Commissioner's business. It was these men who complemented *Caryatid*'s crew, for they cleaned off the rusty buoys that she landed, then scaled, serviced, repaired and painted them, finally preparing them for a further three years at sea. They also ranged worn lengths of chain, cut out weak sections and assembled new moorings by forging new links and joining up existing runs. Stores, engine spares, diesel and lamp oil were ordered and held until loaded aboard *Caryatid* for carriage to the lighthouses and lightvessels in the Silurian Strait and adjacent sea area. In fact, everything from heavy spare anchor cable, to small, light rolls of blue and white lamp wick was prepared for despatch, each item carefully parcelled in accordance with the station requisition order. Marked with its destination these disparate stores were loaded aboard *Caryatid* until her boats delivered them as the tender effected the period reliefs of the crews of each lightvessel and lighthouse.

It was a ceaseless routine that had run for years with the oiled precision of near perfection and it was this very seamless, unglamorous ordinariness of its business that seemed now to be somehow in question. To those men waiting the arrival of Sir Charles Mudge, the air seemed pregnant with foreboding, so charged with rumour had the atmosphere of Porth Ardur become in recent weeks. Men for whom politics was a venal trade with which they wanted no contact, and which they regarded as the improper occupation of public school boys and the sons of miners whose mothers affected exaggerated airs, found themselves arguing about the irreconcilable nature of capital and labour. These men grew eloquent and passionate in expressing half-grasped opinions about the fundamentals of economics as the promised wealth of Porth Ardur failed to materialise. The previous day, when the *Galahad* had arrived, the dockers had mounted a protest and sat down on the railway track to the mine in protest at the loss of jobs, now that the loading of the coal had become fully mechanised. No general cargo trade had materialised, though the management claimed that increased passengers aboard the *Kurnow* had meant that two extra boys had been taken on, and no bonuses were forecast. A noisy meeting had been held the previous evening between labour and management and a compromise had been announced, the port manager guaranteeing that six men would be engaged on every shift as trimmers.

The uncertainty of this industrial unrest was infectious, spilling over into the staid ranks of the stolid labour force who had given their lives to the service of Sir Charles Mudge, his antecedents and, it had been assumed, his successors. Mudge was ignorant of this local dispute, but he was no fool. Despite the confidential nature of the news he and his colleagues were about to reveal, Mudge considered it likely word had leaked out that in the wake of the scrapping of *Caryatid*, more changes would follow. He was not a coward and fully accepted the responsibilities of his high office, but what was easily resolved in the remote fastness of the capital's board room, was less easily argued in the windswept buoy yard while standing on a wooden crate thoughtfully provided by the yard's carpenter.

"My men," he began, clapping his hand on his hat to restrain it in a sudden gust of wind as the Commissioners and the two ships' commanders fell in behind him.

"We aren't *your* men, mate!" an unidentifiable voice called out from the rear, to be ignored by Sir Charles, who may not even have heard it.

"As you know the government has taken a very hard line with all of us in the public service. The Celtic Lighthouse Service has a record to be proud of . . ."

The clatter of shunting came downwind as a load of coal trucks arrived from the Mynydd Uchaf mine to coincide with the resumption of the *Galahad*'s loading. Some of Mudge's words were lost in the racket.

". . . And of course that means many of us will have to work harder. It also means we will all have to make sacrifices—"

"What sacrifices will you make then, mate?" the anonymous

heckler asked, stirring a chorus of assent from the workforce and prompting a low chuckle from Macready. Foster shot his former commander a nervous sideways glance.

"Give up your eight-course dinners, will you?"

Mudge ploughed on, suddenly wishing that Stanier was delivering this unpleasant homily instead of standing behind him, half hidden from the expectant faces staring up at Mudge himself. The heckling in front of, and the distracting racket behind him, had cost Mudge the thread of his logic. He drew a deep breath and plunged on.

"Unfortunately in order to make the necessary economies, the Board have been compelled to retire the *Caryatid* from active service—"

"If you're going to scrap the old rust-bucket, just bloody say so, for God's sake, man." A chorus of affirmative exclamations greeted this unsurprising news and several men relaxed, thinking this was all Sir Charles Mudge had to say.

Mudge detected this softening and hurried on. "She will not be replaced . . ."

The crowd suddenly seemed to stiffen. He was aware that he now had their full attention. Behind him, his heart beating, Stanier was watching the reaction of the men, wishing he was somewhere else, but aware that he had no option but to stand shoulder to shoulder with his fellow Commissioners.

"There will be no replacement for the old ship and . . ." Mudge looked round and waited while the crash, clunk and roar of the first upended coal truck shot its contents down the chute into the after hold of *Galahad*. As the roar subsided, he concluded his speech as hurriedly as possible.

"And this entire facility will be shut down."

There was a moment of silence. Definition of the word 'facility' spread from the startled Dale, through the ranks of the salaried office staff to move among the dismally clad members of the yard labour force.

"Does that mean we've lost our jobs?" a voice called in the wake of the clatter and roar of the second truck depositing ten tons of coal down the much nearer chute into *Galahad*'s forward hold.

"It means you are redundant . . ."

It was at this moment that Foster felt his sleeve insistently plucked by Macready.

"Move back, Bernard! Full astern," Macready whispered as he shuffled back into the shelter of the buoy-yard wall behind them. Then the storm of wind-blown coal dust swept across the yard, scouring the neck of Captain Sir Charles Mudge and his colleagues and blowing full into the faces of the entire staff of the base at Porth Ardur.

As hands went up to faces and the ranks wavered, cries of "Oh, bugger!" and "Filthy shit!" and "Fuck the mine!" mingled with "Redundant, by God!" "You bunch of bastards!" and "What does Jimmy Stanier have to say?"

Then the dust cleared and before the next truck reached the top of the tower, Mudge was waving them away with a dismissive gesture.

"That's all I have to say, men."

But Mr Dale, his face pale with shock, had already turned on his heel and led his stunned staff off towards the office door, while the tradesmen and labourers, less intimidated by a cloud of coal dust, surged menacingly forward.

"Why don't you all come back when you've thought up something worse, you bloody pigs!"

"Where's Stanier?

"Aye, what's he got to say?"

Mudge was off his box now as, with a sigh, Macready detached himself from the shelter of the wall and with a "Come on, Bernard," walked forward through the retreating ranks of the Commissioners.

Macready held up his hands, the sunlight sparkling on the four gold rings on his sleeves.

"Keep order, men! Don't bugger everything up! We've all lost our jobs, me included, but don't put yourselves in the wrong."

Macready's standing was such that his sudden appearance checked the impulsive forward movement. The men surged round him until he was directly confronting the base blacksmith, a huge bear of a man whose heavily muscled, scarred and tattooed forearms were crossed over his leather apron.

"What are you going to do?" Macready asked the scowling

blacksmith. "Throw them into the dock and get yourselves assault charges? They're not worth it and it will prejudice any chance of fighting this whole idea."

The blacksmith and those about him hesitated. "Are you for us, Captain Macready?"

"Aye," said another. "Are you with us in fighting this then, Captain?"

A brief image of Justine waiting for him on Ynyscraven flashed across his mind, but then he was caught up in the mood of the men. He had been part of the Celtic Lighthouse Service all his working life; it was a part of him. It would moreover do no harm to try and help where he could. He had known the fathers of the younger lads and many of the older had served at sea, in *Caryatid* or the lightvessels . . .

"Yes, I'll do what I can."

And then they cheered him. It was quite stupid and the noise brought no comfort to Mudge and his party hurrying back to the sanctuary of *Naiad* through the gritty air, wiping their eyes. For as Macready waved them to silence with the remark that they should all disperse to avoid the next lot of coal dust, the black cloud coming from the after hold struck the retreating Commissioners as they were fully exposed on the quay.

"Damn and blast it!" Sir Charles swore as he blew his congested nose and the impassive Sudbrook handed him a cup of tea. The roar and rattle of another emptying truck came from the far side of the dock and a cloud of black dust trailed across the immaculate teak planking of *Naiad*'s quarterdeck.

"Shut that bloody door!"

The steward obliged as the sooty Commissioners restored their equanimity.

"Ah," said Blake who had regarded the whole proceedings not without a certain humour. He nursed a private envy that he, not Mudge, should have been knighted for his services to safety at sea and Mudge's predicament had amused him. "Ah, the cup that cheers, but doth not inebriate. How very welcome it is."

"I don't think it went too badly, Sir Charles, all things considered and excepting the coal dust." Stanier's smooth smug face mooned over the rim of the porcelain cup and

Mudge found it difficult to conceal his growing dislike of Stanier.

"That is one of your festering ships, Stanier!" Mudge nodded beyond the smoke-room windows. "Now far be it from me to interfere with the trade of our great nation, but you might have had the wit to have ordered the loading suspended while we attended to our business. When she wasn't working cargo this morning, I thought for one indulgent and clearly misplaced moment, that you had actually had some foresight—"

"Sir Charles!" Stanier protested, secretly pleased that the industrial dispute, of which he had been notified by the port manager in the mail arriving earlier that morning, was now over. The slight dusting of coal dust that he had received, while extremely irksome and ironic, had nevertheless arrived like a tactical smokescreen, enabling the Commissioners in general and Stanier in particular, to beat a timely retreat.

"Inconvenient though the coal dust was," Stanier said, "it rather conveniently got us off the hook, don't you think?" The grim silence following this announcement was broken by a grunt of agreement from Blake.

"Stanier's got a point, Sir Charles. The men's mood was turning decidedly ugly—"

"It was old Macready that pacified them," Gostling said and Mudge agreed.

"That's true, Sir Charles," said Stanier, quite willing to give Macready his due if the man was out of earshot and it suited his own purposes.

"I shall have to thank him," Mudge grumbled.

"I entirely agree," said Stanier, reaching new heights of pomposity. "Where we chastise when it is due, we should also praise when it is timely to do so."

Mudge looked at Stanier and grunted. The man was impossible!

The wives of Sudan Road were in raptures when they learned that the two lighthouse ships, *Naiad* and *Caryatid* had been liberally covered with coal dust throughout the day. Held captive by the tides, they were subject to a ceaseless deposit of sulphurous filth and were forced to secure all ports, hatches and companionways to keep the pernicious dust at bay.

The first sign of the success of their own grand plan was whispered up and down Sudan Road, rapidly spreading throughout the town as it emerged that same day. It was another factor, it was afterwards claimed, which showed the workings of fate quite clearly. News came in from the mine that three of the men working there, one of whom was known for his skill with the largest of the grab-cranes, had packed their hands in and moved on. Production, it was said, was drastically affected, an embarrassment to the management who were in the very act of loading a ship.

The actual impact of the defection of the three men was somewhat exaggerated, and the precise cause was uncertain, but since the three young women who had enjoyed the favours of these men swore blind that they had refused their beaux the smallest favours, the Lysistran plan seemed to be working. In fact the men had been summoned to the capital while their three girlfriends, two of whom had recently fallen pregnant, had covered their humiliation by a story of abandonment.

The three women were later mentioned in chapel by a pastor who did not known them, except by hearsay. His sermon, based upon the repudiation of temptation and repentance for sin, was long held to have been an inspiration and was afterwards published in an anthology of original sermons and homilies. For this reason, it was fortunate that he did not know the ladies' reputations, which it would be salacious to expand upon further.

A lady whose sensibilities are more closely associated with the grander events in Porth Ardur was actually that same morning more than two hundred miles away in the distant capital. Tegwyn Pomeroy woke with a vague sense of unease, touched perhaps by ancient, inherited Druidic instincts or by half-dreamed disturbances in the night. It was not unusual that she woke alone, for her husband often slept in his own room, being an insomniac, but something prompted her to get up. Thinking Pomeroy might be unwell, she was about to enter his bedroom when the door opened and the figure of David Smith emerged.

In the split second of mutual surprise, Tegwyn saw – and never forgot – the face of her husband lying on his pillow, his hands behind his head, the look of satisfaction frozen in the terrible rictus of discovery.

The presence of the coal dust persuaded Captain Foster to sail from Porth Ardur as soon as possible. Having announced the closure of the base, Captain Sir Charles Mudge had no desire to stay either. But that afternoon, Mr Dale had sent aboard, by the single hand of Cyrus Jones, a note stating that Lord Dungarth, on his way to Ynyscraven by way of the new service run by the *Kurnow*, had just arrived at the Station Hotel and sought a meeting with Stanier.

The information was, of course, an attempt by his lordship to enjoy a lavish dinner at the expense of the Commissioners, but Stanier took the bait and, pleading that his lordship was both the owner of an island upon which the Commissioners maintained establishments and a member of the upper House whose influence might at any time come in useful, prevailed upon Mudge to send Mr Jones on to the Station Hotel with an invitation to dine aboard *Naiad* that evening.

Captain Foster's plans to sail were therefore postponed to the next morning and he slipped ashore to join Macready and dine with his old commander and Gwendolyn, whom he had not seen for some time.

Curious about the state of the Macreadys' marriage, Foster noticed a change in Gwendolyn. Her bird-like frame seemed to possess even greater energy than the formidable reserves he remembered, as if she had, as it were, taken a new lease on life. This seemed to Foster in direct proportion to the growing indifference evident in her husband who, despite his rhetoric of that very morning, appeared uncharacteristically reconciled to his forthcoming retirement, premature though it was.

While Septimus did not wish him to, he felt obliged to regale Gwendolyn with an appropriately doctored tale of her husband's suppression of the incipient mutiny of the base labour force. Without actually saying so, Bernard Foster managed to convey an impression that Macready had averted bloodshed. Mrs Macready seemed much impressed, particularly when

Foster told of how he had stated publicly his intention to fight the closure of the base. This, too, was somehow embellished to give it the gloss of a sacred vow, so that Gwendolyn, apparently moved by Bernard's account, patted her husband on the hand in what seemed a gesture of admiration. Bernard found this touching and averted his gaze, not noticing the unfeigned astonishment clear in Macready's face. Gwendolyn herself scarcely noticed what she had done.

Mrs Macready was in truth hardly listening to Foster. It was only later that night, as she lay sleepless and hardly knowing what to do with her good fortune, that it occurred to her that Macready's actions of the morning seemed destined to be cast in so favourable a light and that the town might forgive her, her own perfidy.

For Gwendolyn was troubled, hating disruption in the well-organised mechanism of her life, but tempted beyond endurance by the news that had arrived that morning when she had received a letter and an interim prospectus from the directors of the Ardurian Slate Company. It announced their success in securing a highly advantageous contract to supply the navy of the Central American republic of Costa Maya with a regular supply of 5,000 tons of coal a month. The republic's warships, an elderly fleet of laid-up dreadnoughts, had been hastily recommissioned and it was predicted that the state of emergency would last for a period of at least a year. Share prices in Ardurian Slate had rocketed, increased investment was invited from 'esteemed and farsighted investors who were able to see the magnificent, but short-term opportunity thus offered'. In short, Gwendolyn reflected as she stared at the ceiling, the logic of it was incontrovertible: the more coal that could be shipped to Costa Maya, the greater the profit accruing to the Ardurian Slate Company. By the same token, the swifter the insurrection would be suppressed and thus human suffering minimised. There was, incidentally, no doubt about these facts, or so Mr Sinclair had assured her as she considered the matter in his office, her trembling hand holding both letter and prospectus.

"My dear Mrs Macready," Sinclair had said, scarcely able to suppress his own excitement. "*Carpe diem!* Seize the day!"

"But what," she had sensibly prevaricated, "about the stoppage at the docks."

Sinclair had smiled. "It is already as good as over. A small concession is even now being made to keep the workers happy. You will hear those new coal chutes sending the black diamonds, and that is really what they are, Mrs Macready," Sinclair said with unfeigned and surprising enthusiasm, "tumbling into that dirty old ship!"

"But—" She hesitated. How did one explain doubts about accruing wealth? How did one make excuses for greed?

"My dear Mrs Macready, I understand your misgivings."

"You do?"

"Of course, it is natural in one of your probity, but please be assured that nothing but good can come of such an investment, not least to the population of . . ." he looked at his own copy of the letter on his desk, "of Costa Maya who will not long have to labour under the misfortunes of anarchy."

And so she had agreed to substantially increase her shareholding in the company, following his example and assisted by an additional loan secured against the deeds of the house which, many years earlier and against the unexpected death of himself, Septimus had made wholly over to his wife.

Lying sleepless, Gwendolyn was wickedly excited by the prospect of augmenting her windfall, increasingly convinced that she might soon cease to depend upon her husband in any way. Not that she sought divorce, she thought suddenly, only the upper hand.

She might have been even less inclined to sleep had she known that Captain James St John Stanier knew nothing whatsoever of either the news from Central America or the additional flotation of shares.

At the same hour that Gwendolyn Macready lay unsleeping, Tegwyn Pomeroy lay awake on the uncomfortably jolting bed of a first-class sleeper on the Western Night Mail. Having spent a miserable day tramping the streets of the capital, unable to locate the only women with whom she might claim an intimate friendship, she had left her husband. It was as though, at this desperate and unhappy moment in her life, Caroline Stanier had chosen to disappear.

By an odd coincidence, Caroline Stanier was also settling aboard an overnight train. The Pullman express was leaving the capital heading for a Channel port, scheduled to connect with a ferry and sweep her in due course to a new life on the shores of the Mediterranean. David Smith had seen her tucked into her sleeping compartment after they had enjoyed a cocktail together in the station lounge bar. He had also paid off the three men who, in a matter of less than an hour, had cleared her belongings out of her flat, carried much of her own furniture and private effects to a furniture store and taken her personal baggage to the station. As she smoked a last cigarette, Caroline smiled at the curved and fluted ceiling of the Pullman carriage.

The Commissioners and their noble guest lingered for some time over their brandies. The conviviality of the evening had made up for the earlier part of the day. Mudge had not previously met the Earl Dungarth and, knowing him to be an hereditary knight of his own order, found his faith in the ancient institutions of the country restored. He even managed to forgive Stanier much of his stupidity, reflecting that the man's intentions were probably no worse than anyone else's. Moreover, Mudge reflected, as Stanier was so much younger it was not to be wondered at if he embraced some of the more incomprehensible enthusiasms of the modern age. Mudge remembered with a private chuckle that he had himself once argued with a shipmaster who insisted steam would never replace sail. And that had been only thirty years earlier!

That evening, Stanier himself behaved with unassuming propriety. He seemed to have abandoned much of the overbearing pushiness that had characterised his conduct during the last few final days of the Commissioners' cruise. He looked, thought Mudge as he regarded the smooth, urbane young man chatting to Dungarth, rather like a cat who had got the cream.

"Well, gentlemen," Lord Dungarth said, rising somewhat unsteadily and noisily venting wind. "I think it might be time for us to call it a day—"

"Nonsense, my lord. You must have one for the road while we summon a taxi," Stanier pressed, taking the Earl's glass and refilling it.

"Oh, well, if you insist . . . Good of you to get me a cab, though. Save the old pins."

"Of course." Stanier picked up the telephone to the bridge and looked at his watch. It was three minutes to two in the morning. Behind him Dungarth belched.

But Stanier never ordered the taxi, for at that moment Lord Dungarth rose to his feet and, swaying slightly, announced with a faint air of surprise, "Damn me, gentlemen, but the old Queen has just sent for me to form a government!"

And as they all stared at him dumbfounded, he fell dead at their feet.

Moments of Decision

The death of Lord Dungarth further delayed the sailing of *Naiad*, drawing a gloomy pall over the end of the cruise of the Commissioners. Stanier had intended to remain in Porth Ardur and he now undertook to attend to the formalities of registering the death and making a deposition to the coroner's office. Mudge and the other Commissioners, pleading the delay would compromise the work of the Board, fell in with Stanier's suggestion and left the ship next morning, bound for the station and the long railway journey up to town.

"I shall see to all relevant matters here, Sir Charles," Stanier reassured the Chairman of the Commissioners, "before I leave."

"Very well," muttered Sir Charles, who was not looking forward to the journey and had a hangover.

"You have no objection?"

"Uh?" Mudge shook his head. "No, no, do what you suggested."

"What we all suggested, Sir Charles," Stanier said, smilingly reminding Sir Charles that the Commissioners' decisions were all made jointly.

"Yes, yes," Mudge said, increasingly testy.

"Well, you need not concern yourself further, Sir Charles."

Mudge grunted and it was only an hour later when Captain Blake remarked, "I hope we've done the right thing leaving Stanier to sort matters out," that Mudge felt a vague sense of unease.

"It's not that difficult to report a death, is it?"

Blake gave the Chairman an odd look, then shrugged. They had dined too well and too late. If he could not snooze in

152

his cabin, he would have to make the best of the first-class seat. To hell with Stanier. To hell with Sir Charles Mudge, for that matter.

The Earl's death was one more circumstance afterwards indicated as causal in the chain of events now about to engulf Porth Ardur. When his lordship's booking aboard *Kurnow* was cancelled, the clerk shook his head. The new service was not exactly popular, but half an hour later he cheered up when a beautiful young woman, her face pale and her eyes shadowed, arrived to enquire about a passage to Ynyscraven. The *Kurnow*, which had returned to Porth Ardur overnight, was already loading and, taking a cabin, the young woman half-ran, half-stumbled towards the gangway.

Scratching his head, the booking clerk thought the tragic figure looked vaguely familiar, but it was not until after the little ship had sailed that it suddenly struck him.

"By damn!" he exclaimed out loud, "that was Tegwyn Morgan! Her mother used to run that brassiere shop in Chapel Street . . . My word, she had lovely tits though . . ." The astonished baggage boy who had just conducted the beautiful but obviously distressed lady aboard, overhearing this recollection, was uncertain who it was who possessed attributes he was much fascinated by of late. But noticing his boss's introspective air, he decided his own services would not be required for a while, and retired to consider the matter at greater length in private.

Aboard *Kurnow*, Tegwyn flung herself upon the bunk and, in due course, fell into a fitful doze.

Two days later *Naiad* finally sailed. It was a calm day of beautiful sunshine. The lack of wind meant that the instant her ship's company could draw clean sea water into the ship's fire main, every hose in the ship was employed in flushing out the last offending grain of coal dust from the remotest corner of the Commissioners' yacht. She sailed down the bay, watched over the sea wall by Captain Macréady from his viewpoint on *Caryatid*'s bridge. He could guess the activity upon her decks, for *Naiad* was enveloped in a fine cloud of spray which, catching the sun, made her radiate brilliant rainbows, so that she seemed a faery thing as she diminished with distance and headed for the horizon.

Macready turned away from the ineffable sight, his throat choked by a feeling of overwhelming sadness. He stared down across the filthy decks of his own ship. Across the dock the clatter and roar went on as *Galahad* sank her huge chocolate bulk imperceptibly lower and lower in the water. As each truck spewed its contents into her capacious hull, the black dust rose on the still air in a great cloud, to fall, with a soft patter all over the dock area, even on this calm day.

Macready swore under his breath. Somehow the presence of the tramp ship, almost too big for the dock itself, marked the unavoidable march of progress. Its dominating, juggernaut proportions seemed to Macready to be the very agent of change, sweeping him from his hitherto pre-eminent position as the foremost seaman in Porth Ardur. Macready remembered his hubris at Porth Neigwl and knew the gods, having swept him up to the heights in his love for Justine, now intended to humble him. He sighed again. Well, at least Justine had no need to witness this sad end.

He felt the deck cant slightly under his feet and peered over the front of the bridge. The main derrick was lifting a clean buoy aboard. The brilliant red and white of its chequer-work was in odd contrast to the grimy, down-at-heel appearance of *Caryatid*. Oh well, Macready consoled himself and thinking a cup of tea might prove beneficial, there was still some work to be done.

He was sitting in his cabin, the teacup and saucer on his desk as he toyed with some paperwork, when the fateful knock came at the cabin door. It was the base messenger, Cyrus Jones.

"Morning, Cap'n."

Macready turned and, recognising the man, smiled. "Morning, Jones. How are you?"

"Better for knowing you're on our side, Cap'n Macready."

"Oh yes. That." He looked at Jones's expectant face. Jones was a messenger – perhaps he should be sent off with a message. "To be candid, Mr Jones, I don't hold out much hope." Macready watched the man's face fall.

"I couldn't get another job, sir . . ." Jones waved the stump of his missing right arm and Macready recalled the circumstances of the accident. The buoy had been swinging across the deck, dragging its mooring chain as the derrick picked it up and the chain-gang ran in to hook the links. It was a wet day with a miserably persistent westerly wind making life as wretched as possible. *Caryatid* had been rising and falling in the swell, a common enough motion and certainly not one to intimidate either the ship's company or their commander. Then the nose iron by which the lifting gear hooked and handled the buoy, failed. The buoy dropped from a height of about six feet, four tons of riveted steel plate drawn swiftly back to the ship's side as the weight of the mooring took over.

One man jumped clear but Cyrus Jones, his boots slipping on the deck, was caught by the inert mass of metal and, as it leapt clear over the lip of the foredeck, it caught the after end of the starboard bulwark with a savage crash. Unfortunately Cyrus was carried across the deck with it, and his arm was crushed in the impact.

He had never complained; never whined that the Lighthouse Authority owed him a thing. Of course he had received the usual compensation, but this was little enough, quite inadequate to keep his wife and three growing sons. The job of messenger had come up within two months and Jones had been offered it; he was a bright man and made the best of a bad job. Most pleasing was his continuing association with the work he loved and the sight of him standing in the doorway hardened Macready's resolve. He simply could not abandon men like Jones, to go off and spend the remainder of his days living in sin with Justine Morgan!

Macready coughed awkwardly and smiled. "We'll do what we can, eh, Cyrus?" he said. "Never say die until you're dead, eh? You're a good example of that!" and the two men laughed with the black, gallows humour of seamen.

"I'm glad to hear you talking like that, sir, I really am!" Jones suddenly remembered his job. "Oh, there's me almost forgettin', sir, I've a message from Mr Dale, sir. Would you mind very much steppin' across to the office?".

Dale rose as Macready entered the Area Clerks' office. It

was a large room upon one wall of which a fine painting of *Caryatid*'s predecessor, a pretty steam paddle schooner named *Mermaid*, thrashed her way past Mitre Rock light with a distant prospect of the Bishop's Islands in the background.

The painting always pleased Macready and, with the sunlight falling almost directly upon it, he failed to see another figure in the room until Dale indicated the presence of Captain Stanier. The Commissioner was slumped in the single armchair that stood to one side of a large filing cabinet. He inclined his head, but made to attempt to rise, still less to shake Macready's hand.

"Captain Stanier has some instructions for us, Captain Macready." Dale's tone of diplomatic distaste was eloquent of disapproval, dislike and disdain. Macready looked at Stanier as Dale sat at his desk and, picking up a pencil, began turning it in his fingers. The Commissioner's sprawled form bespoke utter contempt and Macready felt his colour rising with anger, humiliation and a dreadful embarrassment. He felt damnably awkward standing there like a schoolboy brought into the headmaster's study. It was unfortunate that Dale's detachment added to his own feeling of isolation, but it was not Dale's fault. Macready knew Dale enough to know the clerk would resent Stanier's presence in his office as much as he did himself. But there was an air of defiance in Dale, a hint of frosty spirit engendered by the revelations of yesterday morning. Emboldened, Macready went to the window and, with his back to it, he turned and confronted Stanier. With no chair to sit on, it was a not unnatural thing to do, but the silhouette of the bulky Macready against brilliant sunshine made Stanier squint. The small inconvenience gratified Macready as he looked at Dale.

"Well, Mr Dale," he said pleasantly. "I gather you wanted a word yourself."

"Actually it was Captain Stanier who insisted on summoning you." Dale smiled thinly, neatly emphasising the subtleties of cause and effect and the capsizing of the normal, civilised rituals of the base at Porth Ardur where Captain Macready was not usually summoned anywhere.

"I quite understand, Mr Dale," he responded, turning to Stanier. "And what can I do for you, Commissioner?"

Stanier sat up. "Well, Macready, you can stop loading those buoys for a start—"

"We are due to lay them this week, Commissioner. We may be about to be decommissioned, but we must tidy the Area up before we hand it over. Besides, you have to give us all one month's notice."

"*Waterwitch* is currently under orders to sail for Porth Ardur in three days. I think matters can wait that long. As for notice, Macready, you will require two weeks to destore your ship, no doubt, and a week to proceed to the breakers. No doubt you and many of the ship's company have leave due . . ."

Macready experienced a sudden, awful pain. It was clear Stanier did not intend that he should ever take *Caryatid* to sea on her proper business again. The whole game was up! He was finished. He was thankful that his stance in front of the window concealed the terrible, overwhelming sense of panic as he felt his whole reason for existence being torn from him.

"I have the authority of the Board in this matter, Macready . . ." Stanier went on.

This was not the right way to end matters, Macready thought, trying desperately to find some reason for persuading Stanier to allow him one last trip to sea, even if for purely personal, sentimental reasons. That he would never, ever again anchor *Caryatid* under the great lee of Ynyscraven seemed a denial of the most dreadful cruelty. Surely his ship's company should be allowed one last fling in the Craven Arms, one last, valedictory roister back down the cliff path to the waiting boat. Even the sad, dawn partings from Justine's bed seemed full of a beautiful poetic sadness which he must experience for one last, lingering time, before such departures came, at last, to an end.

"You should discharge those buoys you have loaded this morning, Macready . . ."

Mr Dale, sitting watching to one side of Macready did not have the sunshine in his eyes. Long association with Macready told him that the Captain would not wish to leave any business in his parish open to criticism and there was one matter which concerned him. He too had noticed a falling off of Macready's devotion to duty, ascribing it to worry and the prospect of unwanted retirement. He had intended to mention the matter to

Macready in as discreet a manner as possible, but the Captain's obvious loss of initiative needed immediate prompting.

"Captain Macready, I have the station fuel figures here." Dale held out a sheet of paper. It was a copy of the figures posted on the after bulkhead of *Caryatid*'s wheelhouse and, to Dale's relief, it triggered off Macready's memory. The Captain grasped at the half-forgotten fact like a drowning man seizes a passing straw.

"There is an urgent requirement for oil fuel at the Buccabu lighthouse, Commissioner," Macready began, his argument gaining momentum as his mind abandoned its personal pre-occupations and shifted into professional gear. "The matter had to be deferred due to the programmed inspection at Ynyscraven and the subsequent problems at the St Kenelm lightvessel. We shall have to attend to that before we decommission."

"That will not be necessary, Macready. I shall signal *Waterwitch* to attend to it. She has to pass the station on her way north."

"The matter is increasingly urgent, Captain Stanier," urged Dale. "Any delay might result in the light being extinguished, sir."

"And the weather at present is ideal," added Macready, gesturing to the window behind him.

But Stanier ignored both Dale and the weather. He rose and drew himself up to his full height. "The matter is not open to discussion, gentlemen. It is an order!" He paused and glared at both men. "Do you understand?" he asked, but Macready had made for the door.

"What a damnably rude man," Stanier said. "Have a signal passed to *Waterwitch* to refuel and water the Buccabu light on her way here," Stanier ordered Dale as he picked up his briefcase. "If you want me, I shall be aboard *Galahad*."

Dale nodded his head in assent. He wondered what Macready would do, for there had been a dangerous gleam in the Captain's eye as he had stalked out.

Back aboard *Caryatid* Macready penned a short note and went down to the saloon for lunch. Sitting down he ordered the steward out and stared at the officers, quickly outlining the gist of his encounter with Stanier. He then passed the note to the Second Officer. "Take off your uniform jacket and pull on a sweater, Mr Wentworth, then take this to the harbour master's office after lunch." He turned to Watson. "Put that load of buoys ashore, but cancel shore leave. Don't tell the men until six o'clock, I want all this kept under wraps until the last possible moment. D'you understand?"

"Aye, aye, sir."

Macready turned to the Chief Engineer. "I want steam kept up, don't blow the boilers down even if Stanier comes aboard and personally orders it. Tell him we need steam to discharge our stores tomorrow. Just to keep up the fiction, Mr Watson, we'll land some slings of chain from the lower hold and leave the derrick hanging over the side when the men go to tea. I want it to look as if we're staying alongside all night."

"So we're not, Captain?" the Chief said, frowning uncertainly.

"No, Chief, we most certainly are not. The Buccabu light needs refuelling and it is our job to do it."

"Our last trip then—" the Chief said, a frog in his throat.

"Sadly yes. I'm asking the harbour master to open the caisson at about 0345 tomorrow morning. We'll slip out on top of the tide."

"I see . . ."

"No disrespect to you, Mr Watson, or your colleagues aboard *Waterwitch*."

"I quite understand, sir. No-one hands the watch over without completing the log, as it were."

"Quite so, Mr Watson."

"Besides," Watson added, "I'm not sure that *Waterwitch* will be able to do the job, sir. The radio news this morning said there's a ship in trouble in the Atlantic. Her cargo of grain has shifted in very heavy weather. It may not be so pleasant in two days' time."

"I had a revision of the figures this morning, sir," put in Wentworth who seemed to have wanted an opportunity to speak for some moments. "They are getting pretty desperate. We've really left the matter a bit too long."

"All the more reason for us to get on with it then," said

Macready briskly, suddenly alarmed by the reproach in the young Second Officer's voice. He had lost his air of conspiratorial bravado. This was no longer a matter of defying Stanier. This was a matter of real urgency, for the gods were surely going to make him pay for his indifference. If the Buccabu light went out his own career would be eclipsed ingloriously.

Septimus Macready did not want that thought to mar the rest of his life.

On Ynyscraven Charlie Farthing had completed his daily round of the island. Sonia had insisted he accomplished this on one of the sure-footed ponies which formed the chief export of the place. It was a day of outstanding beauty and as the two of them had come back across the rough upper pasture of the high ground, having called on the two shepherds who had cottages in the remote northern part of Ynyscraven, they had stopped and made love in the grass.

Craven met them with the tempting invitation to circumnavigate the island that afternoon in *Lyonesse*.

"The breeze is perfect," he said, "I have a lunch aboard and you and I, Charlie, can play with the kites while you, my lady, can sunbathe."

Sonia smiled. Craven delighted in flattering her and she adored his attentions.

Charlie just laughed, never doubting for a moment that Sonia was devoted to him while Craven's obsession with Tegwyn manifested itself from time to time in references he made to her.

They sailed swiftly up the eastern side of the island, standing about three miles offshore to the north to avoid the rocks and skerries which littered the north point, broken off remnants of a larger island which, Craven averred, was once part of the mystical land after which his yacht was named. The afternoon sun shone on the forbidding cliffs of the western coast which rose precipitously to a height in places of 500 feet. They watched a pair of peregrine falcons hawk among the auks, puffins, guillemots, kittiwakes and herring gulls which filled the air with their clamour.

The brilliance and warmth of the sun filled them with an

indolent happiness. While Craven and Charlie pulled up a huge balloon jib, Sonia lay upon the deck, smiling at the gangling form of her husband as he tugged at halliard and sheet. It was five hours later that they doubled the eastern extremity of the Hound's Teeth. The reef looked full of chocolate box charm, a frill of white water which completely concealed the deadly rocks below. It was hard to believe it was the same place upon which they had seen *Sea Dragon* pounded to pieces.

Hardening in the sheets, the ketch stood back towards the anchorage; already the westering sun threw the east coast of the island into shade. The repaired *Plover* lay in the bay ahead of them.

"About time too," remarked Charlie, relaxed after the undemanding sail.

"Oh look," said Sonia suddenly sitting up and pointing to the north. "We've got more company."

"Ah, here comes the new arrival," remarked Craven as *Kurnow*, inbound after a brief call at Porth Neigwl, steamed down the east coast towards them. "I'm expecting my father any day," he added.

"Does that mean you'll get all serious?" Sonia asked.

"But of course, my lady. You don't think that I can continue to live this life of hedonism with my old Pater cracking the whip, do you?"

"I'll have to have a word with him," Sonia said, smiling.

They ran in and doused the sails. Craven went forward and eased the anchor over the bow, waiting until he could see down through the clear water, the chain stretching out ahead of them. He watched the curve ease and waved at Charlie who remained aft. "She's brought up, Charlie. Let's put a harbour stow in."

"I'll do that, Roger. Sonia's gone below to put the kettle on."

"Then I shall take my ease," Craven declared, "as befits the skipper . . ."

He sat in the cockpit and picked up the binoculars, focusing them on the *Kurnow* as the mail steamer glided into the bay, her First Officer and Carpenter on her forecastle, ready to let her own anchor go.

"Tea's up." Sonia appeared in the companionway with a

tray, but Craven had stood up and was staring intently at the approaching *Kurnow*.

"Good God . . . I don't believe it . . . It is! It is!" He lowered the glasses and gestured with them at a lone figure standing on *Kurnow*'s deck. "It's Tegwyn Pomeroy!"

"Are you sure, Roger?" Sonia asked putting down the tea tray. "I'd hate you to be disappointed."

Craven handed her the glasses. "See for yourself," he said happily.

Sonia put the glasses to her eyes and fiddled for a moment while Charlie joined Craven in staring across the water as the *Kurnow*'s anchor dropped from the hawse pipe with a splash.

"It *is* Tegwyn," said Sonia, lowering the glasses. "I wonder what on earth she's doing here?"

"Well," said Charlie dryly, "it's just possible she's come to see her mother."

"Never mind about that. I'm taking the dinghy," said Craven and Sonia and Charlie were left to their tea in the cockpit of *Lyonesse*, while Craven rowed frantically across to the steamer where they saw him attract Tegwyn's attention, saw her bend over the rail and shake her head. The two seemed to talk for a few moments, then Tegwyn straightened up and Craven began to row back. Sonia and Charlie looked at one another.

"He's pushing his luck," Charlie remarked.

"I still feel sorry for him—"

"Well, he shouldn't fall for another bloke's wife. I daresay he could have the pick of plenty of lovely young women." Charlie bent forward and kissed his wife.

"It's all right for you two blasted lovebirds," said his lordship, climbing back over the rail and distracting them from their self-absorption. "Any tea left in the pot?"

Sonia poured him a cup. She and Charlie stared at Craven.

"What are you two staring at? Don't you know curiosity killed the cat."

"Oh, come on, Roger," said Sonia, "you haven't stopped talking about Tegwyn, she arrives like Venus in a machine, you row across and speak to her and then you come back and ask for a cup of tea."

Craven held out his cup for a refill and looked at Charlie.

"Why is it, Charlie, that women are so insatiably curious about the lives of others?"

"I have no idea, Roger. But there are occasions when men share the same vice."

Craven grinned. "She's come to see her mother. She won't tell me how long she's staying, nor whether she will have dinner with me. She refused to come aboard and cruise up to Porth Neigwl, but she did say that she would call upon you this evening. So, if you have no objection, I shall join you for dinner. If you refuse, I shall declare you to have piratically seized my vessel and have you hanged."

Sonia turned to her husband with an exaggerated gesture. "I wondered when he would show his beastly side and claim a *droit de seigneur*."

"I think he needs cooling off," and immediately springing to his feet, Charlie made a grab for his lordship. Craven rolled onto his back and bent his legs, thrusting them at Charlie's belly. Charlie began to fall backward, but grabbed Craven's feet and, with a drenching splash, both men fell overboard.

Tegwyn landed by way of *Kurnow*'s launch. Twenty minutes later, after a punishing climb with her suitcase, she surprised her mother. A few minutes later, the extent of her shame exposed, she was sobbing in Justine's embrace.

"I am so glad you came here," Justine said, crying herself as she stroked her daughter's hair. "You will feel better after a few days of rest with nothing to concern you."

"I'm going to divorce him—"

"Of course, but in good time. When you feel better."

"I left him a note."

"Then so be it." Justine was sure Pomeroy, queer fish that he was, would make a generous provision for his wife.

They had only just landed on the beach and were in the act of dragging the dinghy above the high water mark, when the master of the *Kurnow* approached them.

"Excuse me, but is one of you two gentlemen Lord Craven?"

"Yes," said Craven, "that's me. Don't tell me Pater missed the boat?"

The master of the *Kurnow* looked rather non-plussed. "Well, in a manner of speaking, I suppose he did, my lord, though not quite in the manner you imagine."

Craven saw the serious demeanour of the man, awkward in his gold-laced reefer, his shiny black shoes out of place on the shingle.

"What is it, Captain?"

"I'm afraid your father died last night, sir, at Porth Ardur. I was asked to keep a lookout for you, and let you know. I'm afraid he collapsed aboard the *Naiad*, the Commissioners' yacht—"

"Oh dear," said Sonia, "poor Roger." She put her hand on Craven's arm as he turned away.

"I'm very sorry, my lord—"

"I'm so sorry, Roger," Charlie added.

Craven sniffed and turned back to them, his eyes bright. "Just when we were having a perfect day, too." He paused then swore, apologised and pulled himself together. "Captain, can you hold sailing for half an hour?"

"Of course, my lord. We aren't due to weigh for an hour."

"Charlie," Craven swung round, "take me back to *Lyonesse*. I must pack a bag. Sonia, my dear, you know my situation. Speak to Tegwyn. Tell her I'll be back as soon as I can and that I forbid her to leave the island until I do. You do understand how important this is to me?"

Sonia shook her head, her eyes sad and serious. "Yes, yes of course, Roger, but she's married—"

He leaned forward and took her by both shoulders. Speaking with an intense vehemence, he said, "I don't care. Tell her not to go. Not to go until I get back." Then he turned and grabbed the dinghy. "Come on, Charlie," adding to the *Kurnow*'s master, "I'll go straight aboard, Captain. May I see you on the bridge?"

"Yes, my lord, of course."

Sonia sat on a rock and waited while the two men rowed back to the ketch. Craven leapt aboard, telling Charlie to remain in the dinghy. A few moments later, dressed in blazer and flannels, Craven stepped down into the stern of the dinghy.

Charlie plied the oars and quickly closed the distance between

Lyonesse and *Kurnow*. As he drew under the stern in seach of the accommodation ladder on the far side, Craven looked up at the sky.

"Bugger it. The weather's on the change. Just my festering luck!"

Charlie manoeuvred alongside the foot of the ladder. Craven stood up and handed his bag to a sailor who had nipped down to meet them.

"Goodbye, Charlie. I'll be back as soon as I can. Try and keep Teggy on the island."

"We'll do our best, Roger."

"Yes, I know you will." Craven heaved himself up on the ladder while Charlie trimmed the rocking dinghy. "Oh, by the way, Charlie . . ."

"Yes?"

"Keep an eye on *Lyonesse* for me. Feel free to take her out if you wish. It'll keep the weed off her bottom."

"Yes, of course. Thanks. I hope it all goes as well as it can."

Craven waved, turned, ran up the accommodation ladder and disappeared from sight. Charlie pulled back to the shore where Sonia helped him drag the dinghy up the beach.

"What on earth are we going to do, Charlie?"

"What he asks, I suppose. He is the gaffer, after all."

Fatal Errors

There was an easterly breeze blowing as Captain Macready walked out onto the starboard bridge wing of *Caryatid* at 0300 the following morning. Across the dock the deck lights of *Galahad* burned brightly, but the loading had ceased for the night earlier the previous evening. The stiff breeze on his face gave Macready the first sensation of alarm. Were they already too late to refuel the Buccabu lighthouse?

Within a few seconds he had another problem. Thomas Jones from the harbour master's office was on the bridge asking to see him.

"What's the trouble, Mr Jones?"

"The easterly, sir. It's getting up all the time. I'm going to have to boom the caisson before much longer. I thought I'd let you know, if you're after changing your mind about sailing."

Macready shook his head. "No, Mr Jones, I'm sorry, but we're going out, come hell or high water."

"Very well, Cap'n, but you know what these easterlies can be like, it being a spring tide, like."

"You're thinking it may be that bad?" Macready frowned.

Jones nodded. "Reckon. Once you're out, you'll be boomed out. The *Galahad*'s due to sail later, but I thought I should warn you, especially as you seem to be sailing rather secretly—"

"Well, never mind that. We're sailing and that's that!"

"All right. Give me ten minutes. *Kurnow*'s going to come in after you've sailed. I've told him to let you get clear first."

"Very well, Mr Jones."

"We'll see you when we see you then, Cap'n Macready."

"Yes, Mr Jones."

Watson sent the ship's company to their stations quietly and Macready was thankful he commanded an old steamship with silent, reciprocating engines. The only noise would be from the jangle of the telegraphs and he could keep their movements to a minimum.

The word came up from forward and aft that the mooring ropes were singled up to bights, easily loosed from the ship, and, at the expiry of Jones's ten minutes, as Macready saw the caisson move slowly across the entrance and the popple on the dockwater where it was exposed to the wind, he ordered, "Let go fore and aft," and jangled the telegraphs from Stand-by, to Slow Astern Port, then Slow Astern together. *Caryatid* gathered sternway, seeking the wind, and proceeded stern first out of the dock.

Once clear of the extremity of the lighthouse pier, Macready began to swing his ship and he felt the rising force of the wind properly as it blew on the beam. Then he was ringing the engines ahead and *Caryatid* steamed down the bay.

"It's blowing up a bit and clouding over," remarked Watson, coming up onto the bridge to take over the watch after securing both anchors. He raised his glasses and followed Macready's example, staring at the pale white hull of the approaching *Kurnow*.

"Yes."

"I hope we're not too late," mused Watson.

"So do I," snapped Macready.

Both officers stood and watched *Kurnow* pass, then they lowered their glasses. "Course Sou' West by South, full speed away."

"Aye, aye, sir."

By sunrise, the wind had dropped a touch and Macready was feeling more cheerful as he returned to the bridge, unable to do more than doze in his cabin. He noticed the barometer had steadied and, going out onto the bridge wing, studied the sea and sky. It was cloudy, but bright patches of sunshine blotched the sea with their brilliance and the day seemed full of life and light. Perhaps it was not going to be so bad after all. Macready tended to think the gloomy prognostications of

Jones and Watson belonged to the fearful hours of the night. In daylight the reality was not so terrible. He turned his mind to the more practical aspects of the coming day.

With the ebb tide out of the strait, they would be at the Buccabu light at about three in the afternoon. The tide, approaching high water at Porth Ardur, would already be falling at the lighthouse. If the wind stayed in the east they would be able to land a party on what was normally the windward side of the rocks. It was unorthodox, but they had done it before and he guessed his men would rise to the challenge. He could, if he had the nerve, get the ship quite close and pump oil fuel directly ashore. He had done that before and it would give him a hell of a kick to retire on a high point like that. It would be something they would all remember, by damn! Well, he would have to see. It would be stupid to take a foolish risk on this last occasion. He went below in search of breakfast.

By mid-morning Ynyscraven was dropping astern to the north-north-east. Macready stared at the fading and insubstantial-looking island. It seemed impossible that it was actually inhabited by the only soul in the world who made his life worthwhile.

Stanier arrived at the docks to see the loading of *Galahad* completed and her hatches battened down. From the windows of the port manager's office, he could see the derricks being lowered and it was then that he discovered *Caryatid* missing from her berth. He was about to leave and walk across to the Lighthouse Authority base and demand an explanation from Dale, when the port manager put down the telephone.

"The harbour master boomed the dock gate this morning, he doesn't want to drop the booms and let *Galahad* out at high water."

"Why not?"

"He's unhappy about the easterly wind."

Stanier looked out of the window and up at the sky. "Well, it's a stiff breeze, but hardly a gale. Here, give it to me . . ." Stanier took the phone. "Is that you, Jones? Well, it's Captain Stanier here. Now listen, you can't pull the wool over *my* eyes. Remember I know as much about that bloody dock gate as you.

Now I know you buggers have let Macready out in defiance of my orders . . . What? All right, that may have nothing to do with you, but it's got a good deal to do with me. So has the sailing of *Galahad*. Her fortunes mean a lot to this town and don't you forget it. I want her out at high water. You see to it, Mister, that that bloody caisson is open."

Stanier slammed the phone down and looked at the port manager. "She'll be trimmed and ready by then, I hope."

The port manager smiled. "No question about it, Captain Stanier. Those extra coal trimmers make all the difference."

Both men laughed, then the telephone rang again. The port manager held it out towards him. "It's for you."

Stanier took the phone again. "It's Mr Dale, sir—"

"Yes, Mr Dale. D'you have a message for me from Captain Macready?"

"No, sir, I don't, though I can tell you that *Caryatid* sailed at 0300 this morning—"

"In defiance of my orders, Dale."

"May I caution you before you take a stand too heavily upon that point, Captain Stanier—"

"What the devil d'you mean?"

"Well, I'm ringing you to let you know I've had a message from Cavehaven. *Waterwitch* has cancelled her trip up here for the time being. She's gone to the assistance of a ship in the Atlantic. Apparently the vessel's cargo of grain has shifted and there's a danger she'll capsize. Perhaps it's just as well that *Caryatid* has sailed to look after the Buccabu light."

Stanier spent a moment digesting this fact. He could not stop *Waterwitch* going to the assistance of a vessel in distress, nor would he be wise to compromise Macready's chances of refuelling the Buccabu lighthouse. Then a thought struck him.

"Tell me, Mr Dale, how desperate *is* the Buccabu light?" Had Dale and Stanier been in the same room, the clerk might have seen the look not of concern, but of cunning, in Stanier's eyes. But as the Commissioner was on the telephone, it was impossible to gauge Stanier's motive and Dale responded directly to the question.

"It's a matter of *extreme* urgency, sir," he said.

"In other words it should have been attended to some time ago."

Dale perceived the trap too late. He hesitated for a revealing moment before admitting, "Well, yes, sir."

"Thank you, Mr Dale." Stanier came off the phone smiling and handed it back to the port manager. "Got him!" he breathed.

Stanier had lunch in the Station Hotel where he unexpectedly bumped into Roger Craven. He had almost forgotten the sad business of the previous day and the telegram he had sent to the capital.

"Please accept my sincere condolences, my lord."

"Thank you, Stanier. I gather from my enquiries this morning that you attended to most of the paperwork."

"Yes. You got my telegram, obviously—"

"No, I was on Ynyscraven. The master of the *Kurnow* let me know. How was he told?"

"I'm not exactly certain, but the whole town knew during the morning . . ." Stanier went on to recount the conviviality of the dinner and Dungarth's last words.

"Rum old bugger," his lordship said affectionately. "I've just made arrangements to have the body taken home. I'm getting the afternoon train. It means a long wait for a connection, but I need to attend to a few things in town."

"Yes. Yes of course," said Stanier, who had no idea what protocol had to be followed when one became the umpteenth Earl of Dungarth.

"Well, I'll be seeing you."

"Yes. Yes of course, and my condolences, my lord." Stanier watched him go, looked at his watch and then hurried back to the docks to watch *Galahad* unberth and sail.

The town of Porth Ardur still lay under sunshine, but a curtain of grey cloud was welling up from the eastwards in a great curve, clearly visible from the railings that skirted the descent towards the lower town. Stanier could already feel the thrust of the wind. Behind him, the villas of the better-off stretched up the incline. Somewhere up there in Glyndwr Avenue Stanier had once rented a house and enjoyed the delights of making love to an eager Tegwyn Morgan. The thought stopped him in his tracks and, at the same time, he recalled he had not rung his wife for several days. He paused, he could see a telephone box further down the road and began walking again. As he descended he stared out to sea. It was clearly blowing quite hard offshore. Macready was going to have a job to refuel the Buccabu lighthouse, Stanier thought happily.

"Got him on two counts!" Stanier muttered. Not only would the old charlatan retire and have no job, Stanier would see he lost his reputation as well!

He could not get through to Caroline from the telephone box and walked on. Down at the dockside, Stanier boarded the *Galahad*. Going directly to the bridge he announced he would sail with the ship and come ashore with the harbour pilot.

"I'm not taking one, sir," the master told his owner. "It could be tricky disembarking him outside and pilotage isn't compulsory. I've had some warps run across the dock. We'll heave her off and line her up and then go astern. Piece of cake. Besides," the master said with a grin, "it'll save you a few bob."

"Yes. Oh, quite, yes. Very well, Captain . . ." Stanier held out his hand. "Good voyage."

From the quayside, Stanier watched the tramp slip her moorings and heave herself into the middle of the dock. Suddenly he saw the dark swirl of water under her counter from her deep propeller. She was full to her marks, he observed with satisfaction as she drew astern and her master waved from her bridge.

"Good voyage!" he called out again.

"No problems," the master shouted back.

Stanier stood for some moments until the chocolate brown stem had withdrawn beyond the entrance and Jones's men were sliding the caisson back as he had once ordered them too, in the days when he first seduced Tegwyn Morgan and knew the lubricious delights of her body. With that he turned back towards the port manager's office, resolved to call Caroline. At the end of the dock Jones's men boomed the gates again.

"There's no doubt," Jones told them as they grumbled about the necessity of having to do the task twice in one day, "there's no doubt that there's going to be a bloody hard blow before too long, my lads."

* * *

It was Charlie who first noticed the increasing wind on Ynyscraven. He was making his rounds alone, leaving Sonia to keep Justine and Tegwyn company, shying away from what seemed to be a female occasion. From the high pasture, he caught a glimpse of a distant smudge of smoke on the horizon and, reining in his mount, he stared at it for some time, conjuring up in his mind's eye a picture of *Caryatid*'s bridge, imagining old Macready, his glasses about his neck on their sennit-work lanyard.

He smiled to himself, guessing the ship was off to the Buccabu light. It was amazing how quickly one got out of touch. He felt the pony beneath him twitch and remembered what Sonia had told him about their habit of turning their backsides into the wind. The sensation made him want to look the other way and he saw then the increased number of white horses heaping up to windward and the great swirl of grey cloud which was already covering half the sky. It was this point that he remembered *Lyonesse*, lying at her single anchor, exposed to the increasing wind and tailing back on her cable, with the shore under her lee.

"Oh shit!" he swore and, kicking the pony into a canter, he tugged its head round.

He found Sonia in the cottage, preparing lunch. "She's much better," Sonia announced and it took Charlie a minute to recall Tegwyn's misery. He began to throw some items of clothing into a bag.

"What are you doing?" Sonia asked. "Lunch is almost ready."

"Never mind. Go outside and tell me what you think of the weather." Sonia looked at him as though he had asked her to fly to the moon, then she suddenly caught the tone of alarm in his voice and went to the door. She was back in a moment her eyes wide.

"Well?" Charlie demanded. "You think it looks bad, don't you?"

Sonia nodded. "It looks like an Invaders' Wind."

Charlie nodded. "That's what I thought. Look, I'm going to have to get *Lyonesse* offshore, or she'll be wrecked."

"You can't do that on your own—"

"I'm going to have to, darling, otherwise she'll be smashed to pieces. I haven't time to argue."

"I'm coming with you—"

"No!"

"You haven't time to argue, remember? I'll get some food and some clothes. Give me five minutes. Let Justine know."

Charlie did as he was bid and five minutes later the two of them were scrambling down the cliff path, shooting glances at the breakers already rolling into the bay.

Stanier was unable to reach Caroline on the dock manager's telephone. It was the middle of the afternoon, so perhaps that was not surprising. He set off to walk back to the Station Hotel and on the long uphill haul he was approached by a small, energetic woman. He recognised her and she him.

"Good afternoon, Captain Stanier," Mrs Macready said. "Have you just come up from the docks?"

"Mrs Macready," he said awkwardly, "er, yes, I have."

"The *Caryatid* has sailed, I believe. It is most unusual for my husband not to let me know when he's going out—"

"Oh, there's an, er, an emergency, Mrs Macready—"

"Ah, that explains it, then." She smiled and seemed to want to chat. Stanier tried to disentangle himself but before he could do so, she said, "I suppose I ought to thank you, Captain Stanier. As a benefactor of the town."

"Oh," Stanier said with a self-deprecating shrug, "well, one does what one can for the less fortunate—"

"I'm personally grateful as well, Captain. This new flotation on behalf of Ardurian Slate . . ." She smiled again, seeing the expression on his face. "Surely you've heard? Oh no, of course not, you've been at sea on the *Naiad*, haven't you. Well, you see . . ." and she went on to explain the good news.

When they parted, Stanier hurried back to the hotel and picked up the telephone. Caroline would be having her bath about now, he thought, drumming his fingers impatiently. After several minutes he put the phone down, then after a moment's reflection he telephoned David Smith's number.

"Mr Smith's not here, sir," Smith's manservant said. "Would you like to leave a message?"

"Er, no, no, thank you."

"Would you like me to say who called, sir?"

"Er, no, no, don't worry."

He put the phone down and swore. Then he rang Tegwyn. Pomeroy answered the telephone. "It's James Stanier here, Pom. Is Caroline with Tegwyn?"

"I haven't a bloody clue, Stanier," said Pomeroy with uncharacteristic brusqueness. "Where the hell are you?"

"Me? I'm in Porth Ardur."

"Oh, that dreadful little place. If you see Tegwyn down there tell her she can have the divorce."

"Divorce? What on earth's the matter, Pom? Why should I be running in to Tegwyn?"

"I've really no idea, Stanier, old boy—"

"You're drunk."

"How very perceptive of you, Stanier. You always were brilliantly quick on the uptake."

"You haven't seen Caroline, then."

"You do catch on, old boy, don't you. Quite amazing."

Stanier hesitated before discussing business matters with Pomeroy and in the end decided against it. He was panicking. Caroline would be home by now.

"Well thanks, Pom."

"My pleasure, Stanier, old boy. Any time you like."

All at Sea

Even as the tall finger of the Buccabu lighthouse broke the regularity of the horizon, Macready realised he had run out of luck. The sea was humping up astern of the ship and the wind was blowing past them with considerable force. If one added to it the speed of the ship and that of the favourable tide, one arrived at the conclusion that, if the wind was not already at gale force, it was perilously close to it. Macready swore. He felt the jaws of fate close inexorably round him. This was the final payoff for his hubris, this was nemesis, the final humiliation that wrecked his reputation with his career. The sea, he reflected bitterly, always won in the end.

He was left with no alternative, for he could not run for shelter. He would have to heave-to and await a moderation, seizing the moment when it came. Fortunately an easterly gale tended not to persist. Although there would be no lingering ground swell, as occurred after a westerly blow, nevertheless the next few hours would be uncomfortable enough, requiring a degree of fortitude. While they were still running downwind it would be as well to make sure all was secure on deck.

Charlie and Sonia were soaked through by the time they got the dinghy launched and pushed it through the breakers. Charlie had a stiff pull out to the ketch and, when at last they clambered aboard, he took a few moments to catch his breath while Sonia stowed things below.

Lyonesse was pitching wildly, snatching at her anchor in such a manner as to make it obvious that they had arrived not a moment too soon. Once she broke its flukes out of the sandy seabed, the yacht would fall to leeward in a matter of moments to dash herself to pieces upon the cliffs of Ynyscraven which rose sheer from the sea astern of them.

Pulling himself together, Charlie went below and roused the spitfire jib out of the locker and dragged it forward. Shackling it onto the halliard, he indicated where Sonia should bend on the sheets.

"Use a bowline," he shouted.

"I know."

When the jib was ready for hoisting, they went aft, pulled the mizzen sheet in hard and threw off the sail ties. Then Charlie hoisted the mizzen and, leaving Sonia on the helm, turned to her before going forward again.

"I can't tell which way her head will fall when I get the anchor off the bottom, but get the jib sheeted home as soon as it becomes obvious, all right?"

Sonia nodded, biting her lip. Charlie smiled. "Once we get away we'll be all right. Then we can get some dry gear on. Don't worry."

"I'm not worried, except that you're standing there talking when you should be getting that anchor up before it drags."

As if to add to Sonia's logic, *Lyonesse*'s bow rose and she tugged viciously at her cable. "I'm off." Charlie made his way forward, fighting the wind on the wildly plunging deck.

He hoisted the jib and got the halliard as tight as he could on the small winch. Then shipping the handle in the windlass and trying to dodge the wildly flogging jib clew above his head, he began to crank in the anchor cable. It was hard work. Despite the mechanical advantage of the windlass, he had to bodily haul the whole weight of the ketch, with the drag of wind in her rigging, against the force of the gale and the constant knocking back of the breakers now rolling into the bay, steepening with every moment that the tide fell.

Suddenly he felt the chain snag as *Lyonesse* began to rise to an incoming wave. The chain drew taut, restraining her buoyant bow and a sea crashed inboard, rolling past Charlie and sweeping aft along the side decks and pouring overboard on either side of Sonia in the cockpit. Then the ketch shook herself, parted her anchor chain with a bang and began to fall astern. For a terrifying moment it seemed she would drive directly astern under the beetling cliffs, but then she fell off the wind.

Sensing the moment, Sonia quickly hove in the starboard jib sheet, belayed it and seized the helm. Veering as a wave struck her port bow in an explosion of spray and spent energy, *Lyonesse* began to gather forward way. A moment later she was moving ahead, crabbing across the wind. Pulling the loose end of broken cable in, Charlie scrambled aft. He was shivering with cold, but frantically hauled in another foot on the lee jib sheet as Sonia called out a warning.

"It's no good, Charlie! We'll have to go about, she won't weather the Hounds Teeth on this tack!"

He looked up and saw the foaming maelstrom of the tide rushing southwards through the black fangs of the reef. "It's the bloody ebb tide! Keep her going for a moment or two. We can't afford to risk not staying properly! We must have enough momentum to get her bow through the wind, otherwise . . ." He left the shouted sentence unfinished. Sonia understood.

They stood on for one and a half minutes, then Sonia shouted, "Tell me when, Charlie!"

He watched the crabbing motion of the boat, then at the water rushing past the side. She was certainly driving along. "Now!" he yelled and Sonia put the helm down.

Charlie did not start the sheet until he was certain *Lyonesse* had passed through the eye of the wind. Then he worked frantically as the heavy canvas of the spitfire jig flogged wildly before the port sheet tamed it. A moment later they were heading north-east, stemming the tide and drawing slowly away from the Hound's Teeth.

Sonia cast a glance astern. High on the path she could just see two bright spots of colour that were Justine and Tegwyn.

"You'd better go below and try and get something more suitable on."

"Aye, aye, skipper. Then I'll put the kettle on."

"Good idea."

Stanier was as much at sea in a metaphorical, as were Macready or Charlie Farthing in a literal sense. He consistently failed to get an answer from Caroline's number, while David Smith's manservant grew tired of informing him that his master was at a late sitting of 'the House'. It was only when it dawned upon Stanier that Parliament was prorogued for the summer that he rang back and insisted upon speaking to Smith.

"I have already told you, sir, that Mr Smith is attending a late sitting of the House—"

"Don't fool with me, you damned scoundrel! I know the House of Commons is in recession for the summer—"

"If you'll excuse me, sir, but there is currently a play on in the West End, called *A Late Sitting of the House*, sir. A farce, I believe," the man added dryly.

For a moment Stanier was speechless, then he gave his number and asked that Smith should telephone him the moment he got in. Ten minutes later the phone rang.

"Stanier, old boy, what can I do for you? My man says you're damned jumpy. Sorry about the confusion. Good play though; made me laugh."

Stanier, worked up to a pitch of nervous tension, almost shouted, "Where's my wife?"

"How should I know?"

"I've been trying to ring her number and there's no reply. You haven't seen her?" Stanier mastered himself.

"No, not recently, anyway."

"I tried Tegwyn Pomeroy, but I got Pom and he sounded drunk."

"He probably was, old boy. She's left him."

"What?"

"Tegwyn has left Pomeroy. It was inevitable in the end . . . Perhaps Caro is with Tegwyn, or is it the other way round. Sorry I can't be more helpful."

"There's something else," Stanier said gloomily.

"What's that, old boy?"

"What's this about a flotation?"

"Oh that. Well, we had to act fast—"

"We? You mean you consulted Caroline?"

"Well no, actually she consulted me. That was the agreement, wasn't it, while you were enjoying your own little flotation on the briny."

"So everything's fine?"

"Couldn't be better, old boy. Caro secured a contract for supplying coal to Costa Maya—"

"Yes, yes, I knew about that."

"Well, we had to charter two extra ships, bareboat charters, and wanted some quick funds, otherwise we couldn't fulfil the schedule. Got two tramps on the Exchange and they'll be painting their funnels tomorrow, I should think." Smith chuckled. He could hear Caroline saying, "Tell Jimmy about their funnels being painted in Cambrian Steam's colours and he'll be happy as a sandboy."

"As long as Caro's happy about it all," Stanier said, slightly mollified, but still trying to wrestle with the sequence of events. There was something not quite right about it all, but he could not figure it out for himself.

"Look, Jimmy," Smith was saying, "Caroline is more than happy. She has everything well in hand. I saw her only yesterday and she told me, and I quote, 'Everything is going just as we planned, David.' Now that is what she said to me. I imagine that if you had been accessible, she would have said something along the same lines to you. She's a damned clever woman, Jimmy, you don't deserve her."

And with that Stanier had to be content and take himself to bed.

Having cleared the Hound's Teeth, Charlie stood offshore for a mile of so before tacking again, heading roughly south-east until clear of Ynyscraven when he hove to, backing the jib and lashing the helm down. The motion of the ketch was much easier and although *Lyonesse* pitched heavily, she was no longer fighting the sea, but curtseying to it, acquiescing to its force, while matching it with her own, lesser but enduring strength.

"She's like a woman making love," he shouted to Sonia when she re-emerged in hideous black oilskins holding mugs of hot, sweet tea.

"How many women have you made love to?"

"Enough."

The cloud had covered the sky before sunset and the day that

had begun in bright sunshine ended in gloom, fizzling out in a
long twilight. Macready had turned *Caryatid* about and hove her
to an hour or so earlier. He had also spoken by radio telephone to
the keepers on the lighthouse. They too were concerned about
the state of the oil reserves on the station, but thought they had
sufficient for two more days.

"Mind you, sir," said the Senior Keeper, "we'll be scraping
the barrel by then."

Macready was much relieved. Two days was more than he
could have hoped for, and although the matter might yet reach
crisis point in the coming hours, while the easterly wind wound
itself up to its climactic velocity, he could relax insofar as the
Buccabu light was concerned.

Despite this remission of anxiety, however, he decided that
he would remain close by, ready to seize the first opportunity
that offered to refuel the station. He signalled this intention to
the keepers and as darkness fell, they could see the navigation
lights of the lighthouse tender bucking up and down as, at slow
speed, *Caryatid* shouldered aside the heavy seas that tore down
upon her from the east-north-east.

Charlie decided he must get some navigation lights organised
before the onset of darkness. It took him some time to locate
the brass lanterns, only to find them empty of paraffin. Further
time was lost locating their fuel and then he decided to fill all
the lamps, including those for the compass and the cabin. It
is a difficult enough matter to attend to in still water. By the
time Charlie had replenished the reservoirs of all the lamps
and wedged each filled lamp where it would not move, about
a gallon of paraffin had been used, three quarters of which was
busy finding its way into *Lyonesse*'s bilge, while it stunk the
saloon to high heaven.

Nevertheless, Charlie persisted. He placed two small Argand
lamps in their gimballed sconces in the saloon, then took the
small light out and shoved it into the binnacle.

"Oooh, that's very cosy," said Sonia, curled up in the corner
of the cockpit.

"I'm glad you like it."

"I do. I wouldn't be anywhere else on earth right now."

Charlie looked at her. He could just see her face peeping out from under the turned-back brim of the sou'wester.

"I almost believe you," he said, laughing and ducking back into the saloon where he gingerly lifted the stern light up and, moving aft, hung it over the stern rail where its white light fell upon the oily swirl of the black sea a foot or so beneath him. Returning to the saloon, he next picked up the big port lantern and, bracing himself, carried it through the companionway and out into the cockpit.

"Are you going to open a house of ill repute?" Sonia asked as her face was suddenly bathed in the red glow.

"Yes, I'm going to hang it in the port rigging for all the passing sailors to see."

Charlie struggled forward and set the lantern on the bracket screwed to the painted side-screen. He then locked the lantern in position by screwing the thumb screw as tight as possible. Afterwards he went back into the saloon for the green, starboard light.

"Oh, that's really weird," Sonia said, as the ghoulish glare fell on her husband's face.

Forty miles to the north-east, *Galahad* steered to head through the 25-mile gap between Ynyscraven and Landfall Point. The tramp ship was deeply laden and wallowed in the following sea. As the waves overtook her, they washed along her side, sluicing in through the openings at the foot of her bulwarks, then poured out as trough followed crest, cleaning the accumulated dust of her lading off her well decks.

On the bridge at eight o'clock in the evening her young Third Officer took over from the Mate and settled down to the routine of watch-keeping.

"It's a filthy night," the departing Mate remarked. "And it'll probably get worse before it gets better. Good night."

"Thank you for your cheery encouragement," the Third Mate said.

"Don't worry, sir," remarked the seaman at the wheel. "It'll be four in the morning before he knows what's hit him."

"Well, I'll be bloody glad when it's midnight."

"So will I."

* * *

As the first watch passed, between the hours of eight o'clock and midnight, the wind rose. The waves grew steeper under this assault, their crests toppling and breaking, the thunder of their dissolution adding to the shriek of the wind in the rigging of the three vessels. Then, at about half past eight o'clock off the Buccabu light, the tide turned. The strong force of a spring flood now made against the wind, heaping the seas into steeper and steeper gradients, so that they broke with heavy and destructive force.

One such wave swept *Lyonesse* from end to end, water pouring through the tightly shut skylight and waking Charlie who had sought an hour's shut-eye before taking over from Sonia. Sudden fear for her safety propelled him into the cockpit just as a second wave poured aboard. As he opened the companionway, his eyes unaccustomed to the darkness, there was no sign of Sonia. For a moment his heart stopped, then he saw her lying in the bottom of the cockpit, water sloshing round her. The next wave poured over the low roof of the dog-house and down his back, making him gasp.

"We'll have to turn round and run for it!" he yelled. "I'll have to get the mizen off her!"

He was never quite sure how he got what he had hitherto considered a small triangular sail down and roughly secured to its boom. But sometime later he collapsed exhausted into the cockpit and recovered his breath. *Lyonesse* had already paid off the wind and it took only a moment of easing the jib sheet for her to start scudding before the storm.

"You'll have to steer," he shouted into Sonia's ear. "I'll get a mooring warp over the stern and stream it."

"Be careful—" she urged, reaching out a hand and squeezing his arm.

With a warp astern, there would be less likelihood of the ketch broaching-to and capsizing in a breaking wave crest. Again, the task took him some time but immediately the line snaked out astern, Sonia reported the steering was a little easier.

"Thank the Lord for small mercies," he said. "I'm going below to change again."

"Have you any more dry clothes?"

"No, I'm reduced to wearing Roger's cricket kit."

"He's an earl now."

"That's a bloody funny thing to think of right now."

"I hope he marries Tegwyn."

"That's impossible."

"I'm not so sure," Sonia said enigmatically, but Charlie had disappeared below in search of white flannels.

Fateful Encounters

Charlie relieved Sonia and sent her below to rest, while he concentrated on steering *Lyonesse* downwind. The ketch's motion was still violent, for the hollow steepness of the seas flung her about, but it stressed both hull and crew less than trying to hold on, hove to and head to wind. Sonia, however, did not remain below, but soon reappeared in the cockpit. Even in the mean light diffused from the compass bowl, Charlie could see she was pale.

"Oh Charlie, the stink down there is unbearable." She gasped in the fresh air, staring astern.

"The lamp oil?" She nodded without saying a word. "Sorry. My fault." She put out a hand and touched his shoulder. "Don't look astern, darling. It can be pretty terrifying." She slumped down in the cockpit, curled herself into a ball and tried to sleep. He could see her eyes close and, slipping in and out of the fitful, waking doze that hours at the helm of a sailing yacht can induce, steered like an automaton through the succeeding hours.

On the bridge of the *Galahad*, the watch changed at midnight. The young Third Mate handed over to the Second Mate. In the security and cosiness of the tramp's wheelhouse, the gale did not seem so very bad, not even when the wind rose to hurricane force, slicing the very tops off the tumbling seas, and sending the atomised water along the flattening surface of the sea with the velocity of buckshot.

The Second Mate supped his third mug of tea, enjoying a desultory chat with the helmsman. It was inconsequential nonsense, words intended merely to put the long voyage ahead into some sort of perspective and rationalise the demands of their odd, outlandish profession. It was only when they both heard the lookout on the bridge wing sing out:

"Right ahead! Something right ahead!"

The Second Mate lifted his glasses, saw nothing at all, then a small pinprick of light swung across his narrow field of vision, coming clear of the black column of the foremast. The angle at which he stared down at it, and its swirling reflection in water, made him realise instantly that it was no distance ahead of them.

"Hard a-port!" he snapped.

"Hard a-port!" came the grunted answer as the helmsman reacted. The Second Mate rushed out onto the bridge wing, alongside the lookout.

"What the hell?"

"It's a bloody yacht!" The incredulity in the lookout's voice was not surprising, but his report was accurate. The Second Mate saw it, a low white shape, a thin pale mast beyond which a triangle of sail flapped in the lee of the *Galahad*'s hull, a shorter mizzen. As the apparition drew swiftly astern, he thought he saw a face peering up at him. It was to haunt him for the rest of his life, for it had a spectral quality that, despite subsequent events, he was always to think of as supernatural.

Charlie had no inkling of the overtaking steamer until its approaching bulk blanketed the straining canvas of the spit-fire jib. The sail collapsed, filled, and collapsed again, each time cracking like gunshot. His first thought was for Sonia, but she lay like a dead child in the foetal position, then he looked round.

The bow of the tramp steamer almost overhung him. The wallowing hull pushed a great wall of water before; this was as high, it seemed, as *Lyonesse*'s cross trees. Charlie stared up at the huge, black steel wall, speechless with horror. Then it swung ponderously away from him, exposing the flare upon which he read the stark white letters of the ship's name: *Galahad*. Then the tramp was surging past, the sideways thrust of her bow wave striking *Lyonesse* and flinging her over to starboard. The yacht rolled back to port and was sucked closer as she fell into the trough which succeeded the bow wave. Charlie looked up but could see only the green glow of the ship's starboard navigation light, then she raced past, images of boats and boat davits passing quickly, followed by the low after well deck, a poop deck house and then another slam and roll and the kick of the protesting tiller as, lit by the *Galahad*'s rapidly diminishing stern light, *Lyonesse* wallowed for an instant, then drove after her tormentor, as the wind caught her again.

Charlie huddled shaking with reaction over the tiller. He had never been so terrified in his life and, seeing Sonia undisturbed by the appalling episode, resolved not to tell her.

Slowly he mastered himself. He recalled Macready telling him you could never run down a yacht, for the thing was inevitably shoved aside by the advancing pressure of the bow wave. In the light of his own experience, this seemed a hollow reassurance. They had survived an encounter with death, Charlie thought in that bleak and lonely hour. *Lyonesse* had saved them, he felt sure, and patted the tiller.

"Thank you, little ship," he said to her, and Sonia stirred, waking in an agony of cramp with a whimper of pain. Charlie looked ahead into the screaming darkness, but there was no trace of the *Galahad*'s stern light. Then he saw the loom of a lighthouse. It was the Buccabu light, just over the horizon, a point to starboard. It was an immensely reassuring sight and he was about to point it out to Sonia, but she appeared to have drifted off to sleep again.

Despite the fact that he had had a disturbed night, Macready felt little inclination to retire to his bunk. That this might be his last night at sea in heavy weather was only one reason why he dozed fitfully in the chair provided for him on the bridge. He was also aware that, stout though *Caryatid* was, the conditions were extreme. Her low foredeck made her vulnerable to shipping green seas, and her large hatch, if stripped of its tarpaulin cover, would soon swallow sufficient water to sink her.

Besides, there was a rare majesty to the night, for the wind was scouring the sea so that it no longer presented the serried ranks of wave upon wave marching inexorably down upon them, but was one vast, undulating plain of grey-white and this, at about two o'clock in the morning, was suddenly dramatically lit by the full moon as the first rents in the overcast began to show.

In the next half hour, these first short moments of illumination grew longer. The stabbing light of the Buccabu, some five miles distant, grew less prominent, so that it was a moment before anyone, Macready, Wentworth, or the helmsman, noticed the light had vanished. Then they simultaneously reacted.

"The Buccabu light, sir! It's not there!"

"By damn, you're right!" Instinctively, Macready shook himself fully awake and checked the compass course. No, the ship's head remained roughly north-east, and the wind direction seemed steady. Surely they had not all been asleep and steamed past without noticing?

He went quickly to the wheelhouse door, flung it open and stepped out into the screaming night, almost blinded by the reflection of the moonlight on the sea and grazed by the salt-laden spray that flew horizontally through the air over the bridge dodgers. He stared astern, then swung round again and, leaning into the wind, lifted his glasses. He caught sight of the moonlight on the grey granite tower, a thin, pallid finger not three miles away. He counted the seconds. By the time he reached twenty he knew for certain the light was extinguished.

Well, it had happened. He was shamed by it, but the fact stared him in the face: he had failed in his duty. As if aware of his shame, another curtain of cloud covered the moon and plunged the world into darkness again.

"Sir!"

"I've seen the lighthouse, Mister," he told the Second Mate.

"It's not that, sir, there's a ship beyond the tower, sir!"

Macready lifted his binoculars again, and swept the horizon. He could see nothing. "I don't see anything . . ."

The Second Mate was silent, still peering through his glasses, then he lowered them. "I'm sorry, sir, I could have sworn that I'd seen a ship."

"Let's call up the lighthouse and see what's happened."

"They must have run out of oil, sir."

"Let's check, shall we," Macready said patiently, "before we jump to any conclusions."

*   *   *

From the security of his wheelhouse, the Second Mate of the *Galahad* had seen the light of the Buccubu a few moments before Charlie. Unlike Charlie in the ketch, who, low in the water, had seen only the loom of the light as *Lyonesse* had been lifted up on a swell, the *Galahad*'s Second Mate had seen the sweep of the full beam. He was still shaken by the shock of overtaking the yacht, and deferred taking a bearing, an unpleasant task in the prevailing conditions. The tramp ran on for almost half an hour then, as the chartroom clock edged up to three in the morning, the Second Mate stirred himself. He ought to put a position on the chart and went out onto the bridge wing and clambered up to the compass on the monkey island, the wind tearing at his body as he heaved himself up the ladder.

The moon had ducked in again, and the darkness seemed impenetrable. Then, as *Galahad* lifted on a great swell, he caught a distant glimpse of a ship's navigation light broad on the starboard bow. It was a long way off, he thought, bending over the azimuth mirror and twiddling it to take a bearing. Not as familiar with the Buccabu as the officers of the *Caryatid*, he waited for a full minute before he realised something was wrong. For five seemingly interminable minutes, the Second Mate waited for the Buccabu lighthouse to flash its warning of danger out over the heaving grey-white mass of the sea, but nothing happened.

The Second Mate of the *Galahad* calmed himself with an effort. They were all right. The bearing of the lighthouse had been to starboard. If they maintained a steady course, they must pass it clear. He went below.

"Bloody lighthouse has failed," he said matter-of-factly to the helmsman. "How much are you yawing?"

"Only about ten degrees either side of the course," the man lied. In fact he was having difficulty holding the ship's head within twenty degrees, and once or twice she had nearly got away from him altogether.

"Steer as close as you can."

"Aye, aye, sir."

Aboard *Caryatid* the Second Mate had trouble contacting the lighthouse, but after about twenty minutes a voice came over the air acknowledging the call.

"*Caryatid*, this is Buccabu, over."

"You'd think he'd know what we're calling about," remarked Wentworth to Macready who was leaning in through the radio-room door.

"Well, ask him. He can hardly disguise the matter."

"Buccabu, this is *Caryatid*. We see your light is extinguished. Please report the reason. Over."

"It's pretty bad, sir. We've had the lantern stove in, sir."

"That's the Junior Keeper," Macready said suddenly, pushing his way into the radio room and taking the handset from the Second Officer. "The poor bugger's in shock. Keep a lookout, I'll see to this . . . Buccabu, this is Macready speaking, take your time and tell me what's happened. Over."

"We took a big one, sir. Senior Keeper was on watch and it washed him to the foot of the day-room stairs, sir . . ." That was a fall of at least twenty feet, down a steep staircase, Macready thought quickly. "I think he's concussed, sir. It was some moments before the two of us realised what was the matter. Over."

"And the lantern? What's the score with that? Over," Macready prompted.

"The glazings are stove in, sir, and some of the astragal bars have come loose and damaged the lens. A lot of water got inside, sir. We've tried getting the emergency light going, but the wind up there is phenomenal, sir. Over."

Macready thought for a moment. Then he put the handset to his mouth. "Very well. Make the Senior Keeper, that's Mr Keeble, I take it, make him as comfortable as you can. Hold his head steady if you move him and assume that he's fractured his skull and snapped his neck until we know to the contrary. Then you'll have to go on watch-and-watch. Keep out of the wind, but keep a lookout and call us to let us know if you see any ships approaching. You've a better height of eye than us, tossing about down here, so let us know what you see. It might give us time to intercept anyone hell-bent on dashing themselves to pieces on that reef of yours. D'you understand? Over."

"Aye, aye, sir. Affirmative on Mr Keeble and we'll call you if we see any ships. Over."

Relieved to hear the note of confidence back in the keeper's voice, Macready remembered the distant ship Wentworth had reported. "Go up right away and have a good look round, then let me know—"

"Sir!" Macready turned. The voice was the Second Mate's, calling in from the wheelhouse.

"What is it?"

"There *is* a bloody ship out there, sir. And it's bloody close to the lighthouse."

It was at that moment that Macready thought of the eddies which swirled about the Buccabu reef. Old Captain Jesmond had not believed in them until he had had first-hand experience. On the flood they could set a ship to the east of the reef bodily to the westwards if she hit the inward curve of what was effectively a large whirlpool in the ocean itself.

At that moment several things happened at once. The moon came out from the obscurity of the clouds, the radio handset almost exploded into life and his own Second Mate blasphemed.

"Oh my God!"

"*Caryatid*, this is the Buccabu light. *There's a ship almost on top of us!*"

Macready dropped the handset and strode out onto the wing of the bridge.

On the bridge of the *Galahad*, the sudden moonlight fell upon the granite tower, reflecting pallidly from the smashed glazings themselves. Without orders, the helmsman, who had seen the lighthouse, put the helm hard over to port at the same time that the Second Officer screamed at him to do so. But it was too late. Although the *Galahad* had begun her swing and the eddy assisted the turning moment, her speed carried her down upon the reef and she struck her starboard bilge just abaft the engine-room bulkhead, tearing herself open the whole length of numbers four and five holds. The ship shook violently as her propeller hit an outcrop of rock, mangling the blades and severing two completely so that the engine raced and the tail shaft whipped.

"Oh, my God, my God," the Second Officer whimpered as *Galahad* tore free, then lurched to starboard and began to settle by the stern.

"What in hell . . . ?" Her Master appeared on the bridge wing, staring incredulously aft where, looming over the starboard quarter, the granite tower of the Buccabu light rose above them.

"The light, sir," the Second Mate tried to explain, "the fucking light was out."

"The ship's sinking, sir," the helmsman called, and the Master leapt to the alarm bells and sent them jangling all through the ship.

The Buccabu Light

Captain Macready saw quite clearly the moment of impact, saw the ship swing and strike, heel to port as her quarter rode up on the reef and then, as a gap opened between her and the moonlit finger of the light-tower, she began to fall over to starboard, her stern sinking.

"It's the *Galahad*, sir!" Wentworth called, his binoculars still clamped to his eyes and Macready recognised the ship the same instant. Within the next minute the moon slipped behind the clouds again and all they could see was the dark shape of the stricken ship and the green and white points of her navigation lights.

"Full ahead! Starboard easy!" Macready's seaman's instincts spurred him to action. "Call all hands!"

"Ring the general alarm, sir?"

"Yes! Midships steady!"

Caryatid was thrust forward by her accelerating propeller. Butting through the seas, her bluff bow headed for the *Galahad* as the alarm bells rang throughout the accommodation. Studying the stricken casualty through his glasses, Macready considered what he could do. It was clear that everything possible should be done to save the *Galahad*, but the weather ruled out lowering boats. *Caryatid* had towing gear and rocket apparatus and this seemed to offer the best option. *Galahad* was already lying beam on to the wind and sea, rolling abominably. While she had settled noticeably by the stern, she seemed not to be plunging to her doom. Perhaps they had had a chance aboard her to make an assessment of the damage, in which case it might be wise to try and call her up. Telling the Second

Mate to reduce to half speed and continue to head towards the casualty, he strode into the radio room at the very moment the *Galahad* sent out her first SOS. Picking up the handset, Macready intercepted it.

"*Galahad*, this is Celtic Lighthouse Service Tender *Caryatid*, I am close to your position and have you under visual observation. I have towing capability and am willing to attempt salvage if there is no immediate prospect of you sinking. Please report your current state. Over."

"*Caryatid*, this is *Galahad*. Master speaking. I am holed aft and immobile through damage to the screw. The after peak is intact and the after engine-room bulkhead is holding at the moment. Five and six holds are breached. Your bloody light was out. Over."

"*Caryatid* to *Galahad*, I am aware of the problem at the lighthouse, Captain. The lantern was stove in and a keeper is badly injured. I shall have to consider his life as a priority and will stand by you until daylight. If it comes to it, will you agree to towage under Lloyd's Open Agreement? Over."

"Affirmative. Glad if you would keep us company. Over."

"Very well, Captain. It's a bad night for all of us. Over and out."

Macready emerged on the bridge to find Watson and the Bosun had reported there for orders.

"We've the hands mustered in the messdecks, sir."

"Right," said Macready. "We'll get everything ready to tow, but the Senior Keeper on the Buccabu is suffering from concussion. If we steam away towing that ship, we risk the charge of putting pecuniary gain before safety of life."

"Yes . . . But these violent easterlies usually blow themselves out quite quickly," said Watson, adding, "daylight should give us a better idea of how things stand."

"Civil twilight's no more than an hour away now, sir," offered Wentworth.

"Well, we'll need to get boats and towing gear ready. Get the cook turned-to for an early breakfast, I don't know when we'll have an opportunity to eat again once we commit ourselves to a salvage operation." Macready looked round at them. "Right then. Let's get on with it!"

It was already beginning to grow less dark and an hour later a grey daylight spread across the heaving waste. They were half a mile from the wallowing *Galahad*, a dark shape moving in the twilight.

"Breakfast, sir." The steward arrived with a tray and the delicious smell of bacon and eggs filled the wheelhouse. He placed it in the fiddles on a small table in the corner and Macready fell upon the meal voraciously, unaware until that moment of his hunger. Food put new heart into a man. Behind him Watson relieved the Second Mate who slipped below to gobble up an even larger portion than his commander.

The Mate went out on the bridge wing and sniffed the wind, returning to the wheelhouse to report, "You know, I really think that wind is easing."

Macready sipped his tea and stared through the armoured-glass windows. Certainly less spray was driving aft and the air was no longer white with the suspended and atomised spume. He put his teacup down and began to con *Caryatid* up towards *Galahad*'s bow, seeing how close he could get to her in preparation for when the time came to fire a rocket and line across. *Caryatid*, pitching into wind and sea, edged up towards the tramp, at right angles to the heavily rolling casualty. The *Galahad*'s after well deck was awash, her after mast and Samson posts standing clear of the welter of white water surging across her. The poop looked like an island and a few men could be seen standing up on the docking bridge that ran athwart the poop deckhouse. At the other end of the ship, the bow stood high out of the water.

"I wonder how much of her cargo she dropped through the hole in her after holds," Watson mused as he stared through his glasses.

"With all that deadweight forward stuck up in the air, the stresses on her hull will be immense. She could easily break up," Macready said, raising his own glasses.

"The sea is dying a touch, sir, I'm damn sure of it."

"Tide's turned," Macready responded. "Try not to let the prospect of salvage colour your judgement, Mr Watson." He lowered his binoculars and looked at the younger officer. He wished he had Charlie with him.

"I'm trying hard, sir," Watson said, a lopsided grin on his face. Then his face hardened as he swung his glasses to the right. "What on earth? Is that a *yacht*?"

Macready lifted his own binoculars again and followed Watson's direction. He saw a small speck of white breast a wave and then the narrow curve of a sail above it. "By damn, Mr Watson, I believe you're right!"

Charlie had seen nothing of the drama ahead of him. Huddling cold, wet and miserable in *Lyoness*'s cockpit, the circle of his own visible horizon was limited to a few yards, bound by the restless and heaving seas. Nor had he noticed the Buccabu light had gone out. Navigation in a small yacht in such conditions is not a matter of precision. He had seen not just the loom, but several cycles of the double group flash of the light itself. Since this had shown sufficiently clearly on the starboard bow for him not to concern himself with the danger of hitting it on his present course, he continued to crouch over the compass, drifting half in and half out of a sort of cataleptic trance in which the tired body, like that of the deep-diving whales, simply shut down the extraneous bits of itself. In such a state, daylight came upon him quickly and he became fully conscious as Sonia finally woke from sleep, wracked with painful cramp.

"Ow!" she cried as she tried to straighten her stiffened muscles and finally drew herself up and peered round. "The wind seems to have dropped a little . . ." Charlie grunted agreement. "Oh," Sonia went on, "there's a lighthouse."

Charlie looked up and saw the familiar grey tower on the starboard beam some two miles away. At that distance there was no obvious sign of the damaged lantern.

"Charlie," Sonia said suddenly, an edge to her voice, "there's a ship . . . and that's *Caryatid* . . . Charlie!"

Suddenly desperately eager to relieve himself and have a cup of tea, yet alarmed by Sonia's tone he stood up, stretching and yawning. "What is it?"

"I think I saw a funny ship."

A wave ran up under the ketch's stern and lifted them forward in a great soaring arc of acceleration. Charlie felt the drag of the trailing warp keep them steady, then he too saw Sonia's 'funny ship' and beyond her the familiar, fond silhouette of *Caryatid*.

The wave passed and they fell into the succeeding trough, with a sluggish deceleration. Ahead of them the receding crest drove away from them, hiding the two ships. As *Lyonesse* lifted again, he saw clearly and understood.

"It's a tramp ship, by the look of it . . . Her after part must be flooded and she's broached-to."

"You mean she's in trouble?" Sonia asked, still not quite grasping the fact that she was witnessing a maritime disaster.

Charlie nodded. "Big trouble . . . Look, darling, I need a leak and a cup of tea. Take the helm, will you? I'll get something to eat for us. We may be able to help."

It was only when she found herself alone at the helm that Sonia wondered what on earth Charlie thought they could accomplish.

Macready's attention was diverted from the sudden appearance of the yacht. Yachtsmen were, in any case, a breed with which the good Captain had had only the most basic acquaintance. That this was usually when they were ashore at their most assertively unpleasant, was unfortunate, for it had inculcated a not unreasonable prejudice that they were over-privileged beings who had no business having anything to do with the stern preoccupations of sea-going. Aware that there were yachtsmen who achieved admirable voyages, Macready's attitude towards them generally was, therefore, ambivalent. He summed this up, dismissing the approaching ketch and her crew collectively as 'mad buggers!'

Hardly had this comprehensive assessment passed his lips than the radio telephone boomed into life again. Macready recognised the voice of the Master of the *Galahad* even as he saw what the man was appealing for help over. With a strange, brief but hideous squeal, clearly audible to the watching men aboard *Caryatid*, the highly stressed and neglected hull of the tramp ship twisted as she rolled and tore apart. Relieved of the weight of the submerged after part, the high-riding bow fell back into the sea, to find its own level. With more windage, this forward part drifted to leeward, leaving the after remnant to readjust itself. Consisting of the after two holds which were entirely open to the sea, and the after peak tank, steering engine and poop, this now turned through ninety degrees, the air in the extreme after body supporting the remainder. The most elevated part of the hull was thus the very curve of her stern plating and the rudder. As this small steel islet bobbed in the heavy seas, it alternately exposed and submerged glimpses of what had once been her propeller.

The few men remaining aft, a handful of firemen Macready supposed, could be seen scrambling over the after rail and clinging desperately to the wreckage.

"Looks like we've got three problems now," Watson observed dryly.

Macready went through to the radio room and spoke to *Galahad*'s Master, learning that they had evacuated two men from the poop through the shaft tunnel, but when the tunnel began to leak they had had to close the watertight door and seal the engine room. The engine room after bulkhead was now the effective after end of what was left of the ship and, although it was holding, the Master was clearly consumed by anxiety as to how long this state of affairs would last. When the Master had finished, Macready, well aware that his own part in this drama was as much to support this unfortunate man as to assist him in a more material manner, reassured him.

"We shall remain with you, Captain, and do whatever we can. First I'm going to try and take your men off the stern section, then I'll take you in tow. We'll take it step by step from there. Over."

"Thank you, Captain. Over." The voice was weary with anxiety.

Macready went out onto the bridge wing. "Mr Watson," he said, "send in a signal saying Buccabu lighthouse extinguished through stress of weather, Senior Keeper Keeble believed concussed and steamship *Galahad* breaking up in close vicinity. Say we're standing by and will report situation as it develops. Signal via the coastguard as usual for Porth Ardur Lighthouse Base, to be repeated to headquarters . . ." Macready looked at his watch. "I suppose someone will be interested up there in about three hours."

Watson grunted. "Yes. Fun'll be over by then."

"We'll see."

Charlie was back in the cockpit with two wedges of bread and marmalade and two mugs of tea as they drew past the *Caryatid*.

"What are we going to do, Charlie? What can we do? That ship looks even funnier now—"

"Bloody hell, she's broken up!" He paused, seeing the bow section with its name. "It's the *Galahad*, the bloody ship that nearly ran us down in the night!" Then he regretted the words, recalling that he had not intended mentioning the matter to Sonia. He looked at her, but she had not understood, instead she was pointing, her face screwed up in puzzlement.

"Are those men on there?" Sonia asked.

Charlie stared across the sea for a moment. "Good God! Yes . . . Look, Sonia, we've got to turn round and work our way back to Ynsycraven. You said yourself the wind had dropped and there's no doubt that it'll go down during this morning; it's what always happens—"

"I know that."

"Well then, let's put about now and tack up towards those poor devils—" He never finished, for she cut him short.

"All right then," she said, "let's get on with it."

Charlie looked at her shining eyes. What a girl! "I'll hoist the mizzen—"

"And get that warp in," she ordered.

Charlie laughed. He was tired but suddenly Sonia's spirit invigorated him. What a girl!

"What's that fucking yacht doing?" Watson asked as he clambered up to the bridge from the boat deck. Macready had edged *Caryatid* as close to the *Galahad*'s drifting poop as he dared. Mooring ropes stowed there and now, fouled in the wreckage, trailed about the diminishing refuge of the six souls who stared desperately up at them, their dark faces revealing them as Lascars. Below the surface of the water the after Samson posts and derricks threatened a close approach like the outlying rocks of a reef. To hazard either *Caryatid*, stout though she was, or one of her boats, would be a risky, even a foolhardy business.

But their close approach had given the Lascar firemen hope and Macready felt the moral obligation bind him to their fates. "We'll have to *try* a boat, Mr Watson," he said, lowering his glasses, "that poop section is sinking. You can see air blowing out through an after port. We may not have very long."

Watson nodded. It was not his job to make decisions and he did not envy Macready his responsibility, but the years of training brought his own professionalism unwaveringly to his commander's support. "The men are all ready, sir. Port boat?"

Macready nodded. "Yes."

Watson turned away for the ladder. "By the way, sir, have you seen this yacht?"

"Uh?" Macready turned. A white ketch lay under their port quarter, her sails just full as she edged in and out of the lee of *Caryatid*. A figure stood up in the bows, a hand at his mouth. Macready raised his glasses. "Good God! It's Charlie! Nip aft and see what *he* wants. I'm damned if I can help him as well!"

Watson descended the bridge ladder and ran aft, past the men mustering round the port sea boat. Macready watched as Watson and Charlie exchanged remarks, recognising the ketch as that belonging to Lord Craven, then Charlie turned aft and clearly passed a message at whoever was on *Lyonesse*'s helm: Craven, Macready presumed, as the ketch bore away, disappearing under the stern, out of Macready's sight.

Waiting for Watson to come forward again, Macready recollected that Craven was now no longer the old earl's heir, but had succeeded to the title. He recalled the ketch had probably been off Ynyscraven when the storm blew up, then the irrelevant thought was swept aside as Watson came back up the bridge ladder.

"That was Charlie Farthing," Watson said. "They are going to have a go at picking the survivors off the stern section, sir."

"Is that wise?" said Macready, irritated. "Suppose they get into trouble. Then we've got him to worry about as well—"

"I put that to him. He said it was better to hazard the yacht and get the men off even if it meant damage. We could more easily take everyone off a drifting yacht in the lee of the ship if matters came to the push, and you would be relieved of the need to lower and recover our sea boat."

Macready sighed. "Well, I can see the logic of his argument . . . I suppose it's up to Lord Craven . . . I mean Dungarth. It's his boat, after all, and it might give us a chance to do something about getting Keeble off the Buccabu. Call up the lighthouse and see how he is."

"Aye, aye, sir," and as Watson disappeared into the radio room, Macready ordered *Caryatid*'s engines from slow to half ahead again, to keep *Lyonesse* under observation and try to resolve some of the more pressing of his problems. It never occurred to either Macready or Watson that the half-seen figure hunched over the *Lyonesse*'s tiller was anyone other than her owner, the latest Earl Dungarth.

Charlie scrambled aft and took up a position by the mizzen shrouds, conning Sonia as they steadied on a course which would take them as close downwind of the drifting stern section as he dared. He could imagine all the detritus trailing to windward, and while the windage of the poop would rob their sails of energy, he wanted to close the distance as quickly as possible and make an assessment.

As they beat up towards the *Galahad*'s stern they could see the frightened Lascars waving at them. More ominously, as they drew close, not only did the wreckage loom large and solid, it was also obvious from the jets of escaping air that hissed and poppled about its surging waterline, that it was sinking fast.

Charlie bent and let go the senhouse slips on *Lyonesse*'s upper and lower guard rails, making access to the deck somewhat easier, then he cupped his hands round his mouth. "I come alongside next time – you jump – savvy?"

"Yes, sahib. Next time you come, we jump!"

"Right, darling," he said, leaping down in the cockpit to handle the sheets, "bear right away."

Sonia pulled at the tiller and *Lyonesse* skidded to port, dipped her bow, flung spray high and then lay over as she came onto a broad reach and shot away from the wreckage. As soon as her speed built up, Charlie ordered: "Gybe her!"

With only her small mizzen boom to worry about and the jib

sheets to shift, the manoeuvre was less hazardous than might be supposed. Sonia turned the yacht's stern quickly through the wind, while Charlie worked frantically at the sheets. As the ketch came round, Sonia steadied *Lyonesse*'s leaping bow on the *Galahad*'s wrecked stern.

"Give me a compass course, Charlie, I can't look at this."

"Steady as you go . . . No, port five . . . That's fine—"

"That's one-three-eight—"

"Good, keep on that then." Charlie could feel adrenalin pumping into his system. He did not feel as though he had spent the night at the boat's helm, he just felt a great surge of focused elation as *Lyonesse* stood boldly towards the wreckage on the port tack. He would need all the acquired skill of his years at sea, an absolute faith in his own judgement and in Sonia's skilful obedience, if they were to succeed. For a second he felt the enormity of what he was intending to do and then he gave himself up to it.

"One-three-oh."

She would just hold the wind on that course, Charlie judged, and Sonia said without looking up, "Will she take it?"

Charlie looked up at the jib. The wind was below gale force now, but still blew strongly, while the seas still flung the ketch about as she swooped in towards the waiting firemen who were already clambering down the stern railings, using them as a ladder.

"Yes—"

It looked as though they were going to have to do this six times, Charlie thought, and then they were suddenly up with the rearing steel as it curved away round *Galahad*'s stern.

"Luff!"

Sonia thrust the helm down and *Lyonesse* came upright as she turned into the wind, rapidly losing speed as her rate of turn slowed.

"Jump!" Charlie roared, grabbing the arm of a Lascar who fell on top of Sonia in the cockpit. She caught a glimpse of a rusty plate scabbed with chocolate paint and a row of rivets that seemed possessed of a kind of life of their own as they zipped up, down and then passed out of her sight as the man's weight knocked the breath out of her. Charlie lost his own balance and then felt another man on top of him and flung his own arm about the fellow's waist.

The confusion in the cockpit had thrown Sonia across the tiller, pushing it back to port, so that it arrested the port swing. Charlie frantically fought himself free of the man on top of him who, having reached sanctuary, was not intending to let it go, and required a huge heave. "Get below out of the way! *Jildi! Jildi!*"

Then Charlie felt a thump on the deck followed by a second while the starboard mizzen shroud he was clinging to vibrated and a pair of plimsoled feet crushed his hand as a fifth man swarmed down it.

"Go! Go! Sahib! Go!"

"Hard over, Sonia!" he shouted. *Lyonesse* gave a jarring shudder as she came into heavy contact with *Galahad*'s stern. Charlie heard the splinter of wood and, forcing his way forward desperately, held the clew of the jib to windward.

There was another rending sound and then *Lyonesse*'s bow began to fall off to port, helped by the sudden surge of a wave as it poured round the wreckage to throw her clear. Charlie hastened aft again and flung the starboard jib sheet off the cleat. The sail flogged madly and the cockpit seemed full suddenly of excited, chattering, dark faces with Sonia, black clad and determined in their midst.

"Get below! Go bottomside! Fuck off into cabin! *Jildi! Jildi!*"

He shooed them down below, while trying to catch hold of and haul down the port jib sheet. As soon as he was done he looked at Sonia.

"We got five," she said, her eyes shining with triumph.

"There were six. We've got to go back again," he said.

"Oh no—"

"Not necessary, sahib." A Lascar face in the companionway rocked happily and pointed upwards, over Charlie's shoulder. He looked round. Above his head, his feet on the mizzen cross trees and clinging to the mizzen rigging stood the sixth man.

"By damn, Charlie's done it!" Macready lowered his glasses. "I'd not have believed it, had I not seen it myself."

"Not a moment too soon," Watson said. Astern of *Lyonesse* the stern section of the *Galahad* was disappearing fast. As they watched, it took a sudden plunge and disappeared. "I've got through to the Buccabu, sir," said the Second Mate, coming out onto the wing of the bridge. "I've just spoke to Keeble himself. He says he's all right. He's got a bump the size of an egg on his head, but he's more concerned with the light. He says he's tried to get the stand-by burner working, but the bronze astragals knocked it for six. It's smashed to smithereens."

Macready nodded. The relief on his face was obvious. "Well," he said, his voice suddenly buoyant, "let's see if we can get what's left of that rust-bucket under tow."

No Cure, No Pay

The news of the disaster at the Buccabu lighthouse reached the headquarters of the Commissioners for Celtic Lighthouses about mid-morning. Captain Sir Charles Mudge called an immediate meeting of the Board which was hurriedly scheduled for that afternoon. It was a day of extraordinary activity, unparalleled in living memory for, by a strange coincidence, in addition to the *Caryatid*'s attendance on the stricken *Galahad*, off the south-west coast, *Waterwitch* had just been released from standing by the grain ship whose cargo had shifted, but which was now under the tow of a salvage tug in moderating weather.

The Board was not so much concerned with the deployment of its ships, as the problem at the Buccabu lighthouse which clearly required the issuing of navigation warnings, notices to mariners and consideration of the means by which the effects of so catastrophic an event could be reversed. Reports of the disaster seemed to rule out a quick and easy answer for, in addition to the virtual destruction of the lantern structure and the lighting apparatus, some damage seemed to have been inflicted on the masonry of the tower. This was only discovered after the wind had dropped to a fresh breeze shortly before noon, arriving with the tidings that *Caryatid* had the *Galahad* in tow under the standard salvage arrangements of a Lloyd's Open Agreement.

This extraordinary legal instrument is unique in being the only one binding without signature. The difficulties of obtaining and exchanging formally signed contracts under the extreme circumstances prevailing in a rescue at sea in bad weather clearly preclude such a nicety. It was however,

Macready afterwards thought, clear evidence that that strange brotherhood which existed between seamen of all nationalities, was one of the most civilised if unestablished institutions upon earth. Moreover, the formalities concluded an agreement which was exemplary in its essential fairness for, if the salvage attempt failed, no payment was due. This 'no-cure, no-pay' principle ensured that no salvage was undertaken lightly and for Captain Macready it was necessary that he sought the sanction of the Commissioners. This he did retrospectively, for he had had *Galahad* in tow for some hours before he transmitted his signal.

At about the same time as this intelligence was passing along the wires to reach Sir Charles Mudge's desk at a quarter past twelve, and the Chairman's approval on behalf of the Board was returned as a matter of course, Captain Stanier was sitting hugging himself in a first-class compartment of an express train on the up line. The windy night had turned itself into a day of blustery weather with bright sunny periods sandwiched between patches of scudding cloud. His mood lightened; the forebodings of the night receded, dismissed as he sat and read the share prices in his newspaper. The wisdom of Caroline and Smith in chartering extra ships to fulfil the new contracts, impressed him. It was clearly a clever and necessary move, which would allow Cambrian Steam to maximise its opportunities. He had hoped that the financial pages of his broadsheet newspaper might have mentioned the economic impact of the revolt in Costa Maya, but was not unduly worried by the absence of any report on the event. It was an early edition and foreign news had a habit of taking time to percolate through the filtration of editing desks. There was, however, a fine photograph of the badly listing grain ship taken from an aeroplane. In the foreground of the shot he could see the Celtic Lighthouse Tender *Waterwitch* and it made him think of the more satisfactory events of the last few days. In the end the uncertainties as to the whereabouts of his wife receded as Stanier consigned his panic of the previous day to those recesses of his mind that processed his neuroses. As the journey wore on, Stanier found himself more bothered about where to go first when he arrived in the capital. The train would arrive at the terminus at four o'clock. He could go straight home, but Caro might not yet be there and he loathed going home to an empty flat. He ought to go to the city offices of Cambrian Steam and find out the details of recent events, but these were so clearly all under control and he would learn them from Caro herself later, that he thought it unnecessary. On the other hand, he had a bulging briefcase full of papers connected with the recent cruise of the Commissioners and would be happy to disencumber himself of their deadweight. Moreover, the most pressing matter he had on his own mind, was to report the disobedience of Captain Macready and this finally decided him upon dropping the briefcase off first at the headquarters of the Lighthouse Authority. It would be interesting too, he thought, to catch up on the latest news of *Waterwitch*'s involvement with the grain ship casualty, and to find out when she would head for Porth Ardur.

When Stanier arrived at headquarters, he was asked to go straight to the Board Room where the extraordinary meeting was still in progress. He was not surprised, though he meanly hoped that the Board had yet to hear of Macready's unilateral action. It was clear that Mudge and his colleagues were in sombre mood. Stanier guessed that the near mutiny at Porth Ardur was at the root of their deliberations. Mudge waved him to a seat.

"You've heard about *Caryatid*, Stanier," Mudge said, thinking that Stanier's first preoccupation might be with his damaged ship.

"I know about him sailing from Porth Ardur without orders and in insubordinate disobedience—"

Mudge interrupted, matters were dragging inconclusively and he was anxious to get on. "Well, it's just as well that he sailed, your *Galahad* would be in even deeper trouble than she is at the moment."

"*Galahad*? What on earth d'you mean?" Stanier was frowning with incomprehension.

"You don't know? Damn it! Last night's severe weather stove in the whole upper part of the Buccabu lighthouse. A few minutes later Cambrian Steam's *Galahad* hit the reef and ripped her after bottom out. She drifted clear disabled, having shed most, if not all her propeller blades. Fortunately *Caryatid* was in the offing."

Stanier was white faced and it was a moment before he spoke. Then, in a quavering voice, he asked: "You mean Macready has *Galahad* in tow?"

"Well the half of her that is still afloat."

Stanier looked at Mudge, his face aghast. "She's broken in half?"

"Yes," Mudge nodded. "Well, I'm sorry, but it is the Buccabu that we must consider. It looks as though it is going to be a major operation repairing the lighthouse and Blake is suggesting we may have to lay a lightvessel near the reef—"

"You said the light . . . the Buccabu light was out?"

"Yes," said Mudge impatiently, "that is what we are discussing. How to make good the deficiency as quickly as possible—"

"No, no," said Stanier leaning forward, "I mean, you said the light was out before *Galahad* ran aground and this would have contributed to the grounding—"

"Look, that's as maybe, Stanier," Blake said crossly, "and I daresay you're concerned about your ship but we've a different concern which is our prime preoccupation—"

"While you're here, Stanier, you're wearing the hat of a Commissioner," Mudge reminded him sternly.

Stanier looked from one to the other of them. "You don't understand," he whispered before sitting back and lapsing into silence, his face glazed.

Captain Macready looked astern with some satisfaction. His decision to sail was now thoroughly vindicated. His career was not to end on a note of whimpering, but a classic piece of good seamanship. He was in no doubt of this after the event just as before it, when competing priorities had been removed by Charlie's dashing act and the merciful thickness of Keeble's skull, he had had no doubt that he could do it. Nor did this confidence in himself arise from hubris; it derived from the sure and certain knowledge that, even with Watson as his mate, he commanded a ship and ship's company of unprecedented excellence.

It was in this knowledge that he had manoeuvred *Caryatid* so close in under the bow of *Galahad* that they had dispensed with the rocket line and found the distance could be bridged with a hand-thrown heaving line. This had been followed by a heavier rope and eventually *Caryatid*'s towing wire which, once shackled onto a length of *Galahad*'s port anchor cable, had finally connected rescuer and rescued.

The easterly wind died away as the day progressed, producing an evening of tranquil sunshine and a breeze backing quickly into the north and later the north-west. The sea dropped too, so that by sunset, when Ynyscraven was just abaft the beam on the northern horizon, only a low swell marked the passing of the storm.

Far astern of them on the starboard quarter, now no more than a sunlit speck of white, *Lyonesse* tacked up towards Ynyscraven. She had passed her happy Lascar 'passengers' across to *Caryatid* by way of one of the ship's boats after the tow had been connected, and then with a wave, Charlie had sheered away, setting the mainsail and a larger jib.

Having settled his human cargo safely in the messdeck, Watson came up to the bridge. "D'you know who that was in the yacht with Charlie Farthing?" he said, to which Macready shook his head.

"She had red hair—"

"You mean Sonia . . . his wife?" Macready asked incredulously, genuinely surprised.

Watson shrugged. "There was no sign of anyone else."

After the board meeting closed, agreement having been reached on the necessity of getting a lightvessel prepared immediately, Stanier had left the Lighthouse Authority's headquarters and taken a taxi to the offices of the Cambrian Steam Navigation Company. As the cabbie fought his way through the traffic, Stanier reflected unhappily on how quickly all had been reversed. As he had cosily sought the downfall of Captain Septimus Macready, the bloody man was busy trying to save the wreckage of Stanier's ship. Stanier could hardly bear to contemplate the irony of it.

It was already late and, apart from a cleaner, only the charter manager was left in the shipping company's offices. He was a nondescript, middle-aged man who seemed incapable of existence without a cigarette. He looked up as Stanier approached.

"Ah, sir, thank goodness, do you know about the *Galahad*?"

"Yes. I found out this afternoon—"

"I tried to call you in Porth Ardur, but heard you had left your hotel this morning."

"I was on the early train. What are the chances?"

"Oh, quite good, sir. There's been no loss of life and the men on the after bit were picked up. The after bit has sunk, sir, so there's the loss of that part of her cargo."

"Yes, I know," Stanier snapped sharply. That was another aspect he could hardly bear to think about. Then his other anxiety broke surface. "What was her port of discharge in Costa Maya?"

The man frowned. "Costa Maya, sir? No, she was bound for the Mediterranean."

"Oh, I thought she had loaded under this new contract with the Costa Mayan government."

"I, er, I don't think I quite follow you, sir. We have no contract with the Costa Mayan Government—"

"We've a contract to supply the Costa Mayan Navy with navigation coal. We've chartered two additional ships to service it . . ." Conviction ebbed from him with every word he uttered. To irony was now added terror.

The charter manager was shaking his head. "If we had, Captain Stanier, I'd know about it."

Stanier was feeling faint. "Has my wife phoned? She was going to be in daily contact while I was away."

"Ah, well." The contract manager looked away. "Well, she was, sir, for the first three weeks, then, well, we haven't heard from her recently." He brightened and added, "Everything was fine though, sir, until this morning."

But Stanier was no longer listening, he was reaching for the charter manager's telephone and impatiently tapping the man's desk as the noise of unanswered ringing went on and on.

When he finally replaced the receiver, he turned and confronted the charter manager. "I am ruined," he said. "*Galahad*, like all my ships was uninsured . . ."

* * *

209

From the empty flat Stanier reeled towards the Pomeroys' apartment, unsure why he had gone there, but with some vague idea that Tegwyn could help him, even give him a bed for the night. Pomeroy opened the door; he wore a yellow dressing gown and, with a lop-sided smile, ushered Stanier in.

"My dear James, you have come to tell me Caro has left you." Pomeroy said, handing Stanier a glass half full of neat Scotch whisky.

"How do you know?"

"The whole town knows, my dear, but don't worry, it is quite the fashion. You should count yourself lucky."

"Lucky?" cried Stanier after a large, restorative gulp of whisky. "Lucky?"

"You have only lost your wife . . . I have lost my wife, my lover and half my fortune."

"Your lover?" Stanier's capacity for surprises wearing thin.

"The beautiful, feckless, corrupt, devious and drunken David Smith. I am a queer, my dear. So was he, but he was queer-queer, if you see what I mean. Utterly corrupt, not just oddly orientated. He persuaded me to invest . . . but it is pointless to go over and over the matter. Come with me. Oh, I shan't touch you, Jimmy, you are not my type at all. But just indulge me a little. Come."

Stanier followed Pomeroy through into the room in which he kept his ethnographic treasures. Lighting a single lamp, Pomeroy set his glass down, picked up a Tasmanian wind mask and putting it to his face he suddenly blew through it. The thing emitted a howlingly piteous note.

Stanier stood dumbfounded, then stared as Pomeroy undid his dressing gown and stood naked. He lowered the mask from his face. "Tell them about David, my dear Jimmy, there's a good fellow," he said, advancing with mincing deliberation towards Stanier. "Tell them it was due to David Smith, *Member* of Parliament and much else besides." Pomeroy replaced the mask in front of his face and repeated the howling note.

Stanier dropped his glass and fled. He was seen by the apartment porter and would have been the prime suspect had

Pomeroy not left a long note explaining everything. Nevertheless, the unfortunate Stanier spent a humiliating morning undergoing police interrogation until, convinced that the evidence against him was all circumstantial and Pomeroy's death was indeed suicide, he found himself on the street again.

Once on her homeward passage to Ynyscraven, Charlie inspected *Lyonesse* for damage. He had already ascertained that she was not taking water below, for she was pretty tight and he had pumped little water out of her bilge since he had first sailed on the ketch from Aberogg. But the beautiful line of her sheer was badly chewed in two places amidships, and below three ribs had suffered bad cracks. The most serious damage was down aft, on her starboard quarter, where her counter had been seriously damaged. It was, however, all above the waterline and all repairable.

Charlie was not quite certain how he was going to explain it to Lord Dungarth, for the damage seemed to put him in so untenable a position that he could no longer think of *Lyonesse*'s owner as Roger Craven. This was the only thing to mar the sense of joint achievement he felt. Sonia had proved her mettle, handled the ketch with absolute brilliance and earned herself, if such a thing were possible, an even greater measure of affection from her husband.

It was midnight before they got ashore and wearily tramped up the steep path. In their lit kitchen Justine was asleep at the table, her head on her folded arms. She woke as they came in and got up, her face smiling, her arms outstretched.

"I've a thick vegetable soup for you. I saw you tacking up at twilight."

"Justine, you're an angel," Charlie grinned, hugging her.

"And you two, I understand, are heroes."

It was almost exactly forty-eight hours to the minute since he had left the bay, when Macready slipped his tow and *Galahad*'s starboard anchor rumbled out of the hawse pipe and brought her up, three cables south of the lighthouse pier of Porth Ardur. There was hardly a breath of wind.

Winners and Losers

For a few days Porth Ardur enjoyed a curious period of frenetic activity. At high water later that day, edged inwards by *Caryatid* secured alongside, the forward section of *Galahad* was nudged into the dock entrance and thereafter warped back into her old berth. Here a mass of dusty men dug out the coal so easily poured into her capacious forward holds. It was a brief sunset flurry of laborious work before a prolonged period of idleness while the tortured hull awaited a decision as to its future.

Across the dock, *Caryatid* disgorged her own stores and sank into the inertia that was to precede her decommissioning. It was a state of affairs that lasted some weeks. In the meantime the Secretary to the Board of Commissioners for Celtic Lighthouses sought a buyer for her tired hull, finally agreeing to her being broken up.

There *had* been a revolt in Costa Maya, and the state navy *had* brought out of reserve two ancient monitors. These had steamed down the coast and bombarded half a dozen villages with their huge 12-inch guns, after which Costa Maya sank back into obscurity. That was all; no contracts for navigation coal had been sought on the spot market, no tramps had been taken up on bareboat charter.

In the succeeding months, a society magazine called the *Tittle-Tattler* contained several reports from the Côte d'Azur of the flamboyantly extravagant excesses of Caro Blackadder, a woman, it was averred, whose marital distress had led her to adopt the highly creditable initiative of absconding with a substantial amount of her cruel husband's assets, after acquiescing to his putting them in her name to avoid tax himself.

212

Feminist opinion praised her highly, admired her resumption of her maiden name and in particular, her adoption of what they called 'inalienable rights to pursue happiness through freedom of expression'. Caro Blackadder was thereafter frequently seen assisting the consumptive former Member of Parliament, David Smith, to enjoy the last years of his tragically short life.

By a trick of fate, the cruel husband avoided the scandal of bankruptcy. Tegwyn Pomeroy took pity upon her former lover and, wanting nothing associated with Pomeroy, whose physical betrayal she found herself unable to forgive despite the fact that he had left the residue of his fortune to her, made it all over to Stanier. It was a considerable sum, enabling him to pay off the modest salvage claim submitted by the Celtic Lighthouse Authority on behalf of Captain Septimus Macready and the ship's company of the *Caryatid*. Stanier was compelled to scrap the remains of *Galahad*, covering the cost of her towage to the breakers, and compensate the consignees of her lost cargo. The consignees invoked the reversion clause and cancelled their contracts. The salvaged remains of *Galahad*'s cargo, discharged upon the quay at Porth Ardur, was loaded into four coasters and shipped out, to be resold at a net loss, to another buyer.

Faced by the loss of his job, the Cambrian Steam Navigation Company's contracts manager secured three cargoes for the remaining ships in the fleet. These, two of iron ore and one, oddly a logwood cargo from, of all places, Costa Maya, began the slow process of rebuilding the shipping company. This skilful saving of his Cambrian Steam in the face of extreme difficulties, not only earned Stanier a measure of admiration from his fellow shipowners, but secured his seat on the Board of the Commissioners of Celtic Lighthouses. It was not the business of the Commissioners to kick a man when he was down and, as Sir Charles Mudge remarked, "Any damn fooled can get into a mess; it takes a real man to get out of one."

This fortuitous consequence decided Stanier to promote his contracts manager to a place on his own Board of Directors and the Cambrian Steam Navigation Company entered a phase of its existence characterised by substantial reinvestment.

In Porth Ardur, Mrs Gwendolyn Macready, like Mr Sinclair of the Pendragon Bank, grew wiser, acknowledging the sin of greed. Sinclair, a widower, found himself retired early and, sharing his humiliation with the only other living soul who knew of it in Porth Ardur, formed a scandalous attachment with Mrs Macready. It would be indelicate to pry too deeply into this odd and quite unexpected liaison, particularly as the Macready house was put into the hands of an estate agent and divorce proceedings followed. Both Mrs Macready and Mr Sinclair left Porth Ardur at the same time. Some said together, and occasional rumours surfaced. Families on holiday reported seeing them in seedy seaside resorts and one incredible account suggested they had been positively identified running a troupe of pierrots at an end-of-the-pier show. The truth does not greatly matter; they fade from this history, finding perhaps a small contentment amid the shame in the twilight of their lives.

A month after *Caryatid* had arrived at the breakers' yard and Macready had turned his back on the old ship for the last time, Parliament reassembled. The Upper House was held spellbound for half an hour, while Roger Craven, eleventh Earl Dungarth, lambasted the Government in his maiden speech for its coercive policies towards the public services, policies that reduced them to levels of such penury that they were unable to carry out their functions.

". . . They might just as well not exist!" he declaimed. "Indeed, would it not be better for the Government to approve the complete abolition of these institutions? They could, with the money thus saved, refund every freeholding taxpayer in the land, a measure, my lords, that recommends itself to a self-serving coterie, anxious to secure re-election!

"Consider, my noble lords, the consequences of which you have read in your newspapers of the extinguishing of the Buccabu lighthouse. It is not something your lordships normally worry about! Why? Because for one hundred and nine years a light has shone out from the Buccabu lighthouse every single night in that period. But, my lords, a cut-back on putty . . . yes, putty, caused the glazings to fail, whereupon this structure, my lords, as noble as ourselves, was filled with the ocean which it had withstood for over a century . . ."

Creeping crabwise towards his objective, Lord Dungarth precipitated a protracted debate the result of which, some two years later, led to the commissioning of a new, modern diesel tender, named *Caryatid* after her predecessor. She would be based at Porth Ardur, whose facilities would be modernised.

But we anticipate. Long before this outcome, reading of the decision to build this new ship in the newspapers which had Dungarth brought to Ynyscraven, Macready looked up across the dining table about which were crowded the Farthings, Justine and Tegwyn, and smiled at his lordship.

"That's wonderful," he said, his eyes bright with emotion.

"Someone else will command her of course, Septimus, but you should not let that worry you."

"No, of course not, my lord," Macready said, seeing no obliquity in his lordship's remark, but putting out his hand and squeezing that of Justine, who smiled happily back at him.

"Now, Septimus," Dungarth went on, "I have a favour to ask you. Will you give Tegwyn away? The silly girl agreed to marry me this afternoon."

"I shall be honoured, my lord—"

"Septimus, you will not call me that on this island. Indulge me thus far . . . please, there's a good fellow."

Macready smiled. "On one condition, my lord."

"What is that?"

"You give Justine away!"

"Septimus!" breathed Justine, while Tegwyn reached out and squeezed his lordship's noble hand.

"Honoured, Captain Macready! Charlie, where's that case of bubbly I brought ashore?"

The cork-popping rituals over, the glasses charged, Dungarth gave a series of toasts to which everyone drank enthusiastically.

"Now," Dungarth said as the jollity subsided. "I must not leave you two out of this. Here we are."

He drew a rather crumpled brown paper envelope from his

blazer pocket and tossed it towards Charlie, who caught it. Drawing a linen document from it he unfolded it, then looked at Dungarth, his face puzzled.

"Since you treated the old lady as if you owned her, and since you make such a brilliant crew, you two might as well have her."

Charlie's mouth gaped in incredulity while Sonia lent forward and kissed Dungarth on the cheek. "You absolute sweetie," she said, turning to Charlie. "He's given us *Lyonesse*, you numb-skull."

"But what will *you* sail, Roger? You love that boat."

Dungarth pulled a face and looked at Tegwyn. "I'm not certain Teggy wants to go sailing and, if she does, I've enough spondulicks to build something new. I'd rather set my mind on a schooner." Dungarth turned his attention to Charlie. "Anyway, Charlie, there are a few repairs to see to and, frankly, I can't be bothered."

"Well, thanks, Roger—"

"I think you need to lay a proper mooring for her, but then that's right up your street, isn't it?"

"I'd like to extend the breakwater—"

"Well then, get on with it. Don't keep asking me."

"Right. Thanks."

"There's something else as well. You've both won Lloyd's Medals for your rescue of those firemen. Congratulations . . . No, no, don't thank me. It was Septimus who put in the recommendation."

Charlie looked at his old commander and mumbled his thanks.

"He's a lovely man," said Justine, tears flowing down her face.

Embarrassed, Macready cleared his throat. "There's one thing I must ask you, er, Roger . . ."

"What's that?"

"About the putty in the Buccabu light . . . You know the whole thing was wrecked by a huge wave and the bronze astragals were simply torn out. I doubt if it was just putty. Besides, no-one had stopped any requisition order for putty, certainly not to my knowledge, and I doubt if old Dale would have done it."

"Well, Septimus, politics is the art of the possible. I was pretty certain that no-one in either House would have the slightest acquaintance with the Buccabu lighthouse and I backed my hunch."

"You ought to get a medal for that, Roger darling," Tegwyn said to general laughter.

"I've always," Dungarth said charging everybody's glass, "deeply deplored the effrontery of the peerage. Cheers, everyone!"

That is not quite the end of the story. Its last twist took place not long after this happy evening in the Farthings' cottage on Ynyscraven, in the distant Board Room of the Commissioners for Celtic Lighthouses.

It was, it will be remembered, a tradition of the Celtic Lighthouse Service that every Commissioner had the right to nominate the man he considered best fit to succeed him. It was urged upon Commissioners to make such a nomination soon after their appointment and while their selection was in no way binding upon the assembled Board, it was unusual for a nomination to be black-balled, the nominee usually being duly elected into the vacancy.

In due course that autumn the Board's attention was directed to the matter of filling the post left by the untimely death of Captain Jesmond. The old shipmaster's sealed letter, deposited many years earlier, was reverently opened by the Secretary and solemnly unfolded.

The waiting Commissioners ran through their minds the likely nominees, commanders, no doubt, of ocean liners, large oil tankers or smart cargo-passenger ships, men whose candidacy they would easily approve.

"Captain Jesmond's nominee is . . ." the Secretary intoned, as Mudge struck the bruised table top with his ceremonial gavel, calling the attention of all to this important moment, ". . . Captain Septimus Macready."

There was a stunned silence. The election of a service officer was unheard of! Such a thing was without precedent. The man did not have a formal certificate of competence as master, having been promoted in the days when the Commissioners themselves examined their own officers, unhappy with the government department who seemed insufficiently rigorous in its standards.

"Any objections?" asked Mudge, looking at Stanier, whose mouth seemed about to open.

"He's a damn fine seaman who just about saved your bacon, Stanier," said Captain Blake.

"It's certainly breaking the mould of tradition," offered Gostling, "and we want to be seen moving into the modern world of business practice, don't you agree, gentlemen?"

"Well," asked Mudge, "what d'you say, Captain Stanier? It's traditional to ask the junior man first."

"Like a council of war," added Blake sententiously.

"Well? Any objections?"

Stanier swallowed, then slowly shook his head. The matter was passed unanimously.